Exceptionally Unconventional

by

Victoria Clarke

Exceptionally Unconventional

Cover Art by *Lisa Dawn MacDonald*

The Wild Rose Press, Inc.
PO Box 708
Adams Basin, NY 14410-0708
Visit us at www.thewildrosepress.com

Publishing History
First Edition, 2023
Trade Paperback ISBN 978-1-5092-4618-2
Digital ISBN 978-1-5092-4619-9

Published in the United States of America

They were in a darkened area of the garden, which was no doubt intentional on the part of her captor. Unfortunately for him, the surroundings also suited Lucilla in this particular moment.

London knew her to be an intelligent, aristocratic, prettily behaved young woman with extraordinary horsemanship and feminine accomplishments in droves. What they did not know was that growing up in the company of three elder brother figures had provided her with an education that did not come naturally to other young ladies of her class. It was that education she now called upon to save her the indignity of abduction and social ruin.

Her struggling abruptly ceased. Her unencumbered right hand formed a dainty fist. And her dainty fist connected neatly with her kidnapper's unsuspecting nose. There was a surprising amount of force behind the thrust, and it was so precisely aimed that blood was drawn, and she found herself immediately released.

But the untamed and unladylike streak she was usually at such pains to conceal from Society was suddenly loosened. Instead of escaping while the opportunity presented itself, she made a fist with her left hand as well and swung at the masked man again. So concerned was he with keeping his mask in place that he was unable to deflect the second blow, which landed squarely in the vicinity of his right eye.

Dedication

Dear Mum, I did it.

Chapter 1

The family home of Viscount Iverson, known as Gracewood, stood in a rather lovely park ringed by a grove of cypress trees. The Elizabethan mansion, with its tall frontage and mullioned windows flanked by twin towers to the east and west, was set within an easy distance from the bustling docks of Liverpool. A carefully raked white gravel path, flanked by judiciously trimmed rosebushes, provided an exceptionally picturesque road to the heavy oak doors that decorated the entrance of the house. Built on rising ground, Gracewood was visible from well away, and it was not an uncommon occurrence for the master of the house to be applied to by some painter or other in pursuit of permission to immortalize its likeness.

The inner home park was a dozen private acres, and it was from one of the tall narrow windows that the Honorable Miss Lucilla Iverson sullenly surveyed the view. Presently the prospect of the park was not pleasing to her. The lingering rain had somewhat ruined her plan for the day, so she found herself settled by the parlor window, with several letters scattered across the seat, instead of galloping across the green. She absentmindedly stroked the golden-haired dog curled beside her.

One of the letters was from her mother's cousin, decrying the injustice of being two years younger than

Miss Iverson. The letter was smattered with tearful blotches in which the younger lady fervently wished she could have her own coming-out with her cousin. Miss Iverson was sorry but somewhat less saddened by the situation, for although she adored her young cousin and had many happy memories of her, it would be a pleasant change and rather less daunting prospect to not find herself constantly compared to the fair-haired, blue-eyed beauty that was Miss Jennifer Stanhope.

On the eve of her journey to London for her first Season, one would expect a young lady of eighteen to be full of excitement and perhaps a tiny measure of nervousness. Instead, Miss Iverson found herself entirely devoid of both anxiousness and enthusiasm, for while the other letters were a collection of salutations from various family members wishing Miss Iverson success, one had stood out and dampened her afternoon considerably more than the weather had managed to do.

My Dearest Lucy,

I very much hope that this letter finds you quite well. Mama says that she has written to Lady Iverson and that they have together hatched a plan for your Presentation to Her Majesty and that we should have a lovely party from Lord Iverson's London house. Just think, your First London Season! I'm sure you will be much courted, even though the fashion is for fair hair like my own. It would perhaps be best if you did not spend too much time outside, as it is much better to have fair skin. Tanned skin gives a person a very common appearance, does it not? I am sure Lady Iverson will counsel the same as I have. I have not set foot in the garden for weeks, and I am sure it has done a world of good.

I myself am simply determined to make a match

before this Season is done. Mama says I am sure to do well, and she has taken great pains over my dresses. Grandpapa has spent simply a fortune as he said he would not have me dressed in my gowns from last Season, and he has just yesterday gifted me a pair of emerald drop earrings! My Uncle Cooke was quite displeased and said some dreadfully unkind things, which Grandpapa took him to task over. Uncle is so terribly jealous of Mama and me. It is very unfortunate that he should be so bad-natured.

You must promise me, my dear, that you will not be sad if you do not receive a suitable offer this Season, for it would be quite tedious to have you behave in that missish way you do when you do not have your own way. As your greatest friend, I know you will understand that I say these things with your best interests at heart. It is simply not becoming to put on airs, as I am sure Lady Iverson has said to you. My own dear Mama has said many times that she has told Lady Iverson to tell you, so I am sure she has.

Dearest, I must stop writing now for I am very busy. We will see each other every day once we are both in town, is that not thrilling!

Yours ever,

Tabitha Wallace

Miss Iverson sighed resignedly, then turned and critically studied her reflection in the window. She had never considered herself more than passably pretty, particularly in comparison to her lovely cousin Jenny, but Lucilla could not find anything especially objectionable about her complexion. Dark ringlets framed her lightly tanned face, while the length of her hair was held back by a velvet band and styled in a fashionable pile upon her head. Beneath neat brows were a pair of very dark brown orbs and a small straight nose. There didn't appear to be anything particularly amiss that Lucilla could find.

"Ah, my darling, here you are. I thought you would be at the pianoforte with this provoking weather about!" The golden dog sat bolt upright with its ears pricked, and a startled Miss Iverson looked about the room, her gaze finally landing on her mother standing in the doorway.

Lady Anne Iverson was considered to have been something of a beauty in her youth. She had been educated with exceptional care and promptly presented at Court following her emergence from the schoolroom. Still, the lack of dowry had, at the time, presented something of an impediment to her making a suitable match. Her late papa had been a younger son in a junior branch of the Stanhope family and a distant cousin of the Earl of Chesterfield. The then Miss Anne Stanhope was blessed with well-placed relations who had assisted in ensuring her education was fastidiously attended to in the hopes that should she not make a suitable match, she might at the very least be well positioned to obtain a genteel post as companion or governess within a respectable house. At the expense of an indulgent godparent, Miss Anne Stanhope had enjoyed her first and only London Season, during which she received no offers for her hand. She had then, quite uncomplainingly, retired to the country with her benefactor and enjoyed several years caring for the elderly widow until fate had ordained to intervene.

"Ah, who has written to you? They are quite lucky to have caught us at home," Lady Iverson smiled as she closed the door and walked across the room to sit beside her daughter. She gathered up the letters and interestedly sorted through them, with an absentminded pat to the golden dog as it lay back down between the ladies.

"Jenny and Aunt Mildred have both written. And Aunt Augusta," Miss Iverson replied softly. "And Miss Wallace."

Lady Iverson paused almost imperceptibly and looked at her daughter with a searching gaze. She glanced through the papers in her hand to locate the letter in question and quickly skimmed through its contents, her face betraying some traces of surprise with not a small amount of disdain. After a few moments, she folded the letter and set it aside.

"The girl has not a single sensible thought that is her own," Lady Iverson said with contempt. "I supposed her mother to be more sensible than to allow such a letter to be sent."

"You have spoken to her mama, then?"

"Lady Wallace has written to me several times," her mother replied, "but I have not made any plans with her in spite of what this letter claims. Tabitha has rather a tenuous relationship with the truth, which you know very well."

"Yes, I suppose I do." Miss Iverson sighed and turned her face toward the window again, continuing to study her apparently distasteful appearance.

"Do not let her bother you, dearest. You know she means to be harmless. Tomorrow we will start our journey to London. Your papa and I have some very exciting activities in store. Do not tell him that I have told you, but he is planning to take you to Astley's as soon as he can arrange it."

"Really?" Miss Iverson exclaimed, instantly

brightening. "Oh! That would be perfectly thrilling. Mama, do you mean it?"

Lady Iverson nodded and whispered conspiratorially, "Indeed, but he means it to be a surprise, so do keep the secret."

At that moment, the door of the parlor door opened slightly, and the gentleman of the house peeped his head into the room and exclaimed, "Ah, my dear, here you are. Murray has this moment come to tell me that all is in order for our departure tomorrow."

****

The following morning began in a flurry, with an early breakfast before the party of three and their dog piled into the sizeable traveling coach and set off at a steady pace. They were followed by two carriages carrying essential staff, including Gracewood's incomparable butler, Murray, her ladyship's maid and Lord Iverson's valet, along with all of the luggage conceivably required for an extended jaunt about the town.

The journey to London was to be taken by degrees, the roads being somewhat precarious in early December. It was not in Lord Iverson's nature to abuse his horses, so he fully intended to make the journey very steadily. The family had removed from the country primarily due to Lord Iverson's presence being required in the city on business; however, Lady Iverson had agreed that arriving well before the Season would be advantageous. She had written to several of her friends and relatives who remained in London all year round with the express intention of making an early start in her preparations for her daughter's coming out.

There were dresses to be made and bonnets to be

ornamented, a court dress to be designed and carefully pieced together by her ladyship's modiste, slippers, gloves, and trinkets to be purchased, not to mention the planning of their own ball to be considered. As Lucilla had never before left Lancashire, Lady Iverson also had the idea to introduce her daughter quietly among her friends before the *ton* descended on London *en masse* with the Season in full swing.

Almost four months would allow Lady Iverson plenty of time to organize while her husband was engaged with business and later with his duties upon the opening of Parliament in February. Knowing her daughter to be somewhat restless when she was cooped up in the winter months, Lady Iverson intended to make outings to museums and nearby landmarks. She had written to engage a reputable dancing master and planned several quiet gatherings with ladies of her acquaintance who might be counted on to assist in introducing Lucilla to Society. But before these delights were to be experienced, a singularly long journey was required to deposit them in London.

When Miss Iverson disembarked at The Swan, following the end of the second day of travel, it was with somewhat unseemly eagerness, the golden dog bounding off the step and animatedly stretching and yipping beside her. The time spent aboard the coach as it lumbered along its route through the Lancashire countryside and into Staffordshire had been taken up at varying intervals by conversation, long periods of silence, and sometimes a traveling game or two. The tediousness of the day had left Miss Iverson feeling quite confined, and so the moment she was free of the carriage she begged her mother to allow her to walk with her pet for a little while before dinner.

Lady Iverson looked wearily at her daughter and said, "Oh, Cilla, I am far too fagged to walk just now. I must lie down and rest before we dress to dine."

"Milady, if you please, I should be happy to walk with Miss Iverson if you allow it."

Cilla turned to see her mother's maid had approached them quietly, and she smiled at her gratefully. Looking back at Lady Iverson, she said, "Indeed, surely you will not object if Ellers accompanies me, Mama? We shall not be gone long. I am simply aching to stretch my legs."

After a moment of hesitation, Lady Iverson nodded in acquiescence. "But stay within the square, if you please. And mind the time. Your papa will order dinner, and you must have time to change. I will ask one of the chambermaids to assist me and have a gown laid out for you."

Miss Iverson beamed as the ever-prepared Ellers handed her the hastily retrieved muff from the coach, and the two set off to explore the surrounding square, with the golden dog tugging at its leather excitedly. The thriving town of Stafford boasted a very lovely main street with several exquisite private residences that each possessed a delightful aspect of the buzzing environs. As she walked with Ellers about the square, a sudden and loud clattering drew her attention, and a pair of matched grays appeared in the street, pulling a stylish high-perch phaeton. Of the two gentlemen seated aboard the carriage, it seemed the younger was in control of the reins, if control was indeed a word that could be employed to define the state of affairs. The horses were clearly fine, high-couraged animals, but their mouths gaped and strained at a hard hand at their rein, and their eyes were wide in terror. Miss Iverson had only a moment to make a note of all this before she realized they were wildly barreling in her direction.

The golden dog let out a warning bark, and a hysterical screech came from Ellers as she grasped her young charge's arm and snatched her out of the street. Both ladies fell onto the cobbled stones out of harm's way, with the dog barking angrily as the vehicle flew by. Miss Iverson, recovering from the shock, was assisted to her feet by a nearby shopkeeper, who managed to keep his flat cap on his head as he raced out to aid the two ladies, accompanied by several other witnesses to the incident. Ellers was undamaged, and after graciously thanking their helpers, she set about fidgeting and fussing over Miss Iverson.

The young lady was not harmed. After checking to ensure her pet was similarly uninjured, she began looking around the square in search of the runaway carriage, intent on giving the amateur whip a piece of her mind. Further along the way, the shopkeeper yelled loudly at the two gentlemen seated upon the now stationary phaeton as a groom settled the horses. With a very unladylike snarl she marched toward them, the golden dog at her heels with his hackles raised.

"What is the meaning of this, sir," she shouted as she approached. The two occupants of the phaeton were distracted by the yelling storekeeper and had not noticed her advancing upon them, but when a loud, angry bark sounded from the dog, they both turned and came face to face with the would-be victim of their reckless escapade.

"I say, what is the meaning of this!" she repeated loudly, her color rising and her hands clenched in small fists at her sides. "Have you entirely lost your wits, sir? To entrust the reins to this, this—incompetent idiot? What can have possibly possessed you to allow your horses to be driven by one who is so clearly unworthy of them? It is unfathomable. Unfathomable, sir."

The elder of the two gentlemen dismounted the carriage and faced his assailant. With a methodical stare, he took the measure of Miss Iverson, from her neatly dressed person to her growling golden-haired protector. Gone was the belligerent scowl he had worn facing the shopkeeper only moments earlier, replaced with an ashamed look of concern as he swept off his hat and bowed before her.

"You are quite right, ma'am. I do apologize. Please be assured that the like will not happen again. My young cousin will not be allowed to handle anything better than a donkey until his skills are up to snuff." The older man looked up at the young gentleman who was hunched over in the forward seat of the phaeton. Something in the drawl of his voice seemed almost mocking before he continued in a concerned tone, "I trust you are unharmed?"

"I am quite uninjured, sir," Miss Iverson declared loudly, "despite the best efforts of your companion, I must say!"

"Oliver, my dear boy, dismount the carriage and apologize immediately to the lady for your ineptitude." said the elder gentleman in an irritated tone. The young man shot a resentful glance at his companion, then hurriedly alighted from the carriage and stood before the glowering almost-victim.

"Indeed, ma'am, I am very sorry for almost running you down. You've no notion how strong my cousin's horses are. I'm afraid I was quite out of my depth," the young man said as he stared at the cobblestones. He glanced furtively upward as he ran a hand through his hair and was stunned by the glowing brown eyes that stared back at him. The firmly pursed lips hid clenched teeth but did no harm to the prettiness of her face, and he was in such awe that further words escaped him.

They did not, however, escape her.

"I see now you are certainly older than I am. Pray tell me, what young man of your years has not learned to at least respect his horses enough to resist the urge to tear at their mouths? And ringing your whip over their heads—have you no sense at all? Was it your intent to terrorize them?"

It was fortunate at that moment the elder cousin chose to step in, for the young gentleman named Oliver now colored up defensively and seemed about to find his voice in the form of an indignant retort, but his cousin cut him off.

"There, you're quite deserving of having a bite taken from you, young cub. The young lady is justifiably upset. We shall escort her to her lodgings and ensure she meets with no further harm," said the elder cousin. "My name is Saliston. Please allow us to be of service to you, Miss…?"

Ellers suddenly appeared at her charge's elbow and took a firm hold, saying, "Thank you, sir, that is quite unnecessary. I am sure you are much too busy. We will be on our way."

The man named Saliston blinked in some surprise as the sharp-eyed Ellers quickly looked him up and down suspiciously before inexorably steering Miss Iverson away. Even the dog seemed almost to offer a derisive snort as it followed. Still quite incensed, the young lady strode away with an indignant flounce in her step. The walkway had become crowded with onlookers, but the people parted deferentially for the ladies to pass by. The angry shopkeeper began again to take the two gentlemen to task, railing against young whippersnappers galloping about the streets in racing carriages, running young ladies down and causing trouble for honest tradespeople. As the crowd joined in, Saliston lost sight of the ladies in the babble.

Chapter 2

The private parlor of the small inn was empty of servants, the last having brought in a board carrying cheese and ham sometime before the clock sounded nine tremulous tones. The Duke of Saliston sat across from his young cousin, reclining in his chair with a glass of port dangling languidly from his fingertips and his booted feet kicked up and crossed upon the table. His cousin had remained silent through dinner but had since progressed to offering short replies to attempts at conversation, so after the duke had emptied a bottle of a very tolerable port, he ventured to discuss the topic of the events that had taken place that afternoon.

"Well, dear boy, you certainly have a way of making an impression on the fairer sex," Saliston said blithely before tipping back his glass. "Might I suggest that in the future, you first try conversation to attract a pretty girl before leaping to the act of running her down in the street to gain her notice?"

Oliver Fairley, the Earl of Hartwell, groaned loudly and thrust his face into his hands before sliding dramatically down onto the table. He lay with his forehead down and ran his hands through his hair, letting loose another anguished groan. Then his muffled voice finally sounded an intelligible response to the duke's mocking statement.

"She really was very pretty, wasn't she," Oliver said

13

into the table.

"She was indeed."

"And I could have killed her."

"You could have. Almost succeeded, in fact."

"You are not easing my conscience, cousin."

"Dear boy, it is not *your* conscience that should require easing but my own," Saliston said firmly. He tossed back the last of the port in his cup before pulling his feet down to the floor. Leaning forward, he reached for another bottle. "I ought to have taken a closer interest in your education many years ago like I promised your father I would. If only I hadn't let your blessed mother berate me into leaving you in her charge, you might have learned to handle a horse, and to drive, and fight, and drink, and shoot, like your papa and I did when we were boys."

He paused and considered for a moment before amending his statement to advise that the shooting and drinking had come well after the riding and fighting had. "It doesn't signify when, but you should have been raised by a man."

A sardonic laugh escaped Oliver. He raised his head and stared at his cousin. "Mama says hunting is for neck-or-nothings, and shooting and pugilism are both vulgar pursuits unsuited to real gentlemen."

"I wonder if she had your dear cousin Moore in mind when she said as much," Saliston replied with a snarl.

"Charlie can do no wrong in Mama's eyes, but even he could not convince her to let me learn to ride," Oliver said sulkily. "It always seemed rather unfair that she was proud of his achievements."

Saliston snorted derisively and muttered something

under his breath that Oliver couldn't quite hear. Silence settled on the pair for a few moments before the duke queried why his cousin had said he knew how to drive before being allowed to take charge of the grays.

"Well, Charlie had let me drive his bay pair around in the home park a few weeks ago, and he said I was quite capable, so I thought—"

"Moore let you drive his bonesetters and said you were capable?" Saliston summarized with shock plastered across his face. "I might have supposed that scapegrace was to blame. He was never a good judge of horseflesh—nor anything else, for that matter."

Oliver colored up and instinctively leaped to the defense of his revered cousin Charlie. The sporadic nature of Mr. Moore's visits to the Hartwell home during childhood had made him something of a hero to the younger boy. Small acts of kindness, such as teaching him to play at cards, masked the fact that Mr. Moore's attentions were actually devoted to his aunt, who inexplicably preferred him over her own son. Her favor had expressed itself in not just an emotional sense but also a material way that had not attracted Oliver's notice for many years.

Jealousy was not an emotion Oliver had ever consciously recognized in himself, never having had regular interaction with boys of his own age other than Charlie Moore, who was still nine years his senior. However, at the tender age of twelve, he recalled an overwhelming confusion when he watched his mother present his cousin with a riding horse while loudly rejecting her son's request to *learn* to ride. When he later learned that Lady Hartwell had gifted Mr. Moore his very first pony at a mere seven years of age, the initial confusion developed into profound resentment directed at his mother.

The resentment had faded somewhat when Oliver discovered, quite by accident, that his Mama's strict control would seemingly miraculously dissipate when he reached the age of twenty-one. He would begin to receive an allowance from his late father's estate. The discovery occurred at the ripe old age of eighteen, when a new maid in his mother's household forgot the stern instruction to prevent young Master Oliver from entering the study while Lady Hartwell entertained a visitor.

Mr. White was the man of business appointed as a financial trustee by the late Lord Hartwell, and he had not clapped eyes on the young master since the late Earl of Hartwell's death when the heir was a mere three years old. He had long ago grown suspicious of Lady Hartwell's excuses in preventing him from speaking to her son. When the young gentleman had made his unannounced entrance into the study that day at Calverley, Mr. White had brazenly stared her Ladyship down and declared loudly that she had been permitted to interfere in matters quite long enough. It was time the young master be allowed to understand the position he was someday to inherit.

The provision of an allowance for the young earl would begin at the age of twenty-one. However, the guardianship and estate had been placed in the hands of one Duke of Saliston, his late papa's closest friend and cousin to his mother. The late Lord Hartwell's early demise had ended a sudden and short period of illness, during which time he had taken pains to see that his son and wife were adequately cared for. Still, having come to a better understanding of his wife's manner and demeanor as a parent during their short marriage, he deemed her unfit to be in sole charge of the boy and placed primary care in the hands of the duke.

Unfortunately, Lord Hartwell failed to convey his concerns regarding his wife's fitness as a parent to the duke. When that gentleman unexpectedly found himself charged with caring for his deceased friend's offspring, he was quite as astonished by the bequest as the mother had been. She had immediately rung a peal fit to wake the dead. So shocked was he by her abuses and wishing only to be left in peace to mourn his childhood friend, Saliston had refrained from exercising his rights over the boy and left him to the care of his mother. It was an error in judgment; he now loudly repented over the second bottle of port.

"Settle down, rattlepate. The one to blame is your mama. I know it. And myself, for I should have come to see you long before White ever wrote to me," Saliston said begrudgingly.

Oliver's face remained flushed once the duke silenced his stoic diatribe in defense of Mr. Moore, but he was not a contentious person by nature and so let the matter fall as the duke redirected his ire toward Lady Hartwell. He still held much anger against the lady he deemed personally responsible for preventing his learning regular gentlemanly pursuits as his contemporaries had in youth. Thankfully, not long following the event of meeting Mr. White, the duke had presented himself at the ancestral country home of the Earls of Hartwell.

That day saw an extraordinarily thunderous quarrel between his newly revealed guardian and his despised mother. The young Oliver Fairley, Earl of Hartwell, was immediately placed under the tutelage of an exceptional professor to instruct him, with a view to his one day taking up his deceased parent's seat in the House. The duke also provided a suitable horse and man to teach him to ride, and later a hunter as he progressed in his skills, though his mother flatly refused to entertain the idea of permitting him to hunt. A tailor was also commissioned to produce a wardrobe suited to a young gentleman of eighteen, and he was schooled in archery and fencing, though pistols were also strictly forbidden by his parent.

Not for the first time did Oliver feel intensely aware of gratitude for his guardian's role in changing his life from what it had been three years earlier. He may not yet know how to drive, shoot, or box, but he knew the duke was why his horizons had broadened so significantly since the day he entered the study unannounced. His gratitude also extended to Mr. White, whose interference had brought Saliston back to Calverley to confront the Countess of Hartwell and re-assert his claims over his ward.

After lingering on these thoughts for a few moments, Oliver said earnestly, "I am grateful to you, cousin. I hope you know it."

"Please refrain from expressing your gratitude again, Oliver," Saliston replied sharply and brusquely. "It hardly signifies that I improved your lot for three years when I had left you to your mother for so long. You may thank me once you can handle the grays without trampling ladies in the street, for if there is one thing I will not allow, it is someone teaching you to drive beside myself—and if you cannot learn to tell the difference between my grays and your cousin's horrid bays, I'll wash my hands of you."

Oliver laughed loudly at that and promised faithfully to learn as best he could. After a moment of silence, a slight frown darkened his brow, and he looked at his cousin with confusion before asking, "George, did it not seem odd to you that she was more concerned about—"

"About the horses than she was about being knocked into the street? Yes, I rather thought so at the time myself. Quite intriguing, in fact," Saliston interrupted reflectively. "And the dog. It was not the kind of dog a lady generally would keep, and if I am not mistaken, it was not a common mongrel."

"What do you think it is?"

"Spanish," said the duke absently as he refilled his cup. "A shepherd dog, I think? Seen them in paintings. Not the sort of mutt a lady keeps, not by my reckoning. Not but what it's pleasant to find a lady who doesn't take one of those curst heel nippers about with her. Whoever she turns out to be, I wager she'll make an impression in London. Exceptionally unconventional."

After a short pause to take a swig of his port, he looked at his cousin across the table and said, "I think you will have much to make up for after your less than impressive efforts to make yourself known to her today."

"And what makes you think I have the least interest?"

"Well, I know *she* won't have the least interest," replied the duke with a loud laugh. "And I'll have you know that there ain't a single one of your forebears that wasn't married before his twenty-fifth year. You've got a tradition to uphold."

"Cousin, I've just got my freedom. Why would I leg-shackle myself now?" Oliver said seriously.

The duke smiled thoughtfully. "Well, then, I see

White didn't get to tell you the whole of it?"

"The whole of what?"

"You understand the provision of an allowance, but it never occurred to you to wonder that a young man such as yourself, who has attained his majority, should be entitled only to an allowance and not the entirety of his fortune?"

Oliver's brow furrowed in a frown. "Mama said—"

"My dear boy, any time you want to begin a sentence with 'Mama said'—don't!" cried the duke. "I gave you more credit. Whatever your mama said, I'll wager she lied. A more grasping and scheming wench I never met, by God!"

"Well, then, what is the reason?" said Oliver, a touch of the frustration that had welled up in him tainting his tone.

"I believe your mother wanted to keep you under continued house arrest in an effort to claim your allowance as her own. She has received a stipend to allow her to maintain Calverley and see to your education, though of course that was not done, so I do wonder—well, never mind that. The estate will continue to pay for her maintenance at a reduced rate until you marry or turn thirty, whichever comes first. You will also take control of your fortune and estates for yourself. At that time, you will be able to choose whether to continue to fund her lifestyle or not," Saliston replied. He continued in a sharp tone, "Oliver, my boy, abandon the naiveté of your youth and hear me when I urge you to question everything. Particularly anything your curst mama has told you. You are a man grown now. Do not let yourself be led about."

Oliver childishly dropped his head onto the table

with another loud sigh. His trusting nature had long been used against him, but instead of learning to question her motives, he had relied on White and Saliston to protect him from her for the last three years. Now that Saliston had removed him from Calverley and Lady Hartwell's sphere of influence, he supposed it was time to learn the lesson for himself.

"I shall do my best, cousin," he said with quiet determination. After several moments of silence with no reply forthcoming, Oliver lifted his head and realized his cousin had fallen asleep.

Chapter 3

The remainder of the journey was considerably less exciting for the Iverson family than had been the first half, with the incident at Stafford. Lady Iverson had been greatly shocked to learn her daughter had almost been run down by a neck-or-nothing young man in a runaway carriage, while Lord Iverson expressed much the same disgust as had his daughter when the episode was described to him.

As a member of the Four Horse Club, Lord Iverson was known to be an excellent whip. His boys had been carefully educated from their youth to ride and later to drive with a quiet horse before they were eventually trusted with the reins of his own prized cattle. His daughter was no exception; indeed, Lord Iverson was of the opinion that she outshone her siblings in skill.

Miss Iverson's horsemanship was indeed unrivaled amongst her contemporaries. Other young ladies may have been cursorily schooled to ride and follow the hunt at a sedate pace or perhaps drive a pony and gig, but Miss Iverson proficiently led the chase and was given possession of her own phaeton at fifteen, capable of driving a pair or a team of three, four, or six horses.

With two elder brothers, Miss Iverson had never wanted for amusement, for Richard and Edward were as energetic as their father had been in his youth. With the addition of their orphaned cousin Matthew, the trio had become a very merry four. The three young boys were all particularly kind-natured and doted on the only girl in their group, never allowing her to be left behind when they engaged in some scheme to entertain themselves. Lord and Lady Iverson, being rather indulgent parents, had allowed their daughter to play alongside the boys and encouraged her sporting proclivities, which included archery, fencing, hunting, and shooting. While quietly proud of her daughter's abilities, Lady Iverson made every effort to ensure she would not be seen as a tomboy.

She carefully instructed her daughter in the feminine arts of painting, needlework, dancing, singing, and music. While Lucilla's skill at watercolors was negligible, she sketched prettily, her needlework was quite fine, and she demonstrated a handsome singing voice and genuine enjoyment of music and dancing, which led her to apply herself carefully to these in particular. Her French was passable, but she had taken it upon herself to learn Spanish so that she might impress her brothers when they returned from the Peninsula on leave.

Both Richard and Edward had chosen a military life, the elder beginning at seventeen in the volunteer militia before his father purchased his lieutenancy in the cavalry in 1806. Following close on his brother's heels, Edward took up with the Foot Guard three years later, serving as aide de camp to the colonel of his regiment.

Both brothers had been present at Araplies when Wellington had maneuvered his heavy cavalry to engage the battle that would be called Salamanca. Two days before the battle, Richard had strolled into camp with a basket dangling from his arm, which he had carefully placed beside his brother and begged him to guess what he'd found. Edward had been rather tap-hackled at the time, but in recounting the episode some several weeks later to his family, he had recalled the touching interlude quite clearly. A very excited Richard had lifted the basket lid to reveal a golden ball of fur, peacefully sleeping. The puppy had woken itself with a gentle snore, and the brothers had enjoyed some time playing with the little dog they promptly named Chico. When pressed to divulge how he'd come across it, Richard confessed he had met a Basque soldier whose bitch had recently weaned two pups. The soldier had wanted to sell the smaller one, so, being a kindly young man, Richard had purchased the pup to take it home to their younger sister on his next furlough.

Fate decided that it would be Edward and not Richard who would bring home the downy golden bundle, with a black bandana tied about its neck, and place it in his sister's arms when he finally returned after the battle. He'd sold out his commission immediately after burying his brother and made the trek home to England. By the time he arrived, Lord and Lady Iverson's shock had dwindled into quiet and profound grief. Feeling the loss as keenly as anyone, Miss Iverson had clasped the wriggling Chico tightly, and the two had been inseparable since that day.

He now sat at his mistress' feet as she frustratedly discussed the proper handling of high-couraged horses with her papa over the dinner table while Lady Iverson indulgently listened to the passionate pair debate the topic that had become something of a custom in the four days since the occurrence of the incident.

"Is this a common failing among men in London, Papa?" Miss Iverson sighed.

"I should think not, my dear," her papa replied in a matter-of-fact tone. "I should say that the young chap you encountered would be rather singular indeed. Even the Pinkest of Pinks can drive a pair down a quiet street without running a pedestrian down."

"I cannot imagine how the boy must have spent his time if he's not learned to drive," Lady Iverson wondered out loud. "One never could keep Richard from trying to trick Smithers into handing him the reins, even when he was a little boy. Edward and Matthew too. They were both quite unruly at times. Perhaps the boy didn't have a father to teach him? After all, if you'd not had Papa to teach you, where would you have learned, dearest?"

Miss Iverson pondered her mother's words with a doubtful look on her face. Still, she eventually owned it was possible that such a reason could explain the deficiency. She continued to mourn the evils of being expected to conceal her own capability in favor of behaving in a ladylike manner, which had her papa laughing loudly. Still, as her complaints were delivered in rather a satirical way, her mother took no offense and instead indulged the idea that her daughter was indeed very hard done by.

"Perhaps we ought to talk of merrier things, Cilla. Tomorrow we go to see Madame about the design of your court dress, and we will take nuncheon with Aunt Augusta. Then I believe Papa has a surprise for you. Am I right, my dear?"

"Indeed, I do," Lord Iverson exclaimed with a wink. "An excellent evening to be had by all, I hope."

"Am I to be given a hint?"

"Certainly not. Where is the fun in that?"

"Well, have it your way," Miss Iverson said

nonchalantly.

****

Almost two months later, Lady Iverson and her daughter visited a certain fashionable modiste on Bond Street. The design of a court dress had taken considerable time to meet Lady Iverson's and Madame Barbier's similarly exacting standards and tastes. Several weeks after settling on how the dress should look, that skilled artist had taken delivery of a special parcel that had been sent particularly for the purpose of beginning the arduous task of piecing together the carefully planned court dress. Now having the young lady before her, the Frenchwoman exclaimed over her dark looks and petite figure. She congratulated Lady Iverson on the excellent notion of lowering the waistline to a more flattering level in contrast to the many other court dresses that had been ordered through her little shop.

"La, *Madame*! It is *très infortuné*, these ridiculous waistlines. It makes a young lady look quite squat!" she cried. "*Atroce! Assez horrible! Ingénieux*, Madame, to suggest it. Miss Iverson shall be *très élégant*!"

"Quite so, Madame Barbier," Lady Iverson replied calmly with a contented smile before enquiring as to whether Madame approved of the fabric, which promptly sent Madame into raptures. Madame Barbier had not laid eyes on such fine silks and patterns since she left France, she was assured.

"Indeed, Madame, it has been an honor to have been given the commission."

Some time was spent ensuring the three new morning dresses that had been ordered were fitted correctly, and the court dress had been tacked and sized. The two ladies departed the shop with a footman in tow carrying several bandboxes to secure onto the waiting carriage. The ladies then ventured down the street in search of the necessary accessories for ladies on a London jaunt. An excellent milliner was located, along with a pleasant little shop selling ribbons and silk flowers for finishing the several bonnets Miss Iverson had undertaken to spend time refurbishing in the weeks before the coming Drawing Room at which she would be presented.

A special parcel had arrived containing several tall white ostrich feathers with which she intended to make a banded headdress with some of the silk from her dress. A small length of it was wrapped up in her reticule. The almost shimmering ivory luster would be set off by a row of pearls and matching drop earrings that had once belonged to her late grandmother.

While she contentedly browsed a perfectly delectable pair of long silk gloves with delicately embroidered ends and pondered where she might wear them, she was abruptly drawn from her reverie by a rather unseemly screech. When she turned to locate the source of the awful noise, Miss Iverson's gaze landed on the unwelcome sight of Miss Tabitha Wallace and her mother.

Lady Wallace gave her daughter a look of censure, which the young lady entirely ignored. The two women stood in the shop's doorway, one disapprovingly eyeing her surroundings and the other clapping her hands together excitedly at her luck in chancing upon her bosom friend. The bosom friend did not reciprocate the feeling—in fact, she silently prayed for miraculous intervention as the pair advanced upon her.

"Oh, my dear Lucy, how perfectly wonderful it is

that we have found you this morning. I told Mama that we would just step into this shop for a bit of fun to see what they have, and she was quite against it, but I insisted, and here you are! What do you do in this awful little place? It is perfectly horrid, is it not? You'd do much better to find your long gloves at Dawson's. It is a much finer shop. I'm sure only penny-pinchers would frequent this place." Miss Tabitha chattered unabatedly, taking Miss Iverson's arm in her own and petting her hand as she inexorably dragged her from the shop.

Miss Iverson was quite furious at being approached, but it was considerably more mortifying to be treated so familiarly in public. Even the footman who had come along with her gaped in surprise as he hurried to follow the ladies outside. However, she was unwilling to cause a spectacle. Instead, she calmly and firmly removed her arm from the firm grasp in which it was held and stepped back away from the Wallace ladies.

"How do you do, Lady Wallace, Miss Wallace? You find me quite alone at the moment. I have only William to attend me until Mama returns from an errand. I promised faithfully to wait for her here," Miss Iverson said archly with a smile that she hoped was hard rather than friendly, but her indignance went unnoticed.

"My dear, your mama will not mind in the least when she knows that you came away with us," Lady Wallace replied with a condescending air. "Indeed, I venture to say she will be quite pleased that we have come across you, for I am sure she will have felt that horrid little shop to be beneath the dignity of an Iverson."

"Indeed, as it was Mama who left me here, I do not feel you can be right, Lady Wallace."

Not impressed or at all phased by this mild show of

defiance, Miss Wallace asserted she was sure in any case that once Lady Iverson was told her daughter was with her dearest friends that she could not be anything but pleased. "We are quite a happy party, are we not? Mama and I were about to step over to the tea shop, and you will join us. You may leave your footman here to tell Lady Iverson where to find us."

"I'm afraid that will not do, Miss Wallace," Cilla replied firmly, her temper beginning to simmer hotly under her carefully controlled façade. Lady Iverson had always impressed on her daughter the need to be polite in all situations, however uncomfortable. Still, the Wallace ladies' grasping and domineering behavior had begun to gall long ago, and the present situation did nothing to endear them to her.

"Nonsense, you will come away. I'll brook no refusal," Miss Wallace said with a laugh, betraying no sign that she noticed Lucilla's annoyance as she attempted to take her arm again.

"I must insist, Miss Wallace, it will not do. You must allow me to be the judge of what is expected of me."

"There you are, dear. I was coming to find you."

A loud and commanding yet familiar voice sounded from behind Lucilla, and a firm hand took hold of her elbow. There appeared her Aunt Augusta like an angel sent from heaven, staring down her aquiline nose at the mushrooms before her and immediately taking possession of the situation.

"You really should not wander away. Your mother sent me to this charming little shop, but you are not in it as she promised you would be. How was I to find you? Who are these people?"

"Aunt Augusta, this is Lady Wallace and her daughter Miss Tabitha Wallace," Lucilla said politely, contrasting sharply with her aunt's blunt delivery. "Lady Wallace, this is my aunt, the Countess Edevane."

Aunt Augusta stood as rigid as a post with her lips pursed in a prim line, slowly surveying Lady Wallace from her bonnet to her shoes before eyeing the daughter in much the same way. She did not reach out to shake hands with either lady, choosing instead to keep her hold on Lucilla's arm.

"Wallace? Hm. I assume you are a relation of Sir John Wallace?" the countess said almost accusingly.

"My husband, ma'am."

Thin brows rose swiftly and drew together before Lady Edevane replied archly, "Is that so indeed? Then I was acquainted with your mother-in-law. I was sorry to hear of her passing."

"You are too kind, ma'am," Lady Wallace answered in a gracious tone and seemed about to continue when Lady Edevane broke in loudly and abruptly.

"Well, I must thank you for your care of my niece. However, we really must be going. You there, William. Take this bag, and be sure not to let it drag. Come, dear, your mother will be waiting. Good day, ladies."

Once again, Miss Iverson was borne inexorably away. This time she went willingly after bobbing a quick curtsy to Lady Wallace and singing out a cheerful goodbye. When out of earshot, she turned with a relieved laugh and thanked her aunt graciously for her rescue.

"It was nothing, my dear. You almost have the trick of it. You just need a little more practice."

"Practice in what, Aunt?" Lucilla giggled.

"Your delivery of a set-down needs a little more

polish, of course. Never fear. You will pick it up soon enough. You just need to give it a little more kick," Aunt Augusta said with a wink. "John Wallace, eh? Well, his poor grandmama would be turning in her grave, I dare say. Such a sweet old bird she was. Thank heaven she didn't live to see her grandson marry that female."

"You are a complete card, Aunt. How can you speak so?"

"How indeed. You shall see, dearest. A few years of town bronze, and you'll have the knack. How came you to be accosted by that woman and her daughter? It looked as if they meant to carry you off in their talons."

"It certainly seemed so, though I cannot think why they should want to."

"I cannot think why they felt they *could*, though you were fending them off admirably, my dear. I had thought to let you fight it out alone, but the daughter, in particular, seemed hell-bent on her own will. What a pushy miss! Do you know, now I think on it, I had heard some chatter about a Miss Wallace last year."

At that moment, the Iverson carriage appeared, with Lady Iverson seated docilely inside. She looked to be distracted by something hanging from her sleeve before she glanced up and noticed her daughter and Lady Edevane approaching.

"Ah, you found her. I was sure she would not have left," Lady Iverson called out as they came closer. "I am so sorry, Cilla. Your aunt came upon me quite overcome by heat and said she would fetch you. Did you find anything you liked?"

"A pair of long gloves, Mama, but I shall have to go back for them," Miss Iverson replied, smoothing her dress as she sat facing her parent and aunt.

"Did you not have enough to buy them? Shall we go back now?"

"No, it is quite all right. I shall go back another day. I should have taken them today, but Tabitha and Lady Wallace came upon me in the shop and fairly dragged me out before I could."

"Oh, dear." Lady Iverson sighed.

"A proper waylaying it was too, Anne. But our girl was holding her own." Aunt Augusta laughed.

Lady Iverson's eyes widened, and she stared at her daughter with concern. "Oh, I do hope you were not rude to them, dearest. I'm sure you know they mean well, even though they can be a little vexing."

"A little vexing? Anne, have you suffered a blow to the head?" the countess exclaimed in horror. "A little vexing, indeed."

"Well, perhaps they are more than a *little* vexing," her ladyship replied meekly. "But it is not meant maliciously, Aunt."

"Whether it is intended or not, I can assure you that nothing can be worse than humoring them!"

The two elder ladies being thus engaged in conversation afforded Miss Iverson some entertainment on the drive back to Grosvenor Street. When they arrived at their destination, the countess was still expounding the evils of entertaining connections such as the Wallace family. Lady Iverson continued to interject at regular intervals in defense of well-meaning, if somewhat irritating, persons of one's acquaintance.

Chapter 4

It is understood that the moment in which a young lady makes her curtsy to Queen Charlotte sets the tone of her entire first Season. And indeed, of any subsequent Seasons, should she be so unfortunate as to remain on the Marriage Mart past her debut.

No such misfortune was to befall Miss Iverson, standing beside her mother in an elegantly cut gown of turquoise patterned silk with a round train over a petticoat of ivory and trimmed with matching fringe and threads of gold shimmering throughout. While other young ladies battled with perfectly horrid hoops hitched up in mimicry of the current high-waisted fashion, Miss Iverson's gown elegantly framed her petite waist in a gown reminiscent of a bygone era. While it was absent of absurdly wide panniers, the result was entirely in keeping with the original vision of the Court Dress of the previous century. The ensemble was completed with a matching turquoise band trimmed with tiny pearls and several tall white ostrich feathers, which gave the effect of Miss Iverson being somewhat taller than her usual diminutive size. It was agreed the result was excellent.

After Lucilla executed a well-practiced, deferential curtsy, the Queen condescended to spend two whole minutes complimenting Lady Iverson's choice of dress for her daughter. She was heard to ask her ladyship where she had obtained such delicious fabric, after which she nodded her head with an indulgent smile and watched the Iverson ladies make their retreat.

Such a fortuitous beginning could not go unnoticed, and Miss Iverson soon became the subject of some talk among the seasoned leaders of fashion. However, her gown also drew some ire from less fortunate damsels, and the loudest of these ladies was none other than one who was often heard to declare herself to be Miss Iverson's greatest friend. Although she had never been presented at court herself, Miss Wallace had a very particular notion of how an acceptable court dress looked. Miss Iverson was very loudly informed that her dress failed on every count to meet these exacting standards.

"That shade of turquoise is not at all flattering. Very few people can wear it, and I'm afraid, dear, that you are not one of them," Miss Wallace prated on. She had barely stopped for breath in ten minutes, and Miss Iverson was in no mind to interrupt. Instead, she sat quietly with Chico curled up beside her chair and looked about the room distractedly, her cup and saucer cradled in her lap as she occasionally glanced at the mantel clock.

Lady Wallace was seated next to her daughter, rigidly upright and imperiously nodding along in approval of her daughter's strictures. She would sporadically interject with some severe comment or other, effectively underlining her daughter's criticisms. However, the words of both ladies fell largely upon deaf ears, and though she did offer several small rebuttals to the diatribe, Lady Iverson was mostly quiet, as was her habit in the presence of the oppressive Lady Wallace.

While she was busy ignoring their guests, a fact that

neither of those ladies noticed, Miss Iverson was keeping an ear bent for the sound of a different visitor. She expected that, at any moment, her Aunt Augusta would appear in the doorway to whisk her away from the house for the day on a short journey to visit a friend in the country. After what had seemed like endless weeks in London, Lucilla was fairly bursting to escape the sights and smells of town and enjoy some fresh air. And kinder company.

Just at that moment, the downy golden dog raised pricked ears, and she heard a rap at the door followed by the unmistakable footsteps of the incomparable Murray as he trotted down the hall to greet the visitor. Her immediate relief at knowing salvation was near dimmed when Lucilla realized it was quite unlike the Countess Edevane to knock at all when she was expected. The dimming worsened when she realized the footsteps coming down the hall were far too loud to be Murray escorting a lady—those were boots, if she was not mistaken. And she was not, for a moment after this deduction was made, Chico rose to his feet with a growl as Murray opened the door and announced the arrival of Mr. Charles Moore. Lucilla's devastation was complete.

Lady Iverson stood and greeted her guest, her most affable smile upon her face. Murray backed out of the room quietly, with a parting glance at the young gentleman that masked something looking like disdain, and Miss Iverson, catching his eye, rolled her eyes slightly, which brought a small smile to the butler's face.

The new arrival was entirely unaware of the exchange. Instead, he was engrossed in greeting his hostess expressively before turning his attention to Miss Iverson and gallantly bowing over her hand. Just as he was about to take the liberty of kissing it, Lucilla snatched her hand away and sat primly with a polite smile painted on her face, petting Chico's head as he rested it on her knee protectively.

Lady Iverson then introduced Mr. Moore to the Wallace ladies, and after an appropriate greeting to the older lady, he punctiliously bowed over Miss Wallace's hand. With a kittenish smile, this young lady held the gentleman's fingers in a firm grip until he placed a fleeting kiss on her hand. She tittered prettily before taking her seat beside her mother.

"I had not expected to see you here today, Mr. Moore," Lady Iverson exclaimed. "His lordship is out on business, of course, and so Murray has brought you to us, so I am sorry you must make do with us instead."

"No indeed, Lady Iverson," said the young man courteously. "My mission was to ask Miss Iverson to join me for a drive 'round the Park."

Every eye in the room turned to Lucilla at that moment, and her lips twitched wordlessly as she fought the urge to offer a negative retort. She rather resented being put on the spot, especially with the Wallace ladies as an audience, knowing they would severely condemn her for denying Mr. Moore's request. But instead of issuing a hasty and passionate rejection, Lucilla took a deep breath, crossed her hands demurely in her lap and smiled warmly, much more warmly than she was ever naturally inclined to smile at Charles Moore, and said, "Alas, I am afraid I am spoken for this afternoon, Mr. Moore, for I expect my Aunt Augusta at any moment to arrive to collect me."

"A shame, but so it is. Perhaps another time, Mr. Moore," Lady Iverson said quickly before turning the subject away from her daughter. "Mr. Moore is our neighbor in Lancashire, Lady Wallace. We have known him from a boy. Morcombe has stood not three miles from Gracewood for generations."

"Indeed, and do you have family back home in Lancashire, Mr. Moore?" Lady Wallace enquired in an arch tone.

"My father chooses to stay home to tend our estate, Lady Wallace. I, however, feel the need to socialize, and so I present myself in London. It is gratifying to have such friends in town this year. I foresee an enjoyable Season!" Mr. Moore replied affably, but as he finished his sentence, his gaze drifted away from Lady Wallace and back onto Lucilla with a suggestive smirk. Fighting off a shudder of revulsion, Lucilla looked away.

It was certainly nothing in Mr. Moore's appearance that put her off, for indeed he looked every inch a gentleman in his buckskins, glossy Hessians, and coat of blue superfine. There was nothing in the words he spoke that ought to offend her, either. It was simply an instinct. A feeling that warned her not to allow him too close. She had often felt it in his presence in her childhood, and her brothers had thought just the same, leading them to unceremoniously spurn his friendship in their youth and later in adulthood.

There had been several families in the neighborhood that the Iversons were relatively close to and whose children had visited regularly and befriended the Iverson brood. Raised in a home with rambunctious brothers, Lucilla was no stranger to boyish pranks and escapades.

However, there had often been something malevolent simmering under the surface of Mr. Moore's exceedingly charming exterior that gradually caused the district's young persons to avoid his company. As her brothers had outgrown their childish antics, so too, it appeared, had he, and while he had blown back into her sphere as a clean-cut and smooth-talking young man of seven-and-twenty, she still held him at a distance and with a considerable measure of suspicion. Besides that, Chico held him in decided distaste and never hesitated to growl when he was near.

It had become apparent in the months before the Iverson's removal to London that Mr. Moore sought to make himself agreeable to the entire family, but particularly to Miss Iverson. He had seen fit to accost her while she was alone in the home park exercising her horse on no less than three occasions and had developed a knack for visiting Gracewood at precisely the right moment for Lady Iverson to feel it necessary to invite him to dine. Lord Iverson had even found himself pounced on while conducting business in Liverpool on several occasions and had exclaimed loudly to his family that Mr. Moore was an exceptional pest.

"We'll have the fellow on our doorstep daily if we are not careful, Anne!" his lordship had growled. "Very smooth he is, my word, but he's got the wrong end of the stick if he thinks Cilla will fall for his hums. Just like his father—pockets to let and on the catch for an heiress!"

Politeness had demanded the Iversons not rebuff Mr. Moore too harshly, for he had committed no grievous sin that they were aware of beyond causing irritation and inconvenience. However, his appearance in London so soon after their own had put Lucilla on edge, and her attempts to treat him with cool reserve and keep him at arm's length went entirely unnoticed by him. Lucilla suspected he deliberately ignored her efforts at polite rejection, but the kind-hearted Lady Iverson put it down to blind infatuation.

At this particular moment, he received no encouragement from Miss Iverson to remain, so the ever-forward Miss Wallace stepped in to fill the breach. It had taken her all of half a moment to note Mr. Moore's extravagant attire and immediately identify him as a wealthy young countryman on a town jaunt and obviously hunting for a suitable wife. The fact that he was not unwelcome in the Iverson home could only mean Lucilla's parents did not consider him an unsuitable match for their daughter, which could only make him all the more interesting to Miss Wallace.

"For shame, Lucy! How can you refuse when Mr. Moore has come particularly to invite you? I assure you, sir, that I should never find myself too busy if I were invited," Miss Wallace said in a light voice and waved her hand at Lucilla as she glanced coyly at the young man.

What he would have said in reply would never be known, for at that moment, the door was flung wide and Lady Edevane entered like a whirlwind, causing the golden-haired dog to leap to his feet in excitement and set about yipping around her feet. Lady Iverson was still recovering from a small measure of shock that had accompanied Miss Wallace's extremely forward behavior. Still, she saw her sister-in-law's appearance as ordained by God, for at that moment she was sure nothing but a miracle would have tempered her embarrassment.

"Ah, my dears! I do apologize for my tardiness. My coachman advises me that one of his wheelers was found to be lame, and so he had to arrange a switch—whatever any of that means, I have not the smallest idea, though I am sure Lucilla may instruct me." Lady Edevane said as she kissed her sister-in-law's cheek.

"Indeed, I can tell you, Aunt, though I am sure you will not care in the least," Miss Iverson replied smilingly.

"I'm sure you are right, darling. I am sure you are right. Now go and gather your things so we may leave. Who are these people, Anne?" the countess asked, suddenly realizing there were other people in the room.

The viscountess blushed at her artlessness before she replied, "Sister, you've met Lady Wallace and her daughter. And this is Mr. Charles Moore. I believe you've made his acquaintance also?"

Mr. Moore had stood when Lady Edevane entered the room, and he now stepped forward as his hostess introduced him again to her sister-in-law. He put on an air of charm and gallantry as he extended his hand, but it was flatly ignored by her ladyship, who looked him up and down keenly.

"I see, yes, Philip Moore's boy. Yes, the similarity is unmistakable," Lady Edevane said in entirely uncomplimentary accents. She then turned and addressed her sister—and by default, the rest of the room as well. "I must compliment you, my dear. That dress you chose for Lucilla was simply exquisite, perfection! The whole town is talking of it. She's already a hit, the Queen has seen to that. What condescension! It was remarkable. I've not seen such a flying start in many a year, and lord knows, I've seen plenty."

"Thank you, my dear, you are too kind!" Lady Iverson said, her voice glowing with pride. "Here she is now. Do you have your parasol, Cilla?"

"Murray has it at the door. I will collect it as I pass."

"Have a lovely time."

"Come, Cilla! Milton does so hate to have the horses standing. He's always scolding me. I have no notion as to why, but so it is. Explain it to me in the carriage! Goodbye, Anne. And to you all, as well. Chico, come, you wicked beast," the countess added as she breezed out of the room with the dog eagerly following at her heels.

Aunt Augusta was right. Lucilla hadn't yet learned the trick of blowing in and out of a room with such confidence and carelessness. She hoped one day to manage it, but that day was not today, and she found herself feeling far too embarrassed to flit out of the room without first properly bidding the assembled company adieu. She may not like a single one of them, but she was far too well-mannered to show it. The chore was quickly completed, and she fairly ran out of the room to the front door, where Murray held out her parasol and cloak before advising her none too quietly to enjoy her escape.

Once the Edevane carriage was rumbling its way down the street, Aunt Augusta began an airy diatribe full of congratulations on her apparent success. Lucilla blushed furiously and owned Her Majesty's attentions were extremely gratifying. She had certainly never expected it and had been so very nervous, but Queen Charlotte had been so gracious it had quite washed her terror away.

"I heard many a whisper about you, darling. Everyone present was in a bustle to find out who you were. Lady Jersey approached me herself and said she'd like me to introduce you as soon as possible. I shall arrange it, for your mama will want to obtain vouchers for Almack's. Lady Drummond-Burrell also asked after you. It is quite amusing to have those two in competition for the honor of inviting the Season's Diamond."

"Really, Aunt Augusta! I am no such thing. Just think, if one of them were to know that I'm more at home in the stables than a drawing room, they would surely drop!"

"All the more reason for them not to know," Lady Edevane said archly as she affectionately ruffled Chico's coat while the dog leaned its head out at the side of the carriage. "Although I do think it will not at all harm you for the young men about to see you are quite their match on a horse. It might even drum up more interest. Just remember not to gallop in the Park, I beg of you!"

"Mama has already warned me, and I can assure you, Aunt, that I have no intention of ruining yours or Mama's efforts on my behalf," Miss Iverson replied with a laugh, a merry twinkle sparkling in her dark eyes.

"Good!" said the countess. After a moment of silence, she began a new line of discussion by asking what Mr. Moore was doing in her mother's drawing room.

"He is our neighbor."

"I'm aware of that, dear. I grew up at Gracewood, so I am well acquainted with the Moores," said the countess grimly. "But I asked what he was doing in your father's house."

"Well, I suppose he's come to town for the Season."

"Is he courting you?"

"Aunt!" Miss Iverson gasped loudly.

"Be on your guard, Cilla. All of the Moore men are bad seeds!" the countess said darkly, shaking her finger. "Philip Moore was a gamester and a rake in *my* day. My papa—your grandfather, of course—turned him out of the house when he came asking for my hand. As though

I'd have had him, ha! It was well known he needed to marry a fortune after losing what was left of his at the gaming tables. In the end, he married one of Agarth's daughters. I'm sure she would have had a few pennies, but knowing that rattlepate, he's well and truly lost it all by now, and the son is again on the hunt for an Iverson wife. As though living side by side for generations somehow makes it their right to aspire to the hand of our girls."

"Believe me, Aunt, I have no intention of marrying Charles Moore," Lucilla said firmly. "I've no one to compare him to except for my brothers and Papa when it comes to what a gentleman should be, so I'm afraid the bar is set quite high."

Lady Edevane nodded approvingly and patted her hand, "La, Richard, God rest his soul. And dear Edward and Matthew. If that is the bar you have set, then I need have no fear for you, darling. Lord knows, if anything, I only worry you will end a spinster for being so fastidious."

Lucilla laughed. "That is not a prospect I should fear at all, Aunt. I should be much more comfortable alone than to be saddled with a man I cannot respect."

"Wise beyond your years, my dear. I applaud you. You shall deal famously with Mrs. Carleton, I'm certain! Now, do explain, if you please, what a wheeler is. I am sure I have been duped into thinking this is some serious problem when I am sure it is not."

Miss Iverson smiled warmly and proceeded to explain to her aunt the necessity of having a sound wheeler hitched to one's carriage.

Chapter 5

After a blissful afternoon in the country with her aunt and Mrs. Carleton, Miss Iverson settled back into her town routine of morning calls, dinners, and parties. As the weather had begun to warm, Lord Iverson arranged for the family's riding horses to be slowly trekked by degrees to London in the care of their groom, and so Lucilla finally found herself able to indulge herself with a ride in Hyde Park instead of sitting tamely beside her mama in the landaulet during the fashionable hour of the Promenade.

Along with her hunter, Lord Iverson had surprised his daughter by including her driving pair in his list of requirements, as well as her phaeton. It was not one of those dashing high-perch styles the gentlemen drove, but a perfectly sensible variety with the peculiar addition of blue wheels instead of the customary yellow. It perfectly suited a young lady and the splendid pair of high-stepping white geldings that drew it.

But her first venture into the Park with her horses was aboard the finely built and tempestuous Egyptian blood horse Lord Iverson had seen fit to gift his daughter in her sixteenth year. Many chestnut horses could be seen going about in the Park every day; however, Miss Iverson's striking mount wore a coat of shimmering copper and a unique mane and tail of black mixed with shades of flaxen. Gentlemen and ladies alike watched the elegant creature float by and gasped at its remarkable color, with no one quite able to agree what the name of that color was.

However, the one thing that was absolutely settled upon was that Miss Iverson was an exceptional horsewoman. Her first ride in the Park saw her dressed in a favorite new habit of olive-colored wool that was sharply cut, and upon her brown curls she wore a dashing top hat trimmed with black lace. Lord Iverson rode beside his daughter on a handsome dappled gray, creating a stark contrast between the two animals, and Miss Iverson knew only complete bliss as they cantered gently side by side down the Row. From afar, more than one jealous maiden remarked the red horse was hardly fit for a lady, and their equally jealous mamas agreed that Lord Iverson must be quite mad to have mounted his daughter on such a highly strung creature and declared the young lady was clearly given over to hoydenish behavior.

"Lord Iverson," a lady's voice cried out as the father and daughter had reined in to walk. A quick look about drew their gaze to an elegant carriage in which three ladies sat, but the one who had called out had her arm raised above her head, waving delicately to draw their attention. She was an older woman, dressed in the height of fashion, with a delicately crocheted and netted parasol resting against her shoulder and chestnut ringlets peeping out under her bonnet.

"Maria, what a pleasure to see you," Lord Iverson replied in his booming voice as he guided his horse toward the carriage. "I do not see Dashalong with you. Where is he this fine day?"

"Naughty, Jasper. You're in town now. None of

these country manners, if you please! We must observe the proprieties here, so I must introduce you to my companions, and then you must introduce yours."

"Indeed, you are quite right, Ma—*Lady* Sefton," Lord Iverson replied with a grin that elicited an indulgent laugh from the lady.

"Lord Iverson, this is my cousin Mrs. Craven and her daughter Miss Constance Craven," Lady Sefton said punctiliously. "Constance is just out this Season. I'm sure you saw her at the Drawing Rooms a fortnight since?"

"I believe I did. Very prettily done, Miss Craven! You did not appear half as frightened as most other damsels."

"She managed it very well," Lady Sefton agreed kindly, gently patting her niece's hand with a smile. "Your daughter has been much talked of since that evening. Is this she?"

"Yes, Lady Sefton, allow me to introduce my daughter, Lucilla."

"Miss Iverson, I am very pleased to meet you. Lady Jersey has been chomping at the bit. She was positively determined she would meet you first, and yet, in the end it is I who have the pleasure," Lady Sefton exclaimed jovially.

Lucilla had nudged her gelding forward, but it tossed its head and snorted in protest, so instead of pressing the argument, she tapped it lightly with her cane so she could converse with Lady Sefton alongside the carriage.

"Good day, Lady Sefton. My aunt Augusta has told me so much about you. And I have, of course, met Lord Sefton when he has come to visit us in Lancashire," Miss

Iverson said with a smile. She reached out her gloved hand and gently touched her fingers to Lady Sefton's outstretched hand.

"Indeed, how could I have forgotten," the elder lady replied. "Dear Dashalong was quite enchanted. He has told and re-told the story of your roundly dispatching him in your chariot race. I thought he would have been quite devastated to be brought down a peg by a young lady in her sixteenth year, but there you have it—he was thrilled!"

This drew a laugh from the group before Miss Craven said, "Miss Iverson, your horse is in quite a fidget. How ever do you manage?"

"Oh, he is quite harmless, I assure you," Lucilla laughed as the red horse snorted and pranced in place. "Sierra is all snort and no buck."

"Nonsense, I've been witness to the buck," said Lord Iverson with not a small dash of pride.

"I'm sure I would never manage such a lively creature. I confess I am hardly at home on a *placid* horse," Miss Craven replied with a soft smile. "I am quite envious of you, Miss Iverson. You must be very brave."

The compliment drew a blush to Lucilla's cheeks, but the color was swiftly drained when her eye caught a glimpse of none other than Charles Moore in the distance aboard a fat hack. She forced a smile to her lips and responded kindly to Miss Craven's comment, but with her right hand, she tapped her father's knee with her cane and discreetly pointed in the direction of the approaching rider. The conversation continued with the three other ladies none the wiser for a moment until Lord Iverson suddenly coughed and interrupted the discussion.

"I do apologize, ladies. However, my daughter and

I really ought to keep moving along. This horse of hers is quite fresh and in need of a little exercise before he's handed off to his keepers, and they will surely curse unless he is returned in a less lively state."

Lady Sefton laughed. "Ah, Jasper, you are as bad as my husband, but I am sure you are quite right. My dear Miss Iverson, I shall send your mama my card, and we shall take tea together. I will have vouchers for you both—see if Lady Jersey can stop me. Good day, dear!"

With not a moment to lose, Miss Iverson elegantly wheeled her horse and beat a hasty retreat alongside her father before Mr. Moore and his apparently very sluggish horse could capture them in conversation. Mrs. Craven watched their departure from her carriage and smiled heartily at her cousin before she exclaimed that she'd never seen such a pretty-behaved young lady, present company excluded.

"She is quite charming, is she not? I confess I had expected a hoyden when William gave me an account of his meeting her in the country," Lady Sefton replied merrily. "She's clearly an exceptional horsewoman, but there didn't seem to be anything wanting in her manners at all."

"Nothing at all," Miss Craven said with a wavering smile. "Do you think her a great beauty, Aunt?"

"La! Her mama was a beauty in her day, I will not deny it, but then the fashion was *for* dark girls. Alas, Miss Iverson has come out when men are worshipping fair ladies."

"I do not think it will disadvantage her. Her presentation at court was remarked upon, true enough, but once the gentlemen discover she is more than their match on a horse, Lord Iverson will be swatting them away like flies," said Mrs. Craven in prediction.

"I just had a prophetic vision of the gentlemen of London galloping across the Park in pursuit of the fair Iverson jewel," said Lady Sefton in accents of horror before bursting into a laugh.

The three ladies continued their gentle drive discussing Lady Sefton's ridiculous joke, entirely unaware that the stampede had already begun. Gentlemen bent on catching her during an afternoon excursion in the Park soon learned that in order to keep up with Miss Iverson, they needed to be appropriately mounted, for the days of accosting her whilst she walked with her maid and the growling golden dog were gone.

****

Mr. Moore watched the Iversons' disappearing shapes with irritation. He made absolutely no effort to hide his displeasure, evidenced in the form of a ferocious scowl. Anyone who had considered approaching him soon thought better as he picked his way down the bridle path on his slothful rented hack.

He was an arrogant man to his very core, and so while he rode upon a horse that was not his own, he made sure to be dressed in the peak of fashion with perfectly cut buckskins and a blue coat with a matching top hat. Mr. Moore was the picture of what a young sporting gentleman ought to be.

Unfortunately, he was not much else other than a fine picture, for his peers considered him to be a particularly useless horseman. Whether riding, driving, or betting, he never could pick a good one, and while he himself put it down to poor luck, the wise knew better.

At this particular moment, as he scowled his way up the Row, he knew it had been poor luck that caught him today. It was clear that Miss Iverson had noted his approach and fled before he could reach her. He had been at great pains to make himself agreeable to her before the family departed Lancashire for London—at his father's urging, of course—and he was quite put out that she had not immediately fallen for his charms. He considered it rather irritating that he'd not managed to secure her before she'd been released on the Marriage Mart, but he was not done trying. It was his father's wish to see the Moore family's fortunes restored, and who better to restore them than the heiress of the neighboring estate? It made perfect sense.

He could wish for a less spirited female to chain himself to in matrimony and had indeed said so to his father after receiving another of his haranguing invectives. During that particular argument, he had pointed out to his parent that while Miss Iverson would indeed be handsomely dowered, it was not to be expected that she would inherit her father's seat. She had an elder brother.

But that was before the Hundred Days. That was before Napoleon's escape from Elba and his subsequent rampage upon the Continent. That was before Edward Iverson had left his father seething and re-joined his regiment to take part in the great battle in Brussels—and had not been heard from since.

Mr. Moore the Younger now had reason to believe the Iverson fortunes rested squarely upon Miss Iverson. She might not retain the title, but Gracewood and her father's money would be more than enough to satisfy a fortune hunter. Especially one so conveniently located right next door.

No whisper had been heard of whether Edward had

survived the battle, but in the days before his departure from Liverpool, his father had been heard to loudly and angrily exclaim that he would come home to nothing if he came home at all. A less than discreet housemaid—who soon lost her place within the Gracewood household—was heard to have spread this exciting gossip far enough that it was soon heard in the home of the Moores, where Moore Senior was promptly informed by his toadying butler.

It had settled the question of whether or not Charles could sufficiently manage the feisty personality that Miss Iverson exhibited. He knew she held him in dislike but could not understand why; however, it did not prevent him from trying. He was not yet desperate, of course, but if it should become necessary to use underhanded methods to obtain her, he was not above doing so.

It was, after all, no less than he had done to many other women of a lower order. He was known in the circle of his peers to be a man of carnal habits, and, regrettably, the *ton* did not smile upon rakes lacking in fortune or title—there was so little to recommend such men. However, when a prurient attitude was carefully hidden beneath the façade of a handsome face, fashionable attire, excellent dancing, and enough obsequiousness directed at a hostess—well, much could be concealed.

Thankfully, one such a man could always rely on the graciousness and support of a loving aunt who kept him clothed and mounted well enough to fool the more knowing of the Upper Ten Thousand. He begrudged her only that there'd not been enough funds provided to supply him with a less languid steed, for such a creature could never hope to maintain pace with Miss Iverson's horse, much less catch up to it.

Devil take her! His horse ambled along at a flat jog. *Riding that damned creature, she'll have yet another bloody excuse not to stay still long enough for a conversation.*

Every effort to ingratiate himself with her mother and father had failed. Lady Iverson had at first seemed to encourage his suit; however, he could only assume the daughter had managed to convince her not to. His attention to Lord Iverson had been met with stony silence. He had tried discussing the elder gentleman's sporting pursuits, politics, estate, and business ventures, but the old man had blocked him at every turn. It had never occurred to Mr. Moore that Lord Iverson found him irritating or ridiculous, of course.

Since arriving in London, he had visited in Grosvenor Street every second day of the week. He had invited Miss Iverson to walk and to drive. He had sat talking on mundane topics with her mother for almost an hour in which Miss Iverson had not once raised her gaze from her needlework. He'd resisted the urge to kick that damned dog of hers after it growled at him when he approached her. He was a perfect gentleman. Why did she not see it?

"Lud, what has you in such a foul temper, Moore?"

He was startled out of his reverie by a familiar voice. A wave of loathing swept over him as he looked over his shoulder and saw none other than the Duke of Saliston approaching him in the otherwise deserted area. What had he done to deserve being waylaid like this?

"You look like thunder," his grace said with a contemptuous smile. "What new scheme of yours has gone awry, I wonder?"

"What do you want, Saliston?"

"Nothing at all, lad, nothing at all," replied the duke heartily. "Except to know what you are about, taking Oliver to that hell of yours?"

"What business is it of yours if I show Hartwell the ropes? He's my cousin as much as yours," Moore spat out.

"It is my business to keep him out of trouble. I believe you are making it your business to get him into it," was the venomous reply that dripped from Saliston's suddenly darkened countenance. "Since I cannot prevent him from going about in your company without setting his back up, I will warn *you* instead. Keep Oliver clear of the hells."

"That's rich, coming from you," Moore hissed. "When you have taken him to White's two days ago."

The duke glared at the younger man so rancorously that Mr. Moore momentarily stopped breathing. He knew Saliston's reputation as a Corinthian to be well deserved and earned—crossing him was not in anyone's best interest. But Moore was in such a mood as to risk poking the bear.

"White's was his father's club and is hardly the place where young greenheads will find themselves fleeced of their fortunes."

"Well, I beg to differ."

"And how much do you earn from the keeper when you bring ripe ones to them for the picking?"

Mr. Moore puffed with fury and turned a vicious gaze upon the duke as he whipped his horse around. "How dare you," he shouted furiously.

"I dare! Stay away from Oliver, or it'll be bellows

to mend with you, Charles," the duke retorted before he left the seething Mr. Moore to inelegantly kick his indolent hack into a trot in the opposite direction.

As he cantered his horse toward one of the more frequented areas, the duke's rage subsided into a dull irritation. He supposed it was an emotion not uncommon with anyone who had recently been in the company of Charles Moore. The thought made him chuckle to himself, and it was then that he observed a most elegant creature cantering down the lane, carried by a copper-colored blood horse of athletic proportions.

The elegant creature was, of course, none other than the fire-breathing young lady who had hauled himself and his cousin over the coals in Stafford four months ago.

Chapter 6

Several days later, Miss Iverson stood with her mother outside the steps of that most glorious assembly house—Almack's. Lady Jersey had managed to wheedle her fellow patroness into agreeing to co-sponsor the Season's Diamond, but Lady Sefton did not at all begrudge the contract. She had already attained the distinction of being the first to describe the dark-haired damsel to the other Patronesses, and so she felt satisfied. So, rather than merely forwarding her card to Iverson House, Lady Sefton had actually sent a note inviting the ladies of the house to tea where, together with Lady Jersey, she presented Miss Iverson with that coveted voucher.

Excitement was hardly the word to describe Lucilla's feelings as she realized there would be absolutely no fear of running into Miss Wallace that evening. She had lately suffered through yet another denunciation from that young lady, this time accounting for the evils of such a place as Almack's. However, the lecture had done nothing to dull Miss Iverson's eagerness. Upon entry, she was immediately noticed by her sponsor, Lady Sefton, who swept gracefully across the room to greet the Iverson ladies.

"My dear Lady Iverson, how do you do? And you, Miss Iverson? You look lovely, my dear. Come, I shall make some introductions!"

And with that, the evening began. The number of young ladies and their mothers she met were so numerous that she had lost count of them after half an hour. The gentlemen too. She had already met several eligible young men at the various quiet parties to which she had been invited, and a startling number of them seemed quite intent on furthering the acquaintance. Lady Iverson managed to steer her daughter discreetly away from one or two of the more ardent and less skillful of her admirers, but Lady Sefton and Lady Jersey were particularly adept at filling Miss Iverson's dance card with the better behaved of the evening's attendees. The evening was well underway when Lady Sefton introduced her to Sir Geoffrey Knightsbridge and gave her permission to waltz.

"Sir Geoffrey is an excellent dancer, Miss Iverson. I could think of no better gentleman to guide you through your first waltz than he," said Lady Sefton. Before giving way to the gentleman, she leaned in to Miss Iverson and whispered conspiratorially, "He likes horses. Dashalong tells me he's quite knowing." Then she artlessly gave Miss Iverson's hand to Sir Geoffrey and smiled as the music struck up.

Her first waltz was, in Lucilla's mind, rather unremarkable. Sir Geoffrey was indeed a skilled dancer, and whilst Lady Sefton's estimation of his love of horses was correct, it seemed to Miss Iverson that his ability in conversation with another human was sadly lacking. He talked of poultices and shoeing.

Miss Iverson was next engaged in a country dance with a very young gentleman who made an effort to involve her in discussion throughout, but this was made somewhat awkward by the steps of the dance drawing them away from one another at regular intervals.

As she vaguely listened to her young dance partner marveling at the color of her eyes and the curl of her hair between steps, Miss Iverson noticed Miss Craven standing in the doorway across the ballroom talking to another young lady, one she had not yet met, and made the resolution to excuse herself at the conclusion of the dance immediately, but she underestimated the valor of her cavalier, for the moment the music ended he began begging her to join the next set with him. The very thought of it nearly bored her to tears.

"I'm afraid I must disappoint you, Mr. Russell. I am rather parched, so I think I should like to sit down for a while."

"I will fetch you some lemonade immediately, Miss Iverson. I am at your service." At which Mr. Russell dashed away.

Amazed at her sudden release, Miss Iverson walked quickly across the floor to Miss Craven, fighting the urge to sprint.

"Miss Iverson, how lovely to see you," said Miss Craven as Lucilla approached. "I see Mr. Russell running away. Is he quite all right?"

"Oh, quite. He is gone in search of lemonade," Miss Iverson replied with a smile.

"Heavens, I cannot think when I last saw my brother running. I had always thought his trousers too tight to allow it," Miss Craven's companion said laughingly. "Is he pestering you, Miss…?"

"Where are my manners? Miss Iverson, this is Miss Russell. Caro, this is Miss Iverson, whom I was telling you about."

"Nice things, I hope?"

"All nice things," said Miss Russell. "I do apologize for my brother, Miss Iverson. He is a hopeless romantic. His nose is always in poetry. Fancies himself the next Byron, if you can imagine. Has he bored you to death yet?"

"Rather. Though I suppose I ought not to say so to you," Lucilla replied with a smile. "He's very polite, of course. But I am not really of a poetic mind."

"Has he praised your eyes yet? You can tell when he's losing himself. He starts talking about a lady's eyes."

"He's moved on to describing my hair already."

"Lord, she's done for." Miss Russell groaned and rolled her eyes. "Constance, we really ought to help her escape before he comes back."

"Just send him on his way, Caro. When he was dangling after me, you nipped it in the bud easily enough."

"However did you manage that?" Miss Iverson was suddenly very curious to know by what methods Miss Russell silenced her brother, and she was soon to experience it firsthand as he approached.

"Miss Iverson," cried Mr. Russell in fervent tones. "Miss Iverson, here you are. I have brought you refreshment."

He handed her one of the two glasses he clasped, then uttered a gasp of surprise as his sister relieved him of the other.

"Ah, thank you, Alfred. Most kind of you. But you have forgotten Miss Craven. For shame! You must fetch another," said Miss Russell nonchalantly. Taking her cue, Miss Craven smiled so sweetly at Mr. Russell that the young man's jaw snapped shut before he turned away, muttering to himself.

"Let us move away from here before he returns. I prefer not setting him off into a fit of the blue devils above once an evening," Miss Russell said quietly. "I shall have to listen to him complain for days, otherwise."

The merry trio set down their cups and went on a walk around the room. As they strolled, they chattered happily amongst themselves before Miss Craven was approached by the young man who had claimed her hand for the next dance, and Miss Russell and Miss Iverson were left to their own devices.

"I can assure you, Miss Iverson, that if you show yourself to be a friend of mine, my brother will very quickly lose interest in you," Miss Russell remarked. "He cannot abide me. We are twins, you see, and the thought of my being friendly with his intended wife positively terrifies him."

"I shall take it under advisement, Miss Russell, though I may say it is a small price to pay to be safe from his attentions." Lucilla laughed. "He is perfectly nice but rather too passionate for me, I think."

"He's a bore, I assure you. He simply would not suit a girl with any attachment to the outdoors," Miss Russell remarked. "Connie says she saw you riding in the park on a marvelous horse. My brother rides, but I'm afraid he would be very disconcerted should any perspiration stain his neckcloth."

"I had noticed as much."

"I think you need a Corinthian. Or at least, a young man on his way to becoming one if we cannot find one ready-made," Miss Russell mused. "There are one or two who come to mind, but they are all hardened bachelors, so it could prove a challenge."

Miss Iverson smiled at her companion curiously, her eyes twinkling with mischief. "Do I take it that you are putting yourself in charge of locating a suitable match for me, Miss Russell?"

The other damsel feigned surprise and smiled with a similar twinkle. "My dear Miss Iverson, don't you know I am quite an old maid? What else do I have to do but marry off more fortunate females?"

"An old maid? You? Surely you jest, Miss Russell."

"Indeed, I do not. My mama quite despairs of me. I have been out three Seasons with not a single offer. She says I eat too many biscuits and spend too much time talking. But what else is one meant to do in London?"

"I do miss the country," Miss Iverson replied in a slightly mournful tone. "But I will make the best of things. My papa has had my carriage brought down, so I have something to amuse myself."

"You can drive yourself? How dashing. Will you take me up one day? I should love to take a turn with you."

"But of course. Name the day, and I shall collect you for a turn about the Park," Miss Iverson said with aplomb, extremely happy to have made a new friend. But at that moment her mama approached, and Lady Iverson drew her daughter away to introduce her to an old friend of hers.

Not quite an hour later, after several dances with different eligible young men who had been flung at her by her sponsors, Miss Iverson found herself sitting with her aunt and partaking of a light repast when the countess brought up the topic of Miss Russell.

"I found her quite charming."

"She is, rather. A shame she and that brother of hers

don't have sixpence between them, but so it is," the countess mused. "The right one will come along yet, and it won't matter if the family are as poor as church mice."

"I should never have guessed it."

"Her mama is clever with a needle. She has made every stitch the girl wears, and no one is the wiser. I applaud her for it. The Russells are not nobility, of course, but Mrs. Russell was the granddaughter of a duke and is a sensible woman. They're a lovely family. They're accepted everywhere, and the mother is a great friend of mine," the countess continued.

"I should like to get to know her better," said Miss Iverson, which made her aunt nod agreeance.

"You ought to, much better than that snippet your mother had in the house last week."

"Mama is hardly to blame that they bring themselves to the house, Aunt."

"No, but it is quite her fault that they feel free to do so," Lady Edevane murmured under her breath, causing her niece to smile roguishly. "Have you met anyone else tonight that you think you might like to pursue a friendship with? Any gentlemen, perhaps?"

"I am sorry to disappoint you, Aunt, but pretty well every man I've met this evening has some fatal flaw or another," Lucilla replied with a sigh.

"Don't give me any missish airs, dear. What is wrong with 'em?"

"Well, Sir Geoffrey Knightsbridge spent the entire first waltz telling me about the best way to poultice a lame hoof," she replied purposefully. "Lord Fondant could not keep up with the country dance in which he asked me to join him. Mr. Russell spent the entire time reciting poetry to my eyes and hair. Mr. Brandon kept calling me 'Miss Iverley' though I corrected him several times *and* he kept stepping on everyone's toes throughout the dance. Mr. Palmer offered to buy my riding horse because he said it was unsuited to a lady as delicate as myself—"

"Dear me, what a lot of bumbling idiots," the Countess exclaimed. "Is it any wonder you didn't like any of them?"

"It is only the start of the Season, Aunt. Papa says all of the ones worth *my* while will still be in the country, with the weather being so fine."

"Yes, well, I'm sure he knows a thing or two…"

At that moment they were approached by one of the esteemed Patronesses, none other than Mrs. Drummond-Burrell. There appeared to be someone following close behind her, and Miss Iverson stood along with her aunt as the woman came up to them, assuming correctly that she was about to introduce Lucilla to her next dance partner.

When Mrs. Drummond-Burrell reached them, her follower came into full view, and Miss Iverson's jaw clenched in irritation. It was none other than that conniving creature Mr. Charles Moore.

"Ah, Miss Iverson, I have been approached by this young man who wishes to dance the next waltz with you. I assured him your name was not already bespoken and offered to lead him to you, so here he is. Mr. Moore?"

"We are acquainted, Mrs. Drummond-Burrell, I thank you," Miss Iverson assured the older woman. It took an effort to keep the annoyance from staining her tone, but she thought she must have managed it well enough when she received a smile in response before Mr. Moore led her to the ballroom, and the music began.

But the top-lofty Mrs. Drummond-Burrell had taken note of the interaction, and once the young pair had left them, she turned to Lady Edevane and enquired as to whether she had missed something.

"Miss Iverson has been quite amicable to every young man we have presented to her all evening. Is something amiss, Lady Edevane?"

"Sharp as ever, Clementina. The boy has been toadying her for weeks and does not seem to take a hint."

"I see," Mrs. Drummond-Burrell replied, her gaze narrowed and her lips pursed. She did not appreciate being used as means to force a young lady's hand and made a mental note to mention this episode to her fellow patronesses at their next meeting.

In the ballroom, Miss Iverson allowed herself to be led to the floor and begrudgingly took her place. As the music began, Mr. Moore's arm came about her waist. Her gaze glanced up at his, and she fixed a withering glare upon him. He was undaunted and indeed, barely managed to conceal a smirk.

"Why do you look at me so, Lucilla?" he asked mockingly.

"I do not recall giving you leave to use my name, Mr. Moore."

"Perhaps you did not, but we are such old friends. What is the harm in it?"

"It may not be harmful, but as it is not pleasing to my ear, I will request you not use it, if you please," she replied witheringly as they whirled about the room.

"Whatever have I done to make you so upset, *Miss Iverson*?"

"Other than your underhanded effort to force me to accept a waltz with you, Mr. Moore?"

"I should think the effort was rather successful," was his cheerful reply.

Miss Iverson's jaw clenched. People were watching, she knew, so for quite some time she performed her steps in silence while he spoke on mundane topics and considered himself to have won the round. No one could overhear them, but anyone could surely guess she was angry at her dancing partner, and so she forced herself to fix a smile on her face as she looked up at him again.

"It is clear to me that in spite of my mother's efforts to convince me otherwise, you are quite aware that I do not seek to encourage your familiarity." Her words were deliberately blunt in an attempt to knock him off his perch, and it appeared to succeed, for his brow darkened momentarily. But as suddenly as it appeared, the frown vanished, and he plastered a false smile on his face.

"You wound me, Miss Iverson. What have I done to draw such ire? I have surely not offended you."

"You are well aware that your attentions offend me."

"I am at a loss to understand why, for I am your humble servant."

This drew her gaze up in a flash, and she said scornfully, "Indeed."

"Have I not loved you since childhood?"

"I vividly recall your penchant for tossing spiders at me."

"Only in my childish efforts to gain your notice, I assure you."

"Then I suppose you were also in love with my brothers?" she replied with sarcasm ebbing in her voice.

As he paused to consider the right thing to say in reply, she suddenly pulled away from him, and he realized the music had ended. She bobbed a quick and shallow curtsy before spinning on her heel and marching away. Irritation washed over him at her defiance. Yes, a less troublesome wife would be best. But he might enjoy breaking Miss Iverson of her spirit.

Near eleven o'clock, the Duke of Saliston entered the assembly rooms with Lord Hartwell in tow. He had managed to drag the unwilling Oliver along under the threat of disembowelment. Still, as they stepped into the ballroom barely a moment before the hallowed halls were barred to the outside world, the pair were amicably discussing their plans to visit Tattersalls in search of a new riding horse for the younger gentleman.

"I've made inquiries, and they assure me there are two or three that will suit your needs nicely. We may view them before the auction next week," Saliston said knowingly.

"If you'd sell me that bay of yours, it would be much nicer," Oliver quipped in reply.

"Keep your mitts off my bay and count yourself fortunate that I let you borrow the mare until you find your own."

"Oh, indeed I do, cousin, but a man can hope."

Oliver had thrown himself into learning to drive properly and had finally been allowed to join his first fox hunt, an activity for which he had developed a particular penchant. The duke smiled at his young cousin wryly and considered it a job well done that the boy had increased his skills in horsemanship so speedily in the months since "the incident." Since their coming to London, the duke had seen fit to introduce Oliver to all of his late father's favorite haunts, including White's Club and Angelo's, which was, of course, happily situated right next to the excellent Pugilist's Club. While the latter had not been in existence at the time of the late Lord Hartwell's demise, he had been a keen fencer and spent many a morning at Angelo's Academy.

His efforts to immerse himself in all gentlemanly pursuits had not yet extended to chasing females. However, the duke was certain Mr. Moore would soon introduce the young Lord Hartwell to the Haymarket ware that he hobnobbed with. It was not something Saliston approved of, and while he had been known at various times few and far between to be seen with some barque of frailty or another, he was much more discerning in his tastes than he knew Mr. Moore to be. The late Lord Hartwell had married young and never embarked on such fancies in spite of his eventual distaste for his wife.

Saliston made a mental note to talk to his young cousin about the evils of associating with undesirables. Still, as they had entered the realm of the Marriage Mart, it was hardly the time to begin such a lecture. Instead, he elected to introduce his young cousin to some of the matchmaking mamas he knew had long despaired of attaching himself to their daughters. His hopes were that perhaps some eligible maiden might strike Oliver's fancy and prevent the necessity of a warning at all. The Hartwell men, after all, leapt into marriage at a young age, and Saliston had every hope that Oliver would be no different. More discerning than his father had been, he hoped, but still, no different otherwise.

The fact that the dark-haired firebrand might be present had dawned on him several days earlier when he had witnessed her cantering through the park beside an older gentleman he supposed to be her father or an uncle.

The man was not known to him, so he had not thought it appropriate at the time to introduce himself, but it was with no small amount of hope that he dragged the hapless Oliver to Almack's with the thought that the opportunity might present itself to throw the two in one another's path again.

It didn't take long for a designing mama in the form of Mrs. Palmer to spot his towering figure and make her way over to him, a mischievous twinkle glinting in her eye.

"Your grace," she exclaimed as he bowed over her hand. "It is such an age since we have seen you. Mr. Palmer tells me you were out with the hunt recently?"

"Indeed, I have been, Mrs. Palmer. Allow me to introduce my cousin, Lord Hartwell. He has recently come to stay with me," Saliston responded as he subtly looked about for the hapless Miss Palmer that had been flung at him the previous Season. She appeared to be nowhere nearby, and Mrs. Palmer soon confirmed that her daughter had been recently married, which gave the duke no small measure of relief.

"My son is here somewhere. He had the honor of dancing with Miss Iverson earlier, and her aunt has just now told me he bored the poor girl to death and then offered to buy her horse. Can you imagine? I blame his father, of course."

"I can only imagine it must be an exceptional horse if the purchase of it was foremost in his mind when he was dancing with a young lady," Saliston said with a smile creeping into his features. This went unnoticed by Mrs. Palmer, who had a perfectly acceptable sense of humor but was not particularly adept at grasping sarcasm.

"I am told it *is* an exceptional horse. Even my ridiculous husband says so. Apparently, its coloring is rather unique."

"Is that so," he murmured. "And who did you say this young lady was, Mrs. Palmer?"

The lady looked at him with curiosity. "Don't tell me," she said. "You're keen on this animal too, aren't you."

"I'm sure I do not know what you mean, ma'am," he replied merrily.

"Hm, well. She is just out this year, from what I can gather. The lady was Miss Iverson, the Viscount and Lady Iverson's daughter. I'm rather out of the loop now Millicent has married."

The duke made a pretty comment that caused the lady to blush slightly and Oliver to roll his eyes, but they were soon disengaged from the conversation and made their way around the room. Oliver was entirely unaware of the "exceptional horse" connotation and wondered if his cousin was actually considering offering to purchase this unknown animal. Saliston, on the other hand, was searching the ballroom for Miss Iverson.

And then he saw her, gliding about the dance floor in the arms of none other than Charles Moore, with a thundercloud writ across her face that he would have considered charming had he not felt overwhelming pity for her predicament. Oliver stiffened as he, too, noticed the young lady in a gown of primrose muslin and sarcenet in his cousin's arms.

And, for the first time, the young Lord Hartwell recognized a feeling of jealousy.

Chapter 7

After fleeing Mr. Moore immediately after their waltz, Miss Iverson had sought out her mother and speedily convinced her that the sudden development of a headache required their immediate removal from the building. Lady Iverson concluded her conversation with Lady Jersey, who looked kindly concerned for the young lady as she bid them farewell.

The following day Lucilla reclined on her sofa quietly in her little parlor with a book, and the golden-haired dog curled up on the settee beside her. When Miss Wallace suddenly appeared in the doorway and traipsed into the room with not a hint of awkwardness, Chico growled softly and raised his hackles a little at the sight of the visitor, which caused her to pause slightly and eye the dog warily before he resumed his original position with a loud, disdainful snort.

Miss Wallace was of a tall and slender build, with her blonde hair bound up tightly away from her face. She carried herself with a prideful stiffness in her shoulders, much like her mother. What she thought to be well-bred grace others considered haughtiness, and while the general consensus was that she was pretty enough, upon closer inspection, it was noted that her eyes and mouth were overlarge and her prim smile closely resembled a condescending sneer.

It was the same smile she wore as she sailed into the

parlor, and it made Lucilla stiffen and hold in a moan before she painted a smile of her own onto her face, tucked away her book, and turned to greet the other young lady with at least the appearance of pleasure.

"I thought I should find you here," Miss Wallace began harmlessly enough. "I'm sure you heard the knock at the door twenty minutes ago. You really ought not to be so rude when guests arrive, Lucy."

Miss Iverson fought the urge to point out the rudeness of pushing uninvited into a private room and chose instead to smile urbanely and greet the intruder with well-bred decorum. She thought, not for the first time in recent weeks, that socializing in London had begun to bestow on her a saint-like amount of patience and fervently hoped she would one day be rewarded for her efforts at civility.

"I do apologize, Miss Wallace. I'm afraid I have had a lingering headache, which is why I chose to sit in my own parlor today. I did not know we were expecting your visit," Lucilla replied gently, though she knew no visit had been planned. *You rather just show up uninvited*, her inner self pronounced with exasperation.

"Since when have Mama and I been in need of an appointment to visit this house?" Miss Wallace said in an insulted tone. "I am sure I do not need to stand upon ceremony with any of the Iversons when we have been such friends for years."

Lucilla made no effort to reply, knowing anything she said would have the unhappy effect of either encouraging Miss Wallace to continue believing herself correct or further exacerbating the issue. Instead, she smiled politely again before picking up a piece of needlework from her basket and setting some absentminded stitches.

Mollified by the mistaken belief that she had humbled her hostess, Miss Wallace smiled primly to herself before informing Lucilla that she'd told Murray to bring them a tea tray on her way to the parlor and then began her regular practice of chattering authoritatively.

The tea tray soon arrived, with Murray himself bringing it in and setting it down with a decisive clunk. The dissertation continued uninterrupted throughout, and Miss Iverson mouthed an apology to the stately butler as he passed between the two ladies. Exiting the room, he favored the back of Miss Wallace's head with a sour glare.

"Your mama says that you made the acquaintance of Miss Russell at Almack's."

"Yes, I did. Miss Craven introduced us. Miss Russell is quite charming," Miss Iverson replied with alacrity as she poured and handed her uninvited guest a cup and saucer.

"I suppose it is a habit with her by now," said Miss Wallace mockingly.

"Why do you say so?"

"Well, if charm is all one has to recommend oneself, the person must necessarily make a study of maintaining the illusion, don't you think?" Miss Wallace tittered cruelly.

Miss Iverson's eyes widened perceptibly, and she turned away to survey the tea tray in an effort to regain her composure as the other young lady continued her obnoxious prattle. It occurred to Lucilla that Miss Wallace was always opinionated, and while her comments often irked, she had never before felt such a strong, burning sense of disgust. She had grown tired of

Miss Wallace's friendship many years earlier, but common courtesy required that she behave with politeness in spite of this, as her mama maintained a friendship with Lady Wallace.

The two young ladies were of an age; however, Lady Wallace had declared that as her daughter was exceptionally more mature than other young ladies of her generation, this was reason enough to introduce her into Society early, whilst Lady Iverson had been content to wait another year to present Lucilla. In her characteristic conceit, Miss Wallace had convinced herself this had caused significant misery for Lucilla and had made every effort to console her by way of sending short, boastful letters every other week, recounting stories of her apparent success.

Miss Wallace's comment against Miss Russell struck Lucilla as rather sanctimonious, considering her own origins were hardly noble. Lady Wallace was the daughter of a rather vulgar though admittedly very wealthy merchant. She had married the only titled gentleman to offer for her, and it was well known Sir John Wallace had found himself in dire need of an heiress, in no small part due to his addiction to games of chance. Miss Russell may not have sixpence to scratch with, but her family was old, and she counted herself the cousin of a duke.

"She is rather freckled and pudding-faced, poor dear." Miss Wallace continued her list of Miss Russell's shortfalls. "I cannot imagine a man would consider her countenance in the least attractive."

Miss Iverson's teeth ground together in her effort to maintain her composure. "I saw nothing in her face that was at all distasteful."

"Perhaps you met another Miss Russell, then," Miss Wallace said ironically.

"Perhaps I did. The Miss Russell I met had lovely blue eyes and a positively charming sense of humor. I look forward to knowing her better. Indeed. I will be taking her up in my phaeton tomorrow in the Park," Miss Iverson replied in a clipped tone intended to discourage further negative discourse regarding Miss Russell. She enjoyed a positively exhilarating moment in which Miss Wallace was apparently rendered entirely speechless.

It did not last long, for she breathed the sarcastic retort of, "Well," before taking a sip of her tea and pointedly looking away with a pout. After a moment of awkward silence, Miss Wallace set her cup aside and stood, abruptly declaring she would rejoin her mother in the drawing room. Miss Iverson allowed herself only a moment to reorganize her thoughts before following Miss Wallace out of the room, with Chico tiptoeing behind her.

Upon entering the drawing room on the ground floor of Iverson House, Lucilla found her mother discussing with Lady Wallace the upcoming ball she had been painstakingly planning for weeks. The invitations had gone out only two days earlier, and many replies had already been received to confirm attendance. This greatly gratified Lady Iverson as she had rarely entertained on such a large scale.

"I suppose I have Lucilla to thank for all of these punctilious replies," Lady Iverson said with a proud smile in her daughter's direction. "Every last one of our dinner guests has written to accept. I'm sure I never expected half so much anticipation."

A sudden sense of foreboding washed over Lucilla.

There was certainly nothing innocuous in Lady Iverson's speech. Still, Lucilla knew the Wallaces were not among the guests invited to dinner before the ball was scheduled to begin, and she could not help but feel there was about to be an awkward moment. Her instincts were right, for the ever-undaunted Lady Wallace confirmed the attendance of herself and her daughter at the dinner, and Lady Iverson's eyes widened in shock, her mouth dropping open.

After yet another overlong visit in the Iverson drawing room, the Wallace ladies took themselves off, and Miss Iverson found herself alone with a rather vexed version of her mother. It was very rare for Lady Iverson to complain about Lady Wallace's lack of manners, and Lucilla was not about to attempt to distract her from her exasperation.

"Now I shall have to find two more men to invite in order to keep my numbers even. At least I've some time," Lady Iverson said frustratedly. "Really, what a maddening thing to do. Inviting oneself to dinner—what is she about?"

"You can hardly be surprised, Mama. You've surely known Lady Wallace long enough to know this is exactly the sort of thing she has done many times over."

"It is entirely different when she has imposed on me at home in Lancashire. This is quite another thing to do so here. What can she be thinking?"

"I believe she is thinking that she has got away with it before, so why stop now?" Lucilla said wryly. "Papa has always said one should always immediately correct rudeness in one's young horses, for rude youngsters become unmanageable adults. I expect people are much the same."

This artless and rather pointed speech drew a bitter but amused laugh from Lady Iverson. Lucilla smiled before suggesting that her mama invite her cousin Matthew to join the party and enquire if he had a friend who might accompany him.

"Matthew has come to town? Oh, and he did not breathe a word, the naughty boy." Lady Iverson's suddenly brightened mood just as suddenly darkened again. "I shall invite him and make sure to seat him well away from Tabitha. Your papa would not like to have her flirting with him all evening."

"*Matthew* would not like to have her flirting with him all evening," Lucilla mumbled and rolled her eyes.

****

Matthew Iverson was at that moment strolling down St. James Street with a crony from Oxford. He was a handsome young man of five-and-twenty, bearing the typical dark hair and a straight, narrow nose that marked him as a member of his tribe. The Iverson men were never tall and tended toward stockiness that presented as broad shoulders and a pugilist's musculature. Whichever tailor they happened to favor with their patronage would never find the need to pad out the shoulders of their coats or the legs of their breeches to enhance the shape.

Mr. Matthew was no exception to the rule. He wore a neatly cut coat and an elegant pair of boots, but he did not require extravagance to set him apart. Having been deprived of his parents early in life, he was raised from his twelfth year under the roof of his uncle, Lord Iverson. Like his cousins Richard and Edward, he was a keen outdoorsman, and once he became a man grown, Lord Iverson had seen fit to fix upon him a comfortable allowance. In his early days at Oxford, he had engaged in many a prank and had been no stranger to an evening spent in the company of a bottle, but he had always, in general, been an exceptionally sensible sort. He'd never had an interest in gambling, nor was he in the petticoat line, so it had come as no surprise that after diligent study and taking his degree, Mr. Iverson announced his intention of taking holy orders.

He now served as curate of the parish at Gracewood when the current incumbent called upon him for assistance. That gentleman, though quite infirm, was also exceptionally diligent in his duties, so it was rather often that Matthew had time to spare.

And so, he found himself in London during the Season. His allowance was generous for a conservative young gentleman, but instead of taking up residence with his family in Iverson House, he chose to take rooms at Albany. The idea of having his chums and, by extension, *their* chums hounding him for an introduction to Lucilla was not a thought he particularly relished, and he deemed it safer to be out of the family home.

The gentleman he was currently in company with was rather given over to dandyism and stood in stark contrast to the sportsmanlike Matthew, but Ferdinand Kimbley was a kind-hearted young man and so endeared himself to his present company. As the pair walked along, they reminisced about their time spent in Greece and the Middle East, a journey during which Matthew had facilitated the purchase of several blood horses for Lord Iverson's stable. The Honorable Ferdinand Kimbley had been thoroughly bored during that particular interlude, but the study of exotic locales had tickled his fancy considerably.

As they approached the vicinity of the famous bow

window, Mr. Matthew made a mental note that its usual inhabitant was not currently in residence, but his musing was interrupted when his companion made a loud exclamation.

"Saliston! What do you do here? I was sure you'd not have come down from the country yet," Mr. Kimbley said merrily to the gentleman just now exiting the doorway of the club.

The tall, sharp-featured Corinthian descending the shallow steps made a cursory salute with his hand and replied, "Ferdy, how do you do, my good chap?"

"Quite well, old boy, quite well!"

"Old, indeed!" Saliston chortled. "I certainly feel so on seeing you—quite the dandy you've grown into! Your father must be devastated."

"I am quite a disappointment to him, but Simon seems to make up for it," Mr. Kimbley replied cheerfully. "Have you met my friend Iverson? Matty, this is the Duke of Saliston. My friend Mr. Iverson."

"Iverson," the older man asked curiously, his brows rising slightly. "Any relation to Lord Iverson?"

"My uncle, formerly my guardian," Matthew replied. "Pleased to make your acquaintance."

Saliston replied in kind and made a polite inquiry or two after Ferdy's family. These were interspersed with questions directed at Matthew also, which struck him as almost investigative until it suddenly dawned on him that Saliston might be one of Lucilla's admirers.

He judged the duke to be at least forty-five and supposed him to be what women would call handsome, with sharply chiseled features not unlike the statues Matthew and Ferdy had surveyed during their tour of Greece. He was also rather tall, against which Matthew imagined Lucilla's petite form would stand somewhat ridiculously in contrast.

Ferdy was trying to convince the duke to step back into the club for a drink, but the older gentleman declined, citing an appointment, but he did say, "Do send me your direction, Ferdy. I should like to introduce you to my cousin Oliver. He is in need of friends in town and not much younger than you and Mr. Iverson here. Do you ride, Mr. Iverson?"

"I do indeed, sir."

"Excellent. I'm sure Ferdy here prefers not to risk dirtying his pristine attire, which will probably bore Oliver, so perhaps I might introduce you to him as well?"

"Certainly, I should be happy to make his acquaintance," Matthew replied with aplomb.

The gentlemen parted from one another soon after, with the younger ones entering White's and the elder marching toward Piccadilly and his house in Berkeley Square. The fancy struck Saliston to cross at Dover Street instead of walking to Berkeley directly.

As he walked, the duke pondered why the universe seemed hell-bent on throwing the Iversons in his way. First in Stafford, then during his first ride in the Park since he came down from his estates, then again at Almack's, after having avoided the place for years, and now running into her cousin at the steps of his club.

It hadn't taken much to discover that Lord Iverson was a member of White's, but their paths had simply never crossed before, or they'd never noticed one another. It seemed Lord Iverson's estates were in Lancashire, and he seldom came to London unless Parliamentary duties compelled him, or so the duke had been told when he had made his discreet inquiries.

Saliston was nearing Hay Street, absentmindedly pondering the nature of fate, when that strange beast suddenly struck again, and he was privileged to witness Lord Hartwell descending the stairs of an inconspicuous house a little farther along the street—the sort of famously secret house frequented by pigeons and card sharps.

His grace growled under his breath and steeled himself for an unpleasant confrontation as he marched down the street. An experienced gamester of his years was no stranger to disreputable little establishments such as the one Oliver had just stepped into, but Saliston had long since given up frequenting such places in favor of higher company and more principled opponents. Furthermore, he'd taken the time to warn Oliver against ever visiting such places specifically.

The boy had improved in countenance and skill since he'd left his ancestral home in favor of the duke's country seat in Derbyshire. The events on the street in Stafford had spurred the boy to diligently apply himself to his studies of the manly arts, and he had succeeded exceptionally well in a very short period of time, but his skill at cards and other games of chance was not something Saliston wanted to give any scheming wretch the opportunity to test. Any experienced gamester would have him pegged as a flat before the cards were dealt.

Saliston trotted nimbly down the basement steps where he had seen Oliver disappear minutes earlier. The dragon guarding the door was skilled at deciphering whether visitors were well-heeled gents or men of the law, and he quickly deduced the category to which the duke belonged and allowed him entry. It was only a minute or two before Saliston was walking right back out again, unceremoniously thrusting the young Lord Hartwell along in front of him.

The two gentlemen were soon out on the street, and the hapless Oliver propelled along in the direction of his house by way of Hay Street and the duke delivering a diatribe designed to enlighten Lord Hartwell on exactly what the purpose of such houses were in relation to fat young pigeons such as himself.

"Who introduced you there, Oliver? Who?"

"Charlie, of course."

"Moore," Saliston spat out scathingly. "Have you any idea what the reason for that is? Any at all?"

"He said it's a choice spot. The bank has been broken there three times this month alone."

"Yes, and I'm sure that choice piece of gossip has got about quite nicely. Tell me, was your precious Charlie there when these miraculous events occurred? Have you spoken to *anyone* who was there to see it?"

"Well, no, not exactly."

"I should think not," Saliston growled. The sight of Oliver's flushed and irritable face softened him somewhat. He continued in a softer tone, "Lad, I worry for you."

"I know. But really, cousin—"

"If you are about to start defending Moore, I do not want to hear it. You do not know his reputation in town, and I am loath to be the one to describe it to you, so suffice it to say that while he has not been blackballed from Brooks, he has not been welcome there for years."

Oliver stared at his cousin with a frown and wondered what he meant. Was Saliston implying that Charles was suspected of something dishonorable? He thought back to how often his cousin had soundly beaten him; he had never known himself to win. He was surely a very skilled card player; Saliston must be mistaken.

"I'll let you ponder that at your own leisure. However, it comes to mind that even as I caution you against spending your time overmuch in Moore's company, I have not provided you with any suitable alternatives," Saliston said conversationally now as the pair entered the duke's house.

"So, on that subject, I've just today bumped into the son of an old friend of mine—Ferdy Kimbley. He's a little older than you, maybe five- or six-and-twenty? Not an outdoorsman, but a very fashionable fellow. His elder brother—Simon, I think? Well, he's a bruising rider, rather an out-and-outer, actually, like his father. Well, I met Ferdy outside White's today. He introduced me to his friend from Oxford, Mr. Matthew Iverson. Seems a nice chap, has the look of a sportsman. A wonder what he has in common with Ferdy."

The incident at the gaming house was washed away and neutrality restored as the conversation safely turned in the direction of making new acquaintances; flared tempers returned to normal, and the duo once again found themselves again in perfect harmony.

Chapter 8

"I don't like it," Lady Edevane declared roundly.

It was a day later, and she had just been made privy to the circumstances which now made it necessary for no less than four additional places to be set for the dinner before the Iverson Ball. She had been vociferously against the idea of changing the family's plans in order to not put Lady Wallace's nose out of joint.

"It is absolutely despicable. How could you allow her to run roughshod over you, Anne?"

"I was as shocked in the moment as you are now, sister, and you know how I hate to make a scene," Lady Iverson replied in a tired voice. She was now wading through acceptance of the situation after her initial infuriation, but Lady Edevane was not yet ready to relinquish her irritation on the subject.

"I sent a note round to Matthew's lodgings an hour ago. He ought to be here presently to assist us in singling out which of his companions will be amenable to an evening spent in the company of that awful girl."

"Come now, Augusta, you have not spent enough time with Miss Wallace to determine if she is awful, surely."

"One doesn't need to spend time with a duck to know that it quacks," Lady Edevane replied in disdain. "I've come across enough young ladies just like her to know them on sight. Pushy, conceited little misses, flirting with anything male that is breathing and putting on airs to be interesting."

"Augusta," Lady Iverson scolded in a hushed voice.

"I know, I know, you believe them to be very good people, but I ask you! How good can a person be when they behave in such an underhanded way toward the people they seek to imitate? Breeding will out."

"I'm sure I do not know what you mean."

"I am sure you *do*, Anne. The girl may be the daughter of a baronet, but who is her mother's family, I ask you? You know the answer. I remember when the mother had her come-out, I had been married to Edevane for a year or two at the time, but the woman was throwing herself at anything with a title, my husband included. I asked myself, what well-brought-up girl doesn't know which are the eligible bachelors?"

Lady Iverson pursed her lips and glanced up at her sister-in-law with a sigh, but she went back to her busy-work. Lady Edevane required no encouragement to continue.

"A well-brought-up girl does know, doesn't she? Because she is being brought out by her mama, or an aunt, or some other connection. But the daughter of some vulgar Cit, being introduced by a paid, shabby-genteel hanger-on from the fringes of Society—well, one such as that may not. No sensible man would have anything to do with her, for her vulgarity was obvious. But Sir John Wallace's pockets were so well to let I believe he had no option but to marry money."

"Really, Augusta, must we talk in this way?" Lady Iverson said gently. "I was there, after all, so it really is unnecessary to tell me what happened."

"I will finish once I have pointed out that, between

the two of them, they're hardly as clever as they appear to think themselves. At one point or another, there will be a misstep. I shall say no more, but I shall be watching for it," Lady Edevane prophesied with finality.

The ladies heard the front door of the house suddenly open, and Lady Iverson looked up curiously, wondering who would enter the house without a knock. Matthew appeared in the drawing room doorway with a merry grin on his face as he greeted the ladies. He shrugged off his coat and entered, with Murray appearing right behind him to take Mr. Matthew's garment and hat and lightly scold him in a way only a fatherly retainer could. A bashful smile appeared on Matthew's face while Murray vanished into the hall.

Matthew sat and insisted on knowing why he had been summoned to the house. Upon being apprised of the situation, he offered his friend Ferdy as a suitable guest for dinner before the ball. Still, he clearly stipulated that he be seated as far as possible from Miss Wallace and her mother.

"If I have to sit through another dinner with her fluttering her lashes at me, I shall not be able to eat a morsel."

"I am sure you exaggerate, but I had already quite decided to sit you beside a different guest," Lady Iverson assured him. "When did you arrive in town, dearest? Why did you send word to Lucilla and not to me?"

"I knew you would insist that I should stay here. I simply could not bear it." He stopped short as Lady Iverson's face dropped with hurt, and he hurried to reassure her. "No, dash it, not that I couldn't bear it here. Really! It is just that I know my friends will call, and they'll hound me about Lucilla, and I just cannot do it.

Most of 'em are good enough chaps, but really, I cannot think of one that will suit her. So I really do not want to be involved, if you take my meaning?"

"Of course she does, Matthew. Anne is simply feeling a little overwhelmed at the moment," Lady Edevane said promptly as her sister-in-law clasped Matthew's hand.

"So like Richard. You've always been so like him, dearest," Lady Iverson said somewhat weepily, and Matthew offered her a gentle smile and squeezed her hand affectionately. "He would have said quite the same thing, I am sure. My boys are all so alike."

Matthew beamed widely at her words, gratified to be lumped in as one of Lady Iverson's sons. It was one of many times she had lovingly claimed him, but he never tired of hearing that he was cared for by his guardians. Orphaned though he had been, he had never once felt unloved in the Iverson home.

Lady Iverson, for her part, considered herself to have three sons and a daughter, and anyone who dared to differentiate between her children found themselves swiftly and firmly corrected. Upon her marriage to Lord Iverson, she had been freely labeled Mama or Mother by his two sons, then nine and five years old respectively, and she had similarly allowed Matthew to decide what he would call her. Lord Iverson had remained Uncle Jasper, but Aunt Anne had soon been replaced by Mama. Never Mother, as he had called his own cherished one, but always Mama.

"I am sure you know what is best, dearest," Lady Iverson said with a touch of melancholy. "Though I do wish you'd be home here with us."

"I know, Mama. But really, the last thing you need

is my cronies on the doorstep drooling over Cilla in the guise of visiting me," he said with a hearty laugh that brought a smile to her face.

"I suppose not," she replied wryly. "Now, would it be terribly awful if I put Mr. Kimbley next to Tabitha Wallace? Do you think I'll be forgiven?"

"Oh, he'll forgive you. I think he'll probably not even notice, to be entirely honest."

"Oh, that will be quite impossible. He'd have to be dead not to notice her if she has anything to say about it," said Lady Edevane with a disdainful snort, shuffling through some of the blank invitations for the ball on the table.

Lady Iverson smiled and recalled her other reason for summoning Matthew. "My dear, is there anyone you would like to invite to the ball next week? I had already sent the invitations out, but I did not know you were coming to town."

"Well, I made a new acquaintance yesterday as I was stepping into White's with Ferdy. I could not be sure whether he knows Uncle Jasper or if he is dangling after Lucilla, but he asked a great many ques—"

"Stop waffling and tell us who he is, Matthew, for goodness' sake," Lady Edevane exclaimed impatiently.

He looked a little cross but answered, "The Duke of Saliston."

"Indeed, a duke? Dangling after Lucilla?"

"I do not believe we've met the Duke of Saliston," said Lady Iverson wistfully.

"What does it matter? Send the invitation, and he'll soon present himself at the door."

"He has his cousin visiting with him, a gentleman named Hartwell. Lord Hartwell, I believe."

"Well, we shall invite them both. Is there anyone else you might like to ask?"

"Any young ladies, perhaps?" Lady Edevane said with a suggestive wiggle of her eyebrows.

Matthew laughed heartily at this and disclaimed; however, he gave a list of others of his friends that might attend. Several had already been invited, but others had their names gracefully penned to the blank invitations, and Lady Iverson handed them to Matthew to deliver directly.

The bellpull had just been rung when Miss Iverson appeared dressed in white muslin under a vibrant blue pelisse and a matching bonnet. She was drawing on a pair of tan driving gloves and muttering to herself when she realized her mother and aunt were not alone.

"Matthew! Have you been summoned to assist in the rescue of our dinner party?" she exclaimed happily.

"As you see," he replied gamely. "And what are you up to, may I ask?"

"I expect my friend Miss Russell to arrive at any moment. I am taking her up in my phaeton for a drive in the Park."

"I see, and do you take Smithers up behind you?"

"Yes, warden, we will have Smithers along," Lucilla replied with a smile.

"And do you have your team or your pair?"

"The pair, dear worry-wart, though I do not see what difference that would make."

"It makes a great deal of difference. Your grays were purchased from a London stable, but your bays are country born and bred, and though I don't doubt your skill, I should not like to have you try them in London traffic before Uncle Jasper had done so first."

"Lord, do you hear yourself? You've become an old man overnight, I do declare!" Lucilla laughed and clapped her gloved hands together in amusement. "Fear not, dear cousin, Papa has already read me a lecture when he refused point blank to have the bays brought down from Gracewood. He only consented to let me have the grays and Sierra."

"You've brought Sierra to town?" Matthew said with a gasp.

"Indeed, whyever would I not?"

"How many offers have you had so far?"

"For my hand or my horse?" she replied with a twinkle, drawing a guffaw from her cousin.

At that moment, the knocker sounded on the door and Murray quickly appeared, having been expecting the visitor to arrive. After a few moments he showed Miss Russell into the drawing room.

She had a happy smile on her face as she entered and looked about the room until her gaze landed on Miss Iverson, who rose and stepped forward to greet her.

"Come and meet my family, Miss Russell," Lucilla said, leading her into the room and performing the necessary introductions. Lady Edevane was already known to the young lady, being well acquainted with her mother, but she had not before met Lady Iverson. Last introduced was Matthew, who had risen when Miss Russell entered the room and now had a rather odd look on his face Lucilla did not quite recognize.

"This is my cousin, or my brother if he has not annoyed me too much and I choose to own him. Mr. Matthew Iverson," she said with a sly smile and a curious glance at his face as he bowed over Miss Russell's hand. The young lady's eyes were quite wide and remained trained on Mr. Iverson's face as she whispered a greeting.

"Well, this has been lovely," Lucilla declared cheerfully, looping her arm through Miss Russell's. "We really ought to be going. Murray said the horses have been brought round, so I will risk a scold from Smithers if I keep them waiting."

"You take your life in your hands going out driving with Lucilla, Miss Russell. Are you feeling brave?" said Matthew seriously as he took a seat and picked up his teacup.

"Here now, you have never been turned over in any carriage of mine, which is something *you* can hardly boast," Lucilla cried indignantly. "I still bear the scar from the last of those incidents."

"She's not wrong, Matthew. Between yourself and Edward, I am sure you've tipped your chariots more than most other young men." Aunt Augusta laughed indulgently.

"Lucilla takes no risks—"

"I hardly think that is a fault," Lucilla replied.

Miss Russell stood open-mouthed as the almost-siblings bickered playfully, rather enchanted by the whole interaction and not wanting to interrupt it.

"Perhaps not, but if one does not take risks, one does not know what one can manage," Matthew said airily.

"Or what one cannot manage, in your case?" Lucilla replied. "I hardly think you can say I take no risks, when I can gallop my team through a gateway, and I have soundly beaten several of Papa's friends when they've been visiting at Gracewood."

"I wonder how many of Uncle Jasper's friends were too gentlemanly to school his daughter?"

"You are trying to provoke me, but I refuse to rise to it," Lucilla said with finality, but her color had risen noticeably. Miss Russell determined it was time to intervene since neither of the elder ladies seemed inclined to do so.

"Well, Miss Iverson's reputation precedes her, for my friend Miss Craven tells me her cousin Lord Sefton was routed in a carriage race by a dashing young lady from Lancashire," said Miss Russell with a gentle smile. "I am sure I shall be safe in her carriage."

This caused Mr. Iverson to laugh and reply that she was quite right. "Lucilla is an excellent whip. She'll not overturn you until and unless she intends to, you may be sure of that."

"If your purpose is to earn me a scold from Smithers, I am sure you will have succeeded marvelously by now," Miss Iverson said crossly.

"I should hope so. I have put in a great deal of effort," he replied with a grin.

"Miss Russell, shall we go?"

"Indeed, let's. It was a pleasure to meet you, Lady Iverson. Good day, Lady Edevane," Miss Russell said merrily. Mr. Iverson had risen from his seat, expressing the intention of escorting the ladies to the waiting phaeton and subsequently leaving the drawing room in their wake.

Lady Iverson smiled knowingly at her sister-in-law and received a similar glance in answer as the two ladies each turned their focus back to their invitations.

Outside, Miss Iverson skipped nimbly up the step of her phaeton and took up her reins before fixing her cousin with a curious glance as he reverently handed Miss Russell onto the carriage. It occurred to her she had never before seen Matthew take notice of a lady beyond her mama reminding him to ask one to dance at an assembly room or escort some other upon an errand. He had certainly never before done anything solicitous of his own accord. That is not to say that Matthew was not perfectly gentlemanly; it simply never occurred to him to pay even remote attention to ladies unless he was prompted to.

"Master Matthew, I should ha' known I'd you t' thank for Miss Cilla being late," the Iverson's faithful stablemaster, Smithers, said testily as he came away from the grays' heads. They fidgeted on the spot. The lanky middle-aged groom glared at the young gentleman as he passed by, and Mr. Iverson sheepishly endured a light scolding as his cousin beamed at him winningly.

"You've your just desserts, Matty."

"Indeed, you do, Mr. Iverson," laughed Miss Russell.

"Yes, yes, come along, Miss Cilla," Smithers said hurriedly as he stepped up behind the ladies. Miss Iverson urged her pair on, and the energetic grays leapt forward lightly.

The blue-wheeled carriage rumbled down Grosvenor Street, passing the Square to their right and proceeding on their route toward Hyde Park. The young ladies had chosen their time wisely, knowing an early appearance would find the Ring largely empty of other carriages, and they were thusly rewarded. There were some persons about on foot, on horseback, and upon their own carriages, but not nearly as many as there would be in another hour.

As the horses jogged along spiritedly, the two ladies laughed and talked together happily. Smithers sat up behind, his arms crossed and a contented smile on his face as he watched his young charge expertly guide her horses. After half an hour, the grays had settled somewhat, and Miss Iverson asked Miss Russell if she'd like to take hold of the ribbons. This offer had Smithers sitting up with a sudden start and an exclamation, but Lucilla only laughed him off.

"Dear Smithers, have a little faith, if you please. Here, Caro, watch what I am doing," Lucilla said, directing Miss Russell's attention to her hands as she halted her pair. After showing her friend how to hold the ribbons correctly and how to turn and stop them, the grays were urged into a steady walk, and Miss Russell let out an excited gurgle of laughter.

Miss Russell was soon confidently managing the pair at a sedate jog along the mostly deserted thoroughfare. The horses were well-schooled and perfectly suited to ladies in spite of their occasionally hyperactive behavior and were quite readily managed when they had been warmed correctly. Happy with the success of their lesson, Miss Iverson soon took the reins back, and it was not long before she was recounting the tale of the Stafford episode for Miss Russell's amusement as she steered her phaeton out of the Park with the intention of depositing her companion at her home in Green Street.

"It was quite a singular afternoon. One does not forget almost being run down in the street," she said with a laugh.

"I should think not. I wonder who they were?" Miss Russell replied curiously as her friend cautiously navigated the carriage onto the street.

"I think the older gentleman called himself

Sawstone, or Sallstone, or someth—"

"The *Duke* of *Saliston*?" Miss Russell gasped and clapped her hand across her mouth.

"A duke? Well, that would be quite amusing if it is indeed the man I met," Lucilla replied, arching a brow.

"I do not know him, of course, except by reputation. Mama has never bothered to put me in his path. I believe all of the matchmaking mamas have long since despaired of him," Miss Russell said knowingly.

"And the cousin, do you know anything of him?"

"I cannot say that I do, I'm afraid. I know the Duchess of Saliston was the daughter of the late Lord Agarth, so I suppose the cousin could be from that side of the family."

"How very strange. I wonder that I've never heard of either of the families before," Miss Iverson said wonderingly. "Agarth sounds vaguely familiar, but I am not certain."

"Their estates are in Norfolk, I believe."

"Well, I suppose we would not meet by chance then." Lucilla smiled at Miss Russell, and the two young ladies laughed.

They had arrived at the Russells' small Green Street townhouse, and Miss Iverson drew her horses up before she turned to embrace her friend and thanked her for her company before the two bid one another goodbye. Smithers nimbly leapt off the phaeton and assisted the young lady's descent, and they waited for Miss Russell to disappear into the house before the grays set off again.

As she wound her way along the streets, dodging pedestrians, handcarts, carriages, and dogs, Lucilla thought hard about where she had heard the name of Agarth. She was certain now that it was familiar to her, but she could not recall with any clarity how she had come across it. By the time she had steered the grays onto Grosvenor Street and drawn up in front of Iverson House, Lucilla had decided that she must have heard Papa mention the name. Certainly, if the family hailed from Norfolk, there could hardly be any other place she would have heard of it.

Chapter 9

The evening of the Iverson Ball began well when Lucilla was introduced to Mr. Kimbley once again. The young gentleman had made the journey to Gracewood several times during his school years to visit with Mr. Matthew. Still, he distinctly recalled Miss Iverson as a rambunctious tangle of brown hair and muddied skirts. Now he faced a demure and rather meticulously presented young lady by the same name.

"I'd never have known that chit was your cousin, Matt," Ferdy whispered to his friend. "Grown rather fine feathers, ain't she?"

"Gad, Ferdy, you're not going to start dangling after Cilla, are you?" Mr. Iverson groaned as he poured them each a glass of Madeira.

"Not looking to leg-shackle meself just now, dear boy." Ferdy grinned at his friend. "Just giving credit where it's due. She was always more of a boy than a girl, so I must own some surprise to see her decked out in the family jewels."

"Pearls, you sod. She can hardly be wearing anything nattier than that in her first Season," Mr. Iverson replied as he glanced over in Lucilla's direction to confirm his assertion. He was not typically in the habit of studying what his cousin wore, but he could see she was in exceptionally high form this evening.

She wore a blue silk robe that crossed together over

the bodice. The under-dress of patterned silver was adorned with a fringed hem, and the ensemble was completed with matching silk slippers and long gloves, but only a blue ribbon was woven through her dark hair. It was simple and exceptionally exquisite, or so Matthew thought once he had made a thorough assessment of his cousin's attire. He was made to regret this momentary distraction when before him appeared Miss Wallace, demanding his attention.

"Matthew, I had no notion of your being in town. How have you not come to see me?" Miss Wallace said crisply as she stood before her surprised quarry, fairly glaring at him.

Somewhat aghast, Matthew's eyes widened, and his mouth dropped open, but before he could respond the young lady continued her castigation.

"When we have been such friends, and I have not laid eyes on you in months. You shall sit beside me at dinner. I will not brook a refusal," she said in a pettish voice as she looped her arm in his and turned to look at his companion. "I have not met your friend here."

"Indeed, Ferdy, this is Miss Tabitha Wallace. Miss Wallace, this is my friend from Oxford, Mr. Ferdinand Kimbley," Matthew responded as he attempted to extricate himself from her grasp rather unsuccessfully by gesturing in Ferdy's direction.

Ever the gentleman, Ferdy put out his hand expectantly, which had the desired effect of requiring Miss Wallace to withdraw her claw-like grasp of Matthew's arm for long enough to allow him to sidle away from her slightly. Ferdy dutifully pecked her hand with his lips and muttered his greetings, but there was a certain amount of horror and concern in his gaze that

Matthew recognized as being for himself.

Mr. Kimbley kept Miss Wallace's attention for a short while, but she seemed determined to keep Matthew engaged in the conversation and would not be drawn away from him. After several minutes of unsuccessfully distracting her, they heard her name being called from across the room by her mother.

"Come, Matthew, Mama will want to see you," Tabitha said firmly as she attempted to retake his arm.

But this time, he was quicker. Having had a few moments to collect his thoughts and form a plan of escape, he now put it into action.

"Oh, is that my aunt arriving? Pray, excuse me, ma'am." He bowed shallowly and spun on his heel to beat a hasty retreat with a desperate glance at Ferdy as he hurried away in the direction of the newly arrived Lady Edevane. He breathed a sigh of relief as he heard his friend excuse himself and follow.

"Lord, what a shrew," Ferdy muttered under his breath as he came up beside Matthew.

"You've no idea. When she gets wind of your being the son of a viscount, she'll be digging her claws into you too, no doubt," Matthew replied broodingly.

"Second son. She doesn't seem the type to be interested in a second son, thank the Lord," Mr. Kimbley replied airily with a wave of his hand.

"What is this hand-waving about, may I ask?" Lady Edevane said archly as she looked at her nephew and his friend.

"Nothing at all, Aunt," Mr. Iverson replied. "This is my friend Ferdy. I told you about him last week."

"Indeed, Viscount Kimbley's son," said her ladyship in a tone that ended her sentence with *I have made inquiries* without need of the actual words being uttered. Proper introductions were made, and merry small talk had for a few minutes before Lady Edevane turned the conversation back to the scene she had witnessed ending upon her arrival.

"I do so hate to miss a well-acted set, you know."

"People are but players on a stage for you, aren't they?" Mr. Iverson said with a shake of his head.

"Come now, my boy, was she sinking her claws in? Was she all familiarity and airs?" Lady Edevane replied with a wry smile and a small dollop of contempt.

"Should have seen it, ma'am. She was fairly growing talons." Ferdy made a claw-like gesture with his hand at his friend's elbow, causing Matthew to flinch away and triggering a round of snorts and chuckles.

"What is so funny?" Miss Iverson said with a curious smile as she joined the conversation with Miss Russell approaching at her side.

"Nothing," Matthew said firmly. His gaze came to rest on Miss Russell, causing her to blush lightly and smile at him.

"Nothing at all," Mr. Kimbley confirmed with a nod and a grin that belied it.

"Are you all in one piece after your chat with Tabitha? I saw her approach you. I considered mounting a rescue, but I feared the consequences to myself would be too enormous to bear," Lucilla said smilingly.

"Oh, thank you, dearest," replied Matthew sardonically.

"Shush. Do not speak so familiarly, Matthew. I do not want anyone to assume there is some sort of affection between the two of you beyond that of a brother and sister. I cannot imagine anything more damaging to her chances," Lady Edevane whispered frantically.

"I can't imagine anything more revolting, myself," Matthew whispered in reply.

"Oh," Lucilla gasped, feigning offense. "And here I cherished such hope."

At that moment, Lady Iverson announced dinner to be ready, and the guests assembled in order to make their way into the dining room. Lucilla eyed her cousin and inclined her head toward her friend, and so Mr. Iverson gallantly offered his arm to Miss Russell, whilst Lucilla took the Honorable Ferdinand Kimbley's and followed him out of the drawing room under the contented gaze of Lady Edevane and the vastly irritated Miss Wallace.

It was soon apparent that some matchmaking was afoot, for Mr. Iverson fortuitously found himself seated beside Miss Russell at dinner. Mr. Kimbley was placed between Miss Iverson and Miss Wallace, who spent quite some time attempting to catch Matthew's eye until Lucilla loudly enquired after Mr. Kimbley's father and Tabitha suddenly deduced that she was seated beside the son of a viscount. This had the effect of making him quite the most charming young man in the room, and Mr. Kimbley realized the horrid brown-haired scamp of his youth was still very much alive and well, residing in Miss Iverson's outwardly pleasing person.

*****

After what seemed like hours of greeting guests, Lady Iverson released Lucilla from her duty and the ball was opened with the first dance of the evening.

Mr. Moore was among the earliest arrivals, and Lucilla managed to side-pass answering his request to dance with her at some time during the evening by surreptitiously turning her attention toward a new arrival and feigning deafness. This required her to keep track of Mr. Moore's movements through the room once the dancing began so she might avoid being cornered. In her efforts, she was assisted by Miss Russell, who was more than happy to suddenly notice an acquaintance that she simply *must* introduce Lucilla to immediately if Mr. Moore was seen heading in her direction.

Quite some time after the commencement of the dancing, the Duke of Saliston and his cousin arrived at the Iverson ball. The hostess had abandoned the door and was now engaged in the task of ensuring every young lady in attendance was granted a partner for any dance in which they wished to partake, and Miss Iverson was in high demand. The duke sought out his godmother, Lady Marian Lacock, to make the necessary introductions.

She was quickly located, for it was hard to miss her. She was a stunningly large woman. Not tall, but immense, and dressed rather ostentatiously in a gown of deep red, her hair adorned with black feathers. She waved her fan and called out to the duke when she spotted him among the crowd.

"George? George, dearest! You are shockingly late," Lady Lacock scolded gently and tapped her godson's knuckles as he kissed her hand.

"My apologies, Aunt Marian. I was called away yesterday and have only returned this evening," Saliston replied courteously.

"Yes, I'm sure you have," the lady replied suspiciously. "Oliver, how do you do, boy?"

"Very well, ma'am," the young man replied with a sunny smile. "We've just returned from Kent. Saliston has procured a perfectly excellent team of horses on my behalf."

"Good heavens, let us have no talk of horses this evening," said her ladyship in forbidding tones. "Almost every pretty lady in town has been invited tonight. You must be introduced to them—both of you."

"We are at your mercy, Aunt Marian," Saliston said with a laugh. "Perhaps we ought to begin by being introduced to our hostess?"

"Indeed, you are quite right. My sister, Mrs. Carleton, will introduce you to our hostess." Her ladyship stood precariously and bustled away in search of her sister, motioning to the two gentlemen to follow.

Mrs. Carleton was the antithesis of her sister. They each bore the same fading golden hair and blue eyes, but the resemblance thereafter ended swiftly. Where Lady Lacock was buxom and loud in dress and voice, Mrs. Carleton was slim and quiet of the same.

"Adelaide," Lady Lacock called out as she approached her sister and tapped her elbow impatiently with her fan to gain her attention.

Mrs. Carleton turned slowly and cast a serene gaze upon her sister, a gentle smile spreading across her face as her eye came to rest on the duke. "Ah, Marian. I see you bring George and Oliver. How fortuitous. Augusta, you remember my sister Lady Lacock? This is her godson, the Duke of Saliston. And his cousin, the Earl of Hartwell. Gentlemen, this is my dear friend, Lady Edevane. She is the sister-in-law of our hostess."

Lady Edevane quickly sized up each of the men in front of her before favoring them with a gracious smile. After several minutes of polite idle chatter, she deemed them both to be perfectly gentlemanly and declared that she would introduce them immediately to their hostess, Lady Iverson. Her ladyship was completely unaware of

Saliston's eagerness and Oliver's complete and utter terror of being introduced to Lady and Miss Iverson. She marched through the ballroom in the direction of the supper room, having seen her sister-in-law and niece heading that way only a few minutes earlier.

"Anne, dear, I have someone who has asked to be introduced to you," Lady Edevane said softly as she approached Lady Iverson, who was conversing with Lord Iverson. "Ah, Jasper. How fortunate that you are here. Let me introduce the Duke of Saliston and his cousin, Lord Hartwell."

"We are so grateful to be included in your gathering, Lady Iverson," Saliston said gallantly as he bowed over his hostess's hand. Beside him, Oliver went through the motions of greeting their new acquaintance, but his gaze was fixed on the dark-haired lady in blue and silver who stood with her back to them only a few steps away.

Lady Edevane noticed Lord Hartwell's attention was elsewhere and followed his gaze. She smiled, then stepped toward the young lady in blue and silver and attracted her attention with a gentle touch and a whisper. The girl nodded to Lady Edevane before excusing herself and turning slowly away from her companions. There was a laugh in her gaze as she said something to her ladyship. Then she looked up and her eyes landed on Lord Hartwell.

A flash of recognition swept the mirth from her face. Her laughter died a sudden death, but she recovered quickly and forced a prim smile to her lips as she was finally, formally, introduced to the men she remembered quite clearly from the street in Stafford.

****

Lucilla had been enjoying a perfectly charming

discussion with Miss Craven when her aunt called her away. She was far too good-natured to be anything but amused by the conspiratorial tone Lady Edevane employed in drawing her away from the conversation. Still, when she saw the young man standing before her, she was fairly bowled over. Her months in town had taught her the art of thinking on her feet, so she was able to shrug off her surprise enough to partake in the required introductions.

The Duke of Saliston betrayed not the slightest sign that he had ever met her before as he bowed over her hand and presented his companion, the Earl of Hartwell. As the younger gentleman took her hand, she felt a slight trembling in his touch, and for no discernable reason was compelled to comfort him with a gentle press of her fingertips, an action that earned her an enquiring glance from him in return. She was quite unsure why she had felt the need to offer him reassurance, but the look on his face reminded her somewhat of a lost puppy, and she was excessively fond of puppies.

Lost in her own thoughts, Lucilla was entirely unaware that her mother was offering permission to dance with the duke, who was waiting patiently with an amused smile on his lips for her to acknowledge his request. A well-hidden sharp jab to her ribs from Lady Edevane brought her back to earth, and Cilla was soon being led to the ballroom as the quartet prepared to play a waltz.

After a turn or two about the floor in silence, during which Saliston gazed down at the young lady with barely concealed amusement, he decided to draw her into conversation.

"How do you like London, Miss Iverson?"

She glanced up at him quickly, as though deciding how to respond, before she said flatly, "I like it more than I did Stafford."

Saliston laughed heartily and smiled down at her. "I should think you do. I suppose you have yet to be run down in the street?"

"I have managed to avoid it, so far at least," Lucilla replied wryly.

"Well, I am glad to know it. Please do allow me to apologize once more for that mortifying incident," the duke said lightly as they twirled about the floor.

"I believe I owe you an apology also, your grace," she answered. "I ought not to have shouted at you so."

"Oh, you were quite justified, I assure you. My cousin and I are in complete agreeance on that score."

She smiled tightly in response to his statement but did not reply. Instead, she looked away, and he thought she was perhaps looking for someone in the crowd.

"I should inform you, Miss Iverson, that unfortunate incident weighed on Lord Hartwell's conscience considerably. He has since spent many hours in careful study of proper handling of the ribbons," Saliston said conversationally. "I think he would very much appreciate the opportunity to demonstrate his improvement to you."

Miss Iverson pursed her lips, and her nose twitched slightly as she looked at the duke, and he wondered if it was amusement he could see in her gaze. "I am not sure I should appreciate being at the mercy of your cousin's skill as a driver, your grace."

"I am not surprised that you should say so, Miss Iverson," he said with a laugh. "Perhaps you might view the demonstration from a safe distance?"

This suggestion brought a smile to her face, and her reply came with a soft laugh. "Perhaps that would be best."

After a few moments of silence, Saliston tried once more to engage her in conversation. He thought perhaps a compliment would be a better foundation for discussion, so he said, "I have heard tales of your prowess with horses, Miss Iverson. I have been approached several times now at my club to lay my wager on whether you will part with this legendary chestnut of yours."

"Heavens, I have lost count of how many offers my father has received for him these three weeks. I think he has begun to despair of receiving an offer for my hand, for any gentlemen who approach him are only after my horse," Lucilla said artlessly, smiling up at him.

"Come now, Miss Iverson, you do not fool me. I am convinced you must be turning gentlemen callers away by the dozen."

"I would not say that, precisely," she replied modestly, but a prim smile lurked at the corner of her mouth.

"Have you yet met anyone in town of interest to you?" he enquired, perfectly aware that he was not in any position to be questioning her thusly. But he found her openness amusing, and for the first time in a long time, he did not feel in the least that he was being hunted, which was refreshing, to say the least.

"There have been a few gentlemen who have called upon me, but I cannot say that any of them have been particularly interesting. I am sure the younger gentlemen find me rather dashing, and the older gentlemen…" Her voice trailed off, and she looked away musingly before she focused on his face again and continued, "Well, I am unsure what the older gentlemen think of me."

The duke again threw his head back in laughter. "I wonder if I count as one of these 'older gentlemen' or the younger?"

"I do not think I should answer that, your grace," Lucilla said with a merry lilt in her voice.

"That is an excellent answer."

"I've become quite diplomatic, if I do say so myself."

"Indeed, I do see you have acquired some of what the *ton* would call 'polish,' " he replied perceptively. "I would urge you not to change yourself in an effort to conform. My first impression was of a singularly spirited young lady, and I should hate to see you blending in with the dozens of other simple misses who wander these ballrooms in search of husbands."

"I shall endeavor to defy convention then," she declared cheerily.

As the music ended, the duke led her toward an anxious-looking Lord Hartwell, who stood at the edge of a small group of young people with whom he had been conversing, but he turned away as he caught his cousin's eye.

"Have no fear. You are forgiven," his cousin declared as they approached.

"Not quite," Lucilla countered archly. "I believe I will require a demonstration of your improvement before I am satisfied, Lord Hartwell."

Oliver's gaze darted between Miss Iverson and his cousin in some confusion, unsure which of them to believe. He wondered if they were jesting, but he was not sure until a playful smile slowly spread upon Miss

Iverson's face, and only then did he let his mouth form a smile in return.

"I will, of course, not be seated in any carriage with you until I have seen from a safe distance that you are capable of handling your horses," she said mischievously. "The duke informs me that you've purchased a splendid team. Perhaps we ought to see how they match up against my grays?"

"You drive?" Oliver said in surprise.

"But of course."

"Are there many young ladies that do so?"

"I believe it is a skill that quite a number of young ladies have acquired," Lucilla replied cautiously. "Though perhaps not many would engage in the activity quite as often as myself."

At that moment, across the ballroom, an excessively irritated Mr. Moore observed as his excessively irritating young cousin engaged Miss Iverson in what he could only assume was a riveting conversation, considering both appeared to be in high spirits. She was laughing. *Laughing*! With *Oliver*, damn her! And that infuriating wretch Saliston was hanging about her too. She was already maddeningly immune to his own charms. The last thing he needed was to be in competition with a duke.

Before Moore knew what was happening, Oliver offered his hand to Miss Iverson and led her out of the ballroom. He fought the urge to march across the room and interrupt the situation, but he at least had the sense to acknowledge that assuming familiarity would only set the young lady even more against him. Perhaps he could use Oliver to his advantage? She seemed to be on easy enough terms with the young earl, certainly more so than she was with himself, and he knew Oliver to be a loyal dog. Perhaps a kindly placed word or two might thaw her icicles. He would need to find a way to have Oliver speak of him to her.

In the meantime, he had drawn from the conversation that Lucilla was maddeningly jealous of her friend Miss Wallace, so he considered that perhaps a well-timed dance with that young lady might spark a vein of envy enough to seed a little doubt of his devotion to herself.

Yes, he thought to himself, *this is just the thing to draw her attention.*

He had, of course, been told of Lucilla's jealousy by Miss Wallace herself, but the total illogicality of relying on one such as Miss Wallace for information never occurred to Mr. Moore. He had not spent very much time with the girl; in fact, he found her rather annoying. But she had declared that she was Miss Iverson's oldest friend, and so he had taken some minor pains to ingratiate himself with her.

Miss Wallace, for her part, seeing that her friend had gained the interest of an apparently well-to-do and handsome young man, was instinctively compelled to draw his interest herself. She had twinkled and smiled, fluttered her eyelashes, and supposed she had made some headway in diverting his attention from Miss Iverson. When he approached her at the edge of the ballroom and invited her to dance the next set with him, she was beyond delighted, particularly as Lucilla had just returned from supper. With a flirtatious flounce, she put her hand in Mr. Moore's and allowed him to lead her to the floor.

Entirely unaware that Mr. Moore and Miss

Wallace's dance was a spectacle intended specifically to rouse a flame of furious jealousy within her, Miss Iverson did not even notice that they had joined the set.

Chapter 10

Lucilla was not in love. With anyone, really. She hadn't come to London in search of what the poets described, exactly, but she had hoped to at least find a gentleman interesting enough to consider marriage with. There had been several gentlemen who had shown themselves inclined to dangle after her, had called in Grosvenor Street, and had sent flowers and candies and notes. But not one of them attracted her in the slightest. To be sure, they were all perfectly lovely men, with one or two a little less than lovely, but they all had something about them that Lucilla simply could not set aside.

For example, Sir Geoffrey Knightsbridge was a handsome man of about five-and-thirty years. Since they had met at Almack's, Lucilla had danced with him at least once at every ball or party, and he had called at Iverson House several times. While she was pleased to discuss horses and dogs, it seemed that one ought to be able to talk of more than this, and she had the unhappy impression that Sir Geoffrey had singled her out simply because she was too polite to feign complete disinterest in his favorite topic. He never complimented her unless it was to praise her horsemanship, and while she did not consider herself a vain person, she would have liked to be treated with the same consideration that other young ladies received.

On the other hand, there were several young

gentlemen, much like Mr. Russell, who fawned over her beauty, sending poems and sweet cakes and flowers on an almost daily basis. The excitement that accompanied the receiving of these gifts speedily waned as it dawned on Lucilla that her admirers seemed more interested in out-doing one another than they were in attaching her. Duels of honor were fought by proxy with the largest bouquet or the prettiest poem. Some young men went so far as to beg that she would wear his flowers as a sign of her affection, and this happened so often that she had taken to wearing no flowers at all.

Then there were the older gentlemen, the kindly, fatherly widowers of fortune. Some were titled, others were not, but they all had at least one child in need of a mother, and they had decided a pretty and spirited young girl like Lucilla would liven up their household. While there was nothing inherently wrong with this kind of thinking, it was hardly attractive. She was not necessarily a fervent romantic, but she was undoubtedly not a pragmatist either.

Finally, there were the fortune hunters. There were no less than three, and while two had been speedily routed either by her own efforts or her father's, one simply refused to be dismissed. Mr. Charles Moore made her skin prickle most unpleasantly—even a thought spared for him brought a sour taste to her mouth. She had a distinct memory of her father storming across the home park at Gracewood to shoot a deer that had been wounded through a prank that a thirteen-year-old Mr. Moore had played, involving several wires being strung up between some trees. The poor creature had been found hopelessly, mortally, tangled, and Lord Iverson had rounded on his neighbor's son, who had expressed not even the smallest grain of remorse.

Distaste for the young man had waned and bloomed at turns, depending on the flow of local gossip regarding his exploits. As time had passed and the boy had grown, his lordship had softened. He was more inclined to forgive earlier sins but extended no invitations to Gracewood, and it wasn't until some ten years after the incident with the deer that the young man entered the park again, this time with the intention of courting the daughter of the house.

Lucilla had not forgotten his crimes, but she agreed that the misdeeds of youth should not plague a man for the rest of his life. At first, she had accepted his presence in her life as a matter of neighborly courtesy. Once she understood his intentions, it was too late for her polite rebuffs, for they were ignored altogether, and he had made sure the entire neighborhood was aware that he considered himself to have a claim on her.

Beyond disclaiming any understanding between them to any of their mutual acquaintance that was forward enough to enquire, there was little that Lucilla could do. She made a substantial effort to avoid him whenever they were in public, but as he had made something of a study of her habits, she was now forced to ride with her groom, even nearby her home, for fear he would accost her while she was unaccompanied.

She was well aware he had grown desperate. The elder Mr. Moore was known to have gambled away his money in his youth, and only his marriage had saved his modest estate. But that money had long since been lost to the same habits, and as the son had developed rather expensive tastes of his own, it was generally known in the neighborhood that whoever Charles Moore married would require a sizeable dowry. And Lucilla was determined she would not be that woman.

It was now two days since the Iverson Ball, and the event had been labeled a fabulous success. Ladies and matrons adored the string quartet, gentlemen applauded the excellent choice of liquor on offer in the card room, everyone enjoyed the light repast, and the dancing had only concluded at the early hour of five o'clock.

Miss Iverson walked with her mama toward Hyde Park with Chico in tow. Her ladyship was quite aware of her daughter's reasons for wanting, for once, to walk in the park, and it had absolutely nothing to do with exercising her dog. Lady Iverson had been requested to chaperone a meeting with the Duke of Saliston and his cousin Lord Hartwell, though she was at a loss to know why Lucilla had developed a sudden interest in the two gentlemen. She was not going to discourage a friendship there—a mother would be mad to give a duke or an earl their marching orders—but she was curious as to why, after several months in town, these two men were somehow different from the many others who had been met.

Chico skipped along at his mistress's skirts, sniffing everything that came within his reach and occasionally requiring a tug on his leather strap to remind him that he ought to keep up. Miss Iverson and her mother chattered on, discussing their plans to attend an *al fresco* party the following day and the subsequent assembly at Almack's, until they entered the gate and selected a walking path that would keep them near the carriage drives.

Barely five minutes after their arrival, a rather new-looking high-perch phaeton appeared, pulled by a pair of flashy bays with matching stars and socks, and they appeared to be driven by Lord Hartwell. The yellow-wheeled carriage rolled up beside the path near the Iverson ladies, and the horses drew to a halt, bringing a rather pleased grin to their driver's face. The Duke of Saliston was seated up beside his cousin, leaning back with his arms crossed and a rather lazy smile. When he spotted Miss Iverson and her mother, he sat up and called out a greeting to them.

"How do you do, your grace?" Lady Iverson said as the gentleman stepped down from the phaeton. He bowed over her hand and replied pleasantly before smiling at Miss Iverson and asking if she had seen enough of Lord Hartwell's skill to feel safe in his carriage.

"Well, they are certainly a strapping pair, and he can obviously pull them up, at the very least," Lucilla said laughingly.

"Perhaps your mother will allow you to take a turn about the park?" Saliston queried with a quick look at Lady Iverson. Her ladyship made a note of the liveried groom up behind the earl before she nodded affirmatively, took Chico's leather, and watched as the duke handed Lucilla up onto the phaeton beside Lord Hartwell.

As the carriage rolled away, Lady Iverson clicked her tongue to regain Chico's notice, and the golden-haired dog trotted up beside her. The duke looked at it curiously and queried Lady Iverson on its origin as they strolled along the walk.

"My son Edward brought him back from Spain after the battle of Salamanca. Our elder son had purchased him as a pup from a Spanish soldier and intended to bring him back to England for Lucilla, but he did n-not survive the battle," Lady Iverson said with a slight stutter at the memory. But she smiled through her evident pain and bent down to pet Chico's blond head, earning herself a cursory sniff before he went back to investigating the ground around them.

"I am very sorry for your loss, Lady Iverson," the duke said gently.

"Thank you. I still have Lucilla, of course, and Matthew. He may not be my own, but I feel as though he is."

"Ah, yes, I have met Mr. Iverson. He seems a charming lad."

"He is a wonderful boy. I have every reason to be proud of him," Lady Iverson said simply.

"And your other son—Edward, did you say? Does he come to town?"

Lady Iverson's face froze, looking off into the distance with her brow furrowed and her lips tightened. Saliston frowned a little and followed her gaze, concerned she might have seen something untoward happening, but he could see nothing.

The expression on her face evaporated as quickly as it had appeared, and she forced a smile before responding that Edward had rejoined his unit and been dispatched to Brussels some time ago. "We do not hear from him often."

Her tone did not invite conversation on the subject of her son, so Saliston improvised a new topic to pass the time as his cousin tooled about the park with her daughter.

Meanwhile, Lord Hartwell was discussing his new horses with Miss Iverson. She was quite impressed at how well matched they were and marveled at their movement and temperaments.

"They seem a rather high-strung pair, or is that an illusion, Lord Hartwell?" Lucilla chirped.

"Oh, quite an illusion, I assure you. Saliston says it's the stockings. I think it's their eyes. We cannot quite agree, I'm afraid." Oliver laughed.

"Well, so far, I must say I am quite impressed with your improvement. My brothers and I were taught to drive when we were children. Papa gave us a fat little pony and a cart. He used to set up baskets on the green for us to steer the pony through for practice." She laughed at the memory.

"My cousin had me doing much the same, except with one of his older carriage horses and a jinker."

"It is an excellent teaching method, indeed. You've progressed very well," Lucilla said with an encouraging smile. His color rose slightly at the compliment, and he grinned back at her.

"I think you ought to let me drive them."

"You? Drive my bays?" Oliver said incredulously.

"Why not? I can assure you I am quite capable. I'd wager my grays are rather more of a handful on a bad day than these two are today." She smiled mischievously.

"Are you sure?" he said worriedly. "I should not like a repeat of what happened in Stafford."

"Surely you jest." Lucilla laughed. "I am quite sure I shan't injure you or your horses."

Lord Hartwell glanced at her apprehensively, but she had put her hands out to accept the reins, and while he remained a little uncertain, he handed them to her anyway. With a playful twinkle in her eye, she adjusted her fingers about the ribbons and checked the horses with an imperceptible twitch that caused Oliver to lurch forward at their sudden stop. His expression of shock made her gurgle with laughter, for he had barely enough time to register what had happened before an elegant flick of the whip had the bays clipping from halt to trot in a single step. Shock gave way to a wide grin as he realized she had jerked him back and forth on purpose to exhibit her skill.

"Well, you needn't be a show-off." He chuckled.

She tossed her head gleefully as she urged the horses on. They were soon approaching the spot where they had left the duke and Lady Iverson, and Lucilla spotted them up ahead, seated on a bench, with Chico employed in dismantling a tree branch beside them. They appeared to be deep in discussion and did not notice as the phaeton bowled up the drive.

"What do you think they're talking about?" Lucilla tipped her head in the direction of their respective guardians.

"I wouldn't have the faintest idea," Oliver replied wonderingly. "Perhaps the weather?"

"The weather? Lord, what a tedious prospect."

"Well, what do *you* think they're talking about, then?"

Lucilla looked at her companion from under arched brows. "Well, they aren't discussing the weather, of that you may be certain. I think it is much more likely they are each attempting to glean information from the other—without giving the appearance of interest, of course."

"And what kind of information do you think they would be trying to obtain?"

"My mother will be attempting to ascertain the size

of your cousin's fortune and possibly your own, I imagine."

"What?" He gasped.

"Really, what else would mothers of unwed daughters want to know?"

He frowned thoughtfully before replying that he was not acquainted with very many mothers of unwed daughters, so he could not be an expert in the matter.

"Well, I assure you, that is precisely what they do."

"I see," Oliver mused. "And what are your thoughts on it?"

Lucilla turned her head toward him and fixed him with a curious stare.

"On what, exactly?"

"On fortune and its relevance in a marriage." He shrugged.

"I should not consider it imperative, I suppose," she answered airily. "I prefer to think that mutual respect and affection are of greater importance."

"I rather think I agree," he said with a wry smile.

She smiled back at him. "Here, take back your horses. We ought to rejoin our chaperones."

"Show me how you stopped and started them so quickly before, and then I'll set you down." His boldness provoked another gurgle of laughter from her in reply as he took the reins back.

Lucilla showed him how to adjust his reins in such a way that the horses would feel the driver's fingers more sensitively, and after a few more attempts, he was able to halt the bays rather more quickly than he had previously managed, which pleased him greatly. Once they had come as close by the bench as the drive would allow, he called for his groom to go to the horse's heads so he could assist Miss Iverson down. He climbed down and offered his hand to her.

"I do hope we may do this again, Miss Iverson," Oliver said earnestly before his cousin and her mama were within earshot.

"I should like that very much, Lord Hartwell," she replied with a sunny smile. As she took his hand and stepped down, her boot caught on her skirt, and she tripped, falling into his arms. She burst into ready laughter, resting her hand on his arm to steady herself and regain her balance.

"Oh, dear, anyone will think I am throwing myself at you in rather a literal sense."

His color rose slightly and he forced a laugh, but the rush of emotion he felt as he held her prevented intelligent speech from forming in his mind, let alone on his tongue. He was grateful that she did not seem to notice, as she had begun to address her startled parent.

"I am quite all right, Mama, I assure you."

"Heavens, Lucilla, you gave me a fright," Lady Iverson cried.

"I am quite all right," Lucilla repeated.

"It would indeed have been quite a shame to survive Oliver's driving, only to perish as you descended from the carriage," Saliston said jestingly. His eyes narrowed on his cousin. The boy was utterly tongue-tied.

"It would indeed have been very awkward! But it is no matter, for I am fine," she said firmly in her mother's direction before she continued. "We had a very pleasant drive, your grace. Your lessons have clearly done the trick, or Lord Hartwell is an exceptionally quick student. I am inclined to think it is the latter, for he picked up my little trick very readily just now."

119

"Ah, you forsake me, student," Saliston said with mock hurt. "I am cast off for a prettier instructor, I see."

"Well, I should not think you would be flattered by being called pretty, cousin." Lord Hartwell found his voice and joined the jest willingly.

"Lord Hartwell was kind enough to let me drive his pair, your grace."

"How did you find them, Miss Iverson?"

"They are sweet goers, very well-schooled." She turned her attention directly to Oliver. "I shall let you drive my grays some time, I think. Then you may compare."

"I should like that very much," he answered.

"Well, we ought to return home now, Lucilla," Lady Iverson said gently, and her daughter agreed readily, accepting Chico's lead from her mother.

The little group bid each other farewell and promised to meet again another day. Miss Iverson and her mother walked in the direction of Grosvenor Street, chattering agreeably, the golden dog bouncing along beside them, and the gentlemen mounted Lord Hartwell's phaeton.

After some time driving along in silence, Saliston broke the quiet by asking his cousin how went his tête-à-tête, but Lord Hartwell was too lost in his own thoughts to hear the query, let alone answer it.

Lord Hartwell was not in love. At least, not quite yet. Miss Iverson's face flickered through his mind, the sound of her laugh echoed in his ears, and he remembered how it felt to hold her, however short-lived the moment had been. But he was not in love.

Not quite yet.

Chapter 11

Following their afternoon drive in the park, every gathering saw Lord Hartwell among the earliest arrivals of any party that he attended. He was unsure what compelled him, but he no longer required Saliston's urging to be dressed and ready to depart, and so he was when the carriage arrived at the door to carry them to Almack's several days later.

Saliston was no less eager to catch a glimpse of Miss Iverson again, but he was not so driven that he would arrive early enough to draw the attention of gossips. When they arrived at Almack's, she was already taking part in a lively dance, her eyes brimming with laughter as her dance partner tripped, and she attempted to stifle her mirth behind a gloved hand.

Oliver greeted some of his acquaintances as he made his way through the room, glancing at the dance floor every so often in the hope of catching her eye. Instead, he found himself waylaid by his cousin Charlie.

"Olly, fancy seeing you here," the older gentleman said smoothly.

"Charlie, what do you do here? I thought you were visiting your friend at Melton Mowbray?" Oliver said in surprise.

"Called it off," his cousin replied with a wave of his hand. "Turns out my dear friend Dickie doesn't have a hunting box up there anymore."

Lord Hartwell frowned slightly, wondering how exactly one might lose one's house in the space of two days. Surely there was a logical explanation, but he was also sure it was none of his business to know, and so he forbore to ask Charlie to elaborate on the subject.

"Well, I'm mighty glad to see you, in any case, cousin," Oliver said cheerfully. "Any particular reason you decided to show yourself here?"

"I might ask you the same," Mr. Moore replied rather archly. Seeing his cousin's brows raise at the sharpness of his tone, he quickly softened to a jest. "Thinking about becoming an honest gentleman already, are you?"

Oliver blushed lightly and answered in the negative, but he suddenly realized the music had stopped and found himself looking about in something like panic for Miss Iverson, only to find her leaving the floor on the arm of her dance partner.

"Excuse me for a moment, cousin," he said, abruptly departing and making his way toward Lucilla, leaving his cousin slack-jawed and simmering.

As Oliver approached her, Lucilla glanced around and saw him. She smiled sunnily, calling out a greeting.

"How do you do, Miss Iverson?" he said as he bowed punctiliously.

"I am quite well, Lord Hartwell. Have you just arrived?"

He replied with an enthusiastic nod and was about to enquire whether she was engaged for the next dance when he thought he saw her shoulders stiffen. She had caught sight of something, or someone, past his shoulder, and it was clear she did not like whatever, or whoever, it was. Suddenly her eyes flashed with an emotion he hadn't yet observed in her and didn't quite recognize before she looked at him with a tight, agitated smile and said, "Lord Hartwell, if you should not mind it, would you please ask me to dance?"

Oliver's eyes widened in surprise, and he blinked quickly for a moment before he gathered his senses and obliged her.

"I should very much like to dance," she replied, the thin line of her lips making way for something more like her natural smile as she took his offered hand, and they walked toward the floor past the red velvet ropes. As they took their place, she looked across the room with a glare, and he followed her gaze to see that it rested on his cousin Charlie.

As the orchestra struck up a waltz, she looked at him expectantly, waiting for him to take the lead, and he shuddered with surprise when she placed her hand on his shoulder. She threw another distracted glance toward Mr. Moore as Oliver put his hand at her waist. Her lips curved almost into a sneer, and then they were in motion. She had smiles only for her partner.

"You seem out of sorts, Miss Iverson," Oliver said inquiringly, not understanding why she seemed different.

"Do I really seem out of sorts? I do apologize," she replied gaily.

"That isn't really an answer, is it."

She bit her bottom lip a little and said, "No, I suppose it isn't."

"Well then?"

"Well," she replied, throwing a quick look toward the edge of the ballroom. "If you must know, there is a gentleman I should very much prefer not to dance with.

Or talk to, for that matter."

"Oh, I see," he mumbled. "And who might this gentleman be?"

She laughed. "Clearly, he is not you! Would I ask you to ask me to dance if I didn't want to dance with you?"

"No, but I should like to think you'd like to dance with me because I asked you myself," he retorted.

"Come now, Lord Hartwell, you were about to ask me to dance, were you not?" Her eyes twinkled mischievously as she spoke, and his heart beat awkwardly in his chest.

"Perhaps I was, perhaps I wasn't," he replied with an airiness he was far from feeling. After a pause, he continued, "So, who is the gentleman you don't wish to dance with, now that we've established that you *do* want to dance with me?"

Her head tipped a little and she furrowed her brow, but after a sigh, she answered, "If you must know, it is my neighbor. His name is Charles Moore, and he has been hounding me to death for months on end back home in Lancashire and has decided to continue his assaults here in London."

"Charles Moore is your neighbor?" Lord Hartwell iterated.

"That is what I just said."

"Charles Moore is my cousin," he stated unsteadily.

Her eyes flashed with shock, and she became rigid in his arms, but it was over in a moment and she said slowly, "I do not see a resemblance."

He was suddenly more self-conscious than he had ever been in her presence as he shook his head rather dumbly. "I favor my father, or so I'm told," he said in a hollow voice.

"No, I mean you are not *like* him. As a person." It was a statement, but Miss Iverson was looking at him so warily that he wondered if she was re-evaluating him in spite of the firmness in her tone. It was clear she held his cousin in distaste, though he did not understand how anyone could dislike Charlie. But the thought that she was perhaps measuring him against a man she did not like… That thought terrified him.

"I do not know," Oliver said carefully. "I suppose we are alike in some ways, at least."

The young lady's brows remained furrowed, and her eyes searched his face. He wasn't sure what she was looking for, but he found himself hoping she would find whatever it was she needed to reassure herself of his character.

Lucilla was not concerned that she had misjudged him. What did alarm her a little was his apparent lack of self-awareness and the knowledge that he did not seem to see how markedly different he was from his cousin. Lucilla could see the differences as plain as the nose on his face. Starting with the simple fact that Lord Hartwell wore his heart on his sleeve while Mr. Moore hid beneath a black miasma of languid disinterest, and whatever genuine emotion Lucilla had ever been privy to was not one she could appreciate.

She realized she was frowning, for Lord Hartwell couldn't hide the anxiety writ on his face, so she forced herself to smile reassuringly. "I assure you, I am quite well acquainted with your cousin, Lord Hartwell. I have yet to see a similarity."

Oliver didn't realize he had been holding his breath, but as she smiled at him, his chest loosened with relief.

Then trepidation gave way to curiosity, and he inclined his head as he asked, "How long have you known my cousin, Miss Iverson?"

"Since I was a child. He is a similar age to my brothers, and they often played together," she answered nonchalantly.

"May I ask why you do not like him?"

Lucilla met his gaze directly, and her lips pursed thoughtfully as she decided whether to answer his question. It was obvious he held his cousin in affection, and while she did not flatter herself that anything she might say would weigh on the familial relationship, she hesitated to explain what was essentially an instinct that events and time had strengthened.

Instead, she forced herself to laugh with a roguish lilt and shake her head. "You may ask, but I am not required to answer. Let us talk of happier things, shall we?"

He saw no reason to pursue the subject of Charlie when she clearly did not want to discuss it, and he was not one to dwell on things beyond his control. So he stored away his curiosity for another time, settling that she would hopefully, one day, feel comfortable in answering it.

On the other side of the assembly room, Miss Wallace had observed Lucilla's hasty claiming of a dance with Lord Hartwell and made a mental note to remind her friend that it was unseemly for a young lady to throw herself on the notice of a gentleman. In truth, it rankled her to watch as Miss Iverson was led to the floor for the waltz. As it was Miss Wallace's debut appearance at Almack's, convention required her to wait for one of the patronesses to present her with a suitable partner for the waltz, but as none of them had so far done so, she was relegated to the edges of the ballroom until she was remembered.

She watched Miss Iverson and her partner taking their places. Lucilla seemed to be looking for someone, and as she followed her friend's line of sight, Tabitha found Mr. Moore standing rather broodingly against the wall. The little minx is trying to make him jealous, she thought to herself. Silently applauding her own cleverness at deducing the situation, Miss Wallace decided it would not be too much trouble at all to assist Mr. Moore in giving Lucilla a taste of her own medicine, so she strutted across the room toward him and greeted him gaily.

He was not glad to see her at first, but he saw no harm in conducting a little harmless flirtation in the boredom of the moment. And Miss Wallace had her uses, he supposed. Perhaps there was something she could tell him that might bring Lucilla around. He decided if he was to be her chosen entertainment for the evening, the least she could do was be of use to him.

It did not take much encouragement from Mr. Moore to have her chattering about the Iversons. He decided she was a dreadful gossip and that, lumped with her penchant for issuing lectures, he found rather insufferable.

With feigned interest, he listened to her natter on about Miss Iverson's brothers as she attempted to impress upon him that she'd had a special understanding with the eldest brother, who had been killed at Salamanca. Nothing had been announced, of course, but they had planned to do so as soon as that awful Bonaparte was defeated. Alas, it was not meant to be, and she simply could not bear the thought of transferring her affections to her dear Richard's younger brother.

"I am afraid I have yet to meet another young man I could bear to pledge myself to in marriage," she said, fluttering her eyelashes. "There are so few truly good gentlemen, such as *yourself.*"

She received no encouragement from him to continue, but she didn't require encouragement. Miss Wallace expounded on the virtues of loyal young men, especially those who fought on in spite of adversity such as he faced with Miss Iverson.

"She has always been rather missish, I must warn you. But once you have proven yourself impervious to her mischief, she will become quite pliable," Miss Wallace said firmly. "It is all nonsense, I assure you. She has simply been allowed to become spoiled."

The young lady sneered in her friend's direction as she watched her dancing and a blaze of annoyance at Miss Iverson's good fortune made her say, "She is quite undeserving of your devotion, Mr. Moore. I wonder why you should bother with her, indeed, I do. There are other young ladies who would not give you half so much trouble."

Mr. Moore's brows rose in surprise at the sudden change in her tone, and he looked at her sharply. It occurred to him that he knew nothing about her other than that she was Miss Iverson's self-proclaimed closest friend and rather an odious conversationalist.

It was no matter. He doubted there was anything to learn about her that could possibly render her desirable. He had gleaned from her gossiping that she was in her second Season. Her general manner betrayed her eagerness to marry, so surely she would have been snatched up by now if her dowry would provide the same sort of monetary stability that would come of a match to Miss Iverson.

He had not despaired of his goal yet. She was the daughter of a viscount. In marrying him, she would continue to enjoy wealth and a comfortable home, and he would have what he needed to pay off his existing creditors. At the same time, his social and financial standing would rise above such mundane considerations as tailors' bills and vowels.

Mr. Moore fixed his cousin's form with a glare. He'd never had cause to be jealous of Oliver before; his aunt had showered him with favors whilst mercilessly holding her own son back. Oliver had never beaten him in anything, and he'd be damned if he allowed it to happen now. But the boy had always been pliable and faithful to a fault. It would surely take only the barest nudge to have him singing his cousin's praises in Miss Iverson's ears.

The orchestral wailing died off, and Mr. Moore watched as his cousin led Miss Iverson off the floor. He considered making his way across the room to ask her to dance with him. With an audience nearby she would be honor-bound to accept his request. But he'd now observed Olly with her twice, and they were clearly friendly toward one another. Perhaps he could use his cousin to set her at her ease. As things stood, she was so set against being in his own company at all that it was effectively impossible to contrive a situation in which he might compromise her virtue and force her hand. Friendship with Oliver might just assist him in gaining the sliver of her trust that he needed in order to achieve his ends.

****

Miss Iverson was engaged to dance every dance and only sat out those she chose. Lady Edevane exclaimed that the young men were fairly climbing over one another to gain her attention.

"I declare, if it should come to fisticuffs, we must have a plan in place to assure a speedy escape." She laughed, bringing an amused smile to Lady Iverson's face.

Her ladyship had contentedly watched as the Duke of Saliston had requested her daughter to dance twice, a minuet and a quadrille. Lord Hartwell had claimed a waltz and had begged the honor of escorting her to supper, which had been readily accepted. A gentle reminder that she ought not to show too profound a preference was heeded with no malice, for Miss Iverson had gone on to dance with several other gentlemen whilst carefully avoiding Mr. Moore.

But when Lord Hartwell escorted her to enjoy a light repast, she realized she had finally been cornered. Mr. Moore waved to gain his cousin's attention, and Oliver felt obligated to acknowledge and join him. A glance at his companion was enough for him to know she was not pleased, but she managed a tight smile as she nodded agreeance.

"Well, cousin, how do you fare?" Mr. Moore cried mockingly. "I hardly need ask, as I see you have obtained the highest honor of the evening."

"Charlie," Oliver replied, hoping he conveyed enough firmness in his tone to discourage his cousin from behaving badly in front of Miss Iverson. He had already tried to convince her she had misjudged his relative. The last thing he needed was for Charlie to ruin his efforts by saying something stupid.

"Mr. Moore," Lucilla said hollowly.

"I hope my little cousin Olly here hasn't been boring you to tears?" Mr. Moore grinned.

She glared at him witheringly, and her hand tightened against Oliver's arm. "Far from it, sir. Lord Hartwell is an excellent companion."

"Well, well, high praise indeed."

"Do I interrupt?"

If anything could make the present situation worse, it was the arrival of Miss Wallace on the scene. Lucilla fought the unladylike urge to roll her eyes as she turned to acknowledge Tabitha's arrival. The other young lady appeared at Mr. Moore's side, batting her lashes and smiling in such a sickly sweet manner it made Lucilla's stomach turn.

"I do apologize, Mr. Moore. I quite lost track of time."

"It is no matter, Miss Wallace. Allow me to introduce my cousin, Oliver Fairley, the Earl of Hartwell." Mr. Moore made sure to linger on the title, and he was rewarded with seeing Miss Wallace's eyes light up with interest.

Miss Iverson sighed so softly that none of the others even noticed. The last thing she wanted was to spend the next twenty minutes watching and listening as Tabitha fawned over Lord Hartwell. Unfortunately, there was little she could do to mitigate the situation, short of praying fate would intervene and rescue her from her predicament. The rules of polite Society demanded that she submit to the state of affairs at least for the duration of supper.

While Miss Wallace fluttered her lashes and laughed

flirtatiously, Miss Iverson responded monosyllabically to the queries directed at her. Lord Hartwell, for his part, was so shocked by Miss Wallace's pointed attentions that he also had little to say in reply to anything. Mr. Moore, on the other hand, was thoroughly enjoying watching as Miss Iverson's feathers were ruffled and was pleased to think there was at least one other person in London she treated with as much disdain as himself.

Chapter 12

After once being unceremoniously dragged out of a gaming house by Saliston, Oliver had no intention of entering another. However, after accepting Charlie's offer to dine with him along with some friends, he worried that he would appear churlish in declining the offer to join them on a visit to their den of choice. He did not know Charlie's friends well, but he had a distinct feeling there were one or two older men among them of whom his cousin George would not approve.

He pushed the thought aside and determined that it was just one night, and after observing Charlie's odd behavior at Almack's, he hoped that perhaps having a companion of sound moral fiber, such as himself, his cousin might see the error in his ways and adjust himself accordingly.

The realization that both Saliston and Miss Iverson had now expressed distaste for Mr. Moore had not yet occurred to him. And even had it, he was far too attached to Charlie to abandon him quite yet. He was conscious of a need to enact the hero; having been saved by Saliston, a subconscious need to pay the debt forward had begun to manifest itself, spurred on in part by growing confidence within himself and the encouragement of his advancement by Miss Iverson. That he could have perhaps selected a more worthy candidate for his assistance would have been obvious to anyone else.

And so, Lord Hartwell found himself stumbling out of a somewhat less respectable house than the one which Saliston had previously hauled him from. His head throbbed and his stomach was ill—and he had a terrible feeling that he had played rather deeper than he had ever intended. He had not lost so much as one of Charlie's other young friends. That young gentleman had fairly fainted when the sum of his debt had been read aloud to him, and Oliver's senses, while still considerably dulled, had been shaken enough to cause him to immediately rise from his seat and declare that night was ended.

He had no doubt that had he remained, he could have found himself in a similar state to the other young man. However, he had paid his way before stumbling home with a thick head and enough presence of mind to enter Berkeley Square quietly enough to avoid attracting Saliston's attention.

By midmorning, the duke had begun to wonder why Oliver had not yet made an appearance in the breakfast room. The receipt of a note from an old friend made him growl loudly as he realized what must have been the reason for Oliver being abed so late in the day. He stomped noisily up the staircase and strode down the hall, then rapped loudly on the door of his cousin's bedchamber, but he didn't wait for an answer before he entered.

"What's to do, Hartwell," he shouted with forced gaiety as he slammed the door behind him. The loud report caused Oliver to start upright and look wildly about him. There were dark circles under his eyes, and his usually carefully combed mane of fair hair was tousled terribly.

"Well?" Saliston thundered, throwing himself heavily into the armchair in the corner of the room. "Is there something you'd like to tell me?"

Oliver groaned and fell back against his pillows. "No, not really, George."

"Is that so? Well, that is fair, I suppose, since Knowles has told me what I hope is the worst of it already."

"Knowles? Knowles told you what?" Oliver exclaimed, sitting up sharply again.

"Of your little jaunt last night to that hell run by Gott. He happened to find himself there when the group of good-for-nothings led by your cousin Charlie arrived, and he was surprised that you were among them," Saliston boomed. "So surprised that he wrote to tell me of it as soon as he got himself out of bed this morning."

"I did not know that he intended for us to go there. I swear it, George."

"How badly dipped were you?"

"I paid my way. I have nothing over me, I swear to you," Oliver said earnestly.

"Do you know what happened to Worland? Do you have the slightest idea what has happened to that boy?" Saliston's knuckles were turning white on the arms of his chair. "He has been ruined, utterly ruined! And Charles Moore calls himself the boy's friend. Where was *he* when Worland was being dragged under the hatches? I have no doubt he will sleep soundly in spite of luring the boy to his end. It is not the first young buck he's introduced to such a place, and I'd wager confidently that it won't be the last."

"Surely you cannot blame Charlie."

"Can I not?" Saliston thundered, standing abruptly.

Oliver winced. "Have you any idea of whom you speak? Have you any idea whom you defend so blindly?"

"He is my cousin, George," Oliver replied meekly.

"And for that, you will follow him to such a place as Gott's house and find yourself counted among the string of young idiots who have been cheated of their fortunes?" the duke spat out angrily.

"Yes," was his hasty reply. "I mean— No!"

"Do you have any idea what your precious Charlie is? How do you suppose that one such as he, without a feather to fly with, manages to find himself admitted to such places?" Saliston glowered. "Houses of that kind do not issue invitations to rolled-up young men like Charlie. Not unless they have something to bring to the table. In his case, he brings young sprigs of fortune, following at his heels, throwing their blunt down."

"No." Oliver swallowed, sounding much less sure than he had been.

"Yes," Saliston said firmly. "It is time you were wise to the ways of the world, Oliver. I tell you this because I know you are far more clever than your mother ever allowed. You may hate to believe what I say, but I know that with my saying it you will, at the very least, be more cautious."

Oliver was looking about himself dazedly, his head swimming in incomprehensible thought. He desperately did not want to believe George's accusations against Charlie; every feeling revolted against it. But his mind was still too muddled to make any sense of anything he had witnessed at Gott's house. Surely Charlie could not be held responsible for Worland not stopping his reckless betting. What was it Saliston expected?

"Well, I don't know what you should have expected

Charlie to do about Worland," Oliver said pettishly. "He's a man grown. It is hardly Charlie's responsibility to tell him what to do."

"Adam Worland is twenty years old. He hasn't any family left other than his mother, who is known to be very sickly," Saliston replied bitterly. "He attained control of his estate barely one year ago, and from what Knowles writes, he's lost every piece of it. So I ask you, what is a man's friend honor-bound to do if he sees a young cub such as Worland playing deep? Do you think I would stand idly by if I saw such from you?"

Oliver's eyes clamped shut, and he pressed his palms hard against the sides of his head, nursing a sudden sharp ache. He knew the answer to George's question. George would never allow him to gamble his life away. But Charlie wasn't Worland's cousin—or family at all, for that matter. It was hardly the same situation. No one present had any such claim over Worland and had hardly any right to prevent him from doing precisely what he had done. Oliver was sure that had it been himself in Worland's shoes, Charlie would not have been silent then.

"Well, I have said my piece." Saliston stood. His face no longer held as much anger as it had earlier; that had faded into resignation. He sighed, muttered something about assisting Worland's mother, and strode out of the bedchamber, leaving Oliver to sink back into his pillows.

He thought long and hard through the fog in his mind about the events of the previous evening. He tried to remember where Charlie had been when Worland was playing. He tried to remember where he had been himself and whether he'd seen any of Charlie's other companions nearby. He tried to remember what had happened after Worland had fainted. And he tried to remember what Charlie had said.

After he had finished sipping the cup of coffee that had been brought to him on a tray, Oliver sat in silence. His memory was very hazy. He wasn't sure of many details, but he remembered Charlie's laughter. He remembered his cousin playfully telling his younger companion that his luck would soon change. He remembered a tumbler of gin being poured on Adam Worland's pale, unmoving face. And he remembered his cousin walking away as two other young gentlemen had pulled the unconscious man off the ground.

He remembered Charlie being completely and utterly uncaring. And it was not a pleasant realization.

****

Meanwhile, Miss Iverson was receiving an offer. Her father entered the little blue parlor with a light rap on the door and greeted a happy Chico as the dog pranced around his knees. Lucilla looked up from her novel and smiled tolerantly as Lord Iverson tousled the young dog's ears and cooed at him.

"Really, Papa! If you mean to rile him up, I shall insist that *you* take him for a walk. He's far too boisterous as it is," she said with a laugh.

"I shall take him if you wish. It must be hard for the little fellow to be cooped up here in town." His lordship had knelt down and was fondly petting the golden dog as it sat staring at him blissfully, its tongue lolling out of its mouth.

"He's hardly little, but yes, it is hard," she acknowledged, setting her book aside and sitting up straighter. "Did you need me for something, Papa?"

His lordship gave Chico a final firm pat on his downy head before he stood to face his daughter. He had an odd look on his face, and Lucilla suddenly realized what his purpose in speaking to her was. She managed to hide her amusement and instead bit her lip and looked down at her folded hands as her father cleared his throat and spoke.

"Cilla, I've had a visit this morning—" Lord Iverson's words came haltingly. "Sir Geoffrey Knightsbridge has come to see me—"

"Again?" Miss Iverson said incredulously. She breathed a sigh of relief and stifled a laugh, for she had already long ago rejected Sir Geoffrey's first and second offer for the purchase of her horse.

"Really, Papa, you must know by now that I will never allow Sir Geoffrey to purchase Sierra. We have already discussed this several times, and I thought that we both agreed—"

"Sir Geoffrey did not come to speak to me about your horse, Lucilla," his lordship said with a dismissive wave of his hand. "He has requested my permission to address *you*."

Lucilla's mouth fell open in shock, and she stared at her father in disbelief for several moments in complete silence before she regained her voice and said intensely, "I should hope you did not grant it to him."

"I have given him no answer. He's sitting with your mother in the drawing room, should you wish to answer him yourself, or I shall offer him your rejection if that is what you would prefer."

"I should prefer it, I confess," Lucilla said dully, shifting uncomfortably on the blue satin sofa. It was silent again for a short while before she continued, "He is a perfectly respectable gentleman, Papa. I hope you do not think that I dismiss him without consideration, for I am well aware that he has many good qualities. It is just that he is…well…"

She took a deep breath and held it for a moment before saying desperately, "He's just *so boring!*"

His lordship laughed indulgently as he sat beside his daughter and took her hand. "I am glad you are able to see there are many fine things about Sir Geoffrey. But I am inclined to believe you are right. He seems to be rather singular-minded in the limited time I have been privileged to spend in his company."

"Are you insinuating that he is offering for me with the belief that he will also attain my horse?" Cilla replied with a wry smile.

Lord Iverson laughed heartily. "I must admit, the thought did cross my mind. However, I do trust that is *not* the case."

"I confess that I am less certain. I know that at a glance it must seem Sir Geoffrey would be exactly the sort of gentleman that would please me. He is a sportsman, and he talks of horses and dogs," Lucilla said contemplatively. "But I should like to think I am capable of discussing more than just those two topics. I foresee that if I were to marry Sir Geoffrey, I would be confined to speaking only of dogs and horses for the rest of my days."

"I shall not try to convince you otherwise. There is no need to explain yourself, my dear." His lordship gave his daughter's hand a pat and stood, straightening his coat and clearing his throat. "I will go and speak to him. Stay above stairs for now if you prefer not to see him."

Miss Iverson nodded silently and smiled tightly at

her father as he offered her a reassuring squeeze of her hand before he left her alone. As the door clicked shut, she sighed and wrapped her arms around Chico, who had jumped up onto the sofa beside her and sat staring at her curiously.

The thought of marrying Sir Geoffrey was hardly thrilling, but it ought not to have been as upsetting as she found it. Perhaps it was the knowledge that many of her acquaintance would consider him rather a perfect match for her that left her feeling somewhat deflated. Sir Geoffrey was at least fifteen years her senior, and while he had perfectly respectable manners in company, he was well known to be rather single-minded in his conversations. The idea that she herself had become a simplistic figure in the minds of other members of the *ton* was not something she relished.

After dwelling on this depressing train of thought for nearly twenty minutes, it dawned on her that no one knew Sir Geoffrey had proposed marriage, and she was jumping to conclusions in expecting that anyone would harbor such thoughts or feelings at all. With a shrug, she determined to banish all thought of the worthy gentleman, his offer, and whatever might end up being said of both in relation to herself in the near future.

Chapter 13

The receipt of a note from his aunt requesting the immediate presentation of his person at Hartwell House alerted Mr. Moore of her arrival in town. Lady Hartwell was a woman of uneven temper, and while he enjoyed a certain amount of license with her, he was loath to cause irritation, and so he took himself off to Wimpole Street in some haste.

Upon arrival, the butler ushered him up to her ladyship's boudoir and found her reclined upon a sofa, clutching a cloth over her eyes, a vinaigrette clasped in her other hand. She let out a low moan when her nephew was announced and waved her hand distractedly at the settee beside her.

"Ah, finally," Lady Hartwell said throbbingly.

"I came the moment I received your note, aunt."

Her ladyship snatched the cloth off her eyes and glared at her nephew accusingly but did not reply. He shifted uncomfortably, and she was satisfied to have unnerved him. Instead of responding bitingly, she busied herself with carefully folding the cloth and allowed several moments of silence to shame him further.

"What brings you to town, dear aunt?" Charlie said quietly.

"What else but your letter?" she said archly, raising her thin brows in feigned surprise. "Surely it was your purpose in writing to have me come down from

Calverley, was it not? I must say, your papa will be quite cross to hear you have not secured the Iverson chit."

"I assure you, ma'am, it will be done. By hedge or by stile," Mr. Moore said confidently.

"Well, whichever way you intend it, let it be soon, if you please," her ladyship replied caustically, pursing her lips. "I am sure it will ease your dear papa's worries to have the thing settled. I myself have no preference for the girl. I will be happy to see you in charge of a fortune, whether it is hers or some other's, for it is my dearest wish to see you settled as you ought."

"I own I would prefer to have a less willful wife," he said in reply. "But it is neither here nor there. One way or another, I am in need of funds to keep the estate afloat, and as I have reason to believe Miss Iverson will inherit all from her father, it would be in my interest to secure her rather than another girl."

Lady Hartwell's head tilted slightly, and she stared at her nephew curiously. "I do wonder how that could be possible. It seems rather unlikely. She has brothers, does she not?"

"Two, but the eldest was killed at Salamanca, and the other re-joined before Waterloo and has not been heard from since." Mr. Moore sat back in his seat and shrugged nonchalantly before he continued. "I've had it from a female in service to the family that Lord Iverson was heard declaring he would disinherit his son."

"I assume there is no entail, if that is the case. There are no cousins?"

Mr. Moore started suddenly. He had utterly forgotten about Matthew Iverson's existence. It had not occurred to him Lord Iverson might choose to settle his estate on his nephew instead of his daughter. The idea that anyone would prioritize their sibling's child above their own was so absurd that it had never entered his head.

"I am certain Lord Iverson would not settle on his brother's son when he is so particularly attached to Miss Iverson."

"Are you indeed?" Lady Hartwell replied in a haughty tone. "It seems not so foreign a concept to me. I am sure I know of a dozen gentlemen who would prefer to see their family name remain attached to their estate, no matter the daughter."

Mr. Moore was a little rattled but shrugged and muttered that he would make discreet inquiries on the matter. "Either way, her portion will be considerably larger than most of the females being trotted out by their mothers this Season. And if I have to create a ruckus in order to force her hand, so much the better. I will have the leverage I need to drain Lord Iverson further."

"It would be best to avoid scandal. Can you not put your mind to charming her?" Lady Hartwell sighed with exasperation.

"I own it would be preferable, but she has been entirely impervious so far and is quite adept at avoiding my company," Charlie said irritably. "And now, with Olly sniffing around, not to mention Saliston—"

"Surely not!" Lady Hartwell gasped. "Well, you must cause a to-do as soon as possible, if that is to be the only means of securing her. My cousin is far too high in the instep to attach himself to a chit that another man has blemished, and I shall be able to manage Oliver easily enough. He shall not trouble you."

Mr. Moore cringed. "I'm afraid she has shown some partiality to him already."

"Well, to be sure, she only does so to attract Saliston," Lady Hartwell sniffed haughtily. "No one would prefer a simpleton like Oliver."

"Have you seen him lately, aunt?" Charlie asked carefully, with a raised eyebrow.

"I have not, and he's not written to me either," her ladyship said crossly. "I do not see how that would signify, in any case."

"You may be rather surprised in his transformation, ma'am. He has sprouted rather fine feathers."

"Even so, I am sure I will manage him. He's always been a biddable boy. I shall nudge him out of this Miss Iverson's path."

Mr. Moore was not so sure, but he did not say so. Until recently, he'd thought his influence over Oliver to be unquestionable, but he was not so confident anymore. He had managed to drag the boy to Gott's, but it was plain that Oliver joined the party out of social obligation rather than because he *wanted* to. It was unfortunate the lad had borne witness to Worland's downfall. One could not always predict when one's plans would come to fruition, and Adam Worland's staggering loss had lined Moore's own pockets quite nicely, so for that he was not at all sorry.

He could feel some of his control slipping away. It was plain his aunt was not yet conscious of the same feeling, but he doubted it would be long before she was. The son she had raised to be meek and compliant had been replaced by a rather different kind of young man. Oliver seemed taller, more confident, and certainly less obedient than he had been mere months earlier. The development of his skills in a social setting had grown immensely, as was evident by his invitation to pretty well every social event of the Season. While Charlie found himself working to gain admittance to some more select gatherings, Oliver found no impediment. The leaders of the *ton* had declared the young Lord Hartwell to be unexceptionable, and beside his cousin Saliston, he had become something of a pet. The fact that none of this was evident to Oliver made it all the more galling to Charlie, who had been on the town for so long that he liked to think of himself as well-liked among the ladies.

It made Miss Iverson's rejection of his advances all the more irritating, particularly as she seemed to encourage Lord Hartwell and Saliston's acquaintance. Since his own financial situation was not widely known, he could hardly write Miss Iverson off as mercenary; he had a respectable estate situated not five miles away from her own home in the country. He dressed in the newest fashions and made sure to spend enough in Liverpool for the local inhabitants to believe he had money to burn. It was, of course, all an act, but he had no reason to believe the charade was failing in any way. But pride would not allow him to think that Miss Iverson could find him objectionable for any other reason. That his personality was the cause of her dislike never entered his head.

While Mr. Moore dwelled silently on these thoughts, Lady Hartwell considered what her nephew might do to make himself more agreeable to Miss Iverson. She knew very little about the young lady except that her family's estate was extensive and included several smaller properties scattered about the kingdom. This had the effect of making Miss Iverson a much more interesting figure, and she saw the advantage of her nephew aligning himself with the girl. Even one of the smaller Iverson estates made Mr. Moore's plot of earth appear tiny by comparison, and should his lordship choose to settle one or even two of these upon his daughter, well, it would set Charles up for life.

She had no reason to want her own son to marry a fortune—his own was exceptional—but Lady Hartwell had no intention of handing over the reins of Calverley to Oliver and his wife any time soon, if at all. It would suit her much better to have him remain a bachelor, and in time she could direct him to marry some suitably demure miss who would not interfere with the current Lady Hartwell's running of the estate.

It would satisfy two of Lady Hartwell's causes to see Miss Iverson married to her nephew, so she determined to assist him in his efforts to attain the young lady's hand. It would, of course, be preferable to have her accept his suit without staining her reputation. However, if circumstance necessitated that Lady Hartwell devise a plan to push her in the right direction, it could be easily arranged. For now, she thought, it would be proper to insist that Charles press his suit by conventional methods.

"To begin, you will take her flowers. Daily. Discover which are her favorite if you do not already know," Lady Hartwell said authoritatively. "I recommend poetry—young ladies adore poetry. If you do not know how to write prose, find some other person to write it for you, and be sure to copy it out in your own hand. And you will invite her out to walk, or to drive if you have a suitable carriage."

"I do not," Mr. Moore replied thinly.

"Then we shall remedy it. I will pay for a suitable carriage to be hired for you for however long you require. And the horses, of course," his aunt continued. "Does she ride?"

"She is rather a famous horsewoman," was his answer.

"Well, then you must exhibit your skill," she said firmly. "Make inquiries about a curricle, or gig, or whatever you think is best. I expect it will take a few days to secure one, so in the meantime, you will go to her home now and invite her to walk with you. Or to ride, if that is more to her taste. You must make yourself available to her at all times. If you should hear her mention something she would like or enjoy, you must facilitate it at all costs. Do you understand me, Charles? There will be no more of this here-and-there-again. You will devote yourself wholly to this courtship."

Mr. Moore had interjected once or twice to insist that he had tried such methods, but his aunt cut him off and firmly served him with her opinion of his half-hearted efforts to attract Miss Iverson. She called him a shameless gadabout and determined that he had met with rejection because Miss Iverson was clearly too clever to be taken in by wishy-washy behavior.

"You must prove to her that you are entirely at her feet. Nothing but devoted worship will turn her head," Lady Hartwell said resolutely. "If in a few weeks we do not see a change, we will discuss a different course of action. But for now, you will do as I say."

"Fine. I shall, but you will see that it will not work, aunt."

"With an attitude such as yours, it is certain to fail, indeed," she exclaimed. "Pluck up, Charles. It is time to play the star-crossed lover. It will not be for long, I assure you. Once the knot is safely tied, you may do as you wish."

Mr. Moore did not relish the thought of acting like a mooncalf in full view of Society, particularly as he believed it would ultimately be a complete waste of his time and efforts. He had reached the conclusion that a dastardly plan to seduce the girl—or at least give the appearance that she had been seduced—would serve his purposes. Unfortunately, his aunt's plot would cost no small amount of his dignity, and he was not particularly willing to pay it in service of an idea that he felt sure was doomed to failure.

But beggars (and a beggar he most assuredly was) cannot be choosers, and so he went on his way with every intention of following through on Lady Hartwell's demands and every expectation of meeting with a rebuff at each turn.

After taking leave of his aunt, Mr. Moore took himself off to a flower mart and paid a pretty sum to ensure Miss Iverson would receive a fresh bouquet each morning with the breakfast gong, courtesy of Lady Hartwell's bank notes. He then stopped off at the hiring stable and requested his hack be brought around to his lodging at an assigned time before hurrying there himself to dash off a note to a pal enquiring about the cost of hiring a phaeton and horses. By the time this task had been completed and he had changed his dress to ride, the fat horse had arrived and he paid off the groom with another of his aunt's coins.

By the time he had ambled the fat horse down Grosvenor Street, Mr. Moore was in a much merrier frame of mind. The effect of having a full purse was wonderful for the mood, and so he was quite pleased with his prospects and rather more determined to play the part Lady Hartwell had envisioned for him as he rode toward Iverson House.

But this newfound positivity was washed swiftly away when he observed Miss Iverson skipping down the steps of her home to be handed into the Duke of Saliston's waiting phaeton. He watched as his grace handed the reins to Miss Iverson and the young lady gleefully took control of a particularly famous team of bays that many a gentleman whip had jealously dreamed of driving and wondered to himself how his aunt had ever imagined that someone such as himself could compete with the Duke of Saliston for the hand of the exceptional Miss Iverson by anything resembling fair means.

Chapter 14

There was a sharp scowl etched into Oliver's features that warned Saliston something was seriously amiss. He was himself in rather a good mood, so to find his young cousin in a sour disposition was disconcerting, considering they had parted amicably not two hours earlier. Saliston had just returned to his house in Berkeley Square after a pleasant afternoon drive with Miss Iverson in which he had discharged a promise to allow her to drive his famous bays. He had been impressed with her ability to handle a pair, but her prowess with a team was exceptional, and he quickly came to consider her a rival in skill.

Oliver had not yet realized that he was no longer alone in the library and was still staring into the fire. Saliston could only see his profile, but it was evident the boy was in a wretched state. He cleared his voice as he stood in the doorway, and Oliver turned his head in surprise.

"Oh, George," he said with a forced smile. "I didn't expect you so soon."

"What's amiss, Hartwell?" Saliston asked as he walked to his armchair and sank into it heavily.

Oliver snorted, and the scowl returned as he shook his head. "Funny you should ask," he snarled.

Instead of elevating the level of his concern, Lord Hartwell's expression and the venom in his tone only further piqued the duke's curiosity. The young gentleman was generally very easygoing. Anything that could inspire such wrath in him must be truly terrible, but he so rarely got riled that Saliston felt sure there would be a simple explanation. His brow furrowed and he gave his cousin a questioning glance but remained silent.

"My dearest Mama has written," Oliver spat out. "She informs me that she has arrived in town today and demands that I immediately remove from here to join her at Hartwell House."

The news was indeed rather a surprise. Saliston had certainly not expected Lady Hartwell to make an appearance in town during the Season. In fact, she had explicitly declared that she would not be doing so when they had last spoken during his visit to Calverley in November. Her reason had been unclear at the time, for she mainly had screeched and stamped her feet at him once he had revealed the purpose of his visit was to remove Oliver from her custody. After Lady Hartwell began to carry on, Saliston had largely paid no mind to most of her diatribe.

"Well, it is rather inconvenient that my cousin has decided to grace London with her presence," Saliston began carefully and with no small amount of sarcasm. "But there is certainly no reason for you to take up residence in Wimpole Street if you do not choose. She may have use of your properties for a few more years, but her authority over you is at an end, dear boy. Do not let her anger you. We have Mr. Iverson dining here tonight. Put the note out of mind. Or, even better, send round your own note declining her invitation. That ought to put you in a lighter mood."

Lord Hartwell snorted again, but his demeanor had lightened along with Saliston's tone. The frown started to lift from his brows, and his smile became more genuine. He fiddled absentmindedly with the screw of paper in his hand that must once have been the source of his irritation.

"You are quite right. I think it is only polite that I reply to dear Mama's letter." A mischievous grin curled his lips as he jumped up and went to the writing desk. "I shall thank her for her kind offer to join her at Hartwell House."

The duke laughed and lightly applauded before he stood and declared he ought to wash up and dress before their guest arrived. "And you ought to trot upstairs and do the same," Saliston called out as he left the room.

Oliver replied affirmatively as he flourishingly penned his note. He ensured that it was polite enough to border on impertinent before he took the trouble to seal it with wax and stamped it with his papa's signet ring. His mood was transformed, and with a jaunty smile, he handed it off to his cousin's butler before he ran upstairs to change his dress.

By the time he had bounced back downstairs, the dinner guest had arrived. As he marched down the hall, he could hear his cousin's voice emanating from the library, and he entered the room to find Saliston handing a glass to a stocky, dark-haired young man. His cousin called out a greeting and offered a glass of port, which was declined with thanks, and then he introduced Mr. Matthew Iverson.

"Iverson, this is my cousin Oliver, Lord Hartwell."

"I am pleased to finally meet you, Hartwell," Mr. Iverson said seriously, but there was a slight twinkle in his blue eyes. "Your reputation precedes you, I'm afraid, for my dear little cousin has apprised me of the tale of the Stafford Affair."

Oliver blushed furiously and stammered a reply but was waved off with a bursting laugh from Mr. Iverson. "I assure you, you are quite redeemed. I must congratulate you on it, for Cilla rarely changes her mind about anyone, particularly men."

There was something curious in the way Mr. Iverson was looking at him that made Oliver a little nervous, but he had learned to laugh about the Stafford Affair, and so he managed to reply in a similarly rallying tone, earning an encouraging smile from the other young man that settled his nerves slightly. Oliver managed to wade through a few minutes of mildly uncomfortable conversation before Saliston's butler interrupted to inform the three men that dinner was ready.

They then adjourned to the dining room, where a hearty repast had been laid out. The dinner conversation ran heavily on the subject of Mr. Iverson's travels to Greece and the Middle East. Oliver asked a great many questions, beginning with the different climates and architecture, before he focused on Mr. Iverson's reasons for traveling.

"Is there a particular reason you chose to travel away from England? And during wartime too. Surely there must have been a mighty compelling reason for you to go," Oliver queried.

The younger man's earnest expression amused Matthew. He had heard that Lord Hartwell's home life had been rather sheltered and correctly deduced that he was being asked whether he had fled England for the Continent, but nothing was further from the truth for

Matthew.

"In all honesty, being a rather boring sort, as my cousin likes to remind me, I am rather keenly interested in art and history," Mr. Iverson replied matter-of-factly. "My cousins had both joined the war effort, and I knew that my uncle would not prevent me from doing the same but would indeed be very disheartened if I followed them. I had intended to join the church, in any case, and my uncle encouraged me to travel if I should choose. Obviously, France and Italy were not as safe as they once were, but in Greece, Ferdy and I were able to go about relatively easily. And in Egypt, I was able to combine pleasure with business and arranged the purchase of some horses for my uncle."

"You bought horses in Egypt?" Oliver exclaimed with awe. "I think I should like to see Egypt, George."

"Well, you've seen my cousin's chestnut?"

"Yes, I think it is a rather famous horse about town these days," Saliston replied with a smile.

"Well, one of the mares I purchased foaled that colt not three months after arriving in Liverpool." Mr. Iverson laughed. "Cilla was there when it was born and decided it would be hers, on the spot. And so it was. The little red devil won't suffer anyone else aboard."

"Well, that explains why she can't be brought to part with him. I hear Sir Geoffrey Knightsbridge has been rejected several times."

Mr. Iverson guffawed loudly and put down his wine glass heavily. "Oh, yes, he's been rejected one final time, in fact. Silly fellow offered for Cilla herself this time, but my uncle delivered her refusal and advised him not to try again."

While Matthew and George laughed heartily over

this new information, Oliver was conscious of his stomach flipping uncomfortably, but he managed to smile weakly as his companions continued to speak. Oliver couldn't hear anything anymore; his ears were filled with a strange buzzing noise, and all he could think about was that someone had proposed to Miss Iverson. It hadn't occurred to him that another man might offer for her hand. It seemed a strange thing not to realize, for he was himself very conscious of her beauty, but that another man might actually approach her? That another man might be sure enough of receiving a positive reply from her that he would be motivated to ask? It had never entered his head.

"Hartwell? Oliver!"

Saliston's voice broke through the buzzing, and he realized he was staring blankly across the table, wearing the same odd smile he had plastered on moments earlier.

"I'm sorry, what?" he said, shaking his head distractedly.

"Are you all right?" Saliston asked concernedly. "You seem to be off somewhere else."

"I'm fine. What were you saying? Sorry."

"I was just saying that my cousin has gotten quite tired of Sir Geoffrey always talking about her horse," Mr. Iverson replied with an amused smile as he raised his wine glass to his lips.

"Oh! Yes, I imagine it would be very aggravating to her," Oliver said with a forced laugh as he, too, took a long gulp of his wine.

"Seems she has got it in her head that men are only interested in her because of her horses. Speaking of which," Mr. Iverson continued conversationally, "Saliston says you're in the market for a hunter or two?"

"Indeed, I am."

"Well, a friend of my family recently passed, and my uncle is assisting with the dispersal of his stable. The widow is selling up everything to go live in Bath, or some such," Mr. Iverson said. "The old gent was a keen rider, so I think there might be several of his horses to suit you. My uncle bred some of 'em, exceptional stock. Are you interested?"

"I'm sure that I am," Oliver replied, all thoughts of Miss Iverson flying from his head.

"Excellent. I shall talk to my uncle and arrange a suitable time for you to discuss it with him, and perhaps we can make a trip to see 'em," Mr. Iverson declared with a grin, lifting his glass again.

The evening wore on, and discussion meandered from horses to hunting, to sports and travel, before looping back again. Mr. Iverson was a learned young man and had, in Oliver's opinion, already lived so very much. He admired the methodical way the other gentleman had traveled, cursorily recounting his visits to landmarks but dwelling on his descriptions of the cuisine, colors, and art that he'd enjoyed.

Oliver realized Mr. Matthew Iverson's youth had been very much the opposite of his own. Where he had been closeted and reined back in every way, Mr. Iverson's family had allowed him to open any door he had seen fit to choose and then supported his endeavors wherever they led him. It dawned on Oliver that, in spite of the exemplary tutor the duke had provided him, he wouldn't really know anything unless he was able to see and touch and experience things the same way that Mr. Iverson and George had once done.

As the three men talked on and on, Oliver wove

ideas for his own cultural education. By the time the table had been cleared, and the trio had decided to fetch some playing cards to idle away the time over their chatter, Oliver's ideas had become fixed plans in his mind.

He was not insensible. With the war so recently ending at the final battle in Brussels, he knew travel upon the continent would remain rather tricky and dangerous for some time. But Britain was a land full of culture if one knew where to look, and Mr. Iverson certainly knew where one might seek it out. Question after pointed question drew the answers that Oliver needed to begin a mental list of places he wished to visit and things he would like to see.

It had not taken Matthew long to realize the reasons for Oliver's inquisition. The boy was artless and exceptionally eager, and as he himself found historical buildings and fixtures and art excessively interesting, he was all too happy to oblige.

"I have every printed issue of Ackermann's magazine. Would you like to borrow them?" Mr. Iverson asked. His offer was accepted with alacrity, so he continued in the same vein by enquiring as to whether Lord Hartwell had heard of Lord Elgin's collection.

"I gather there is still some discussion going with that mess?" Saliston drawled.

"Yes, I'm afraid there is," Mr. Iverson replied in a mournful tone. "My uncle tells me there is much talk of it within the House. Of course, I ought not to discuss it myself, but I believe some changes will be made soon regarding the housing of the sculptures. Perhaps you might care to see them when the matter is settled, Hartwell?"

"I should like that very much," Oliver replied promptly with a grin. He had not the slightest idea of what he'd agreed to see, but if Mr. Iverson was interested in them, then surely they would be worth seeing.

"I shall send Ackermann's magazines round to you tomorrow," Matthew said smilingly. "And I'll enquire with my uncle as to the marbles. I believe there will be some movement on that score soon."

"I should hope so. There's been enough talk of it over the last decade," Saliston replied. "Byron has certainly had enough to say of them."

Mr. Iverson laughed. "There are arguments for both sides, I gather."

Oliver was thoroughly lost during this discussion, but what he managed to gather was that the marbles were a controversial topic that had been the cause of much talk for many years. When Saliston asked a more pointed question about the moving of the marbles, Oliver interjected to enquire whether they would be taken to Tinsley Green. His question drew confused stares from both of his companions, and they were entirely silent for a moment before he clarified his question.

"Is the championship not held at Tinsley Green?"

"Championship? What *are* you talking about?" Saliston asked, completely stupefied.

"Marbles?"

"Marbles. You're talking of marbles," Mr. Iverson repeated confusedly. He stared blankly at Oliver for several more moments before cautiously asking, "Do you mean the game of marbles?"

"Of course. What else?" Oliver looked between his two companions curiously.

"Oh, lord." Saliston crowed with laughter while Mr.

Iverson grinned and downed his drink with a shake of his head.

"Dear boy, Lord Elgin's marbles are a collection of marble sculptures," Mr. Iverson said with a cheery smile. "But that is quite clever of you to think of sending them to Tinsley. I should think they'd be quite out of the way there."

Oliver's cheeks flushed, but he was quite willing to laugh at his own silliness. Matthew smiled encouragingly and drew the discussion away from the contentious artwork. Instead, he asked Oliver a series of questions about his knowledge of the game of marbles, successfully quelling any awkwardness by giving the younger man a chance to show his cleverness in a different subject. Saliston watched as Matthew expertly maneuvered the conversation and congratulated himself on finding his young cousin an excellent companion.

Some hours later, the three men bid one another farewell. Matthew faithfully promised to send his magazines to his young friend and confirmed they would meet soon to discuss hunting mounts, while Oliver confirmed his interest in viewing potential purchases before he waved his new friend off and went back into the house.

"I like the fellow," Saliston said firmly as he climbed the stairs beside Oliver.

"So do I. He's very clever."

"He is exactly the sort of friend I think you ought to have," his cousin continued. "He's not wild, but he's clever and is a very sporting chap. You should cultivate that connection."

Oliver pursed his lips in an amused smile. "I quite agree, and I intend to."

"Excellent," Saliston replied with a firm nod. "We shall see about those horses as soon as possible. If they're the ones I am thinking of, Lord Iverson will have several buyers lined up already."

He bid Lord Hartwell good night and closed his door softly, leaving his young cousin to walk the remaining few feet to his own bedchamber alone.

As he prepared for bed, Oliver mulled over the events of the evening, and he eventually found himself considering the uncomfortable question of Sir Geoffrey's proposal to Miss Iverson.

Knowing that the other gentleman had been swiftly and firmly rejected was, in many ways, a relief. But as he considered it further, Oliver realized there were many unobjectionable qualities to Sir Geoffrey's suit. He was reasonably handsome, and he possessed a comfortable fortune. His contemporaries considered him to be an excellent chap, if a little obsessive about sports. According to Saliston, nothing was lacking in him, yet he had met with rejection.

Mr. Iverson had declared his cousin was very put off by Sir Geoffrey's constant talk of horses. It seemed reasonable enough that a female would not wish to discuss such things all the time. Indeed, he could not remember his mother ever talking of horses unless it was on the subject of having them called round to transport her to some party or other. But Miss Iverson had always seemed to him to be knowledgeable on the subject and happy enough to discuss sporting pursuits—now he wondered whether he too had been relegated to the ranks of tiresome young men who droned on about hunting and hounds simply because she had shown interest in a topic that other young ladies had no ability to converse on.

Oliver decided to take his new friend's advice and avoid the subject of Miss Iverson's horse. He had not taken very much notice of the animal when he had seen it—he was far too preoccupied with admiring its rider. However, he supposed it was a singular creature. It would not be too difficult a topic to avoid.

Chapter 15

Charles Moore walked along one of the many lanes in Hyde Park several days later, swinging his cane and whistling to himself. In spite of his misgivings, he had meticulously followed through on his aunt's instructions, and Miss Iverson had received a bundle of flowers each morning for the last four days. That morning she had also received a prettily worded poem requesting she meet him during the fashionable hour of the promenade.

There had been no reply—he had not expected one—but he had dressed himself smartly and trotted down to the park well before the time he had specified, with the intention of watching for her arrival. During the preceding days he had been encouraged to believe in his chances by his aunt, who had commended the efforts he had gone to and thus emboldened him to put a small amount of pressure upon the young lady to test her.

As he walked along, he enthusiastically greeted the people of his acquaintance that he passed. He was somewhat optimistic about his prospects. That very morning, he had received word that a wager he had made several weeks prior would be paid in his favor, and all was right in the world.

But yet again he was to receive a blow where Miss Iverson was concerned. He rounded a corner to see none other than Lady Iverson walking with her maid trotting along behind her and that curst yellow-haired dog on a leather. Her ladyship was walking along a different pathway and did not notice him, but he could see that she was clearly not in the company of her daughter.

Mr. Moore growled quietly to himself and glared at Lady Iverson's retreating form while she, of course, remained in complete ignorance of his presence. As he stood clenching his fingers tightly around the top of his cane, he considered catching up to the lady and enquiring after her daughter, but his attention was drawn by someone calling his name.

As he turned in search of the source of the voice, he momentarily let himself think the feminine tone belonged to Miss Iverson, but instead, his gaze came to rest on Miss Wallace's decidedly less welcome form.

"Oh, Mr. Moore," she cried out again as she waved and walked quickly in his direction. "How very fortunate. I am so very pleased to see you, sir. My mama is not feeling quite the thing today, so I am rather alone, except for my maid, of course. *Would* you be so kind as to escort me? It seems an age since we last spoke!"

Miss Wallace beamed at him. She had spoken quite loudly, and several passing pedestrians had turned to look at them curiously, so he had hardly any choice but to greet the young lady in kind and agree to walk with her. It would not do to appear discourteous, for he could not be sure who had seen them.

"I feel sure I ought to give you a scold, Mr. Moore," Miss Wallace tittered as they proceeded along the path. "You have not called to visit at all. I am sure my mama has expected you to."

"I apologize, Miss Wallace. I have been very taken up with business these weeks," Mr. Moore answered with a supercilious air and a sneer.

Miss Wallace pouted, but she continued on, undaunted by his manner and instead intrigued by his apparent business endeavors. "The running of an estate must be a gratifying task, I am sure!"

"It is, indeed," he replied. The fact that he had absolutely nothing to do with the running of his family's estate was of no importance, as was the knowledge that most of it was in complete disarray from a lack of management and care on the part of his father and grandfather before him. Just because he knew this didn't mean anyone else needed to, particularly someone like Miss Tabitha Wallace.

"Where is your estate, Mr. Moore?" she inquired.

"Our boundary at Morcombe stands beside Gracewood, near Liverpool," he answered proudly and was satisfied to see her eyes widen in surprise.

Miss Wallace had been sure that Mr. Moore was a gentleman of substance, but to have a property neighboring Viscount Iverson's ancestral home raised him in her estimation. He was not titled, which was a shame, but he was handsome, and he was obviously heir to a considerable estate. Lucy's imperviousness to his charm was baffling. Tabitha certainly saw nothing to sneer at, and yet it was just like the missish Miss Iverson to take someone into dislike for no good reason.

"La, and to think we might have one day been neighbors, Mr. Moore," she said in a rallying tone. In answer to his silence, she launched into yet another soliloquy detailing her doomed love with the late Richard Iverson.

Mr. Moore had, of course, already suffered through one such retelling of Miss Wallace's imagined romantic history. Any other time, he would have looked for a way to divert her attention elsewhere, but it served him to have her nattering to herself while he looked about in search of Miss Iverson. He had not seen hide nor hair of her except the brief glimpse of her mother, but he knew the young lady never missed a day in the Park, and he assumed she was either driving her grays or riding in her father's carriage. He had begun to consider the best method with which to dispose of his unwanted companion when he heard her say something about Gracewood.

"After all, it will be a great shame to see the estate go to wrack and ruin with such a silly little miss as her as captain," Miss Wallace said bitingly as she continued on her monologue.

"I am sorry, but how should Miss Iverson come to be captain of Gracewood? She has an elder brother, after all," Mr. Moore said with feigned ignorance and an air of wonderment. Miss Wallace was entirely taken in by his obliviousness, though a little irritated to find he had not been listening to her closely enough.

"Edward has not been heard of in months. He's quite disappeared, and no one has had so much as a note from him since the battle at Brussels," she said crossly. "At least, not that I can discover, anyway. I've questioned Lucy about it several times, and she refuses to tell me anything. It is enough to put one quite out of patience with her, as though I ought not to be told. When I have been her nearest friend for years! It is extremely vexing. I should have been her sister had my darling Richard lived, but it means nothing to her, I think."

"But surely his regiment would have told Lord Iverson by now if he had been killed, and the family would have gone into mourning," Mr. Moore continued to gently nudge the young lady back toward the subject he wanted to discuss. He succeeded.

"I am not entirely certain that they would, for I heard Lord Iverson declare that he would disown Edward if he went back to his regiment."

"I cannot imagine Lord Iverson would follow through on such a threat," Mr. Moore exclaimed. It was rather a relief to have found someone that could corroborate the story that had been given to him months earlier by the errant Gracewood maid. But his relief was misplaced; he was entirely unaware that Miss Wallace was in no position to provide him with confirmation of any such facts, and anyone of sense who was acquainted with her knew she had a talent for make-believe. She need only hear a tale before she was suddenly the hearer, seer, and heroine of it.

And so, Mr. Moore found himself regaled with a retelling of the same story he had first heard from the maid—for it was through a similar channel Miss Wallace herself had heard it. But it was no longer a story she had heard from someone else; it was she herself who had listened to the thunderous threats Lord Iverson had hurled. She had witnessed his fury at Edward's departure from Gracewood, and she knew that he had declared her dearest friend Lucy to be heiress of all in the aftermath. All was presented to Mr. Moore as fact, and he took it as such, for he had no reason to disbelieve Miss Wallace's recitation of the episode.

He listened to her confirm all he had so far managed to glean and was pleased. With a little more nudging, he managed to get her to admit that Matthew Iverson would retain the title. Still, she included the valuable titbit that he would only be given one of the smaller estates whilst

Gracewood would remain in Miss Iverson's hands. It was at this point that she returned to her initial lamentations that an immature, morose female like Lucilla would one day have sole charge of the grand old estate.

"It is shocking. Quite shocking," she said disdainfully.

As they continued along the path, he allowed Miss Wallace to continue her pointless babbling, and his attention began to drift off again. He digested the information he had received and was considering his next steps when he heard the sound of a familiar voice, and through the brush beside the path, he saw none other than Miss Iverson herself.

She was once again in the company of the Duke of Saliston, sitting aboard a racing curricle drawn by a pair of black horses. The duke was leaning his head down toward her, and she was laughing innocently at something he was saying. It was rather a pretty picture, but it was entirely wasted on Mr. Moore.

"La, what a spectacle," Miss Wallace hissed spitefully from beside him. He had quite forgotten she was there. "This will not do—she ought not to behave so. If no one will correct her, then I *shall*!"

Miss Wallace made as if to march toward the carriage, but the two paths were divided quite neatly by a row of hedging. She had no way of reaching Miss Iverson without either climbing through the bushes or walking all the way around the path, and either effort would have been in vain, for the duke's curricle was now in motion and heading away from them at a clipping pace.

****

"No, you shan't drive this one," the duke said with a smile.

Lucilla laughed artlessly and said in reply, "I'm quite certain you will change your mind."

"Indeed, I shall not!"

She smiled sunnily and shrugged as Saliston cued the black horses into a jog. It was no surprise that the duke had declined to allow it. The curricle was well-balanced and had obviously been carefully designed, but it was still a racing vehicle and not at all suitable for a young maiden to be driving in the Park. She could see no harm in asking, though.

"Well, it is no matter," she chirped. "It can only increase my consequence to be seen in any carriage with a duke."

He laughed loudly. "You hardly require my influence to increase your consequence, Miss Iverson, I assure you."

"Do you know, I am not so sure that is true," Lucilla replied thoughtfully.

"What troubles you, child?" the duke asked sympathetically.

She looked up at him with an almost melancholy smile. "I am afraid I have become interesting only to dead bores, Duke."

"Dear me, have I become a dead bore, then?" He gasped in affected shock, drawing a bout of musical laughter from her.

"Most assuredly not."

"Well, I shall have a long talk with Oliver, then, for clearly you mean him."

"No! I mean pretty well everyone but yourself and Lord Hartwell, incidentally." She laughed quietly.

"Surely you cannot mean to lump every young man in town in the same basket as Sir Geoffrey Knightsbridge," Saliston said seriously.

Lucilla glanced up at him with a start. "You know about Sir Geoffrey?"

"Your cousin mentioned it, but I assure you it is not commonly known," he answered promptly in response to the horror that he had seen in her face. Her reply was a loud sigh of relief, and he found himself smiling at the dread with which she had responded to a rather simple situation. "Come now, Miss Iverson. There is nothing to be worried about. I can assure you that no one will judge you for refusing an offer from Knightsbridge. You are not the first, and likely you will not be the last, either."

"He has proposed to other young ladies?" Lucilla gasped.

"But of course. He's what, five- or six-and-thirty now? I assure you, he's made an offer for every young female who has politely conversed with him on the subject of horses or dogs."

This drew from her a snort of laughter. "Well, you must think me very conceited."

"Not at all," the duke replied with a smile. "Amusing, but not at all conceited."

"Truly, I think his reason for offering for my hand was because I have not accepted his offers to purchase my horse," she said humorously.

"Believe me, Miss Iverson, he's not quite clever enough for that."

She smiled at him under lowered eyelashes. Silence reigned for some time as the horses jogged along. Lucilla waved at a few of her acquaintances as the curricle whipped along the path, and several cried back greetings in return. She had made jest of her acquaintance with the duke. She knew he was considered a prize among the matchmaking mamas of Society, but while she considered him very amusing and an excellent friend, there was no more that she expected or desired from the association.

Lady Edevane had made a number of comments on the subject, but Lucilla firmly rejected any suggestion that she was interested in more than friendship with the duke. Her aunt had sighed loudly and called it a sad waste of the connection. She insisted that in all of her years she had never seen the Duke of Saliston pay such pointed attention to any young woman, at least none since his youth. There had been a pretty little dab of a girl at one time, but she had been betrothed to some country squire well before Saliston met her, so nothing came of it.

"She was rather an original, little Josephine was," Lady Edevane had declared. "Rather like you, come to think of it, Cilla. Oh, no, not to look at. She was very fair, but she was a dreadful scamp, always smelling of the stables and never comfortable in company unless it was a hunt."

"Heavens, is that what you think of me, Aunt Augusta?" Lucilla had exclaimed with no small amount of shock.

"Oh, of course not, dear. You are much more civilized than Josephine ever was. Perhaps that is why the duke has developed a tendre for you?" the countess mused innocently. Her statement was rebuffed neatly, and the subject changed, but Lucilla had later been left to wonder what had been the fate of the mysterious Josephine.

As she sat beside the duke in the curricle, Lucilla's thoughts again drifted toward the other young lady. She was probably not a young lady anymore but likely the middle-aged wife of a country squire and mother of his children. Lucilla glanced at the duke and wondered if he knew where Josephine was now.

"What have I done to earn such a pitying stare, I wonder?" Saliston said suddenly, breaking through her thoughts.

"Oh, I am so sorry!" Lucilla gasped, clapping her hands over her mouth. "My mind wandered."

"To where, may I ask?" he enquired, peering at her curiously.

"I do not think I should say," she replied meekly.

"Come now, Miss Iverson," the duke said in a rallying tone. "I should think we are friends enough not to be standing on ceremony. Out with it, if you please."

Lucilla gave him a tremulous smile and wondered if she ought to excuse herself again, but after a moment of hesitation, she saw him about to continue his badgering and decided to take a chance.

"Do you remember a young lady named Josephine?"

She instantly regretted her question—her conscience and propriety demanded that much. However, the Duke of Saliston only smiled sentimentally and nodded.

"I do indeed remember her. How do you come to know of her?" he said, perfectly calm.

"My aunt, Lady Edevane, mentioned her name."

"I am sure I know why," the Duke said with a chuckle. "I suppose she said you are rather like her?"

"Yes, she did," Lucilla confessed. Her relief to find the duke was not at all offended by her query was

172

immense, and it emboldened her to press on with her questions. "Aunt Augusta said she has never seen you court any other young lady since Josephine, though she neglected to tell me much else."

"There is not much else to be told, I'm afraid," Saliston replied frankly. "She was betrothed. She married and went to live in Hertfordshire. Her husband was rather older than she and, as I understand it, they never had any children."

"Oh," Lucilla sighed despondently.

"You do remind me of her. It has been many years since I have thought of her," he said with a nostalgic smile as he gazed down the path ahead.

Lucilla became uncomfortable as silence descended again. Something in his tone made her a little concerned that she had perhaps misread the duke's intentions and wondered whether she had just inadvertently encouraged attentions she had no idea of reciprocating. She was thankful Lady Iverson had appeared on the path up ahead, waving and smiling.

"Ah, there is my mother," Lucilla said cheerfully, but Saliston had already seen her ladyship and was drawing his horses to a sedate walk. They came to a halt nearby to Lady Iverson, and the duke's groom immediately jumped down from his perch to take hold of his master's horses. At the same time, Saliston stepped nimbly down from the curricle and offered his hand to Miss Iverson as she descended.

"Thank you for joining me, Miss Iverson," he said, bowing over her hand dutifully after a brief word with her mama. "I am most grateful to you for our conversation. Perhaps we know one another a little better than we did before."

His smile unnerved her, and she was not certain she understood his meaning, but she answered politely before they bid one another goodbye. The exchange had not gone unnoticed by Lady Iverson, but though her curiosity was burning, she refrained from questioning her daughter. At least for the moment.

Chapter 16

The Countess of Edevane's elegant annual *al fresco* nuncheon favored only a very select few matrons with invitations. The pretty little rose garden was carefully planned and prepared several months in advance each Season. When the day arrived, her guests were always suitably amazed by the skill and superiority of her gardener. It was always a small party, specifically to ensure that an air of exclusivity would surround the receipt of one of the crisp white invitation cards. Lady Edevane prided herself on that score.

The afternoon came, and no less esteemed persons than Lady Sefton and Lady Jersey promptly attended in the company of Lady Iverson, Mrs. Craven, and Mrs. Russell. Several other ladies of Lady Edevane's acquaintance made up the rest of the party, which was merrily situated on the polished stone terrace at the rear of her London house. Tea was served along with nuncheon, and after half an hour, the party broke up into pairs or trios and scattered about the rose garden and the terrace.

"My dear, it is lovely to see your daughter about town. It is quite excellent that she has caught Saliston, but I am sure you know it," Lady Jersey said eagerly as she sat beside Lady Iverson in a quiet corner of the terrace. "I'm sure that we had all quite given up hope of ever seeing him settle down, but he is so attentive to Miss

Iverson. You must be very proud."

"Oh, I am sure that I would be," Lady Iverson replied meekly with a gentle smile.

"*Would* be? Whatever do you mean?" Lady Jersey gasped.

"Well, the duke has not offered for Lucilla," the viscountess replied cautiously. "But as you say, he has been very attentive."

"Indeed, he has. Markedly so, I should say."

"She is young yet. Perhaps he is not certain he would be comfortable with such a young wife."

"Heavens, if that is the case, I am sure we must all be in despair, for he is not going to get any younger *himself*!" Lady Jersey laughed. "Your Lucilla does not want for suitors. Saliston will need to make haste."

Lady Iverson was quite elated by the compliment and consequently sat in dumb silence whilst Lady Jersey recounted several tales of similarly situated gentlemen who had been roused to activity by carefully orchestrated methods involving the pointed attentions of another man. As she recalled the nuptials of a third young lady who had caught her husband by similar means, their conversation was stopped by the approach of their hostess.

"Anne, what is this I hear of Cilla being driven in Saliston's carriage again?" Lady Edevane cried excitedly.

"It is quite singular, is it not?" Lady Jersey answered with a bright smile showing no trace of malice at being interrupted.

"I should say so," the countess replied promptly as she took a seat.

"The Duke of Saliston is a confirmed bachelor."

Lady Iverson waved a hand.

"But all men are confirmed bachelors until they wed." Lady Jersey laughed.

"How many times has he invited her to dance, I ask you?" Lady Edevane asked rhetorically. "How many times has he taken her up in his carriage? I dare say he seeks her out whenever he is present at a ball. I have seen it with my own eyes."

"It is all very flattering, but I am not sure if Lucilla would accept him even if he were to offer."

This statement was met with shocked silence, which in and of itself would amaze anyone acquainted with either Lady Edevane or Lady Jersey. Neither was able to formulate a reply for several moments, and when they did it was with a flurry of confusion, entirely unable to understand how any young lady could be impervious to the charms of a handsome and personable gentleman, particularly one that also happened to be a duke of wealth and importance.

The idea that the duke was too old for a girl of eighteen was swiftly pooh-poohed. Such matches were made all the time, and Saliston was not much older than forty-five, in any case. It was argued that he was eminently well placed to provide for a wife, particularly one with a nature such as Lucilla's. It was owned that she was not quite conventional, but in a charming and somewhat eccentric way, and her temper being what it was could be easily managed by a husband who was older and more experienced than herself.

"For the Lord knows, if she were to land a husband who kept her locked up indoors, she would go mad within a se'nnight," Lady Edevane declared knowingly, sipping at her tea. "At least with Saliston she'd be allowed a free rein, so to speak."

It was not in Lady Iverson's nature to do more than pose seemingly disinterested questions on topics she wanted to understand. As yet, she had not found herself in a situation where it would be appropriate to ask her daughter to explain the exchange she had witnessed in the park. It was not at all distasteful to Lady Iverson that her daughter might be on the verge of contracting such a spectacular match, but the expression she had seen on her daughter's face and her subsequent silence after the fact did not raise a spark of hope within her, but rather one of concern.

Lady Iverson was privately of the opinion that Lucilla considered Saliston to be rather more of an uncle than a lover, no matter how their interests might align. Having been raised in a household that regularly saw the likes of Lord Sefton and other sporting men visiting during the hunting season, Lucilla had developed an easy-going manner with men of her father's generation. They were companionable, fatherly, and her talent as a horsewoman went a very long way toward encouraging them to treat her as the daughter they wished they had. Lady Iverson feared that the Duke of Saliston, no matter his own feelings, might have found himself relegated to the same ranks as these fatherly gentlemen. And Lady Iverson had never yet seen her daughter change her mind about a man—with the exception of her turnabout regarding Lord Hartwell.

Lord Hartwell. Well, he was very young, and apart from Charles Moore, Lucilla had not been exposed to the attentions of young gentlemen before their arrival in town. While Lady Iverson might harbor some curiosity about the young earl, she was more than half convinced that his was a calf-love if it was anything at all, and as likely to be transferred to some other young lady within a month. In her experience—and with three sons she considered this to be vast—young men were rather more likely to be unfaithful in young love than ladies. Her ladyship did not have serious hopes for the pretensions of either gentleman. And absolutely none at all for Mr. Moore.

The attentions of Mr. Moore rather concerned Lady Iverson more than anything else. His conduct was that of a lover, but the escalation of his romantic behavior without any reciprocation on the part of the young lady was disquieting. For all her protestations to her sister-in-law, whenever the subject of Mr. Moore was raised Lady Iverson would confess to feeling apprehensive in his presence. She had no outward reason to be suspicious of him, but there was something instinctive churning within her that warned her not to trust that particular young man. Lady Edevane certainly held him in particular dislike, but neither could she accuse him of anything improper in his attentions toward Lucilla.

The remainder of the afternoon was taken up with discussing the upcoming masquerade to be held at Vauxhall the following week. Lady Iverson was not entirely convinced such an outing was exactly proper. However, with the promise of a party being made up of several intimates and the assurance that a close eye would be kept on the young ladies, in particular, she allowed herself to be persuaded to attend with Lucilla. Lady Edevane declared that young people ought to be allowed to have their fun, and a close group of friends would ensure nothing untoward could possibly happen.

"Lucilla will stay close in any case, Anne. She is a

sensible girl, and I see no harm in it. We shall be a merry party," Lady Edevane said decidedly as they sat together after the party guests had departed. "I think we ought to include Miss Russell, and I will insist on Matthew attending with us. He might balk at the idea of a masquerade, but I am confident of bringing him round once he knows Miss Russell is to come."

"I am sure he will, but please do be sure her mama is comfortable with the plan," Lady Iverson pleaded.

"Tush, Alvira will be quite pleased, I assure you! I have not spoken to her of this little romance with her daughter and Matthew yet, but I am certain she will be excessively pleased if we can make a match between the two of them."

"If it is Matthew's wish, then I am sure I shall be very happy with it too," said Lady Iverson with a contented smile. "Miss Russell is a delightful young lady."

"She is, indeed, and from what I hear of her through Lucilla, she is not nearly as mouse-ish as I had previously thought. She will suit the boy very well, much better than Lucilla herself ever would. A little too much spirit there—she would chafe him excessively, but Miss Russell is quite another matter."

"I know there was more than one time you hoped to see Matthew and Lucilla wed, sister. But I am glad you now see that they would not at all suit. They are very much brother and sister, and I do not see the habit of a lifetime fading."

"You are quite right, of course. Matthew is not at all like my dear little brother, but he is very much like Jasper. I should like Matthew to find a young lady who suits his temper as well as you do Jasper, for he chose well when he married you, Anne."

Lady Iverson blushed pleasantly and protested the compliment but was brushed off before they were interrupted by a footman who entered to inform the ladies that the Iverson carriage had been brought round and was waiting for her ladyship at the door. The sisters-in-law said their goodbyes and fondly departed with the promise of a visit to discuss the particulars of their attendance at Vauxhall.

"And do not forget Mrs. Russell's dinner party on Friday. I will send a note round and persuade her to invite Matthew, though I am certain she will have done so already," Lady Edevane said with a gleeful wink as she bid Lady Iverson adieu at the door.

Upon her return to Iverson House, Lady Iverson wandered into the library in search of her husband and was rewarded for her efforts. His lordship was seated behind the brobdingnagian desk that took up a large area within the room, his nose buried in a ledger. The tome appeared to be of considerable interest, as he did not notice when his wife entered the room but continued to pore over the pages until she offered a quiet cough, drawing his attention.

"Ah, my dear. I did not see you. Did you enjoy your party?" Lord Iverson asked jovially as he closed his ledger.

"Thank you, I did," her ladyship replied with a gentle smile as she lingered in the doorway.

There was a slight tension in the air. Both husband and wife knew why, regardless of what was generally known about town. Her ladyship's expression was somewhat mournful, but Lord Iverson had no news for her. A slight shake of his head was enough for her to understand, and so she gave a small sigh before plunging into another topic.

"I hope you do not mind it, dearest, but your sister and I have made up a plan to attend the masquerade at Vauxhall. Perhaps you might join the party?"

"Indeed, I shall, if that is what you would like, Anne," said Lord Iverson in light reply.

"I should," his wife answered. "I own I am not quite comfortable with such themes. However, Augusta is quite determined, and she has promised no harm will come of it."

"I am sure she is quite right."

"I will ask Matthew to accompany us. Augusta has rather a plan to throw him together with Miss Russell, which I hope you will not disapprove of?"

"No, indeed. She seems quite a sensible girl," Lord Iverson exclaimed. "I am sure he has nattered on about her well enough of late. I should think he would need no encouragement."

"She has no dowry, I'm afraid."

"That hardly signifies. He is quite well accounted for, regardless of what may come—" His lordship paused as he glimpsed a flash of pain across his wife's face. "Regardless of her situation, that is."

Lady Iverson was nodding absentmindedly by way of reply as she stared at her knuckles grasping the doorframe. She bit her lip and her brows furrowed in thought as she fought the urge to give voice to the question she wanted most to ask, but having asked it so often in the months since Waterloo and meeting the same answer, she had almost entirely given up hope of hearing the news she longed for. Watching her face concernedly, Lord Iverson took several long strides across the room and grasped her hand gently, applying a reassuring pressure to it and smiling rather sadly.

"My dear, nothing good can come of constant worrying. When there is news to be had of Edward, you may trust I will inform you before all others."

Tears were forming in her eyes as her ladyship peered up at her husband, and her lips formed a tremulous smile as he pressed a kiss to her hand.

"Thank you, dearest. At this moment, I am resigned. I do not know whether I want to know or not anymore."

Lord Iverson, still carrying no small amount of guilt at the manner of his parting with his only surviving son prior to his departure for the Continent, quite understood his wife's sentiment. After months of uncertainty, he was no longer sure he wanted to know if Edward had not survived the battle. Not knowing Edward's fate allowed him the freedom to imagine that his son was alive and well, even if his absence must indicate that he was unwilling to return home. Hope was fading, for surely Edward's affection for his stepmother, sister, and cousin would prevent him from allowing them to continue grieving in uncertainty if he had indeed escaped the battle unscathed. His father's declarations against him had been uttered in fear and grief after the loss of Richard at Salamanca, but understanding could not erase the words themselves. His anger and disappointment with his father must assuredly have been acute, but Edward would surely never punish the rest of his family for Lord Iverson's heated declarations.

And yet it was many months since the war had ended, and no word had reached England either to assure or to devastate the Iverson family. No corroboration could be drawn out of the regiment, and not a single one of the returned men who had known him would confirm or deny his condition before or after the battle. The losses had been significant, and so the Iversons were left to wonder and wait.

Lord Iverson was in an unhappy predicament, with no way to attain closure. He knew not whether his nephew and daughter were to serve as his heirs or if he indeed had a living son who simply had no wish to return home.

Chapter 17

Mrs. Russell's small dinner party was an extravagance the family could afford only by means of strict economy in other areas of their finances. The family was an old one with an illustrious background, gradually reduced to penury through the poor behavior of previous generations. The marriage of a duke's granddaughter to the current incumbent of the family manor had been considered fortunate, as the modest dowry the lady brought had managed to cover the more serious debts. Still, it would be many years before the estate regained its independence.

Thankfully, Mr. John Russell was an anomaly in his line and had long since determined it to be his lot in life to repair the fortunes of the Russell family. He took pains to raise his children with an understanding of careful economy, and in this he was aided by an excellent partner in his wife. Though she had been born into grander surroundings and raised with higher expectations, she was a kind and gentle soul who had chosen her lot willingly and with a complete understanding of what her life would be, and never did she begrudge the change.

It was with this same unstinting generosity of spirit that she forbore the purchase of a new frock for herself, among other things, in exchange for the opportunity to repay her friends the kindness that had been shown to her children with invitations and outings throughout the Season. As she sat at the dining table surrounded by her guests, Mrs. Russell decided she had every reason to be satisfied with her efforts and was exceedingly happy to think of her daughter's improved prospects.

Mr. Matthew Iverson's partiality for Miss Caroline Russell's company had not gone unnoticed by her mother, and his name had been flourishingly included on the invitation she had written to Lady Iverson. Mrs. Russell had quickly decided he was an excellent young man. His prospects as a member of the church and the restraint he displayed in comparison to other young men of his age in every way recommended him to Mr. Russell, who valued a moderate temperament. The smile he brought to her daughter's face was quite enough to recommend him to Mrs. Russell, regardless of his material expectations.

The party was relatively small and made up mostly of older company who were inclined to sit about and chat over tea after they had dined, but the five younger members of the gathering subsequently begged to be allowed to dance.

"Indeed, it seems a shame not to, Mama," pleaded the younger Mr. Russell.

"But there is no music, Alfred," his mother said gently.

"I would be quite happy to play at your pianoforte, Mrs. Russell, if you would allow it," Miss Craven volunteered.

"As would I, ma'am," Lucilla chimed in, with Miss Russell offering her own agreeance to the scheme. "Perhaps we three can take turns dancing and playing?"

"An excellent notion," Mr. Alfred exclaimed. "Do

say yes, Mama."

"Well, if you are all so determined, I see no harm," Mrs. Russell said with a fond smile.

The young people scattered to make room, with the young men moving several chairs away and pushing a small table to the side against a wall while the three young ladies went to the instrument to inspect the suitability of the music sheets. When the corner of the room had been cleared satisfactorily and music decided upon, Miss Craven settled herself at the pianoforte, and the pairs met to begin the steps of a cotillion.

The elder members of the party smiled upon the proceedings indulgently. The gentlemen had not lingered long after dinner, so they were present to enjoy the spectacle of energetic young people getting up a jolly jig. Lord Iverson looked knowingly at his wife as he watched Matthew laughing with Miss Russell as the four dancers jested and chatted throughout the steps.

Sitting beside Mrs. Russell upon a little sofa across the room, Lady Edevane was also watching the activities interestedly. With an expressive smile, she inclined her head toward her hostess and said, "Well, what a pretty pair."

"Which do you mean?" Mrs. Russell replied with wide eyes.

"La, my nephew and your girl, of course." The countess laughed. "Heavens, I think Lucilla would eat your poor young man alive if anything came of *that*."

"I quite agree. He's far too much the puppy for a lively girl. But yes, Caro looks to be quite taken with Mr. Iverson," Mrs. Russell replied candidly.

"And he with her, it seems."

Mrs. Russell glanced at her friend apprehensively

before asking, "You do not mind, do you, my dear?"

"Heavens, no! Why, I cannot imagine a better match for Matthew. He will be well placed to provide for her, come what may, and he can quite afford to marry without a dowry, so it is rather perfect for all involved," Lady Edevane said frankly.

"You have always been kind to Caro. I cannot thank you enough for offering your blessing to her joining your family, if indeed the young man does come to the point. It is very early yet, of course."

"No one is getting any younger, my dear. I shall speak to him," the countess said firmly, directing a determined gaze at the entirely ignorant Matthew, who was bowing to his partner at the end of their dance. The music had stopped, and Caroline was now hurrying to take possession of the pianoforte so that Miss Craven might dance.

Miss Iverson was heard to say that they all ought to take turns changing partners, as the ladies changed at the instrument, so she would next dance with her cousin while Mr. Russell should dance with Miss Craven. This brought a dejected look to the young man's face, and he declared it was not at all the thing.

"Lord, I wouldn't dance with Caro for anything. Did you not say that you are like brother and sister? How can you bear it? Dance with me instead!"

"Come now, Mr. Russell. I learned my steps with Matthew when we were children, but I am quite happy to dance with him. And it would not do for you to so insult Miss Craven, in any case. That would not be at all gentlemanly," Lucilla said firmly but laughingly as Miss Craven approached.

Mr. Alfred begrudgingly allowed himself to be

beaten as his preferred stepped away from him and took her place beside her cousin. The exchange had been closely watched, and Lady Edevane let out a mournful sigh.

"Well, if only Edward were here, we'd have a full set and no mistake."

"Your other nephew?" Mrs. Russell asked. "Have you had word of him?"

"Not a peep. It is rather disconcerting."

"Surely, if he had been killed, the regiment would have given notice of it."

"One would hope. However, there were men who simply vanished, apparently. It seems Edward is among their number, although it is left for us to wonder if it is because he wishes it to be so, or if it does indeed mean the worst," Lady Edevane said sadly.

"I cannot imagine a quarrel with one's father would lead a young man to abandon his family so completely."

"Sadly, we have no way of discovering the truth. My brother has twigged every string he can think of, and he knows a great many people within the House that ought by rights be able to assist in the inquiries, but nothing has come of it. It is most peculiar."

"Indeed, it is," Mrs. Russell replied, a frown wrinkling her forehead as she digested her friend's words.

Across the room, Lady Iverson had heard Edward's name mentioned, and while she had overheard no more of the conversation, it brought a flutter of sadness to her heart. She stared dejectedly at Lucilla and Matthew enjoying the dance and the company of their friends. She pictured Edward appearing in the doorway. She imagined him greeting the room before joining in the dancing. She envisioned him laughing and playing with the other young people. But there was no Edward.

After the lively group of five had taken their turns several times over, the young gentlemen declared themselves exhausted, and the young ladies, after a playful attempt to cajole another set from them, allowed that they were content to stop. Mr. Alfred was called by his father to request his input on a trivial matter, while Lucilla and Constance Craven went in search of a music sheet for a duet they had earlier noticed, pointedly leaving Matthew and Caroline to their own devices in a quiet corner of the room.

"What an agreeable evening it has been," Miss Russell said breathlessly as she sat and smoothed the wrinkles from her skirts.

"I can scarce remember a better one," Matthew replied with alacrity. "I had meant to ask you something, Miss Russell."

She stiffened imperceptibly, and her eyelashes fluttered as she looked up at him searchingly before inviting his query as nonchalantly as she could manage.

Matthew was entirely oblivious to the terror and hope he had inspired within her. His question, as it happened, was absolutely nothing to do with what she was expecting.

"Has my cousin said anything to you about the Duke of Saliston?"

As quickly as it had come on, the stiffness in her shoulders relaxed, and she breathed a gasp that sounded much more like a laugh. She was sensible of disappointment coursing through her, and her heart was pounding uncomfortably, but she covered the emotion with amusement instead.

"What is it you would like to know, Mr. Iverson?" Caro said with a smile and mocking tone.

"Only if she has mentioned him of late. I am merely curious."

"Suspicious, you mean? You are asking whether you might have a duchess for a cousin, are you not?"

"Well, I suppose I am." He shrugged, his gaze wandering toward Lucilla as she sat beside Miss Craven, studying a music sheet and laughing.

"Would it be so terrible if she were to marry the duke?"

"No, not at all."

"So you are subscribing to frivolous gossip, then?" Miss Russell asked with a sly grin. She had regained control of her countenance and posture now, but there was a sliver of suspicion beginning to grow where the hope had been only moments before, and it was causing her to lose command of her tongue. She had thought there was something of an understanding between herself and this young man, but she was suddenly uncertain of it. He had made no declarations, of course, but he instead singled her out in company. But then, she had never been pursued before, and she began to wonder if she had imagined it all.

"Gossip is not at all something I routinely partake in," he said firmly. "But when my family is the subject, I prefer to know the facts so I can at the very least rest easy in the knowledge myself."

"I see." The young lady pursed her lips. "Are you certain it is not because you nourish hope there yourself?"

His bark of laughter surprised and relieved her entirely of her fears even before he replied, "Good God, can you imagine? Lucilla is hardly the wife for a clergyman, let alone me as I am."

Miss Russell found herself laughing along with him, for it was indeed true she had witnessed enough of their constant bickering like cats and dogs to know they were as unsuited to one another as, indeed, a cat and a dog. Now that her fleeting suspicion was gone, it was, in turn, replaced with shame.

But Matthew continued in complete ignorance of his companion's feelings. He began to list the things he found utterly irritating about his cousin, and Miss Russell was allowed quite a reasonable amount of time to regain her composure. As he reached the end of his list, she interjected with acknowledgment of his entirely unrelatable complaints.

"I must confess, I do not find Lucilla at all irritating. Perhaps it has become something of a habit for you to be annoyed with her all of the time," Caroline said with a gentle laugh.

"I imagine you are right," he conceded.

"In answer to your question, she has mentioned the duke to me."

"She has? In what context?"

"I am not sure what it is you want to hear," Miss Russell said cautiously. "I do not know if being told what she has said will prove a disappointment or not."

"I have no preference, I assure you."

"Well, she does not consider the duke more than a great friend, I am afraid. I rather think she finds him very diverting. The way that one would find a dashing uncle to be diverting, if that makes any sense at all."

"It does. I worried that it might be the case."

"Worried?" Miss Russell asked, utterly confused.

"Why ever would that worry you?"

"I like the man. He's everything one would wish for Lucilla," Matthew replied ponderously.

"He's a little old, don't you think?"

"Perhaps, but he's certainly no decrepit. I do not hold his age to be a factor."

"Well, I rather think Lucilla does."

"How do you know?"

"Because she said so, of course." Miss Russell laughed. "In any case, I think one need not look too much farther abroad to locate a suitable match for her that is rather more appropriately aged."

Matthew raised an eyebrow in question.

"Lord Hartwell," Miss Russell said, shaking her head in wonder at his ignorance.

Now both eyebrows shot up in surprise, and his eyes widened, but he remained silent as the lady continued.

"Before you ask me, no, she has not said anything of note about Lord Hartwell. She is quite oblivious and sees him as an excellent friend, rather like a brother," Caroline chattered, barely stopping for breath. "I think it is rather the fault of having had three brothers similarly aged to his lordship, but I expect it will not be long before she realizes he is mad for her. I'm sure you have noticed."

"An inkling, I suppose. I suspicioned he liked her, of course, but—"

"But like everyone else, you've been taken up with your hopes for the duke." Miss Russell rolled her eyes and shook her head. "Well, it is no matter. One way or another, she will decide a path for herself. I am sure Lady Iverson is not the sort of mama who would force Lucilla's hand."

Matthew stared at his companion curiously for a moment, and before he realized what he was saying, he asked, "Is your mama the sort who would force her daughter's hand?"

Now it was Miss Russell's turn to be shocked, but she recovered quickly, and an amused smile spread across her face.

"She most assuredly is not."

Across the room, Miss Iverson and Miss Craven were discussing their individual plans for the forthcoming masquerade at Vauxhall. Miss Craven would not make one of the Iverson party, but the ladies had every intention of passing at least some of their time together at the event. The only question left was the most appropriate method of recognizing one another when the entire congregation would be masked.

"Perhaps we ought to arrange a clasp or brooch to identify ourselves?" Miss Craven suggested.

"There might be any number of people wearing such things," Lucilla replied in a thoughtful tone. "What of a ribbon? A ribbon tied in such a way over one's glove, maybe? We could choose a particular color, and each wear the same."

"Yes, I think that will do just nicely." Miss Craven exclaimed, clapping her hands delightedly. "We've only a few more days to prepare, and we ought to tell Caro, too. Is she to attend with your party?"

"She will dine with us before, and then my cousin and Papa intend to escort us. I believe Alfred will be joining us, too."

"Well, I think Mr. Matthew will be rather busy dancing attendance on Caro, so you will be stuck with Alfred." Constance giggled. "There is no harm in him, at least. Even if he plays the sulky bear rather too often."

"If it helps to move Matthew along, I will bear it, for Caro," Lucilla said solemnly, but a playful note tickled the edge of her words, and Miss Craven laughed along with her.

"Will Lord Hartwell attend, do you think?" Constance asked wonderingly.

"He says he will."

"Perhaps we ought to let him in on the secret of our ribbons as well," she pressed.

"I suppose we ought," Lucilla replied in a thoughtful tone. "I expect there will be a great many people there. I expect he will call tomorrow as he usually does. I shall tell him then."

"Excellent," said her friend with decision. She peered at Lucilla, trying to find any sign of partiality in her fine features, but saw nothing. "We shall all then make up a merry party."

"I expect we shall," Lucilla answered smilingly.

Later in the evening, the two young ladies brought the other young people in on their little plan. The idea caught quickly, and Caroline fled the room in search of a length of ribbon to immediately make up the tokens. She soon returned with a bundle of yellow ribbon that was conspicuously dotted with purple marks.

"Heavens, what a hideous color," Constance exclaimed. "It is perfect."

"I had thought to give it away ages ago, but here we are finding a use for the stuff," Caroline laughed as she drew out a pair of sharp scissors and snipped the ribbon into suitable lengths for tying before it was distributed among the group.

Matthew and Alfred each took a single length, as did

Constance and Caroline. Lucilla took one as well before Constance handed her another and reminded her to give it into Lord Hartwell's hands.

"He will surely be disappointed if he cannot find you," she reminded gently, trying to provoke some sort of response from her friend once more. She was somewhat rewarded this time with what she thought was a slight reddening of Lucilla's cheeks.

"Darlings, we ought to be going," Lady Iverson said quietly, approaching the group of young people. "The carriage has been brought round, and you know how Papa hates to have the horses standing."

The party was thusly broken up, and the plan made to meet together at Vauxhall.

Chapter 18

Several days later, the Russell siblings were collected from their home at Green Street by the Iverson carriage and deposited in Grosvenor Street in time for dinner. Chatter was loud and constant around the dining table, over which Lady Iverson benevolently presided with her sister-in-law. Both ladies had caught wind of the young people's trick with their ribbons, and it was with a laugh that they informed the merry people that Lord Iverson had bespoken a supper-box at which they had arranged for Miss Craven to meet them for the evening's festivities.

"I do wish you had said so this morning, Mama," Lucilla said. "I would have told Lord Hartwell to meet us at the box, too."

"Ah, well, dear, perhaps it is a good thing after all that you have your ribbons." Lady Edevane chuckled, wiggling her eyebrows and looking at Lady Iverson pointedly. "He shall be able to bring Saliston to our little party. You must be sure not to wander off too far with the duke, Cilla. It may be a masquerade, but one never knows who may be watching and recognize you."

"I assure you I have no intention of wandering off anywhere with the duke, Aunt Augusta," Lucilla replied hotly, her cheeks flushing furiously as she glared at her aunt. Her invective was brushed off with a chuckle which served only to annoy her further as she looked about the table to find a mortified expression on Miss Russell's and Matthew's faces.

Mr. Alfred heard only that he would have competition for Lucilla's attentions and took the liberty of demanding the first two dances with her, so she was obliged to agree for the sake of civility and found herself all the more irritated with her aunt for provoking Alfred's request.

Dinner continued with several more twitty remarks being directed at Lucilla until Lady Iverson changed the topic by declaring how fortuitous it was that the inclement weather had cleared long enough for the ball to go ahead. Soon after the meal had been finished, the carriages appeared at the door to transport the party to their destination. They were to travel by way of the new bridge, a prospect that somewhat unnerved Lady Iverson in her trepidation of the new and unknown. Her husband, however, declared it an excellent solution to the old wherry and determined it would be a much more pleasant experience to no longer rely on such an incommodious form of transport.

Before they stepped out onto the street, the ladies took pains to arrange their masks and ribbons carefully. It was around this time it was learned that Alfred had mislaid his token, for which he was chastised severely by his sister.

"I am certain that it was in my coat pocket when I was at the club," the young poet cried mournfully. "Absolutely certain. I drew it out only for a moment and put it back again."

"For shame, and I have not brought the rest with me, so we have no more to cut another piece. Really, Alfred," Caro scolded, muttering under her breath as they stood a little away from the rest of the group. His apologies were sincere, and her exasperation had mostly abated by the time they alighted the carriage at the entrance of the gardens, by which time she was concerned only with ensuring she could adequately recognize her friends and guardians for the evening.

Miss Russell herself was easily identifiable, for she had worn her puce satin gown many times, but this evening she paired it with creamy satin gloves and an olive-green silk domino, the half-mask edged in gold-colored paint. Her brother, meanwhile, thought himself excellently rigged out in dark tails and knee breeches with a black half-mask and cloak. Matthew, for his part, was similarly dressed; however, he'd chosen to wear a dark green coat and mask. Whether his choice of dress was by design to match Miss Russell was to be hotly discussed between his two aunts once they were later left alone in the supper-box.

Lucilla had also chosen a favorite dress. Hers was an ivory satin ornamented with spangles that twinkled under the net of lights hung about the gardens. She wore a bright red domino over it and a matching half-mask edged on the left with two tall white feathers. The ensemble was completed with a pair of red silk slippers and elbow-length white gloves over which she tied her token yellow-and-purple ribbon.

Soon after their arrival, the orchestra struck up the first dance of the evening within the ballroom, and having promised to participate in the first two at the very least with Alfred, Lucilla allowed herself to be borne away from the supper-box with her aunt loudly promising to send Saliston to her as soon as he was to be found.

She suffered through two dances and narrowly avoided having a third demanded of her by the intervention of Matthew, who was sent on Miss Russell's orders to rescue Lucilla from Alfred. She worried he would allow himself to push the boundaries of propriety simply because the setting in which they found themselves was rather more liberal than usual. She had confided her concerns to Matthew in advance of the ball in order to ensure herself of his assistance should it be required, and while she was glad to have been prepared, she was conscious of some annoyance that intervention had been required quite so early in the evening.

As Alfred pettishly stormed away from where Miss Iverson and her cousin were now beginning the steps of the next dance, Caro put herself in his way and laid an admonishing hand upon his arm before whispering that he ought to check himself and not take liberties.

"Why should I not?" the young boy demanded irritably. "It is not as though anyone will notice—we are masked. And if anyone *should* notice, what matter is it anyway?"

"It is not polite to force yourself upon a lady's notice, Alfred. Lucilla has given you rein because she is fond of you and me. Do not take advantage," Caroline urged.

Her brother pulled his arm from her grasp and stalked away in search of refreshment, and Miss Russell watched him go. As she turned back to look toward the dancing, a figure cut in front of her for a moment, almost bumping her. She gasped in surprise and stepped back quickly to avoid the collision. The cloaked and masked man was as surprised as she, for he stumbled back too, muttering an incoherent apology before striding away quickly without waiting for a reply.

The masked man hurriedly retreated, but as he rushed off, she caught sight of a yellow ribbon tied around his wrist and realized that since Matthew and Alfred were accounted for, the man could only be Lord Hartwell. He had disappeared into the crush of people, so it seemed pointless to call out or go in search of him. He had his token. It would not be long before he made his way back to the group again.

Once the dance had ended, the Iverson cousins rejoined her. The trio decided to stop by the supper-box, which was fortunate, as the newly arrived Miss Craven was waiting for them. Having recovered from his sulking, Alfred decided to join the group on a tour of the pleasure gardens, but they could not depart without another clever remark being heard to fall from Lady Edevane's lips about being sure to tell the duke where Lucilla was to be found.

"I am sure he will show himself before the night is through," the countess called out after them.

"I wonder whether she has had rather too much to drink at dinner," Mr. Iverson muttered as the little group left the box. He escorted both his cousin and Miss Russell while Miss Craven had taken Alfred's proffered arm. He seemed in significantly better spirits, and his sister wondered whether he, too, had taken something to smooth off his nerves.

"I do wish she would not talk so. I do not find it amusing in the least," Lucilla grumbled under her breath. Both Miss Craven and Miss Russell offered sympathetic glances while her cousin advised her firmly to ignore their aunt's jibes.

"You know that if you react, it will only serve to

encourage her."

"What I think you ought to do, Miss Iverson, is show your aunt that you have a marked preference for *another*. That will surely persuade her that your interests lie elsewhere," Alfred chimed in.

"Speaking of another," Caroline interrupted before her brother could continue, "I believe Lord Hartwell is here somewhere. I saw his ribbon."

"Oh, ought we to look for him?" Miss Craven asked.

"I'm sure we will come across him before long. He was wearing a black velvet cloak and silver mask," Miss Russell replied.

The group of young people decided to take a walk through the Prince's Pavilion. They wandered aimlessly, enjoying the entertainments they passed along the way before entering the building and meandering through the crowds to view the various pieces of artwork on display. The five young people broke off a little from each other once or twice as one or another took particular interest in a painting at different times. It was at one of these moments that Lucilla, lingering over an exceptionally fine picture of a stately home that reminded her of Gracewood, heard her name whispered.

As she turned to see who had called to her, she felt fingertips graze her wrist and looked down to find a gloved hand reaching for her. The yellow-and-purple ribbon encircling the wrist matched her own. Upon glancing up, she found herself staring up at a black hooded figure wearing a silver mask that obscured most of the wearer's face. He did not speak her name again, only raising a finger to his lips as though to hush her as he took hold of her hand.

Lucilla smiled warmly and allowed him to lead her,

assuming him to be Lord Hartwell. As they were near a doorway, they did not need to wade through many people before the crush was no longer upon them. He did not speak. Instead, he inclined his head to suggest that she follow him and drew her hand around his arm. She went willingly, amused by his strange behavior. He led her from the Pavilion toward the Grand Walk and proceeded up it, passing the Rotunda and hurrying by the supper-boxes.

As he bore her along, Lucilla laughed lightly and exclaimed that he had not yet spoken. He looked at her quickly, and she thought he must have smiled beneath the mask, and she was pleased to have had some small success without ruining his romantic efforts. At length, they came to a halt before a behemoth object concealed by a curtain. In front of it stood a crowd of people that seemed to be waiting for something to happen, and then the sound of a bell rang loudly.

There was a sudden loud rushing noise, and the curtain was drawn back to reveal a spectacularly lit cascade of water. The people crowded about cried out in admiration, and Lucilla stared in wonder at the spectacle, her mouth dropping open in a wide smile.

"Oh, how wonderful," she gasped, mesmerized. "How ever did you know about this?"

Her companion made no reply, only grasped her hand tighter, a gesture she reflexively returned as she smiled up at the concealed face. She turned back toward the magnificent fountain that was on display before her and immersed herself in the moment.

He had still not spoken when the performance was over. Instead, he led her away down another path. Lucilla, still reeling somewhat from his surprising and romantic gesture, had not yet considered whether there might be a reason for the sudden change in his manner. She had surely sensed in recent weeks that Lord Hartwell's attentions might be serious in nature, and the recent teasing of her aunt had forced Lucilla to ask herself some rather solemn questions, resulting in something of a revelation.

She decided she liked Hartwell quite as much as she liked Saliston, but in rather a different way. Her feelings for Saliston were for that of a dear friend or uncle, whilst her liking for Lord Hartwell seemed to be something more. The escalation of his behavior in the romantic and rather scandalous setting of a Vauxhall masquerade was quite enough to convince her his attentions were indeed *very* serious in nature.

While Lucilla's thoughts wandered, she neglected to notice precisely where her companion was taking her. By the time she had shaken off her dreaminess, she was quite unsure of where she was. The area seemed darker than had the rest of the paths, she could see no distinctive arches like those decorating the more populated walks, and a new thought crept into her mind.

"My lord, we really ought to re-join the others," she said gently, peering up at him. "It has been a lovely interlude, really, but for the sake of propriety, we should not be alone like this."

Her companion did not reply. In fact, he acted as though he had not heard her at all. She frowned a little as she watched him, trying to distinguish the expression under the mask, but only his mouth was visible.

She focused on his mouth. His lips. They were set differently than usual. She knew he had a pettish streak, not unlike Alfred's, but he smiled more often than not, and she could see no reason for the grim set of his mouth at this moment. She glanced at the ribbon tied about his wrist to assure herself of its authenticity; placed close to her own, she knew it to be precisely like her own, but she could not shake her uncertainty.

"My lord, I must insist that we return to my family," Lucilla said lightly, forcing a teasing note into her voice in an effort to hide her rapidly growing concern. She gave a friendly squeeze to his arm to enforce her words and to guide him back the way they had come, but instead of giving in to the pressure of her hand, her companion suddenly tightened his grip on her arm and quickened his pace.

She gasped in shock and struggled against his hold; there was now no doubt in her mind that she was not in the company of Lord Hartwell. Whatever reasons this imposter had for assuming his position could not be honorable. As she pulled against him and he struggled to hold her, his velvet hood fell away from his head, revealing dark locks and a dark blue coat with silver buttons, but the mask continued to hide the man's identity admirably.

Lucilla forbore screaming. Attracting attention now would only serve to damage her own reputation, and the chances of a masked man slipping into the crowd with no one the wiser was a chance she was unwilling to take. They were in a darkened area of the garden, which was no doubt intentional on the part of her captor. Unfortunately for him, the surroundings also suited Lucilla in this particular moment.

London knew her to be an intelligent, aristocratic, prettily behaved young woman with extraordinary horsemanship and feminine accomplishments in droves.

What they did not know was that growing up in the company of three elder brother figures had provided her with an education that did not come naturally to other young ladies of her class. It was that education she now called upon to save her the indignity of abduction and social ruin.

Her struggling abruptly ceased. Her unencumbered right hand formed a dainty fist. And her dainty fist connected neatly with her kidnapper's unsuspecting nose. There was a surprising amount of force behind the thrust, and it was so precisely aimed that blood was drawn, and she found herself immediately released.

But the untamed and unladylike streak she was usually at such pains to conceal from Society was suddenly loosened. Instead of escaping while the opportunity presented itself, she made a fist with her left hand as well and swung at the masked man again. So concerned was he with keeping his mask in place that he was unable to deflect the second blow, which landed squarely in the vicinity of his right eye.

He let out a loud exclamation, and upon hearing his voice, she recognized it but could not immediately identify who he was. She was determined to know and so went in to swing again, but her hand was caught midair.

In shock and irritation, she spun to find a second male figure had appeared, and it was this man who held her raised hand captive. With an unladylike growl, she tried unsuccessfully to shake her arm free, but as she did so, the newcomer said her name and tore off his mask to reveal himself.

Lord Hartwell's face was awash with so many emotions that Lucilla did not immediately grasp his intent. His hold on her wrist did not slacken as he attempted to pull her away from the masked man. But her fury was unabated, and with her loose hand, she managed to land a final glancing blow on the masked man's jaw. He gasped and reeled away before turning and sprinting away down the path, with Hartwell in pursuit.

After briefly following the would-be-abductor, Lord Hartwell regained enough presence of mind to realize that continuing the chase would leave the young lady as vulnerable as ever on a dimly lit path and quite alone. His quarry was rather faster and had already gotten well ahead, so he frustratedly gave up the chase.

"Lucilla," Lord Hartwell cried in a panicked voice as he approached her, his hands grasping her shoulders firmly as he peered into her eyes. "Are you all right? Are you hurt?"

"I am fine," she practically shrieked in answer. The anger that had flowed so intensely in her veins only moments before had evaporated as suddenly as it had come on, and in its place was shock and terror. She was trembling violently. Her hands ran up and down the lengths of her arms. She stared at Lord Hartwell with widened eyes, and he stared back at her. She could see fear writ across his features, mixed with a jumble of indistinct emotions that neither she nor he could quite decipher.

Without realizing what she was doing, she rushed toward him and threw herself into his arms, where he instinctively clutched her to himself, his chin finding a natural resting place at the crown of her head as she sobbed into his cloak. They clung to one another for a long while. As she cried softly, he whispered consolingly until she at length regained her senses. She slowly backed away from him, muttering apologetically.

"I am so sorry, my lord." She glanced around fearfully. The spell was broken, and with relief she observed the area around them remained entirely deserted. She spied his discarded mask upon the gravel path and reached down to retrieve it.

After successfully re-establishing his disguise, the pair turned back down the path, heading in the direction of the more well-lit walkways. Painfully aware of the awkwardness of the situation, neither one was willing to touch the other or to speak, but it was Lord Hartwell who caved first by asking the dreaded question that hung between them.

"Whatever possessed you to come down such a path with a stranger?" he said, rather more harshly than he had intended.

She stopped and looked at him for a moment, forcing him to meet her eye before saying, "I thought he was *you*."

"You what?" he blurted confusedly. "Why on earth would you have thought he was me?"

"He was wearing a token. A yellow-and-purple spotted band," Lucilla whimpered, wringing her hands together nervously. "Caro said she had seen you and that you were wearing a black velvet hood. She was clearly mistaken, but how could she have known? She never saw the man's face—she only knew that whomever she had seen was certainly not her brother or my cousin, so she assumed it must have been you."

She paused, realization flooding her face. "Alfred. Alfred lost his token. He was not wearing it."

Lord Hartwell stared at her blankly, digesting her

words carefully, but he did not reply because she had begun to tremble again, and her hands covered her mouth in horror. He put a protective arm about her shoulders, pressing his forehead to the side of her head as she tried to understand what had so recently been attempted against her. Soon enough, her voice returned.

"Whoever he was, he must be known to us if he had Alfred's token," she murmured as she pulled away slowly. "We ought to return to the others. I can only hope to have avoided scandal this night."

She put her hand through his arm and let him lead her. They walked slowly in order to regain their collective composure, and before long, they arrived at the Rotunda. The box Lord Iverson had rented was empty, but the various personal items belonging to its owners indicated they had not vacated the area entirely. The pair were allowed a few minutes of solitary quiet, which they spent avoiding the topic that occupied the forefront of both their minds before they were interrupted by the arrival of her cousin and their other friends.

While Miss Russell and Miss Craven chastised her for disappearing, Matthew's knowledgeable eyes were drawn immediately to the smear of red that adorned Lucilla's knuckles. He said nothing, only looked searchingly at her companion's face and was satisfied that whomever she had struck, it was most definitely not the young man seated in the box with her. He listened to her explain the accidental spilling of a glass of wine in answer to Miss Craven's noticing the stains, but as there was not so much as a speck of color anywhere on her very white dress, he doubted the truth of her story.

Matthew watched his cousin closely for the

remainder of the evening. Throughout, she never strayed far from Lord Hartwell's side, even when Saliston finally appeared and attempted to draw her into conversation. No one else seemed to notice anything amiss, but as Miss Russell had pointed out once before, his knowing Lucilla was the habit of a lifetime, and he knew something must have happened. That something obviously involved Hartwell, but what part the young earl had played was as mysterious as the event itself.

As the clock sang midnight and masks were removed, Miss Iverson searched the crowd for a bruised countenance among the naked faces but could see none. It was a vain hope to believe her attacker would have remained long enough to be unmasked, but she found herself searching, nonetheless. She looked up at Lord Hartwell, who was standing beside her, and realized that he, too, was searching the crowd. He felt her gaze and attempted a reassuring smile. Her body swayed toward his unconsciously, but she stopped short of touching him. The masquerade was over; there could be no hiding behind the safety of their disguises any longer.

Chapter 19

For a week after the incident at Vauxhall, Lucilla complained of a headache and begged off from every engagement she and her mother had planned to attend. Lady Iverson could see nothing amiss, putting her daughter's lethargy down to overexertion. There was no reason to hurry Lucilla's recovery; rest would be beneficial. Instead of sitting at home herself, she indulged herself by attending several smaller gatherings, given by her friends, that her daughter would have found a complete bore.

During that week, Lucilla saw only her family and Miss Russell, who visited several times to sit quietly with her friend and while away the day bent over some mending or an embroidery frame. They spoke very little; other than a brief query regarding the change of Lord Hartwell's mask and cloak, nothing about the masquerade was discussed at all.

Miss Wallace made an attempt to breach the sanctity of Lucilla's private parlor, but this was skillfully thwarted by Lady Iverson's maid, who succinctly decried the behavior of anyone so poorly bred as to force their presence on an invalid. This had the effect of neatly clamping Miss Wallace's mouth into a venomous pout before the young lady removed herself from the hall at speed and took herself back to the drawing room where her mother sat with their hostess.

Lucilla's mood brightened only when Lord Hartwell presented himself at Iverson House, which he did several times. He was not accompanied by his cousin Saliston, much to the chagrin of Lady Edevane, who had begun to worry that his interest in her niece was waning. When Lady Edevane noted his neglect, Lord Hartwell apologetically informed her that his cousin had been called suddenly out of London the morning after the party at Vauxhall. Her ladyship was slightly mollified but remained concerned. Lucilla, though, was glad to see the only person who understood the cause of her present demeanor.

At first, Lord Hartwell was disposed to agree that she had a right to sit about despondently, but after a week had passed, he gently reminded her that it was not at all like her. He assured her that not the smallest word of gossip had been heard, and he was confident the episode had passed unremarked by the *ton*. Surely, if someone had witnessed the attack, the whispers would have begun by now. And if it so happened that someone *had* seen it, they clearly didn't know who the persons involved were.

Lucilla heard his words but decided to remain home for a few more days in any case. It was not merely the attempted abduction she meditated on in her solitude. She was also mulling over the implication of her feelings for Lord Hartwell. Of his affection she was quite certain, but the last thing she wanted was the kind of scrutiny that her friendship with the duke had garnered from her family.

And so, precisely nine days following the horrid evening at Vauxhall, after spending each of the preceding mornings lying abed with a breakfast tray, playing the invalid, with Chico curled at her feet, Miss

Iverson agreed to meet Lord Hartwell for a morning ride in Hyde Park.

She thus returned to her previous schedule of waking early and enjoying breakfast with her father in the parlor. From there, she made the unconventional choice of walking to the rear of the house and meeting Smithers in the mews, where she groomed and saddled Sierra herself before being tossed into her saddle and riding toward the park with her faithful groom beside her astride one of Lord Iverson's hacks.

She arrived at the gates of the park somewhat earlier than she had arranged to meet Lord Hartwell. The Wellington ball the previous night meant that at this early hour the park would be almost entirely devoid of anyone she knew. Entering the park near Grosvenor Street, she guided her excitable chestnut to a path on the left and headed directly for Rotten Row.

As expected, the Row was empty. Throwing both caution and propriety to the wind, she loosened her reins and let the horse run. She heard a shout of surprise from Smithers, but after a moment, he spurred his horse onward and closed the gap until he was galloping right behind her. The tension and weight of the distressing events at Vauxhall were lifting from her shoulders. The clatter of hooves on the gravel seemed to chase away the terror she had felt that night. But, too soon, the end of the Row came in view, and she unwillingly reined Sierra in. The horse tossed his head in protest and pranced in place. All at once, the park came to life as pedestrians, carriages, and mounted horsemen alike began to appear.

"We best be headin' back the way we come if you be wishin' to meet the lad, Miss Cilla," Smithers said crisply.

"We are rather ahead of time, Smithers," she replied. "There is no need to hurry."

"No need t' hurry? Then why did y' decide t' take an unseemly gallop, may I ask, missy?" he said in a rather smug tone.

"To blow away the cobwebs, dear one, why else?" Lucilla answered coyly, a cheeky smile creeping onto her face.

It was the first genuine smile he'd seen on her face in over a week, so the faithful groom was satisfied that whatever had ailed his mistress had passed. He reined his master's hack in alongside Sierra, and they rode in companionable silence back down the Row. They were still relatively early for the rendezvous by the time they reached the gate, but there was not quite enough time to take a stroll down another path.

Instead, Lucilla chose a shady spot along the edge of the drive to halt the horses. She and her groom were engaged in discussing trivial stable matters when another horse was heard approaching, which was not surprising since they were expecting an arrival. Smithers discreetly drew his horse a small distance away, but alas, the horseman who reined in beside her was not Lord Hartwell but his cousin.

"Good morning, Lucilla," Charles Moore purred.

Miss Iverson's skin crawled in response to hearing his voice so near to her. She flinched away, causing the fiery chestnut horse to skitter sideways beneath her saddle. The horse tossed its head and hopped on its front feet irritably. She glared at the man unwelcomingly and offered a very curt reply as she attempted to settle Sierra.

"He is too testy for you. Your father really ought to provide you with a more suitable animal."

"I am quite capable of managing him, I assure you," she replied through gritted teeth and a false smile as the horse continued to snort, shuffling on the spot.

"That does not at all seem to be the case, my dear," he said silkily.

To this comment she did not bother responding, and silence reigned awkwardly supreme for several moments while she focused on the task of calming her horse. She rather hoped that her concentration would encourage him to leave her, but he had never been the kind to take a hint. Instead, he continued to talk to her.

"I hear you are becoming rather friendly with my cousin," Moore said in an airy tone as he lounged languidly on his fat, lazy hack in the shade.

Lucilla looked across at him sharply, her lips pursed. "And who, may I ask, is your source?"

"No one in particular." He shrugged.

"And what is it to you if I were?"

"Oh, it is nothing at all to me, I assure you," Moore replied, but the feigned disinterest in his voice was evident even to his own ears. "But I am fond of the boy. He is excessively green about the ears, of course. I should expect he will fall in and out of love a dozen times before he settles on a suitable female."

"Is this an attempt to offer a warning, Mr. Moore? I am much obliged to you, I'm sure," Lucilla said bitingly with an indignant shrug.

He had the audacity to laugh, which set her teeth even more on edge. Sierra stirred beneath her again, mirroring the irritation he felt through the reins as waves of frustration rolled off his rider.

"I assure you, Lucilla, I have only the best interests of yourself and my cousin at heart."

"I do not recall giving leave for you to use my name, particularly in public, sir," she replied hotly, her fury flowing freely.

"What, when we have known one another for so long? We are neighbors at the very least, if not friends," he said in honeyed tones. "I had always thought we were rather more than friends, though."

Bile rose in her throat, and her eyes stared daggers at the dark-haired gentleman smiling at her so suggestively that his thoughts would be apparent to anyone who chanced upon them. Just as she was about to spit furious words at him, a new voice rang out.

"Is something amiss?"

Lucilla's gaze darted around to see Lord Hartwell had finally arrived, riding a very fine black courser belonging to the duke. Seeing the two men side by side, one astride a magnificent high-bred animal and the other atop a fat hack, she almost forgot her fury enough to laugh at the comparison. But the mirth that rippled up within her throat died a quick death when Mr. Moore replied nonchalantly to his cousin's query.

"Ah, Olly! What brings you here this morning? I swore you'd be abed at this hour. Were you not dancing the night away with Miss Craven at Wellington's last night?"

The confusion plainly written on Lord Hartwell's face was enough for Lucilla to understand. The hesitant answer served to confirm her suspicion that Moore was making a feeble attempt to sow doubt within her mind.

Lucilla snorted derisively under her breath and rolled her eyes. If her mother had been present to witness the unladylike spectacle, she would undoubtedly have read her daughter a strict sermon. Still, Lady Iverson was not present, and her daughter had been driven so near the edge of her temper that appearances hardly seemed to matter any longer.

"I am meeting Miss Iverson this morning," Lord Hartwell said in answer to his cousin, his gaze darting from Charles to Lucilla in turn. They then lingered on his cousin until the look became rather more like a stare.

Lucilla, still simmering in irritation, took no notice of the exchange but said distinctly, "I think it is time we moved on, Lord Hartwell. It will not do to keep our horses standing in the shade here all day." Sierra tossed his black-and-flaxen mane and jigged excitedly.

His lordship dragged his gaze away from Mr. Moore's face and murmured agreeance with Lucilla's declaration. He urged the black horse forward a little, then fumbled with his rein suddenly, causing his horse to bump into his cousin's. The fat hack staggered sideways a step out of the shade of the tree they had sheltered under.

"Oh, I do apologize, cousin," Lord Hartwell cried out miserably. "Dear me, how very clumsy of me."

His cousin, a little flustered, waved off the apology. Lord Hartwell peered at him rather curiously before excusing himself and collecting his reins and his horse once more.

"I have not seen you much of late, Charlie," he said suddenly. "I shall pop in to see you this evening if you are at home."

"Dining with Finch at Robinson's," Mr. Moore muttered.

"I'll come by before, then," Hartwell replied before tipping his hat and riding after Lucilla and her groom.

****

Since the masquerade at Vauxhall, it seemed as though the Earl of Hartwell had grown from boy to man in one night. Saliston had found a note awaiting his return to Berkeley Square in which a crony had taken the time to pen an interesting tale of Lord Hartwell's exploits during the duke's absence from London.

Instead of indulging in drink or gaming, it seemed he was likely to be found at an evening party or playing at cards with one or other of the sober young men he'd met by way of Matthew Iverson. Failing that, Oliver was apparently content to while his evenings away by the fireside, engrossed in some book or another. By day he engaged in exercising his horses or visiting one of the sporting clubs to which he had been introduced. Particularly, he had begun to frequent a famous boxing saloon.

Saliston sat at his desk, pondering the change in his cousin when a slamming door alerted him to Oliver's arrival in the house. He'd disappeared early in the morning on the black gelding that had become something of a favorite, but there was nothing unusual in that. He had himself only returned to London the evening before and had not yet seen his cousin.

"Hart!"

"George?"

"In the library, Hart!"

"Ah, there you are," Oliver said as he entered the room. "We are invited to dine at Lady Iverson's this evening. Had you any plans?"

"I confess I do not. It is frightfully embarrassing." Saliston laughed.

"I heard you had come home before I left the house this morning, so I accepted the invitation for you, in any case," his cousin answered distractedly. He was peering at Saliston in a strangely searching way. His brows furrowed slightly as though he was looking for something until Saliston broke the silence.

"Is that all?"

"Oh, yes. That's all."

"Is something amiss? You seem out of sorts."

"No, it is nothing," was the unconvincing reply.

"Come now, what is wrong?" Saliston prodded, leaning back in his seat and feigning unconcern in an effort to draw out an answer. Lord Hartwell looked at him with a curious expression and was silent for a moment before he replied.

"How came you to get that bruise on your cheek, George?"

Saliston's hand flew quickly to his jaw, and he rubbed a distracted hand over the fading mark.

"Oh, that bay of mine took exception to a hedge and sent me to earth! I thought it had quite gone. Is it very noticeable?"

Oliver shook his head in answer and abruptly left the room when Saliston remembered there had been a message received for him in his absence.

"Oh, hold on a moment! This arrived while you were out," the duke said, plucking a folded note from under his ledger and handing it into his cousin's outstretched hand.

"From whom?"

"The messenger didn't say. It arrived not ten minutes before you did."

Hartwell unfolded the paper and quickly read the one or two sentences it contained, scowling and scrunching the note distractedly.

"What is it?" Saliston asked with concern.

"Nothing," the young earl replied. His tone did not match the frown that was wringing his brows together. He gave a tight smile and a nod to his cousin before striding toward the door, parting with, "Lady Iverson's at half-five this evening."

There was no doubt Lord Hartwell had changed drastically—he stood taller, walked with a firmer step, and had developed an edge about himself that Saliston had never known existed.

Chapter 20

Having shaken off her decline, Lucilla lost her excuse to avoid the company of the Wallaces. The morning after the Iverson household had entertained Saliston and Lord Hartwell, the ladies were subjected to a morning call from the indomitable Lady Wallace and her daughter.

"I am told that you entertained last evening, my dear," Lady Wallace said imperiously as she settled herself on a chair. Before her hostess could reply, she continued, "We had no engagements, so we passed a very dull evening at home. A shame that we had not been invited to dine."

Lady Iverson quailed under an accusatory glint from her friend and hurried to explain the circumstances when she was interrupted by her daughter.

"I am afraid that was my doing, Lady Wallace," Lucilla declared. "I invited the duke and Lord Hartwell to dine. I'm afraid Mama had quite a time of it ensuring that dinner would stretch to accommodate even just the two extra places."

"Well! You are becoming very forward, Lucy," cried Miss Wallace archly. "I cannot think it at all proper for an unmarried young female to be inviting men to dine, and without her mother's express permission, too. What right have you?"

"Seeing as they have become rather particular

friends to my cousin and me, I think I have every right, Tabitha," Lucilla replied. "And I'm sure Mama will confirm she was glad to have them."

"I was, indeed," Lady Iverson agreed immediately. It was her habit to be flustered by the Wallaces' accusing manners, but with her daughter's act to follow, she found it was easier to keep her composure.

"Well, I still say it is unbecoming behavior to invite unrelated persons to dinner without your mama's leave, Lucy." Miss Wallace pouted.

"I quite agree," her mother said dampeningly, peering at Lucilla down her nose.

"A relief, then, that you were not subjected to the invitation," Lucilla smiled angelically.

The retort that rose on either lady's lips was halted by the arrival of the tea, and as the maid lingered over the tray in a fussing manner, the visitors were forced to find a different avenue of conversation.

"How is your dear father?" Lady Iverson asked Lady Wallace before the other woman could land on an alternative subject.

This vein of conversation was surprisingly embraced by Lady Wallace, who had long ago cast herself in the role of longsuffering devoted daughter. In the play that was her life, the lady was used cruelly by her jealous, self-serving elder brother, who prevented her from seeing their dearly loved parent. The reality of the situation was somewhat different.

Lady Wallace, born Miss Cooke, was the daughter of a man referred to by Lady Edevane as a vulgar Cit. Mr. Amos Cooke, Senior, was in late middle age when he made his fortune by way of a mercantile venture that he had entered with his then nineteen-year-old son. The fruitful partnership endowed both men with more than enough funds to make a crack at entering the fringes of Society, but both were content with their personal position in life and uninclined to change it.

All of Cooke Senior's social ambitions were funneled into his daughter. She had been almost seven years of age when her father and brother had begun to make their mark in business. When her mother died suddenly three years later, her father decided it would be in her best interests to go to a school where she could be educated. There she would be able to rub shoulders with the fancy young ladies and befriend daughters from noble families who would potentially enable her to break into the upper echelons.

As Miss Cooke, she had been sensible of her advantages but conscious of her shortcomings. She was not a beauty and lacked the breeding of her classmates, but she was a considerable heiress. Unfortunately, money was not enough to allow her entrance into the hallowed halls of the *ton*. All of her flirting and scheming could not attract the men she wanted to notice her. She was well aware of the reasons that Sir John Wallace, her eventual husband, made his offer for her hand, and his gaming proclivities were not cured upon gaining control of her significant dowry.

After squandering the funds he had so cleverly obtained through his advantageous marriage, Sir John found himself bound to a thoroughly unlikeable woman. Thankfully, her own considerable haughtiness prevented her from recognizing her good-natured but rather vulgar parent until she found herself in need of money.

In all honesty, Lady Wallace could see nothing wrong with her behavior. She had learned that ill-bred mushrooms were below the notice of the landed gentry and aristocrats to which she aspired and so treated even her own family in a similar manner. As the daughter of a wealthy man, though, she considered it her due to be allowed to call upon the family bank when it was needed. It was this attitude that irked her elder brother, but he was in no position to prevent her from calling on their father for money while the parent lived.

Her father's illness greatly concerned Lady Wallace. That gentleman had handed much of his business to his son, and Cooke Junior was not inclined to pay the rather hefty bills that their father would have signed away without a thought. She had every reason to wish her father would soon recover, but she was beginning to worry her creditors might begin to talk about her inability to pay her way.

Recently, she had found herself desperate enough to have made a furtive call to her brother's home to request the money she required to settle her significant debts. His response had been less than satisfactory, for he had given her a fraction of what she needed and counseled her to make adjustments and economies.

Lady Iverson's polite inquiry as to her father's health was all Lady Wallace needed to let her grievances flow fully. Her tirade mainly consisted of accusations against her jealous brother and over-seasoned affection for the father she would have turned her nose up at had she seen him in the street. Lady Iverson, of course, took her friend at her word. She had no reason to discount the version of events as Lady Wallace gave them, and as she was unacquainted with either of the Cooke men herself, there was little expectation of hearing a rebuttal.

"Uncle Cooke is exceedingly disobliging," Miss

Wallace pouted between her mother's complaining. She received no encouragement to continue, for Miss Iverson had picked up her tambour frame and was engaged in setting a neat row of stitches instead of taking part in the conversation.

Lucilla had heard the same grumbles many times over the years of their acquaintance. Being an observant individual prone to meditative reflections, she was not at all convinced that Miss Wallace and her mother were victims of a jealous and vindictive relative. Her own opinion was that, like a piece of paper, stories also had two sides, and she had so far only read the side that the Wallace ladies had written on.

After what seemed like an age to Lucilla, the unbidden guests finally stood to take their leave.

"I have a mind to step over and visit dear Lady Jersey," Lady Wallace declared, waving off her hostess's offer of a carriage to take them home. She finished pulling on her gloves and waited impatiently as her daughter completed the same task while chattering incessantly on some subject or other at a rather bored Miss Iverson a little away from their mothers.

"Tabitha, do come along! We'll walk to Berkeley Square before we return home," Lady Wallace said in a hurrying tone.

"Yes, Mama," Miss Wallace answered in a sweet tone before turning back to Lucilla with an even sweeter expression. "Dear Lucy, I shall no doubt see you at the Walsinghams'. Do be sure not to make a spectacle of yourself. It is not at all the thing to favor gentlemen with more than two dances together, you know."

"We do not go to the Walsinghams'. But as I have yet to do what you warn me against, I confess I am at a loss as to why you would feel the need to counsel me," Lucilla replied, clasping her hands lightly behind her back and smiling docilely.

"Only it is just the sort of thing you would do, dearest, and as I have been about town longer and know how to behave in company, I feel it is my duty as your closest friend to school you."

"Let me assure you, Tabitha, that I am quite capable of navigating Society by my mother's side."

"La, as though you would listen to your mama," Miss Wallace tittered.

Lucilla, annoyed by this overstep, blinked slowly and forced a smile to her face that admirably mimicked Miss Wallace's own sickly sweet and sanctimonious expression before replying, "And what exactly makes you think I would listen to you, Tabitha?"

Miss Wallace's smile died, and an irritated glare took up residence in its place, but before she could reply, her mother called out to her again, insisting that they immediately depart.

"Good day, Miss Wallace. Do have a lovely evening at the Walsinghams'," Miss Iverson said, smiling wholesomely.

Miss Wallace turned on her heel, bobbed a quick curtsey to Lady Iverson, and departed Iverson House in her mother's wake with a furious flounce to her step.

"Lucy has become incredibly impertinent!" she muttered furiously as she walked beside her mother down the street in the direction of Berkeley Square. "It is high time someone gave her a talking to about her manners. Did you hear what she said to me, Mama? It is not to be borne. I am sure I should not be expected to bear such treatment. You must talk to dear Lady Iverson before she says something outrageous in company."

Lady Wallace did not answer, and when she finally drew a breath, Miss Wallace realized that they had walked straight past Lady Jersey's house, continued through Berkeley Square, and turned down a quiet street.

"Mama, where are we going?" she asked exasperatedly.

Lady Wallace still said nothing but handed a dirty-looking urchin a small coin and requested a hack be fetched on her behalf. An exceptionally ratty-looking hack eventually drew up to collect them. As the vehicle lurched into motion, she glared at her mother and said pertly, "Must we really hire such horridly cheap little carriages, Mother? It is quite beneath our dignity."

"Yes," Lady Wallace spat out venomously. Such an outburst from her rigidly composed and imposing mother had the profound effect of rendering Miss Wallace entirely speechless, and she reeled back in horror. "Really, Tabitha! You haven't the slightest notion how abhorrent it is to me to be seen in such a state. If word should get out that we have been reduced to such straits, we shall be done for."

"I do not understand, Mama. Surely Grandpapa—"

"My father is in no position to assist me," her mother practically screeched. "Stupid girl! My brother will soon be master of all, and he is no friend of ours."

"But Grandpapa would not—"

"Did you not hear me, you foolish girl?" Lady Wallace shouted. "Your grandfather made no provision for you, and as your blessed father has squandered what was mine, it is only so long before we are cast out by Society. It is as important as ever that we keep the Iversons close, and even more important that you make yourself agreeable to a suitable gentleman and marry."

"How can this be, Mama?" Tabitha said, terror coloring her tone as she stared wide-eyed at her parent.

"How? How can this be? It can be because your stupid grandfather is under my brother's thumb, and my brother wills it so."

"Why does Uncle Cooke hate us so?" her daughter exclaimed tearfully. Her mother only laughed mockingly and reiterated the oft-sung song of jealousy and spite.

"Hear me, Tabitha!" Lady Wallace said firmly. "You must marry, and soon. My father is not long for this world, and the money is already gone. Title or no, you must marry a gentleman that has money and can take care of us, for the lord knows your father and mine are no longer of use to either of us."

****

That same day, Lady Hartwell received her nephew graciously when he appeared in her drawing room and exclaimed when she spied the fading, yellowing bruises under his eyes.

"Heavens, Charles, have you met with an accident, dearest?" she gasped, her hands flying up to her face in horror.

"Not an accident. I'm afraid it was quite intentional," he said after greeting her, languidly throwing himself onto a sofa and putting his feet up.

Her ladyship's lips twisted irritably, and her manner flipped instantly from concern to exasperation. "Do remove your boots from my satin, if you please," she barked. He complied, but not without a sideways glare that escaped her notice.

"I've never understood this predilection your sex has with pugilism. Really, the idea of hitting one another for amusement—it is ridiculous!" Lady Hartwell said irately, fidgeting on the sofa.

"Which is why it is a pastime for men, not ladies," her nephew muttered under his breath. She raised an arched brow at him but refrained from requiring him to repeat himself.

"I should like to know why you are wasting your time in boxing saloons when you ought to be making yourself agreeable to Miss Iverson."

"I can assure you, ma'am, that I have been doing my level best in that quarter."

"Well, what do you have to show for it?" she asked mockingly. "Have you made any declaration? Has she accepted you?"

Moore's face twisted belligerently in response, but he had no words of rebuttal to offer. He had indeed done all that his aunt had suggested, and yet it seemed the temperamental young female pulled farther and farther away from him. When he had come upon her by chance in the park, his intention had been to charm her, but every syllable seemed only to annoy. He was at a loss as to why, for he had never failed so miserably to charm a woman before. The appearance of Oliver had rankled.

"I would perhaps not have quite so much trouble if your troublesome offspring would keep out of my way."

"Do you mean to tell me you find that boy to be a threat to your efforts? Oliver is a puppy, so green about the ears that he could be mistaken for grass, and you, with your airs and graces and fine clothes, are not capable of putting him in his place?" Lady Hartwell sneered.

"Have you seen Oliver lately, aunt?" Charles snapped back at her. "I tell you that he is not the little boy who left you last year. Saliston has quite transformed him. I dare swear you would not recognize him."

"I should recognize my own child anywhere," she snarled spitefully, for once feeling unsure of her own words. In truth, she had not laid eyes on Oliver since he had fled Calverley with the duke.

That she had lost control of her son was evident, but she had been confident her efforts to stymie him would be successful. After Saliston had re-asserted his interest in the boy and begun providing him with tutors and clothing, Lady Hartwell had sunk to devious methods to frustrate her son's progress. Whether it was the "accidental" staining of a coat or shirt, directions to the stablemaster to keep his horse unshod, or incessant bullying of his instructors, she had done her level best to prevent his growing in confidence.

She had yet to witness proof of the disappointment of her efforts, and she was such a woman that only the evidence of her own eyes would be sufficient to confirm her failure. Perhaps even then it would not be enough.

"Perhaps you would recognize his face, ma'am," Charles said mockingly. "But I can assure you that the boy is not the incompetent little fool you were at such pains to design."

"Pooh! He may dress as differently as he pleases, but he will surely bend to me, as he always has."

"I am not so sure, but do prove me wrong."

Lady Hartwell glared at her nephew, a violent glint shining in her eyes. It was a sparkle that was well hidden and rarely recognized by anyone of consequence around her, but it was well known among her staff and by her son. Mr. Moore was one of a sacred few who had never yet been subjected to the more sinister side of her, but his irreverence of late had begun to gall. As she was predominantly a selfish creature, full of her own importance, the affection she held him in was beginning to fade rapidly.

But he was still of use to her, for now.

"In any case, it is becoming more difficult for *me* to steer him. He's refused every one of my invitations to dine, and he won't come out with me to any of the clubs," Moore said complainingly. "I sent him a note yesterday to invite him to dine with Finch and me at Robinson's den, but he didn't even reply."

"Well, we must find another way to part them. If we cannot keep Oliver at the tables, we must find a way to turn him off the girl," Lady Hartwell said decisively. "We must make her undesirable. Nothing is quite as useful as a little rumor to tarnish a pretty gleam."

"I've already tried to warn *her* off *him*," Charles replied.

"Yes, well, pressure applied on both ends is more likely to be successful, I imagine. I will think on it," she said dismissively.

"I am for the ball at the Walsinghams' this evening," Moore said stiffly, rising and taking his leave of her. Both had their feathers ruffled by the visit, but they parted on cordial terms, both determined to succeed for their own reasons.

Several hours later, he entered the Walsingham ballroom and was disappointed to learn Miss Iverson was not in attendance. But Miss Wallace was present and put herself in his way almost as soon as he arrived.

He found her insipid, but it would not do to be rude to her and bear the consequence of having her whisper against him in Miss Iverson's ear, so he indulged her laughable efforts at flirtation. She was excessive in her flattery this particular evening, but after the bruising his ego had received from her friend, it was rather soothing instead of galling.

For her part, she had taken her mother's warnings to heart. In Mr. Moore, she saw a fashionable but untitled young man who aspired to the hand of a viscount's daughter. Not a negative word had she heard uttered about him. Indeed, if he was a suitable match for Lucilla, he would be an excellent one for the daughter of Sir John Wallace. The satisfaction of stealing one of Miss Iverson's suitors would merely be the cream on top. So she flirted, she simpered, laughed at his jokes, and flattered him.

Moore took care not to appear too eager. He danced twice with her but then favored another young lady with his attention. She, too, was at least mildly conscious of observing and falling within the social boundaries of a ball, so she engaged in dancing with other gentlemen during the course of the evening.

During one of these interludes, Mr. Moore found himself standing in just the right place to overhear a particularly useful conversation. Who the ladies he could hear were, he did not know, and they were clearly not aware that their conversation was of interest to anyone but themselves, for they made no effort to lower their voices.

While Miss Wallace twirled around the floor with some sallow youth of uncertain years, Mr. Moore became apprised of the knowledge she was, in fact, the granddaughter of an exceptionally wealthy merchant. The two ladies decried the manners of the lower classes and laughed at the girl's efforts to snare a landed gentleman.

"She may be the daughter of a baronet, but really, just look at the mother," one of the women chattered.

"If I've said it once, I've said it a thousand times, blood will out," her companion agreed.

"Sir John does not go out in company with her. Is it any wonder? Frigged out in fine clothes, but you can still see she is a vulgar."

"Well, he saw fit to marry her, in any case."

"His pockets were to let. Can one blame him for snatching at the chance to be free of his debts, poor dear?"

"Still, it is because of him that we must accept his wife and this daughter of his. None of us benefit from the money, so we are not compensated," said the woman disdainfully.

"I suppose you are right, my dear. It shall be interesting to see whether she makes a match this year," the other replied.

"Nothing but a title would do for the mother in her day. Sadly, for the daughter, I cannot think of any that would take her even with all that money behind her."

Chapter 21

Lady Hartwell had shunned the company of the *ton* since her arrival in town. She paid no calls, made no invitations, and received the same in return. Since her youth, she had held the annual Marriage Mart in disdain, but for the purpose of obtaining freedom from her controlling mother, she had chosen to marry and make her own way.

Marriage had not been what she expected. Her father's disinterest in his family had meant her mother was free to do as she chose, leaving her son and two daughters in the care of an army of indulgent nannies, governesses, and tutors, so it was only once her girls had reached a marriageable age that she took any interest in them. At that point, she busied herself with settling them in their own establishments as speedily as possible in order to return to her own pursuits, which essentially involved gambling and other unspecified pastimes.

With such an example, it is not to be wondered at that both her daughters grew to be self-absorbed and spoiled young ladies. The elder was married off to Mr. Moore, to whom she would bear a son and then succumb to influenza before the child's third birthday. The second daughter, seeing the state of her elder sister's life married to a fortune-hunting gamester, refused to be drawn into a similar situation and instead set about making herself agreeable to the young, handsome, and wealthy Lord

Hartwell.

His lordship's early death caused her considerable inconvenience. The spark of affection she had carefully cultivated and nourished during their courtship died in the early days of their marriage. Lord Hartwell had quickly developed a horror for his wife's unbridled anger and sought to shield their son from her, his efforts ultimately failing. However, while he had not successfully prevented her from raising their son, he *had* managed to hamstring her financially, for her abilities and rights over his fortune were limited, and those limits were guarded diligently.

Unfortunately, her predilection for games of chance was unabated, and the fact that she frequently lacked the funds to cover her losses was not enough to curb her habits. Her stipend was paid by Mr. White out of the estate for her personal use, and additional funds were given to provide for the needs of the household and her son. However, much of the latter money never made it to where it was supposed to go.

To be sure, outwardly, there was no reason to suspect anything was amiss in the running of Calverley. But had anyone thought to enquire of its staff as to whether they were content or if they were reasonably compensated for their work, a different picture might have been drawn.

Her ladyship dressed herself in the height of fashion, taking herself off to London often but only rarely making appearances at the social events of the Season. She cultivated a few friendships she felt might be useful, but on the whole, no one really knew her well or saw her often. The words "poor Lady Hartwell" were habitually used in description of her, for she had taken great care to maintain an image of heartbroken widowhood and maternal dignity.

It was upon one of these friends that she now imposed herself and successfully gained herself an invitation to a select ladies' evening card party at which the likes of Countess Lieven and Mrs. Drummond-Burrell would also be in attendance. As her object was to begin a quiet assault on Miss Iverson's otherwise unimpeached reputation, she felt all of her good luck in discovering two of the haughtiest Patronesses in the room upon her arrival at the party. She made her way to the table where they were seated and was greeted and invited to join their set.

"Did you hear that Sir William Morris died last month?" said one of the women as her ladyship seated herself.

"Oh, how very sad," Countess Lieven exclaimed mournfully. "And that poor little wife of his, no children in the ten years since they wed."

"None from his first wife either, mind," another lady replied. "Everyone blamed her, of course. But little Josie has given him none either, so I can't but feel the first Lady Morris was shamefully used in the end."

"The estate will go to his nephew, I hear. He is nearer to little Josie in age. I wonder if there will be anything in *that*?" the first lady mused.

Eventually, introductions were made, and the first woman was identified as Mrs. Hurst. Her companion was introduced as Mrs. Fernsby, and Lady Hartwell eventually deduced they were, in fact, sisters and close friends of the Countess Lieven. She smiled inwardly at her luck and eagerly awaited an opportune moment in which to inject a word in edgewise on the subject of Miss

Iverson. Fortunately, she had not long to wait.

"Have you seen that horrid Wallace girl lately? Heavens, what a sight," Mrs. Fernsby exclaimed.

"I confess I am quite shocked at her, but then, what can one expect with her breeding?" Countess Lieven replied austerely as she examined her cards.

"That's as may be. There is money in the mix," Mrs. Hurst added. "I am at a loss as to why she is throwing herself at every single gentleman. Surely the mother has enough sense to know if the thing were to be carefully cultivated, and with a dowry from that rich grandpapa, it would go a long way to securing a good match."

"It is an odd thing, to be sure," the countess mused. "The two of them make such a show of their friendship with the Iverson family; one would have thought they'd take a leaf out of *that* book."

"Indeed. A pretty-behaved girl, the Iverson Jewel," Mrs. Fernsby replied. "Lady Sefton's little nickname for her, I hear."

"She's quite the thing, isn't she? All the gentlemen are mad for her, but she's quite enamored with your boy, I hear, Lady Hartwell," Mrs. Hurst said in a congratulatory tone.

With an opening so fortuitously presented, Lady Hartwell jumped in with both feet and said, "Alas, I do not see it ending favorably."

"Heavens, why ever not?" Mrs. Hurst exclaimed, making no effort to hide her shock. The other two ladies also looked askance at her, a mixture of disbelief and concern swimming about their countenances.

"I'm afraid I have heard a little rumor about Miss Iverson," Lady Hartwell answered in a melancholy voice, intending to arouse sadness and pity in her audience. While Mrs. Hurst and her sister seemed open to hearing her "little rumor," it was plain that Countess Lieven was not teetering on any edge.

"Absurd," the countess said dismissively, tapping her cards on the table impatiently.

"I am quite certain she has set her cap at my dear son in an effort to snare my cousin Saliston," her ladyship continued, undaunted by the contemptuous glint in Countess Lieven's eye. "I have heard they were seen stealing away together at a gathering recently. It is such a shame, truly. My poor Oliver is quite besotted. But I felt compelled to warn him. He is young, though. He will find another."

The countess did not miss the dramatic flair in Lady Hartwell's delivery. She pursed her lips carefully and stared at the other woman as if she were sizing her up. Mrs. Hurst and Mrs. Fernsby, both prolific gossips of great renown, looked to their formidable friend for their cue and, seeing the suspicious gaze upon her sharp face, looked back at the downcast Lady Hartwell with curiosity.

"Dear me, I am sure I've never heard a whisper," Mrs. Fernsby said archly.

"Nor I. How very strange," her sister continued. "At which party did this event occur, Lady Hartwell? I should very much like to know."

"Oh, I should not at all wish to contribute to gossip about a young lady, I'm sure," she replied.

"I confess, Lady Hartwell, I am unsure of your motive, " the countess queried. "If you do not wish to contribute to gossip, I see no reason to mention such a scandalous titbit to us now. I do not believe it at all, myself, and I shall certainly not repeat it anywhere."

"Nor I," Lady Hurst said archly. "Indeed, now I think on it, I can scarcely recall a single moment when the girl is ever unaccounted for. One can see the satellites about her wherever she goes."

"Now that *I* think on it, Lady Hartwell," the countess said accusingly, "did you not some years ago tell me that your son was a simpleton?"

Lady Hartwell had the grace to blanch at the question. She had indeed made slight comments about Oliver throughout his youth in an effort to convey the idea that he was perhaps a little impaired, seizing upon the opportunity whenever an acquaintance would ask after his schooling whether he might be sent to Eton or later to university. It now came back around to bite her, for the Countess Lieven was a formidable woman to annoy.

"I am surprised, for the young gentleman that I have gotten to know these last few months is anything other than an imbecile," she continued. "Indeed, he is quite the reverse. How do you answer, Lady Hartwell?"

Lady Hartwell stuttered an incoherent reply, and Countess Lieven rose abruptly from her seat, staring at the other woman distastefully. She leaned in so the rest of the party guests would not hear as she whispered harshly, "I am at a loss to understand your reasons, madam. But I will not be a party to whatever scheme it is you are hatching."

With that, she walked away from the table. Mrs. Hurst and Mrs. Fernsby both pursed their lips and stared at Lady Hartwell disdainfully before rising and following the countess. A few confused glances from other ladies followed them, but as their hostess chose that particular moment to announce supper to be ready, the baffling exchange was speedily forgotten.

Lady Hartwell, shaken somewhat by the direct reproof she had received, made no further attempts that evening. She decided the years of carefully grooming her façade would not go to waste on such an endeavor as besmirching Miss Iverson's name. Another method would need to be found, something real, something tangible that would prevent the backlash she had gotten from the frigid Countess Lieven and her cronies.

She spent the rest of the evening with cards in hand, smiling jovially whilst playing at loo. In her efforts to appear congenial she, unfortunately, caused a little chatter to begin. Mrs. Hurst watched her lose again and again. She made several lighthearted but vociferous attempts to convince her companions to increase the stakes. Still, she was laughingly shouted down each time and reminded that it was not a gentleman's club.

Mrs. Hurst continued to watch and came to the disturbing conclusion that Lady Hartwell might be a rather dangerous woman. She was pretty and could undoubtedly make herself agreeable, but there seemed to be something menacing lingering under the surface, and Mrs. Hurst decided quite firmly to avoid her in the future.

****

While his mother spent her time plotting new methods of causing disturbance in his life for reasons unknown, Lord Hartwell was to be found by Miss Iverson's side. Whether at a ball or other gathering, riding or driving their respective horses in Hyde Park, or quietly talking or reading together in her mother's drawing room, there was scarce a day during which they did not spend a portion of their time together. During their assignations, they were strictly chaperoned, and neither for a moment thought of or suggested the idea of dispensing with this particular convention. Both of them still keenly felt the extreme luck that had favored them in not being seen the night of the masquerade.

They found themselves, this particular afternoon several weeks after the event, sitting together by the cold fire-grate in the drawing room at Iverson House, with Chico seated under Lord Hartwell's chair, poring over a stud book Miss Iverson had drawn out of her father's office. She had been explaining the origins of several of Lord Iverson's blood horses when it occurred to her that the stud book would serve as an excellent guide. It was meticulously organized, from the birth dates to the strains, the tribes they had been procured from, and the color, height, and prices.

"It is marvelous, pretty well a work of art," Oliver exclaimed as he ran down the list of births and deaths by year, which was then cross-referenced into a list of mares served by studs each season.

"Papa will be so pleased you think so." Miss Iverson laughed. "It is rather his life's work."

"I should like to begin a venture somewhat like this," he replied almost distractedly as he continued to pore over the pages. "It would be a fascinating thing to travel the world, collecting horses wherever one went."

"Lord Iverson is content now to remain at home, watching his collection grow and thrive in England, I am pleased to say," Lady Iverson remarked smilingly from her place upon the sofa where she sat listening to the conversation and idly mending a linen shirt.

"Mama did not like to be left at home, nor did she like to leave it herself," Lucilla said lightly, smiling fondly at her mother.

"I'm sure I quite understand why Lord Iverson would not want to be away from home," Oliver remarked in a knowing tone, which had the effect of gratifying both ladies.

Lady Iverson watched the couple from her seat across the room with an indulgent eye. In the preceding weeks, it had become profoundly evident to her ladyship that her daughter was well on her way to falling in love. The young gentleman she had apparently settled on was improved in leaps and bounds upon closer acquaintance.

He had seemed at first to be clumsy and childish, with a puppyish ardor that was not unlike Alfred Russell. But by steady degrees, he had found his feet, and the immaturity waned and suddenly disappeared entirely overnight.

What had passed between her daughter and Lord Hartwell at Vauxhall was a mystery to the viscountess. It had taken quite a bit of time and reflection for her to see it was in the wake of the masquerade that Lord Hartwell had emerged as the clear preference for Lucilla's affections. After consideration, she realized the Duke of Saliston's efforts in that quarter had fallen flat that evening. And Lady Iverson had not for a moment entertained the thought that Alfred Russell would arise as a victor.

Lord Hartwell was still something of a dark horse himself, though, until his visits were a regular occurrence. He was now so often in the house that Lady Iverson had at one time risen to leave the room during a visit and was only called to earth when Lucilla had squeaked loudly at her as she passed through the door.

He would often remain for several hours at a time, but not always was he occupied with Miss Iverson. On one day he was closeted with Lord Iverson and a sketchbook that had been the viscount's constant companion in his youth while traveling through France and Italy. It had inspired many questions from Lord Hartwell, and they were all gladly answered, right up until the dinner gong was rung and Lady Iverson appeared in the doorway to good-naturedly inform the young gentleman that a place had been made up for him at the table and he was expected to remain for dinner. She had rather hoped the conversation would eventually end with an engagement. She was disappointed, however, for the only engagement formed that particular day was between the two gentlemen to tour the gallery at Gracewood.

As Lady Iverson sat watching the young people, she marveled at how well suited they were. Lucilla was not an idle girl, nor a flighty or nervous one, but of late it seemed anything might make her jump. Chico had scarcely left her side and had taken to following Lucilla about with his hackles half-raised in anticipation of a threat.

In contrast, Lord Hartwell had grown steady, the sort of steadiness that could only leaven Lucilla's suddenly tremulous energy. Besides that, their shared interests were abundant, and he being a humble and amiable sort, was not averse to letting a young lady teach him anything. He acknowledged her superior learning and skill in the saddle but was eminently teachable and was well on his way to being on par with her.

Lord Iverson was very happy with him, as was Matthew, and Lady Iverson knew herself to be growing extremely fond of him. Lady Edevane was unwilling to relinquish the idea of a match with the undoubtedly excellent but less youthful Duke of Saliston.

Lady Iverson lingered on the thought. She had wondered at the whole thing many times before and did not know what to make of the duke's attentions, let alone Lucilla's response to them. As the younger cousin had surged forward in favor, there did not seem to be any change one way or the other from Saliston. He still joined Hartwell and Lucilla whilst riding or driving and chatted amiably with her or asked her to dance. There had also been no change in Lucilla, except that it was now rather marked that Lord Hartwell was her preference and her smiles were for him.

They were laughing softly now at some remark Lucilla had made, her dark head and his fair bowed together over the table. Chico had risen and put himself between them, adamantly demanding attention from them, which was willingly given.

"How did you come to have this chap?" Oliver asked as he stroked the soft golden head that had been impatiently nudging at him.

"He was given to me by my brothers. Richard had got him from a soldier and was to bring him home to me, but in the end—" She had continued rather matter-of-factly but suddenly broke off. "Well, you know. So Edward brought him home when he returned from Spain."

"Ah, I see," he replied softly, letting the subject fall. They had spoken of her brothers before. He had been very interested to learn they had both served in the army. Lucilla's descriptions of them had sounded much like her cousin, who had become a rather good friend.

"I think you will like Edward," she said suddenly, in a happier voice.

"Will? Have you had word from him?"

The furtive glance she made in the direction of her mother made him suspicious of the following shake of her head. But she smiled, and he smiled back at her in return, as he always seemed to whether he meant to or not.

"But I hope he will return soon," she answered, an oddly knowing glint in her eye. It made him wonder if she knew more than she said.

"In any case, I am sure to like him, if he is at all like Matthew."

"Two peas in a pod, although Edward is somewhat less provoking," she said wryly, making him chuckle.

"He does so to annoy you."

"I know, which is all the more annoying," she exclaimed, her hands waving emphatically in mock annoyance.

"I shall endeavor to imitate Edward rather than Matthew in future, then," he replied, his shoulders shaking with laughter.

Her giggles softened, and she looked at him with amusement in her dark eyes. There was an almost expectant expression in them the longer he held her gaze. Then she glanced away and began to talk of other things.

Chapter 22

Matthew Iverson did not require anyone's permission to marry. He belonged to indulgent parents in his Uncle Jasper and Mama, and never having met with a denial of his requests, he had no expectation of receiving one now. But he wanted their approval all the same, so he took himself to Iverson House one morning when he knew Lord and Lady Iverson would be home, for the express purpose of gaining it.

He met first with his uncle and made the declaration that he intended to seek Mr. Russell's permission to propose marriage to Caroline, at which his Uncle Jasper engulfed him in a good-natured embrace, enthusiastically slapping his back and exclaiming that it was about time he got up the nerve.

"I dare swear her parents have been expecting it for weeks," Lord Iverson chortled. "Go on, then, and tell your mama and Cilla. They'll be that pleased."

Lord Iverson then thrust his nephew out into the hallway before retreating into his study with the promise to join the family party in just a few minutes.

Summarily dismissed, Matthew went to share the news with the ladies. Cilla went pink with pleasure and congratulated him with almost as much hearty excitement as her father had. On the other hand, Lady Iverson, immensely overjoyed, was inclined first to become something of a waterpot before she finally reached out to the young man she had raised and clasped him tightly, whispering her congratulations and sureties of his future happiness.

They were interrupted by Lord Iverson, who entered the room with a spring in his step and a small box in his hand that drew a startled gasp of recognition from his wife.

"Here now, my boy," he said in his deep baritone, holding the box out reverently with both hands toward his nephew, encouraging him to take it. The tears streaming down Lady Iverson's face caused Matthew to hesitate for a moment. When he opened the box, he found a gold filigree bracelet, a rather stunning piece of craftsmanship, with elegant little flowers and beaded with tiny pearls.

"Heavens, what a pretty piece," Cilla whispered, reaching out to touch it reverently with her fingertips.

"It is rather exceptional," Matthew murmured thoughtfully, picking it up out of the box and inspecting it closely.

"It was your mother's," Lady Iverson said with a sad smile.

"My brother had it made for her before they wed," Lord Iverson added. "I should think it is only right that the new Mrs. Iverson wear it."

"She's not accepted him yet," Cilla warned humorously, shaking her finger and wrinkling her nose.

"But of course she will." Her mother gasped in horror at her daughter, not understanding the jest.

"It's quite all right, Mama," Matthew said, gently patting Lady Iverson's hand. He looked at his cousin with a rather wicked smile before continuing, "Cilla may joke, but she will come by her desserts soon enough, I'm sure."

"*I'm* sure I have not the slightest notion what you mean, Matty," his cousin replied coyly. "But in all seriousness, I wish you all the happiness in the world. You are making an excellent choice, and I am very glad of it for myself as much as for you."

"I am glad to hear it."

"In fact, I think it would be wise for you to make haste and visit Mr. Russell immediately."

"What? Miss Russell is sure to be at home now. I should have better luck making an appointment to see her father another day," Matthew said hesitantly.

"Not at all, for I happen to know that Caroline is visiting her aunt today and will not return until this evening," Lucilla replied with a serene smile. "You will be quite safe in visiting her father today, I can assure you."

Her cousin was quite perplexed and said hurriedly, "I had only intended to inform you all today. I confess, I am quite unprepared to complete the task."

"Well, there really is no time quite like the present, dear Matthew," Lucilla said sweetly. She intended to play with him, but if gentle cajoling sent him on his way to Green Street, she would not consider it a bad thing. She was sure he would obtain permission quickly and had every expectation that Caroline would receive his addresses with pleasure. There could be no possible negative to urging him on his way.

He hesitated only for a few minutes more. Lady Iverson was able to confirm Mrs. Russell and her daughter had indeed gone to visit a family member outside of London, which had the effect of calming Matthew's slightly ruffled nerves. The final clinch was applied when Lord Iverson offered him a nip of his favorite port and talked sensibly of why it would be very reasonable to get the thing settled with the girl's father straight away.

"I will call on him to discuss the settlements as soon as you give me the word, my boy," Lord Iverson said in his cheerful, confident voice. "I expect we will be able to come to an agreeable understanding. Russell is a sensible man."

His nerves quelled by the sip of port and his uncle's confidence, Matthew declared he would go to Mr. Russell that very minute and promptly took himself off to Green Street.

Lucilla was soon proven to be correct, for the very upright old butler who answered the door informed him gently that the ladies were from home. Upon being told that he wished to see Mr. Russell, the butler's eyes widened and brightened, and he hurriedly led Matthew to his master's study.

Permission to address his daughter was speedily given. However, Mr. Russell felt it of vital importance to discuss the financial implications of the match. He spoke plainly on the subject, wishing to be certain Matthew understood that Miss Russell would receive only a small portion, for the family was fixed in such a way that there was very little to be set aside for her. These concerns were acknowledged, but Matthew cared not for such considerations.

"I am not my uncle's heir, Mr. Russell," he stated firmly and calmly to his prospective father-in-law. "But a very handsome living will come to me, and my uncle has made further assurances to me. In all honesty, sir, I am not concerned with the financial aspects. I have what

I believe is a reasonable understanding of how you are fixed. Now that I have your approval, I will tell my uncle, and he will call on you to discuss the settlements and make sure that all is as you would wish for Caroline."

This information caused the careful and reserved Mr. Russell to express a sensibility hitherto unseen by any of his acquaintance. He was an affectionate parent and would have been an indulgent one had he been in possession of the funds his forbears had squandered. As it happened, the meager figure that he was able to bestow on his only daughter had been the result of much scraping and saving, and it was a source of considerable pain to him that he had so little to give her. The knowledge that the young man before him was not only a sensible and well-brought-up gentleman but one who had every intention of supporting his daughter regardless of her situation was gratifying and comforting to her father.

The elder Mr. Russell spent almost an entire hour talking with Mr. Iverson and found him to be even more exceptional than he had previously determined. He had, of course, heard talk of nothing and no one else but Mr. Matthew and Miss Lucilla for months, but he had not so far been allotted a tête-à-tête with either. Now the thing was done, it was gratifying to know that the young man was a learned and grounded one rather than a neck-or-nothing—or worse, a gamester.

After a comfortable cose in which the two gentlemen developed a better understanding of one another, Matthew rose to take his leave of his host and was about to depart when the younger Mr. Russell appeared. Seeing their guest was leaving, Alfred volunteered to escort him to the door and was given the news in the strictest confidence.

"Well, I must say it'll be a relief to my mother to have her settled," the younger Mr. Russell remarked, making an effort to sound knowing as he walked the length of the narrow hall with Matthew. "I myself am quite well read when it comes to the subject of proposals. Perhaps I might be able to offer a suggestion or two?"

"I assure you, Alfred, I am quite capable," Matthew replied with an amused smile.

"Really, I am sure I can assist. Have you thought of a gift, perhaps?" Alfred inquired helpfully.

"I was actually given something today that I think will be suitable on that point."

"Come now, you can't be giving my sister some cheap little trinket. It must be something romantic," the younger Russell declared emphatically.

"Would my late mother's bracelet be sufficient, do you think?" Matthew asked quellingly.

"I should think so. May I see it?" Alfred answered, innocently ignorant of his companion's tone.

Matthew found himself unable to maintain his momentary pique. Instead, he burst into laughter, owning to himself that in spite of his varying moods, Alfred was charming in his own childish and disarming sort of way.

"I should let you see it, but I would be afraid that you might lose it," Matthew replied with a grin.

"Here now. That's vastly unfair," Alfred exclaimed hotly. "A little piece of ribbon is hardly the same as a bracelet."

"All the same to you, I think I'll keep hold of it. No telling where it might end up, otherwise."

"I know you are bamming me," the young man said

indignantly as his companion laughed. "But it's mighty unfair to bring that up."

"I'm sure Caroline has mentioned it more than once. Would that be right?"

"Yes, and it is mighty mean of her, too."

"Well, what can you expect, dear boy?" Matthew asked, still smiling. "It was a very simple thing to hold onto."

"The fact of it is that I had to write a note when I was at Gott's, so I took out my pocketbook, which is where I had expressly tucked the damn ribbon for safekeeping, and when we all came together for the party, not an hour later, I found it was gone," Alfred explained in a hushed and irritable voice. "I swear, when I saw it fall out of the book, I put it directly into my coat pocket. I recall it perfectly because I was with Ponsonby, and he asked me why I was carrying a piece of ugly ribbon, so I had to explain it to him."

"Well, I'm sure it is out in the world somewhere," Matthew chuckled heartily, clapping his hand on Alfred's shoulder companionably.

"It is most unfair to have it constantly brought up," the other young man huffed. "It is not as though any harm came of it anyway."

Matthew agreed with him consolingly and promised never to bring it up again and engaged even to convince Caroline to refrain from needling him on the subject also, which successfully mollified her brother's ruffled nerves.

****

While Lord Hartwell had managed to admirably conceal his concerns regarding the identity of her abductor from Miss Iverson, his cousins were both considerably stung by the obvious suspicion with which Oliver regarded them. Saliston, upon his return from the country sporting a livid bruise on his jaw, had been questioned several times about the reason for his leaving town so suddenly after the masquerade.

Oliver's queries were careful and pointed, intended to determine if any discrepancy might be found within the answers he received. Saliston answered promptly and without guile, but after a day or two, it seemed to Oliver that there was something he was not saying about his trip to Derbyshire. For instance, the bay horse he claimed to have taken a fall from while he was away had been present in the London mews the entire time the duke had been out of town.

Oliver did not intend to leap to a conclusion. There were undoubtedly many reasons for George to go into the country. Why he would then conceal those reasons was of mild concern, but Oliver was conscious of an innate trust in his cousin that was not easily shaken. He wanted to believe there was a reason for the concealment that was not connected to the attempted kidnapping of Miss Iverson.

Where he stood on the subject of Mr. Moore was entirely different. Having come upon Charlie talking to an obviously irate Lucilla was disquieting. Still, to then notice the faint yellowing bruises across his cousin's face—well, that was not just disquieting, it was downright alarming. The fact that the bruising had gone unnoticed by Lucilla was merely a trick of the light, for the shade of the tree and the way Charlie had tipped his hat brim had admirably concealed the contusion.

He still wanted to give his cousin the benefit of the doubt. Still, after carefully considering the various incidences in which Charlie had behaved with odious over-familiarity with the young lady, Oliver began to wonder if he really knew his cousin and his motives. And the more he thought along that particular vein, the more he wondered if he really knew the same of Saliston, too.

While Matthew Iverson was tasked with gathering the approbation of his family and Miss Russell's and studiously planned his proposal to the lady herself, Oliver was putting his mind to cautiously determining the cause of Mr. Moore's bruises in order to weigh up whether he believed the answer.

They sat together in a cushioned booth at one of Charlie's favorite clubs. It was a quiet afternoon, but the rooms would shortly begin to fill with young bucks and sharps, all bent on an evening of frivolity and wastefulness that had long since died out of Oliver's blood. He nursed a glass of liquor but refused any suggestion of playing cards with anyone. Instead, he talked, and ever so slowly and deliberately, he worked his way around to the subject that was at the forefront of his mind.

"I was surprised not to see you at the masquerade," Oliver mused as he swirled his glass and lounged back against the cushions in the booth. His cousin sat across the table from him, carefully counting and sorting a jumbled deck of cards.

"What? Oh, at Vauxhall," Mr. Moore said quickly and rather dismissively. "Not generally my sort of thing."

"I should have thought it was exactly your sort of thing."

"And what do you mean by that, may I ask?" Moore looked up from his deck and eyed his young cousin suspiciously, but Oliver was not looking at him. Instead, he was peering into his tumbler curiously as though searching for something, admirably concealing interest in his cousin's response.

"Hm? Oh. Only that it seemed the sort of thing you would like. Masks, intrigues, a little debauchery, perhaps."

"You have odd ideas of what I find amusing."

"If I have, it is only because you gave them to me, cousin," Oliver said with a disinterested shrug. "Either way, I should have thought you'd make an appearance."

"I intended to," Moore admitted. He did not take his gaze from Oliver's face as he continued, saying, "But I got rather carried away in the sport at Gott's. By the time I took note of the time, it seemed late to make my way to the gardens, so I stayed."

"Fair enough," Oliver replied as he refilled his glass, and silence descended on the table. With another wary glance at his cousin, Charlie went back to his sorting, glancing up every now and then in an effort to gauge Oliver's mood. He chose to change the subject and suggest Oliver take part in a little jaunt about the town with him and some cronies.

"It'll be a jolly good evening."

"I don't suppose that is what you told Worland," Oliver muttered under his breath.

"I'm sorry?"

"It is nothing. No, I don't think I'll join you."

"Whyever not? Is Saliston keeping you locked up?" Charlie said sarcastically.

"George is not my keeper. I do as I please. I do not find evenings spent drinking and gaming in excess to be particularly fulfilling."

"He says, as he takes another glass of port," his cousin replied, rolling his eyes.

"It is watered, and it is only my third."

Moore frowned. Oliver's behavior was markedly changed to an alarming degree. He had himself warned Lady Hartwell that the boy was different, but the idea that Oliver was not even mildly susceptible to suggestion as he had previously always been was becoming even more a matter of concern.

For his part, Oliver considered his cousin's excuses and behavior carefully in return. Having chosen in recent weeks to spend his time with such young gentlemen as Matthew Iverson and Ferdy Kimbley, it dawned on him that his cousin was rather low company by comparison. He was unconvinced by Charlie's excuses for his absence from the masquerade, but he was still not sure it meant he was responsible for Miss Iverson's assault. Oliver decided to try one last direct question, as he had with Saliston previously.

"How came you by that bruise on your face a few weeks ago? I had meant to ask at the time, but it quite flew out of my head."

Moore blinked quickly, and a slight frown creased his brow for just enough of a moment that Oliver took note of it. Then he said, "Got myself into a brawl, I'm afraid."

"Lord, with who?" Oliver exclaimed. He had never known his cousin, whose rather keen sense of self-preservation was well-tuned, to swing a punch at anyone, so he considered it rather unlikely that Charlie had been in a brawl, but for the sake of hearing the excuse further expanded, Oliver put on his best effort to appear shocked and dismayed.

"Geoffrey Knightsbridge, if you can believe it." Moore snorted distastefully.

Oliver frowned at this but managed to conceal his concern by asking another question. He did not follow much else of the conversation and soon made an excuse to leave, but the idea that his cousin might not be lying about the cause of his injury was now a strong possibility. And it would now be rather a simple task to confirm it—all he needed to do was ask Sir Geoffrey if it was true.

Chapter 23

It was becoming a more frequent pastime for Mr. Moore to spend several minutes at a time burning the irritating notes he received from his creditors every few days. It seemed that patience was ceasing to be a virtue with several of them in particular, and it was never very long before the papers that fed his fire were replaced afresh. He was himself losing patience with the situation, so the frustration was rather evenly spread about, but it would serve no one if he sat doing nothing. So instead, he took himself off to the Westrop ball where he had every expectation of meeting Miss Iverson.

When he arrived, he found that she was indeed in attendance. She was deep in conversation with a freckled young woman, and her cousin Matthew Iverson was hovering nearby. Charles was about to make his way over when a voice checked him.

"What a perfect shade of blue your coat is, Mr. Moore. I do declare, it is as though you are dressed especially to match me."

He turned to find Miss Wallace smiling at him coquettishly, holding her fan very deliberately across her chest. He saw immediately that the color of her dress was not at all the same shade of blue as his coat and was annoyed she had distracted him from his course. Then he recalled the conversation he had overheard at the Walsingham party and found it much easier to plaster a smile on his face.

"Indeed, Miss Wallace, it is positively providential," he purred.

She fluttered under his gaze and laughed for no apparent reason as she inexpertly flapped her fan. "I am so delighted to see you here this evening. It seems an age since last we spoke."

"It seems an age whenever a day passes without seeing you," he replied, laying it on rather thicker than he normally would when engaging in a flirtation. But if she was as wealthy as he had heard, it might be worth the effort of stroking her self-importance.

"La, what a thing to say." She giggled, flicking her fan closed and playfully rapping his knuckles.

Mr. Moore put his hands behind his back and rubbed his stinging fingers but managed to hide his irritation behind an indulgent smile. She really was quite horridly familiar, but it wouldn't do to put her off when she might be of use if Miss Iverson remained aloof. He fought the urge to look around for the other young lady and instead showered pleasantries and compliments on the one before him. As he did so, he looked at her more closely and found that while she was pretty enough, everything about her seemed a little too much—too much mouth, too much forehead, too much nose and eyes. Once these imperfections were noticed, it was all the harder to look past the inherent arrogance in her posture and the artificial nature of her laugh. But all of this could be forgiven if the fortune was large enough.

Across the room, Miss Iverson was entirely unaware that Moore had arrived. She was engrossed in conversation with Caroline Russell, who had earlier in the day accepted Matthew's proposal of marriage. The engagement was to be announced within days and would be general knowledge before the evening was up. However, the newness of it was still felt among those nearest to the couple, and the two young ladies, in particular, were still very caught up in the moment.

"I have never worn anything so fine before," Caroline said as she gently touched the delicate gold bracelet that Matthew had bestowed on her as a wedding gift. "I am quite overcome. I never expected such a handsome gift."

"There is none more deserving than you, my dear Caro," Lucilla replied, smiling.

"I'm sure there are, but I am flattered you should say so, all the same." Her friend laughed.

"I've not seen my father so excited as when he brought that out for Matthew to give to you. It was made for Matthew's mother, my uncle's wife."

"Yes, he told me so. It is so very special. I shall treasure it always."

"As he will you, or he shall have me to answer to." Lucilla laughed in mock warning, looking in Matthew's direction and arching her eyebrows.

He stood only a few feet away but was engaged in conversation with another young gentleman. When he caught Lucilla's eye on him, he disengaged himself and made his way back to the two ladies, and as he approached them, so too did Lord Hartwell. He greeted the other young man enthusiastically.

"Hart! How d'you do, dear boy?"

"I am quite well, Matty. What has you grinning ear to ear?"

"Heavens, you've not heard yet?" Miss Iverson broke in. "He has asked my dear Miss Russell to marry him. Is he not the luckiest man alive?"

Caroline blushed pleasantly at her friend as Lucilla looped their arms together.

"Undoubtedly so. My felicitations, Miss Russell," said Lord Hartwell, punctiliously bowing. "And to you, Matty. Rather sly of you. You never said a word."

"Well, I'm surprised Alfred didn't let it slip." Mr. Iverson laughed. "I couldn't let it go more than a day for fear he'd say something. In the end, it was all rather hurried and anticlimactic, I'm afraid."

"It was perfect," replied Miss Russell, looking affectionately up at her betrothed.

"Dear me, an excess of emotion in public! Whatever will happen next?" Lucilla said banteringly. "Come, Caro, I have someone to introduce you to. Will we see you at supper, Lord Hartwell?"

"I should like that immensely," he agreed, and the two ladies departed.

"Well, I shan't beat about the bush, dear boy, but when are you going to work up *your* nerve?" Matthew asked pointedly when they were finally alone.

"I'm sorry?"

"You will be, I imagine," his friend said with a substantial dollop of sarcasm in his tone, taking a sip from his glass.

Hartwell stared blankly, unsure how to reply. It was the first time anyone had passed comment on the seriousness of his association with Lucilla, and it was plain that Matthew was rather confident in his assessment. Hartwell was aware of some mild discomfort under Matthew's steady gaze but managed to hide it admirably by feigning ignorance of the meaning in his friend's statement and awkwardly steering the subject toward Alfred instead.

"How came you to tell Alfred? I was sure you were not particularly close to the fellow."

"No, I am not, but he happened to come in when I was with his father, and so he was told," Matthew replied. "Let me tell you, do not mention that episode about the ribbon unless you want to set him off on a story. He gets mighty put out. Caroline has not let him forget it."

Oliver's ears pricked, and his eyes narrowed suspiciously. "Indeed? What sort of story does he have to tell about it?"

"Apparently, he dropped the thing when he was with Ponsonby at that horrid little house that Gott runs," Matthew said, offhandedly summarizing the debacle.

"I see," Oliver murmured thoughtfully. "Ponsonby, eh? I don't know him well, do you?"

"I'd have thought you'd know him very well. He's rather chummy with your cousin Moore, I believe."

"With Charlie?"

"Yes, practically joined at the hip during school. Never quite understood why. Ponsonby has always been a rather sensible sort. Can't imagine what he sees in Moore," Matthew said bluntly but suddenly paused as he recalled to whom he was speaking. "My apologies, he's your cousin, and I should not have said that."

"Not at all. I'm sure you have your reasons for thinking as you do, Matty."

"Well, yes," said his companion matter-of-factly. "But all the same, it is not for me to say so."

They turned the topic again, this time choosing their subject more carefully, but after a few minutes they were interrupted by Mrs. Russell, who requested that her future son-in-law accompany her to meet a distant relative who had expressed interest in making his acquaintance.

"Now that you are to be one of the family, we must show you off a little," the lady said cheerfully as she bore him away, with Matthew smiling apologetically to Oliver as he went.

While he was not glad to be left alone, Oliver made use of it by taking himself to the refreshment table and quietly slipping behind a curtain that led onto a long balcony, which he found to be quite fortuitously vacant. Walking to the very end, he leaned on the marble balustrade and gazed out over the small garden while he mulled over the information Matthew Iverson had inadvertently provided him.

It was becoming evident that all roads led back to Charlie in one way or another. He claimed to have been at Gott's the night of the masquerade, and now Matthew had confirmed Alfred's presence there in the company of one of Charlie's closest friends, too.

The story that he'd brawled with Knightsbridge was absurd. Charlie was always far too careful of his appearance to get himself into a scrap, but it was also entirely out of character for him to fight. He was altogether untrained and unskilled in pugilism, having always preferred to play at cards or dice and charm his way out of a confrontation. Corroboration from an eyewitness was required, and who better to ask than the opponent himself? Perhaps Sir Geoffrey could also confirm whether Charlie had indeed been at Gott's the entire evening or not.

Oliver sighed loudly, steeling himself for an unpleasant conversation that he knew he must have if he was ever to experience another moment of peace in the presence of his cousin. Just as he was about to return to the ballroom, a sliver of light suddenly shone from behind him, and he turned to see Miss Iverson standing in the archway.

"Lord Hartwell, whatever are you doing out here?" she whispered loudly. She did not come out onto the balcony but remained in the archway, holding the heavy curtain open wide enough to see him. With a conspiratorial smile, she said, "I thought I saw you come this way. Are you hiding from someone?"

"No, not at all," he replied with a laugh. "I was merely in search of some fresh air."

"Well, as much as I should like to join you, I'm afraid it would be quite improper," Miss Iverson said, taking a step back and letting the curtain fall. He waited a moment before returning to the ballroom, choosing to enter through one of the other archways on the balcony.

She had lingered near the curtains, so it took only a moment for him to find her in the crowd. She smiled brightly as he approached. He smiled back at her and almost reached out to touch her. Thankfully he regained his senses before he did so, and his hand fell, but not before she noticed. Inwardly she hoped no one else had, and she glanced around and was relieved to see no one looking in their direction.

"Will you sit with me, Lord Hartwell?" Lucilla asked, gesturing to one of the small tables set up along the wall of the ballroom. He nodded in acquiescence and followed her, his hands carefully crossed behind his back.

"You seem out of sorts suddenly. Is something wrong?"

"Oh, no," Oliver answered, too quickly to provide reassurance. "Nothing at all."

"I do not believe you," she remarked with a gentle smile and a tilt of her head.

"It is nothing I wish to trouble you with, then."

"Ah, so there is something," Lucilla said playfully, her eyes twinkling with laughter. A rush of anxiety coursed through him, demanding that he confide what he knew about her attempted abduction. Hiding anything of importance from her felt unearthly, but Oliver remembered too keenly the depression she had fallen into after the attack. He refused to burden her again.

"Nothing of importance, I assure you. How do you like this match of your cousin's?" he asked, steering her away from her questions with one of his own.

"I am thrilled. He cannot have chosen better."

"Miss Russell certainly seems to be the right sort of lady for a man like Matthew," Oliver mused.

"Indeed, she is a very steady character, and clever," she agreed. "They are exceptionally well suited. I hope I might make a match half so happy."

He looked at her sharply, "Only half?"

"Well, one hardly has the right to assume better for oneself than others have. If the gentleman I marry makes me half as happy as Caroline is with my cousin, I should count myself very lucky, indeed," she answered. With a casual shrug, she glanced across the ballroom at the couples stepping elegantly through a country dance.

Oliver watched her face carefully and was about to speak when, out of the corner of his eye, he caught sight of someone entering the ballroom. It was Sir Geoffrey Knightsbridge. Urgency filled him, but he suppressed the urge to leap to his feet, instead choosing to maintain a calm exterior.

"I certainly hope you will be as happy as Miss Russell and more so," Oliver said pleasantly. She glanced at him with a quick smile and seemed about to speak, but he excused himself abruptly before any words could pass her lips, and she was left staring at him, mouth open, in bewilderment and amused surprise as he stood and walked quickly away.

Oliver was too focused on chasing down his quarry to worry that he might have been hasty in his departure. Knightsbridge hadn't seen him yet, so as he approached the other gentleman, Oliver called out a greeting.

"Knightsbridge, where have you been hiding yourself this age? I dare swear I've not laid eyes on you in weeks," he said enthusiastically, coming to stand beside Sir Geoffrey, who had turned to see who addressed him. He recognized Oliver and nodded a greeting.

"Ah, Hartwell," he replied with an edge. "Yes, I had occasion to leave London."

"On an errand of pleasure, I hope?"

"No, unfortunately not."

"Lord, I hardly dare ask what you mean, but I shall," said Oliver with a bright grin, endeavoring to lighten Sir Geoffrey's apparently rather sullen mood by way of overt friendliness.

Knightsbridge stared at the younger man with slightly narrowed eyes and an expression of distaste that Oliver recognized but had no cause to understand. For his part, Sir Geoffrey was carefully questioning whether Oliver's approaching him was part of a scheme to cause him further embarrassment or if he was genuine in his attentions. He had reason to believe the former but reasoned that he had not witnessed any maliciousness in him in any previous interactions. But he knew Oliver to be Charles Moore's cousin and regarded him with suspicion for this.

"I am unsure if you are mocking me, sir," Knightsbridge said carefully, but the flicker of confusion that crossed Oliver's face was quite enough to convince him the younger man was genuine in his friendliness.

"Whyever would I mock you, Sir Geoffrey?" Oliver answered with a frown.

"Forgive me, Hartwell," the other man said apologetically. He continued bluntly, "I misjudged. It is only that I have lately had a…an…altercation. With your cousin Moore. I know you to be close to him and thought the scoundrel had sent you to further his efforts to embarrass me."

Oliver blinked rapidly, amazed the information he sought had so easily fallen in his lap. Now that it had, he hardly knew what to do with it, for it made things all the harder to understand. If Knightsbridge had indeed been in an altercation with Charlie, surely that meant Charlie was telling the truth about his whereabouts the night of the masquerade. Which also meant that he could not have been responsible for abducting Miss Iverson.

"Lord, an altercation? With Charlie?" he said in a remarkably believable tone of shock. "I can scarce believe it."

"Yes, nor could I, as it happens." Sir Geoffrey's generally congenial countenance twisted with disgust at the memory of the incident.

"How came it to happen?"

"I can hardly recall," Knightsbridge spat venomously. "The devil came upon me where I sat at

Boodle's and was mighty insulting—"

"At Boodle's?" Oliver interrupted suddenly.

"Yes, at Boodles. He's always been prickly—"

"Are you sure you weren't at Gott's?"

"Whyever would I be at Gott's? No, it was Boodles. I recall the color of the carpet in particular since the rogue threw me onto it."

"Threw you onto the carpet? Charlie did?"

"That's what I said."

"Lord, whatever for?" Oliver exclaimed.

"I hardly know. He came up to me, smooth as you like, and started throwing around the most ridiculous accusations," Knightsbridge fumed. "Said he'd proof that I'd fuzzed the cards when we played a hand of loo. Can't even remember ever playing with the fellow in my life. Said so, I did. Before I knew it, he was swinging at me. Hardly knew what he was doing, but he managed to get a knock in and loosened a tooth. Had to have it taken out—mighty painful it was, too. Was all over very quick—I never even swung at him myself, for someone picked him up and threw him out."

"You didn't hit him? Are you sure?"

"Quite sure. Been regretting it ever since," Sir Geoffrey said irritably. "Either way, took myself off to the family shack in the country for a time. Hoped the nonsense Moore spouted for all to hear would have died down by now. Seems to have done so."

"Well, I've not heard a whisper," Oliver replied reassuringly.

Sir Geoffrey, finding himself a sympathizer, decided to change the subject to his favorite one—horses. Oliver obligingly said all that was necessary to maintain his side of the conversation, but his mind was now far and away on other matters.

The incident had been at Boodles, not at Gott's like Charlie had said. And if Sir Geoffrey's account were to be believed, he'd not been the cause of Charlie's bruises, either. There was no reason to discount Sir Geoffrey's version of events, for no man would willingly admit that he'd not managed to defend himself. It was only human nature to puff one's chest and declare oneself the winner, but Knightsbridge was very frank in his acknowledgment that Charlie had gotten a swing at him and he'd not managed a reply. It seemed likely that Sir Geoffrey was the truthful party.

Oliver was as confused as ever. On the one hand, there was compelling evidence that Charlie was the culprit. On the other was Oliver's heart and childhood friendship, willing him to believe it was not true.

Looking up, he spied Charlie standing to the side of the ballroom with the fair-haired Miss Wallace. The pair appeared to be making every effort to be agreeable to one another. Charlie was whispering something in her ear, and the young lady was laughing with her usual artificial amusement that Oliver still managed to hear across the din in the room, and it made him shudder involuntarily.

Then his eyes narrowed on the coat Charlie wore, which was a particular shade of dark blue with silver buttons that he had seen only once before. When it had been worn under a black velvet cloak with a silver mask.

Chapter 24

Mr. Moore had no opportunity to approach Miss Iverson at all during the Westrop ball, though not for want of trying. Every time he made his way toward her, she managed to slip away. It seemed that even his cousin was making an effort to avoid his company, though that instance concerned him somewhat less.

An evening spent in the company of the insipid Miss Wallace could hardly be considered to be an entertaining one, although he managed to survive the interaction. He quickly learned that the mere mention of Miss Iverson was enough to bring blazing irritation into her gaze, which in no way improved her appearance. He also learned that she was as quickly charmed out of her temper as she was put in one, for it took minimal coaxing to reassure her of her own importance.

He found her not unlike his aunt, who was always susceptible to flattery. Both craved obsequiousness from their companions and had the habit of believing themselves to be quite the cleverest person in the room, no matter the company. Mr. Moore had dealt with his aunt's varying fits of temper and affection for long enough to feel himself capable of managing Miss Wallace. He had, after all, lived off Lady Hartwell's gifts and scraps for most of his years. While the walls were now beginning to close in, he had every expectation of being able to manage Miss Wallace's fits of ill-temper if the need arose and Miss Iverson continued to elude him.

Climbing the short steps of Hartwell House, he knew he'd face his aunt's ridicule and no small amount of disparagement if he chose to connect himself with Miss Wallace. Still, if he was entirely honest, he knew the chase of Miss Iverson was well over, and there was very little hope of picking up the scent again. At least, not without some exigent circumstance to force her hand. He wondered if his aunt's efforts in that area had seen success, but as he'd heard nothing in the weeks since she had declared that she would see to it, he had no reason to expect a favorable result had occurred.

Lady Hartwell reclined on her velvet chaise in her upstairs parlor. A dour footman announced his arrival, but she didn't stir from her lounge. Lazily lifting her shawl off her face, she pursed her lips distastefully as she looked her nephew up and down and slowly sat upright.

"Tell Gibbin I want tea, James," Lady Hartwell said imperiously to the footman before he withdrew. "And I want it hot. Do not dally!"

The footman nodded and exited the room without a word, leaving Mr. Moore alone with his aunt, who was apparently in one of her irritable moods. He put on his most charming smile as he greeted her with a kiss on each cheek, but she did not melt even a little.

"Well, what news have you?" she asked icily as he settled himself on the sofa across from her.

"News, ma'am?"

"Yes, news. What else would you bring yourself here for if not to tell me you've made progress?"

"Progress?" he stammered.

"Good God, don't play the coy idiot with me, Charles," Lady Hartwell snapped impatiently. "Have

271

you managed to charm the Iverson chit or not?"

Ruffled and not a small amount rankled by this reception, Moore bristled and sneered, "No, I have not managed it."

"Well, what are you waiting for?"

"Waiting for? I've more than half a mind not to bother with her at all."

"Don't be ridiculous," she hissed. "She's the heiress of the Season, and your father has his heart set on the match. You cannot just give way," Lady Hartwell exclaimed exasperatedly, rolling her eyes and throwing up her hands.

"She's also entirely unmanageable. I've a mind for a wife that would be less troublesome."

"She's a child. How much trouble can she be? Say pretty things, send little gifts—it's not that difficult."

"Unfortunately, the little minx is not that simple," he growled, running his hand across his jaw. "Besides, she's not the only heiress to be had."

"Oh, so I suppose you have found some other? I've certainly not heard of any nearly as promising."

"In fact, I have," Moore replied tartly. "Miss Wallace."

Lady Hartwell's eyes grew wide, and her hands clenched into fists. In a chilling tone, she said, "No."

"No? What do you mean, 'no'?"

"I mean no," his aunt screeched. "I'll not have it. That simpering, vapid creature? It is not to be borne."

"Is this the foundation of your objection? I confess I find it rather hollow. I imagined money would more than cover such petty sins."

"Petty sins? To smell of the shop? I've heard her called a vulgar, and the mother even worse. It is suddenly clear why Sir John Wallace has withdrawn from Society. Why, such a handsome rogue he was, no doubt that vile creature got him by devious means."

"I doubt that was necessary. I heard the fellow's pockets were entirely empty. No doubt his choice of wife allowed him to very easily remedy that situation."

"And where has that got him?" she said venomously. "He has his country house and a toffy-nosed wife with a daughter to match, wearing his name to further their connections in spite of their low breeding."

"I'll beg you to recall that Miss Wallace is the daughter of a baronet."

"As though she would let anyone forget it." Lady Hartwell laughed contemptuously.

The door of the parlor opened, and the ancient butler tottered into the room with the tea tray, something of a glare on his face. Mr. Gibbin had served the Hartwell family for several decades, having begun as a footman in the time of Oliver's grandfather. Raised on the Calverley estate, he had chosen to remain after the reign of Lady Hartwell had begun with the hope of the future in Oliver's hands. Still, his disdain for his mistress had become rather harder to conceal in the last twelve months, now Oliver had come of age.

Lady Hartwell ignored Gibbin's scowl, incorrectly assigning its origin to resentment of Mr. Moore's presence in the room. Her sense of self-worth was set far too high to allow her to consider that she might be the cause, and being irritated with her nephew herself, she was quite willing and able to imagine that her servants would instantly feel as she did.

As Gibbin tripped out of the room with stiff

shoulders and an icy glare, Lady Hartwell turned back to her nephew and scowled.

"I will not countenance a match between you and this Wallace chit until and unless absolutely necessary. I think it is time instead that you consider taking steps to put the Iverson girl in your power so that she has no option but to accept you," she said with frosty deliberation.

"Well, that has been tried and failed."

"I beg your pardon?"

He had been leaning forward with his elbows on his knees and his face in his hands, sheer frustration overcoming him, until Lady Hartwell's blunt suggestion. Now Mr. Moore glared at her resentfully and let out a guttural groan of pent-up anger before launching into a vivid recounting of his attempt to abduct Lucilla from the Vauxhall masquerade several weeks prior, starting with his overhearing Alfred Russell's conversation with Ponsonby and his subsequent theft of the token he'd dropped at Gott's. When he had done explaining his effort, it was Lady Hartwell's turn to glare at him instead.

"Do you mean to tell me," she said slowly and deliberately, setting her teacup down, "that this entire issue may have been resolved weeks ago if you had merely prioritized getting the girl safely away over being recognized? If you hadn't been so concerned with keeping your infernal mask on, you might now be married to the girl. What would it have mattered if she saw your face or not? She was bound to eventually."

Her ladyship's voice, which had begun low and careful, had gradually become loud and shrill with indignance. She had stood halfway through her speech and was now towering over her nephew with her arms rigid by her sides and her fists clenched. Like a frightened dog, he hunched his shoulders and shrugged away from her, and she let out a screech of frustration and flung away from him, spinning on her heel. As she moved away from him, his resentment came to the surface again, and he unfurled.

"She would have, yes. But your wretched son was there, so how was I to get through the thing without him coming for me or setting Saliston and Iverson on my heels?"

"I should have thought you'd have skill enough to have dispensed with Oliver."

"And so I should, if it weren't for the girl managing to hit me," Moore snapped spitefully. "Not just once, I might add."

"How much damage could one little female do, pray?" asked Lady Hartwell, sarcasm dripping from her tone and causing Moore to flinch involuntarily at the thought of the gloved little hand neatly striking his jaw with a level of precision he had never managed to attain.

"I'll have you know that size and gender are not a factor in a well-landed punch."

"Evidently so. I suppose we ought to be glad she was not able to land another—you may have been knocked out cold." Lady Hartwell tittered mockingly.

"I had a difficult enough time finding an excuse for the bruises she gave me as it was," he said pettishly. "In the end, I went and started a scuffle so that word would get out. Luckily I did because Oliver ended up asking me how I came to have a bruise on my face."

"And you told him you were in a brawl?"

"Yes."

"Well, I suppose I can applaud your forethought in

developing an alibi," she said dryly, sitting down on her lounge again and smoothing her skirt. "Do you think he suspects you?"

"No, I should think not. He asked why I wasn't at the masque, so he clearly believed I was not there."

"Good," her ladyship said firmly. "Now, what we need is a better plan than your last one."

"What?"

"A better plan so that you will succeed in whisking her away this time."

"But it didn't work last time, so why would I try again?" he asked. "I am sure of a favorable response from Miss Wallace. I think I shall spare myself the indignity of marriage with a female as willful as Lucilla Iverson."

"In favor of the indignity of marriage with the granddaughter of a vulgar tradesman?" Lady Hartwell asked in disgust. "I will not countenance it unless another attempt on the Iverson girl fails. No, you will try one more time. And this time, you will be sure of the result because you will do it the way I tell you."

"And what exactly would you have me do?"

A scowl marring her pretty face, Lady Hartwell rose and walked across the room to the mantelshelf. She lifted several of the figurines that decorated it, apparently looking for something. Tipping one over cautiously, she made a quiet exclamation before taking a key out from under it and replacing the figurine. Key in hand, she went to the writing desk, unlocked one of the drawers, and after a moment of shuffling about, drew out a singularly ornate silver pistol.

"Here," she said distastefully as she paced back toward her nephew, the pistol hanging limply in her hand from her forefinger. "Take this, and for heaven's sake, do not shoot her. The sight of it will frighten her out of her wits, sure enough, so I do not think you will need even to load it."

Moore took hold of the pistol carefully. Upon closer inspection, he realized it was a dueling pistol and must surely have had a twin at one time or another. It was styled in French fashion, with a slim barrel roughly nine inches long and an elegantly engraved hilt. He frowned over the item and glanced at his aunt suspiciously.

"How came you to have this?" he asked.

"It was my late husband's. It has not been fired since before his death, so I suggest you have a care and make sure it is inspected and cleaned properly before you set about your task," Lady Hartwell said carelessly as she seated herself once more.

"And do you have any other suggestions on how I might complete this 'task'?"

"My suggestion, Charles, is that you do not bother with dancing around the issue. Hire a carriage and rooms at an inn outside of London, preferably off the main roads, and abscond with the girl. At gunpoint, if necessary," said the lady menacingly. "Broad daylight or no, it matters not. What does matter is that it is done, and quickly, so that anyone who might notice her disappearance will be too slow in their pursuit."

"You make it sound all so simple, aunt," Moore replied archly.

"It really needn't be otherwise, nephew," she said haughtily. "Do not make a meal of it. Make the arrangements for a carriage and an inn, and for god's sake, do not use your own name. If you are followed, it will not do to be using your own name."

"I'm not an idiot—"

"Well, you do a marvelous impression of one, I must say," Lady Hartwell tittered.

Mr. Moore's face twisted into an ugly scowl, and he was about to snap a retort, but his aunt waved her hand dismissively.

"It is imperative that you get it right this time. There is much at stake," she said tersely. "I expect that you will do all that is necessary."

He pouted childishly. "I really do not see why it makes any difference whether I marry Miss Iverson or Miss Wallace—"

"You owe it to your father to make the best match possible, Charles," Lady Hartwell said irritably.

"I hardly think Father will care one way or another as long as the female I marry has deep pockets."

"It will be of no use to me to have you marry Miss Wallace."

"No use to *you*?" he repeated.

"No," she said firmly. "Exchanging one for the other may suit you and your pockets quite well, but it will not prevent my stupid son from attaching the Iverson girl, will it?"

"He must marry one day. What has it to do with me?"

Lady Hartwell's eyes flashed dangerously, and her nephew flinched unconsciously. Her jaw clenched and unclenched slowly, then she said, "Do I need to remind you how much and how often I have extended my hand to you over the years? The very clothes on your back you owe to me, dear nephew. It would be wise for you to remember it."

This had the effect of somewhat mollifying Mr.

Moore. He was unconvinced that marriage to Miss Iverson was a necessity, but he owed a modicum of loyalty to his aunt, and so he consented to the creation of a plan to abduct the girl. The execution of the plan would hinge primarily on careful timing, but steps first needed to be taken to ensure that a suitable escape route was in place to allow for a speedy flight from London to Scotland.

He left his aunt's house with strict instructions to begin setting everything in order. Lady Hartwell's determination had begun to give him confidence in his capacity to perform his task, but natural ability was less likely to stand him in good stead. He was not a marksman, but rationalized that it was not necessary for him to be so in order to wave a gun about and make empty threats. He was also not adept at fighting, but he was confident that Miss Iverson would not again gain the upper hand on him now that he knew what she was capable of. No matter her skills with her fists, she was far too petite and slim to be able to stand up to brute force, which he was quite capable of utilizing if required. The heaviness of his riding and driving horses could attest to his heavy-handedness.

With a resolute step, he took himself off to begin his preparations.

****

"Do you have a moment, George?"

Saliston looked up from his paper to see Oliver standing in the doorway of the library. He looked concerned most of the time, but except for their brief discussion some weeks prior in the very same room, nothing more had been said. The lines on Oliver's brow had grown deeper and deeper, but his cousin had avoided questioning him in the hope that he would eventually confide his troubles. The day, it seemed, had finally arrived.

"Of course, dear boy! Do come in," the duke said invitingly, gesturing to one of the empty armchairs.

Lord Hartwell had an air of unease as he sat, and he continued to fidget once he had settled himself into the chair. Biting his lip anxiously, he looked at his cousin and said, "I believe Charlie has done something unforgivable."

Saliston's brows shot up in surprise, and with some effort, he contained the sudden urge to laugh. He managed to admirably cover the effort with a muffled cough.

"Indeed?" he asked interestedly. "What exactly do you consider to be unforgivable?"

Oliver pursed his lips and looked at his cousin with a sardonic glint. "I know you have not liked Charlie for a long while, George, and I confess that until recently, I have been at a loss to know why. You mock me quite rightly. I well deserve it."

"I am sorry, my boy," Saliston said genuinely. "Do, pray, tell me what you mean."

With a deep breath, Lord Hartwell stood and wandered over to the fireplace and poked at it contemplatively, leaning an arm along the mantelshelf. His cousin regarded him with some concern and waited for his explanation, and, at length, the younger man spoke.

"I believe Charlie is responsible for a recent attempt to abduct Miss Iverson," Oliver said slowly and deliberately toward the fire before he turned a resolute gaze toward the duke. He searched his cousin's face for any emotion that might not fit the declaration and was relieved to see total and unhindered shock flood Saliston's face before an involuntary shout of surprise sounded from him.

"I lately witnessed a masked man attempt to carry Miss Iverson off," Oliver explained in reply to the duke's exclamation. "It happened at Vauxhall—you may have noticed Miss Iverson was out of sorts that evening."

"Yes, I do recall she seemed restrained," Saliston murmured thoughtfully, casting his mind back to the night in question.

"I recognized her immediately, but the man I could not make out. He was careful with his mask. I came upon them just as she realized the man was a stranger and had begun to struggle with him," Oliver said gravely. "I was about to intervene when she hit him. Twice!"

"Well done, Miss Iverson," the duke mused with a smile.

"Indeed, it was very well done. Drew his cork very neatly." Oliver laughed hesitantly. "In any case, the man fled, and when I questioned her, she said—" He stopped and frowned. "She said she thought he was me."

"She thought he was you?"

"Yes, she said she only went with him because he was wearing one of the ribbons our party had agreed to wear. Miss Iverson and Miss Russell had made up their minds with Miss Craven that we would all wear them so that we might recognize one another, and the fellow who had tried to take her was wearing one."

"How very peculiar," said the duke ruminatingly. "So you have reason to believe it was your cousin Moore?"

Oliver sighed and nodded.

"It is all very complicated. I confess, at first, I held you in some suspicion also, George."

"Me?"

"Yes. You left London that night, and I didn't see you for a week after," Oliver explained. "And when I did see you, you had a bruise on your face."

"And you thought Miss Iverson was responsible?" The duke laughed.

"For a moment, I considered it, but I'd also seen Charlie that morning, and he looked to have bruises as well."

"Lord, no wonder you've been out of sorts of late, boy."

"I asked Charlie where he'd been the night of the masquerade, and he told me he'd been at Gott's. Lost track of time, he said." Oliver pressed on. "Then last week, I asked him how he'd come to have that bruise on his face, and he claimed to have got into a brawl with Sir Geoffrey Knightsbridge."

"Knightsbridge? Whatever for?"

"I asked Knightsbridge if it were true, but he swears he never hit Charlie. Says Charlie came at him swinging, and he felt it necessary to take himself out of town for a few days after, for the shame of it all," Hartwell said disgustedly. "But the real problem with the story is that Knightsbridge says it didn't happen at Gott's but at Boodles. Has witnesses, too, so I've been able to confirm that Charlie was not at Gott's when he told me he was, and also that Knightsbridge never landed a blow, too."

"Well," Saliston breathed. "You have certainly been busy. Have you considered a career as a Runner?"

"Don't poke fun, George, please," Oliver said earnestly.

"I'm sorry, I'm sorry. But in all honesty, you've done well to put so many pieces together." Saliston clapped his young cousin on the back consolingly. "Is there a final nail in the coffin for this puzzle?"

"Yes. I recognized Charlie's coat. He was wearing the same one at the Westrop party two nights ago," the younger man said miserably.

The duke sighed. He was glad Oliver's infatuation with his cousin Moore was finally broken, but it seemed a very hard way for that to happen. Rather harder than Saliston had expected it would be. It was not hard for him to imagine Charles Moore in the role of would-be assailant of feminine virtue, and it was not hard to imagine the failure, either. He enjoyed an inward chuckle at the image of Miss Iverson landing not one but two sound punches on the ingrate.

"I have a confession to make, Oliver," the duke said suddenly.

Lord Hartwell's downcast face came up quickly, confusion and suspicion lingering behind his gaze.

"I told you that business took me out of London the night of the masquerade," he said carefully. "But the truth is that I had received word about an old friend of mine, and on a whim, I decided to visit her."

"Her?"

"Yes. You will not have heard of her, but very recently I was reminded of a young lady I once knew by the name of Josephine. Miss Josephine Dudley, or as she is now, Lady Morris," the duke explained. "Josephine was considered rather a hoyden when I first knew her ten years ago. Her father was a well-born country squire, and she grew up without a mother, so she was not a typical young lady—rather like Miss Iverson. She was more at home with dogs and horses than in company, and she and I developed an attachment, but her father had arranged a match for her and refused to break it. The man was some thirty years her senior and has recently died."

Oliver blinked, slowly comprehending and digesting his cousin's words.

"I see," he said carefully.

"No, you do not. At least, you do not see everything," the duke replied with a gentle laugh. "I went to see Josephine for the reason you can imagine—I intend to marry her. During my visit with her, she shed some light on the reason she was forced to marry her late husband."

Saliston paused and a distasteful sneer appeared on his face as he continued. "She explained to me that her father had significant gaming debts, and Sir William Morris agreed to waive these in exchange for Josephine's hand in marriage. It turned out he was something of a prolific gamester, and Josie was expected to act as a hostess to all manner of persons who entered the house for his regular 'meetings.' "

"I assume you mean that her husband was running a gaming den?"

"Of a sort, yes. They were house parties in which the guests were specifically invited for the purpose of gambling the time away," the duke said sarcastically. "But the rather interesting piece of information Josie imparted was that your mother was a frequent guest there."

"My mother?" Oliver shouted.

"Yes."

"Are you certain?"

"Yes, I am afraid so," Saliston said almost

apologetically. "I am also told that she lost heavily and often. I am at a loss as to how she has been covering the losses, for I am quite certain she has not been paying it out of the estate. I visited White, and he assures me it is quite impossible."

"Perhaps she's been able to recover her losses, then," said Oliver blankly.

"Perhaps," his cousin replied, clearly unconvinced.

Silence descended upon the two men, each of them wrapped up in their own thoughts and both relieved and concerned in turn by the information they'd given one another in the course of their conversation. They mulled quietly for some time before the silence was broken.

"I think I want to marry Lucilla," Oliver declared suddenly.

The Duke of Saliston eyed his young cousin with a soft smile that seemed out of place after the heavy topics they'd just bandied about, but Oliver's words brought him a measure of relief.

"Finally," he cried out in amusement. "I had begun to think you were never going to come round."

Lord Hartwell stared at his cousin, a crease slowly appearing between his brows as confusion spread across his features.

"No, I'm not surprised," the duke said with a smile.

"To be honest, I thought she might prefer you," Oliver said seriously.

"Nonsense. I am an elderly uncle in Miss Iverson's eyes."

"Well, the same cannot be said of Lady Edevane." The young earl snorted.

"Lady Edevane means well, but she is quite off the scent, and I can assure you that her opinion will weigh very little on balance," Saliston said with a soothing air of authority. "In light of your declaration, I think we need to discuss the implications with White, as the estate will need to be wound up and settled on you."

"Should I perhaps ask the question before you go to the trouble of summoning Mr. White?" Oliver asked with a wry smile.

"I think we can be reasonably certain you will receive a favorable answer, dear boy. But if you are going to be superstitious about it, we may hold off on contacting White." The duke laughed. "The only loose end to be tied up, that I can see, is the matter of the Calverley jewels that are in your mother's care. Yet another regret for me to carry."

"What do you mean?"

"When your father died, I was meant to take charge of the jewelry collection that belongs to the Calverley estate. But when my cousin—your mother—learned of it, she threw another one of her legendary tantrums, and I let her keep them to keep the peace. I am somewhat concerned that you may have trouble wresting them from her now," the duke explained.

Oliver sat up slowly in his armchair and smiled widely as he reached out to clap his cousin's back consolingly. "Well, since you started this, you'll have to come with me to retrieve the damn things then, won't you?"

With a dramatic sigh, Saliston agreed.

Chapter 25

The following day as the afternoon neared four o'clock, Saliston accompanied his young cousin on a visit to Lady Hartwell in Wimpole Street. Sitting beside Oliver on his high perch phaeton towed by the flashy bay pair, the duke reflected on how different things were from the last time the young earl had stood before his mother. There was no sign of the anxious, fretful child who had so eagerly fled his home in November. Gone was the over-eager young boy who had replaced him for a time. And now a young man in his image sat in his place, conversing animatedly whilst confidently twitching his reins and flicking his whip, steering the top-heavy sporting carriage skillfully through the busy streets of London without pause.

Calm and collected, this new Oliver spoke with no trace of concern or apprehension at the thought of facing his formidable parent. Saliston glowed with pride as his young cousin prattled on. They had reached the Hartwell town residence, and Oliver reined his pair in with a proficiency that had long since rivaled Saliston's. He had recently hired his own groom, and this young sprite now leapt eagerly down from his post and went to the horses' heads.

"I really am lucky to have found the boy, you know," Oliver said conversationally as they mounted the steps of the townhouse. "Has a way with the horses, very calm young chap. Ah, Gibbin! It seems an age since I saw you. How are you, old chap?"

The aged butler stood in the opened doorway and smiled fondly at his young master, his face faintly coloring with pleasure at being so greeted. Taking the young earl's cue, he answered in kind as he instructed one of the footmen to take the duke's hat and cloak while he attended to Oliver's belongings himself. Once these articles were neatly bestowed, he led the two gentlemen, with an energetic step, to the drawing room in which Lady Hartwell sat alone.

With uncharacteristic glee, Gibbin flung open the drawing room doors and announced his young master's arrival. His voice was simultaneously formal and derisive, and the glance he allowed to land on Lady Hartwell was contemptuous, but as always, she failed to notice this. It was usually missed because she was too conceited to consider whether her staff might dislike her. Still, on this day it was due to surprise at her son's unexpected arrival and displeasure that the duke accompanied him.

Lady Hartwell had been engaged in reading a note as the two gentlemen entered, and this was speedily folded and tucked away under a book before she hastily rose to receive them.

"Oliver, my dearest," she exclaimed with an exaggerated smile as she approached him, arms wide as though to embrace him.

"Mother," Lord Hartwell answered coolly, stiffening as she came toward him but allowing her to kiss his cheek. He did not reciprocate the gesture, pursing his lips in displeasure and nodding as she invited the two men to be seated.

After acknowledging her cousin Saliston, Lady Hartwell sat herself down and smoothed her skirts. She wore a gracious, beaming smile that fooled no one in her audience. Both gentlemen were aware of the tactics she was capable of employing to achieve her own ends and understood the need to remain in control of their own speech and actions. Playing the innocent was merely the beginning of an effort to appear victimized should the conversation displease her, and there was very little doubt that it was going to do just that.

"Well. It has been far too long since you last came to see me, my darling," she cooed affectionately. "You are quite changed, I see. Have you been well? I confess I had thought to see you when I came to town, but you did not come."

Lord Hartwell replied firmly that he had been very well. He was determined to remain civil in spite of the irritation rising within him and was under no illusions that beneath the glowing exterior she was putting forward lay the controlling, heartless woman he had always known her to be. A glance toward Saliston gave him a surge of courage. Ignoring the better part of her speech, he decided that reacting to the silky, sweet tone she had adopted would only encourage her to continue, so instead, he opted to push on with the reason for his visit.

"I am pleased to find you well. However, I am not here to exchange pleasantries, Mother," Lord Hartwell said stiffly. "I am come to inform you that I intend to propose marriage to a young lady who is as yet unknown to you. She is the only daughter of Viscount Iverson, and I am sure that you will approve of the connection."

"Miss Iverson is a considerable heiress, cousin," the

duke interjected as he lounged back in his seat and fixed a rather devilish smile on her ladyship's suddenly very still face. "It is an exceedingly suitable match. He has yet to speak to the girl's father, of course, but I have every expectation that Lord Iverson will give his approval. You will be very proud, I daresay."

Lady Hartwell's expression was frozen in the same beaming smile, but Saliston saw something malicious flash through her gaze. It was gone as quickly as it had appeared, and she blinked rapidly in admirably feigned surprise and delight.

"Oh, how delightful," she exclaimed rapturously, clasping her claw-like hands together. In any other person, one would have seen happiness in the motion, but Oliver thought it looked like she would like to be clasping her hands about someone's throat. Who she envisioned was unknown, but he rather thought it was likely to be himself.

Her ladyship began to say all the right things and behave the way any casual observer would expect the mother of a soon-to-be-married young gentleman to act, but the inner thought did not match the external actions. Lady Hartwell's thoughts had flown immediately to the note she had received not moments before Oliver's arrival, and her mind was now repeating the words it contained as though it were a prayer. Outwardly, she excitedly prattled about the virtues of a country setting for the wedding and when a date might be set. She continued to talk as Gibbin re-entered the room with a tea tray.

"There will be time enough to make preparations after I have spoken to Miss Iverson, Mother," Lord Hartwell said with a dismissive wave of his hand, stemming Lady Hartwell's flow of chatter. "The second purpose for our visit today is to retrieve certain items that you were allowed to keep in your possession after my father died. George tells me there is a rather large collection of jewelry that belongs to the estate and that these remained with you."

"I believe it is customary for a widow to retain the use of such articles, particularly if the heir is not yet of age or is unmarried," Lady Hartwell replied, stiffness creeping into her tone suddenly.

"That as may be, the collection was supposed to be held by my cousin, and he allowed you continued use of the pieces at your request. Is that right, George?" Lord Hartwell said authoritatively, glancing at his cousin, who answered affirmatively. "As I have now stated my intention to take a wife, I think I am within my rights to request the return of these items, Mother."

"But you have not yet married, dearest—" she began to argue, but the duke interrupted.

"I should remind you, cousin, that the late Lord Hartwell's will was specific in this matter," Saliston said in a commanding tone. "The collection of jewelry, except those that were yours before your marriage, was to be held in trust by the Executors until the heir came of age. As Oliver is now twenty-one, the pieces are to be turned over to him. There was no stipulation that he must be married in order to have them."

Lady Hartwell glared at the duke with venomous dislike and remained noiseless, but her flaring nostrils betrayed her indignation and the rage that battled within her.

It was Oliver who broke the silence. "I expect the collection to be delivered to George's house in Berkeley

Square within the week. If you have not all of the items with you in town, I expect that you will have them sent from Calverley immediately," he said firmly, standing as he made his declaration. "I intend to make a gift of one of the pieces to Miss Iverson and will appreciate the time to select something suitable."

Looking over to his cousin, Lord Hartwell nodded resolutely, and the duke rose from his seat.

"We will take leave of you now, ma'am," the younger gentleman said. He bowed formally to his obviously displeased parent and left the room with Saliston following closely behind him. The elderly butler, who had been entirely forgotten, hurried to open the door to escort them out of the house, but the young earl waved him off and said with a friendly smile, "No, no! We will see ourselves out, Gibbin. It is quite all right. Good day to you, Mother."

Gibbin closed the door behind the two gentlemen and returned to the tea tray he had been arranging with painstaking slowness whilst listening to the conversation between the lady and her son. Pouring the tea into one of the cups and handing it to his mistress, the butler enquired as to whether she wished for him to have the jewels sent for cleaning before they were taken around to the duke's residence.

"Whatever for?" her ladyship asked irritably, a surprised expression on her face.

"Why, so that they are presentable for his lordship when he receives them, your ladyship," Gibbin replied confusedly.

Lady Hartwell snorted derisively. "That will not be at all necessary, Gibbin. My son will not require the jewels."

"I beg your pardon, ma'am?"

"My son will not require them," she repeated, a malicious glint in her eye. "Because he will not be marrying Miss Iverson."

Gibbin, entirely at a loss, bowed his head and left the room with a concerned frown. As the door clicked shut behind him, Lady Hartwell withdrew the folded note from under her book and read it once more:

God willing, by the time you have received this note I will have Miss I in my charge. I arranged a room and private parlor at the inn you suggested, though I know not how you came to know of such a place, it being so far off the post road. I dare not write before we reach Scotland for fear of discovery, so I will send word only once the knot is safely tied.

Yours, etc.

Charles

With a prim smirk, her ladyship refolded the note and tucked it away again.

****

Not half an hour earlier, Miss Iverson had been enjoying a quiet walk in the park. Chico tugged on the leather strap she held, plunging down the pathway in pursuit of a delectable scent, and her maid tripped along beside her with a bright smile.

Before the Season began, Miss Iverson had never had the services of her own maid. Upon their settling in London with the intention of being in residence for some months, Lord and Lady Iverson had engaged for her a young female whose services had been recommended by Lady Edevane's personal dresser, who happened to be her aunt. The two girls had taken an immediate liking to one another, and Alice Bevan, given charge of Miss

Iverson's wardrobe and hair, soon proved herself to be something of a wunderkind in spite of her youth. She took pride in turning her young mistress out in style, and Miss Iverson immensely enjoyed her company.

It was not uncommon for the pair to take exercise with the golden-haired hound energetically towing them along, but it was with religious regularity that they would do so on a Friday afternoon. Other days of the week might see them aboard Miss Iverson's phaeton instead, or not at all. But Friday had become something sacred to them, and this circumstance had unfortunately not gone unnoticed.

It was for this reason that Mr. Moore had selected the particular day and hour as the one in which he would execute his plan. Miss Iverson could be depended upon to enter the park at a specific gate, proceed down an apparently favorite walk, and make a circuit before returning home by the same gate. This afternoon was no different. He was sitting somewhat impatiently in the nondescript closed hackney carriage that he had hired when Miss Iverson, talking animatedly to the unassuming young female walking beside her, finally came into view on the deserted laneway.

As the two young women came closer, he carefully fixed his silver mask over his face and pulled up the black velvet cloak. Then he raised his cane and tapped it loudly on the roof of the hackney. Almost immediately, the two men seated upon the rear of the carriage leapt down, and Mr. Moore heard a brief scuffle ensue on the street. Barely a moment later, the door was flung open, and Miss Iverson was unceremoniously thrust inside onto the floor, followed immediately by her maid and the yellow-haired dog before the door was slammed shut again, and the carriage lurched into motion.

The dog was the first to regain its senses. It leapt up and bristled immediately at the sight of Moore, growling menacingly.

Second to recover was Miss Iverson. She sat up, and her gaze darted around, taking in her surroundings before landing upon the masked Mr. Moore, and she said one distasteful, spiteful word, "*You!*"

The dog began to bark and Alice began to shriek, but Miss Iverson stared back at their abductor with an angry and indignant glare. Deciding that she was not suitably frightened, he slowly took the silver pistol out from under his cloak and had the satisfaction of seeing the young lady's eyes widen slightly.

Had he been dealing with a young woman of Alice Bevan's mettle, he might have fared better, for at the revealing of the weapon, the maid lost all sense of self-control and seemed almost about to leap from the moving carriage before she was brought back down to earth by Miss Iverson taking firm hold of her shoulders, shaking her roughly, and insisting she stop screaming. Alice calmed, but tears of terror continued to fall.

Lucilla knew that any man who would attempt an abduction only behind the safety of a mask must be a cowardly man at heart, but that he would do so twice and then think to use a gun to silence his prey marked him as a desperate man, too. And desperate men, not unlike cornered dogs, might bite with little to no warning. With this in mind, she prioritized quieting the panicked Alice before their kidnapper decided to quiet her his own way.

Succeeding in her first task, Miss Iverson then restrained her dog. Chico was not usually an aggressive animal, but he was a protective one. His instincts told him that the masked man was not to be trusted, but as yet he had made no move to touch the women, so the dog merely growled. With a tug on his leather collar the growling ceased, and Chico backed away slowly but kept his gaze on the dark-haired, threatening human in the corner of the coach.

Mr. Moore was off the mark when he thought he had frightened Miss Iverson. Unfortunately for him, when her eyes had widened at the sight of the pistol it was not from fear, but from recognition. At that moment, she was willing to wager that the gun in her captor's hand was familiar to her and that she had held its twin in her own hands not so long ago. With perfect clarity, she recalled the length of its barrel, the tooling of its hilt, and the uniquely twisted hammer, and she had weighed it with her fingertips while she listened to the duke talk of how the pair had come to be separated.

It was quite enough information for her to deduce the identity of their abductor accurately. Seated opposite him, Miss Iverson held Alice's hands as the girl wept silently, but her own large dark orbs were not even slightly damp as she glared at the masked man furiously.

"I suppose it would be pointless to ask where we are going," she growled through gritted teeth.

"Quite," he replied cordially, deciding that keeping verbal interaction to a minimum would be wise until he had dispensed with the maid and the dog, and being entirely unaware that Miss Iverson had already guessed to whom she spoke.

Lucilla glanced out of the window. The carriage was now out of the park, and she caught the barest glimpse of Astley House as they passed by it. She thought they were traveling east on Piccadilly, judging by the swing of the hackney as it slowed for a corner. When she looked again out of the window, the sight of the garden that surrounded the Queen's House confirmed her suspicions, and an idea suddenly came into her mind.

Forcing an expression of worry to her face, she glanced at the masked man and said contritely, "Please, you have what you want—let Alice go."

Mr. Moore inwardly congratulated himself on his luck and made no effort to hide the smirk that grew on his face. He lifted the pistol and waved it threateningly. The sight of Miss Iverson retreating back into the dilapidated cushions in fear was rather pleasing to him. Still, the effect on Alice Bevan was somewhat more substantial, and her tears were no longer silent as she squealed loudly in fright and began to sob again.

He rolled his eyes disdainfully, already tired of the display of feminine sensibilities. He had thought to leave the girl somewhat farther out of the way than the middle of St James's, but she was in such a state that he was beginning to believe it would be unlikely she might be able to provide any valuable information to anyone who might ask of Miss Iverson's whereabouts. On foot and hysterical, it would take her some time to reach Grosvenor Street to raise the alarm with the family, but he was mindful of his aunt's instructions and decided to wait at least a *little* longer.

"Not yet," he said shortly, hiding the gun away.

Alice's crying was obviously causing him irritation. He was looking away from her now, and with a full view of his profile, she wondered how she could have been so blind as not to have recognized him all those weeks earlier in Vauxhall. Catching herself scowling, she forced herself to appear fearful instead, sensing that it pleased him to feel in control of the situation.

The hackney carriage was bumping along rather more quickly than she would have expected, and Lucilla keenly felt the growing importance of disposing of Alice and Chico safely and strategically along Piccadilly before they were much farther past Albany. In her most convincingly fearful voice, she begged for her maid's release, hoping that further hysterics might force his hand—and it worked.

Scowling horridly, he looked at Miss Iverson, his body rigid with irritation.

"Please," she repeated pleadingly. "Please, only set down my maid and the dog, and I will go with you willingly!"

"Miss Lucilla, no!" Alice screeched and sobbed, clutching at her young mistress desperately. Lucilla ignored her and kept her gaze fixed tearfully on the masked man. After another minute of Alice's screeching and Lucilla's pleading, he finally reached the limit of his patience.

"For God's sake, woman, enough," he yelled furiously. "I cannot take another moment of this incessant screeching, let alone another hour of it. I refuse to carry her all the way to Finchley." He lifted his cane and sounded a series of loud bangs on the roof of the hackney to signal the coachman to stop, and the carriage came to a halt near Coventry Street. The masked man remained seated but flung open the door and gestured for Alice to get out, causing her to scream again and throw her arms around Lucilla. Taking advantage of the outburst, Miss Iverson whispered an instruction to her maid.

"Go to my cousin at Albany. Moore is taking me to

Finchley!" she said urgently in a whisper so that their abductor would not hear her, then loudly she said, "I will be quite all right, Alice! Go!"

Miss Bevan pulled back and stared at Lucilla, suddenly understanding what her mistress wanted her to do. She blinked rapidly through her tears and gingerly took hold of Chico's leash, giving her mistress's hand a reassuring squeeze before she stumbled out of the carriage with the growling dog.

Alice Bevan stood tearfully on the side of the street with the golden-haired dog and watched as the shabby hackney coach lurched into motion and began lumbering toward Shaftesbury Avenue. She watched until it disappeared from view, then turned on her heel and scurried along the footpath in the direction of Matthew Iverson's apartment at Albany.

Chapter 26

Matthew sat in his armchair and stared blankly at his unexpected visitor. Surprise would be an appropriate word for his current state of mind, for the visitor had a rather fantastical story to tell and had appeared rather suddenly at his door. He had not expected to see him for at least another week.

Edward Iverson was none worse the wear for his year-long sojourn upon the Continent. He was a little thinner, perhaps, but in one piece at least, which was more than could be said of many of his comrades. He was still broad-shouldered in spite of his slimmed appearance, but he seemed to have developed a hardness to his features that had not been there before he left so suddenly to rejoin the war effort.

And now he sat across from his cousin, a glass of Madeira in his hand and half a smile on his face as he recounted his crossing from France, in which the weather had been so particularly horrid that he wondered if it was an omen for his return to England.

"And when am I to meet the poor girl you've managed to humbug a betrothal out of?" Edward said laughingly.

"You've not even seen Mama and Uncle Jasper yet, and I was not expecting to see you for at least another week," Matthew reminded his cousin accusingly.

"Yes." Edward paused, the smile on his face fading

sadly. "How is the temperature with Father? I expect he is still angry with me?"

"As I said in my last letter, he was at first very angry, but all said and done now, I believe he is merely anxious to know that you are alive."

"Thank you for keeping your word. I know it must have been difficult not to tell Mama," Edward said apologetically.

"I would have kept it from Cilla if I could have, but when she came upon the letter that was sent to Grosvenor Street, she knew your hand. I was relieved that she came to me and not Uncle Jasper, at least."

"She's always been a knowing one. She thrashed me right proper in her first letter to me, and I was glad to be well out of range of her fists."

"I think she resented keeping the secret from Mama," said Matthew.

"Well, there will be no need for it any longer, soon enough."

"How do you think to set it all at ease?"

"I have not yet decided," Edward said thoughtfully. "Perhaps your looming nuptials will suitably overshadow my reappearance?"

"But the date is set for next month," Matthew sputtered in surprise. "I think I have kept your confidence long enough, Ned. It is time to come clean. I refuse to conceal your return for an entire month."

At that moment, Matthew's valet knocked on the door and summarily entered the room without waiting for a response. Jenkins was about to explain this irregularity when he was thrust aside by a bounding yellow dog that both young gentlemen immediately recognized as Chico. The dog was barking anxiously and refused to be still, rushing about the room between the two men who had risen as he appeared and were doing their best to calm the jittery animal.

"Is my cousin here, Jenkins?" Matthew demanded of the flustered valet, who stood in the doorway with his hands across his forehead and an unusual amount of concern on his face. "Surely she would not dare to come here…"

"No, sir, it is Miss Lucilla's maid. She's downstairs with the housekeeper, in a rare state, I must say. Saying all manner of odd things, she is, and mighty upset, sir. Can I trouble you to come down?"

Jenkins rushed from the room, followed closely by the Iverson men and the skittish Chico. They found the elderly housekeeper hovering over the red-faced and flustered Alice Bevan with smelling salts while the maid cried that she must *immediately* see Mr. Matthew. The girl was sitting on a stool in the entrance hall, but as soon as she saw Matthew and his companion, she leapt to her feet and rushed forward.

"Mr. Matthew, sir. She told me to come directly! She wanted me to come to you, which is so very clever, for you are closer than Grosvenor Street," she cried histrionically, gasping for breath and waving her hands emphatically. "You must do something, sir. You must go after her, for the Lord knows what he means to do!"

"Alice, you must calm down and tell me what has happened," Matthew said soothingly, taking her by the shoulders and guiding her back to the stool. "Now, from the beginning, tell us what has happened."

"We was walking Chico, sir. In the park, like we are used to do every Friday, if there is no party to be prepared for." Miss Bevan stopped to take another raspy breath and hurriedly rambled on. "We was coming along the path we likes to take, because it is always quiet-like, so we can let Chico run a little, you know? Well, we was walking along and passing a hackney cab standing away from the path, and two men sitting up behind it, and as we goes by, they jump down and grab us up and into the hackney."

"Good God," Jenkins gasped in horrified accents.

"Please, continue, Alice—your name is Alice, is it not?" Edward interjected. His voice was calm, his face concerned, but there was tension in his shoulders.

"Yes, sir." She nodded. "The two men what threw us in runned off, but there was a man in the carriage with a black mask on. Reckon it was he that tried to kidnap the mistress at Vauxhall, I do."

"Someone tried to kidnap her at Vauxhall?" Matthew cried out in alarm. "But never mind that right now. Did you recognize the man, Alice?"

"No, sir, but I reckon the mistress did. She was mighty keen to have him set me and Chico down, never seen her lose her head before, but she was screeching fit to raise the roof of the coach. Set the man off right proper, it did! He yelled that he wouldn't have me in the coach another minute, nor an hour," Miss Bevan said theatrically, glossing over her part in the hysterics that had taken place in the hackney. "Tells the driver to stop and flings open the door—and as I'm about to get out onto the street, she clasps me to her bosom and tells me to come here and to tell you the oddest thing!"

"Well, what is it?" Matthew demanded. "What did she say?"

" 'More is taking me to Finchley,' she says. What's she say 'more' for? Don't understand that bit, meself, but it's neither here nor there," the maid said informatively. "But I do recall him saying something about Finchley, and now I've told you, sir, so you must go at once and rescue her before he shoots her!"

"Shoots her?" Edward shouted. "What do you mean, 'shoots her'?"

"Had a gun, he did," Alice cried dramatically.

"Please repeat what she told you to tell me, Miss Bevan," Matthew said curiously, a frown creasing his forehead as she said the sentence once more.

"Moore," Matthew growled, turning to his cousin. "She recognized him. Charles Moore has her."

"We must go after them at once," Edward snarled through gritted teeth. "How far have you come, girl? How long ago did you leave my sister?"

"We was set down at Coventry, sir. I watched the hackney going down Shaftesbury."

"All right," Matthew said. "We will take Cilla's grays. Jenkins, send a boy directly to the stables at my uncle's house. Instruct him that Miss Iverson's grays are required with all haste and that I shall be there to collect them presently. And call for a coach to carry us to Grosvenor Street. Go, man!"

Matthew and Edward immediately ran upstairs to retrieve their coats, then came bolting back down. The housekeeper was instructed to ensure that Miss Bevan reached Iverson House safely while the gentlemen bundled into the waiting carriage and were driven directly to the mews. Upon arrival some few minutes later, they were met by a frowning and anxious Smithers. The aging groom had already set about supervising the task the breathless messenger boy had given him minutes earlier, but the entire thing being so strange had concerned him greatly. He met Mr. Matthew at the foot of the hired carriage and asked him what was wrong when his gaze landed on the second gentleman emerging from the coach.

"Lor', Mr. Edward, as I live an' breathe!" He gasped in shock.

"It is good to see you, Smithers," Edward said tersely. "There will be time enough for greetings later, but we must have the horses without delay."

"O' course, Mr. Edward, o' course. But what be the urgency?"

"Never mind that just now. We'll explain later."

"Yes, sir, only Miss Cilla and Bevan has not come home yet, an' her la'ship being in a bit of a stir, the duke and the young feller being 'spected for dinner," Smithers said, peering at Edward's face worriedly.

"Oh, Lord, I forgot," Matthew groaned.

"What?" Edward asked impatiently.

"Saliston and Hartwell—they're in the house, or they will be," his cousin replied, rubbing his brow distractedly.

"What has that to do with anything?"

"Nothing," Matthew said, firmly shaking his head. "Smithers, you'll go with Mr. Edward. I'll go in and talk to Uncle Jasper and explain everything, Ned. For goodness' sake, don't come home without her, or we'll be in the suds."

"Come home wi'out who?" Smithers shouted.

"I'll explain on the way, Smithers," his young master exclaimed. He ran to mount the blue-wheeled phaeton, and without further query, the loyal Smithers bounded up after him and found himself clutching the seat for dear life as Edward flicked the whip over the horses' ears and urged them into a trot. Matthew watched them flying away and then took himself into the house through the back of the building, considerably frightening several staff members as he sped through the kitchen.

As he entered the main corridor of the house and paced quickly toward his uncle's study, Matthew paused and took a moment to calm himself. It would not do to put his Mama into a panic. He calculated that it must have been at least an hour since his sister had been taken, and the duke and Hartwell were expected to attend for dinner at six. A quick glance at the hall clock confirmed they might arrive at any moment. Matthew looked at his reflection in the glass of the clock and hastily smoothed his hair, then turned to face the study door, steeling his nerves to enter and break the news to his uncle. The door handle gave way under his palm as he went to turn it, and he gasped in surprise when he came face to face with his Uncle Jasper—and their dinner guests, who appeared to be about to file out of the room in an orderly fashion.

Lord Hartwell and the Duke of Saliston stood a little way behind their host, and each of the men wore smiles that turned Matthew's stomach in anticipation. Without a word he knew precisely the reason for their early arrival and what his dreadful news could potentially mean. Frozen in horror, he stood, mouth agape and his hand still resting on the doorknob.

"Matthew? Are you quite well, my boy?" Lord Iverson asked frowningly, the smile disappearing from his face immediately as he sensed that something was very wrong.

"I'm glad you are all here," Matthew said firmly, putting his hand on his uncle's shoulder and guiding him back into the study before closing the door softly behind them. "Something has happened. We need to talk."

Lord Iverson stared at his nephew suspiciously, wondering what information he could possibly have to convey that ought to be said in front of their guests, but he walked steadily to his desk and seated himself in his armchair without a word.

"I will not ask what you have discussed between you just now, because I am sure I know the subject. We are near enough friends for that, I think, Lord Hartwell." Matthew, his voice grave, remained on his feet while the three other men seated themselves, and he fancied he understood how an actor might feel standing before a critical audience, for none of them were smiling, only gazing at him apprehensively. "It grieves me greatly to tell you this, but I received word half an hour ago that my cousin has been kidnapped."

The room exploded around Matthew's ears with a cacophony of exclamations from the three men, who each leapt up from their seats. Lord Iverson thundered and shouted, standing so quickly that his sturdy leather armchair rocked back like a tree in the wind and fell against the bookshelf behind him.

"Please," Matthew yelled above the noise. "Please, I beg you, stop shouting."

"Why are you not in pursuit?" Lord Iverson cried, anxiously running his hands through his hair.

"How come you to know this?" Saliston asked loudly, but somewhat softer than he had moments earlier.

"Lucilla's maid was thrown out of the carriage," Matthew explained. "It seems Lucilla was able to identify her abductor and made an excuse to get the girl set down near to Albany so she might raise the alarm.

307

Quite by chance, she also managed to get him to say where he was going, too."

"Where are they going? We must go after her at once," Lord Iverson bellowed feverishly.

"Please, Uncle, calm yourself," Matthew yelled back at his uncle frustratedly. "I am here to tell you what I know, but there is already someone in pursuit. It will be fruitless to chase after her for the moment, unless we presently receive word that she has not been found."

"Who? Who has gone after her?"

"Please, Uncle, there is more I must tell you, but you must calm yourself."

"Lord Iverson," the duke said gently, placing a soothing hand on the viscount's shoulder. "Drink this. I believe we must hear what Matthew has to tell us, and it would be best to have it out without interruption. Go on, Mr. Iverson."

Mollified, Lord Iverson sat on the sofa with hunched shoulders and wide eyes, nursing the tumbler of port Saliston had put firmly in his hand. Breathing a sigh of relief, Matthew continued his tale, beginning with Alice Bevan's arrival at his set at Albany and what she had told him, including details about the mask and the pistol. All the while, Lord Hartwell sat incredibly still, leaning forward in his seat with his hands covering his face— Matthew wondered if he was even listening.

"Hartwell, have you heard me?" Matthew asked concernedly, a quizzical frown on his face. Oliver emerged from behind his hands and let out a long, loud breath before he looked at his friend directly.

"You said she identified the man," he stated rather than questioned, and Matthew nodded almost apologetically in reply. "It was my cousin Charlie, wasn't it."

"How do you know that?" Matthew demanded, his eyes widening in surprise.

"Suffice it to say that I have reason to believe he has tried once before to kidnap her and failed," Oliver said through gritted teeth, running a frustrated hand through his hair.

"You mean to tell me this scoundrel is your cousin? Charles Moore?" Lord Iverson bellowed.

"I believe it to be so, Lord Iverson," Oliver replied almost dejectedly.

"This is all very interesting, but it is not at the moment helpful," Saliston said suddenly, standing and looking straight at Matthew. "You said someone is in pursuit. Who is it? Can they be trusted with Miss Iverson in the event she is recovered?"

"You can depend on the discretion of the man, sir. It is my cousin Edward, with Lucilla's groom, Smithers," Matthew answered heavily, glancing quickly at his Uncle Jasper to gauge his reaction. He was relieved to see the fear and concern momentarily leave his face, but in their stead were regret and, perhaps, hope.

"Edward…" his lordship said breathlessly. "He's returned?"

"Yes, Uncle, he was with me when Miss Bevan came to tell me that Lucilla had been taken. He insisted on going after them himself and has taken Smithers with him in Lucilla's phaeton with the grays," Matthew explained, his voice softened considerably under the anxious gaze his uncle had fixed on him. "He was, I judge, an hour behind them—or a little less. In any case, it will be fruitless to go after them now. If Ned can't locate her tonight or we have not received word through the night, then we will go to Finchley after him."

"Yes," Lord Iverson whispered as though in a daze. "Yes, that seems reasonable. I must go and tell your mother."

With that, his lordship stepped slowly and deliberately out of the study, a shell of his usual boisterous self. His nephew watched him go with concern but knew he would be best left to manage Lady Iverson alone. Matthew turned to the two other men in the room. Saliston was watching Hartwell with much the same concern. His face dangerously darkened with a scowl. They had been whispering to one another, but the conversation ceased as Lord Iverson left the room.

"What did you mean when you said Moore has tried to do this before, Olly?" Matthew asked the young earl suspiciously as he poured himself a glass of Madeira and sat in one of the heavy armchairs.

Lord Hartwell's lips pursed distastefully as he recounted the tale of the events at Vauxhall and how he had come to suspect Charlie's involvement in the episode. Matthew stared at him as he wove the story together, his eyes by turns concerned, angry, shocked— and very amused as Hartwell described the exemplary blows Lucilla had landed on her attacker.

"So you bore witness to just how decidedly unladylike my cousin's education has been, then?" Matthew asked with a snort of laughter. "My aunt would be grieved to hear it. I think she regrets allowing Lucilla free rein. It has concerned her greatly during these last few months that she might do something embarrassing— though, in my opinion, these quite 'unladylike' traits have clearly been a good thing more than once."

"I am inclined to agree," Hartwell said with a placid

smile. "Indeed, I can only hope that she shows the same presence of mind again and will come home unharmed."

"Hear, hear," Saliston murmured quietly, throwing back the port in his tumbler and frowning into the fire.

****

It was going to be a long night, but more than half an hour had passed since Edward and Smithers had raced away from Grosvenor Street mews in pursuit of Lucilla and her abductor. The traffic had thinned as they got away from Mayfair, but they had a distance to make up for in their chase. The grays were fresh and in fine fettle, agilely flitting through the streets at a plucky trot, but their driver was noticeably concerned that they were not moving quickly enough. The grays were fit and sensitive, and eminently capable of maintaining a speed that the job horses Moore would have hired would not, a fact which was pointed out by Smithers early in the piece in an effort to calm the young master down.

"Do y' mean t' search every house in Finchley, Master Edward?"

"There can't be more than a handful of public houses in the area, Smithers," Edward said tersely. "And knowing that beast as I do, he will think that he's gone far enough off the beaten path that it will not be necessary to hide his tracks."

"I dinna think it'll be so easy t' find 'em, sir," the stable master replied grimly. "Pr'aps we ought to split up, might 'ave a better chance of findin' Miss Cilla if we do that. Mustn't be more than—"

"Perhaps, but for the moment, let us just get to Finchley," Edward answered firmly. In a moment of silence, he considered the route that he had taken to get to his destination and wondered what had possessed the idiot Moore to go by Albany after taking Lucilla from Hyde Park. It seemed absurd, but upon reflection, he supposed it to have been an effort to throw any pursuers off the scent. With the blood freezing in his veins, he could only hope that speaking the name of his destination was a colossal blunder on Charlie's part and it was not also an attempt to mislead Lucilla's rescuers.

Finchley being barely above seven miles from Grosvenor Street, Edward expected to arrive there quite soon, but after thinking on it for a time, he wondered if there was more to Mr. Moore's strange path around Mayfair than at first met the eye. With the Great North Road in easy reach, Finchley was a perfectly reasonable place to stop over if one was leaving London, but it was rather too close for an elopement. If he did indeed intend to stop there, he must not intend to seek shelter in one of the coaching houses, for it would be too easy to be discovered there.

"I think we will begin on the eastern side of Finchley, Smithers," Edward said suddenly.

"Why for, sir? Would it not be best to stop at a house on the road?"

"It would if we were not following someone traveling clandestinely, old chap," he replied. "And there must be a reason for this bizarre route he has taken. Why would he go so far around Mayfair? He was in an unmarked, hired carriage, so he had no reason to expect to be recognized. I think he means to stay on the other side of the village. We will make inquiries about any small inns that are well off the highway."

"So be it, sir," Smithers said with a nod. "Sensible, by that reas'nin', I think."

Chapter 27

As soon as the door of the coach had slammed shut and the driver was whipping his horses up again, Miss Iverson's demeanor changed entirely. In the moments leading up to the maid and dog being deposited safely on the sidewalk, she had been frightened, pleading, even tearful. Now that she was alone with the masked man, one would have expected a lesser female to dissolve in a puddle of blubbering tears, but not she. Miss Iverson was made of sterner stuff.

Upon closer inspection, Mr. Moore realized that her face was not even slightly moistened. Her eyes had no redness, and the tearful glistening had vanished. She sat across from him, staring at him calculatingly but silent, and so she would remain until the cobbled London streets gave way to the countryside.

She had worried that he had deliberately mentioned the wrong destination in order to misdirect Miss Bevan should she try to send assistance, but after taking careful note of their direction she determined that they were now traveling in a more northerly direction at last, which relieved her considerably, though she made sure not to show it. The coachman had slowed his horses much earlier, and since Moore had made no move to hurry him, she assumed the change of pace was by design. Evidently, he was confident that he either was not being followed or would not be caught before they reached a safe haven in Finchley.

Now that she was reasonably certain his outburst was a genuine slip of the tongue, and she had had time to consider her next steps, Lucilla decided it was time to give him a reason to stop smiling so smugly every time he glanced in her direction. The mask still hid his face effectively, but as she gazed at him, she wondered how she had not recognized him at Vauxhall. He had donned the same outfit, but the lower half of his face was uncovered. How could she have failed to identify that self-satisfied turn of his lips? How could she possibly have mistaken him for Lord Hartwell, even for a moment? It was absurd. She glared at him, eyes narrowed.

"I think we are quite far enough from prying eyes that you might remove your little mask, Mr. Moore," she said with an air of docility, her lips pursed as she looked at him with distaste. She had the satisfaction of seeing his eyes widen and his nostrils flare as he breathed in sharply in shock. His mouth dropped open slightly, but he slammed it shut again and ground his teeth together audibly, obviously annoyed. She was glad to see that he did not instinctively reach for his weapon, but he tore the mask from his face irritably and tossed it aside.

"How came you to guess?" he snarled, glaring at her.

"Do you think me a fool?" She tittered. "Your disguise may have worked in the crowd at Vauxhall, but it will not conceal you a second time. But I confess, it was actually your weapon that gave you away."

"What, this?" Mr. Moore asked quizzically, pulling the pistol out from under his cloak and inspecting it with concern and confusion. "Why, how could it identify me?

It is not even my own."

"I assume you have it from Lady Hartwell," she replied casually, forcing a calm disinterest into her tone.

He stared at her suspiciously. "And why do you assume that?"

"Because it is one of a pair, and the other belongs to the Duke of Saliston, to whom the original owner bequeathed it."

"The original owner," he said wonderingly. Then his voice became thick and dull as he said, "My aunt's husband."

She nodded and shrugged.

"It is unfortunate for the both of you, I suppose, that the duke had occasion to show me the pistol only a short time ago," Miss Iverson continued nonchalantly, gazing out of the window at the fading countryside. "And to explain the loss of the other."

Mr. Moore's eyes narrowed as he glared at her, his whole aura emanating irritation as he wondered to himself why he had allowed Lady Hartwell to convince him to go along with this ridiculous undertaking. He had long ago realized that her money would not make up for the trouble a clever and spirited girl would cause for him when she was crossed. At least the Wallace chit was easy enough to tame out of a fit of temper.

Miss Iverson turned her head, her lips twitching into a subtle smile.

"May I ask what it is you intend to gain by this havey-cavey adventure?" she asked with unimpeachable politeness.

"I should think that would be obvious, my dear," he answered, matching her tone as best he could, forcing a smile he was far from feeling.

"Yes, well, I should like to hear you say it, all the same."

"I intend to gain a wife," he said simply. "And I intend to gain the ability to meet my financial obligations."

"Oh, how very romantic that sounds." She laughed. "I should dearly like to know how Lady Hartwell came to be involved."

"My aunt has been a source of constant support in my life from when I was a child."

"If only she had been so for her own son."

"My cousin never wanted for anything," Mr. Moore growled. "He was born into privilege few enjoy."

"Yes, I suppose he was," she replied urbanely. "Fed, clothed, uneducated, kept away from the world—it seems a perfectly excellent life for a child."

"He wanted for *nothing*," Mr. Moore repeated angrily but somewhat feebly.

"It tells me not why his mother would assist you in this shameful endeavor."

"My aunt wants me to have what is my due—"

Her snort of laughter stopped him, and he glared at her, open-mouthed.

"Oh, yes, your due," she gurgled, gesturing for him to continue. "Pray, go on, Mr. Moore! Do tell me, what do you deserve?"

He could not find the words to retort, so much fury welled up within him. His mind raced, searching for the right thing to say to regain control of the situation, but all he could focus on was the contemptuous glint in her eye and the taunting note in her voice. His fingers twitched at his side, and he imagined wrapping them around her neck. He had longed to for several years, but the reason had changed dramatically. He realized that his finger was pressing against the trigger of the pistol, and he forced himself to set it aside, placing it on the seat beside him carefully and within easy reach.

Lucilla smiled inwardly. It had not taken much to anger her abductor. She supposed he was used to having his own way and did not like that she was not intimidated by his loud voice. Having the gun in plain sight now gave her a fresh idea.

"Well, you have yet to explain Lady Hartwell's place in this despicable scheme. Am I ever to hear it?"

"No," he snapped.

She sighed loudly and looked away. Seated as she was, diagonally across the cabin from him, the pistol lay roughly halfway between them but somewhat closer to him. He crossed his arms and looked out of his own window. As she watched, he clenched his eyes shut with frustration and ground his jaw left and right as though fighting the urge to scream his irritation for any and all to hear. It was the perfect moment, and possibly the only chance she'd have. Soundlessly, she inched forward and grasped the pistol. He heard nothing, but then came an unmistakable click, and his eyes flashed open.

She was sitting bolt upright with a soft smile, the elegant silver pistol pointed at him very deliberately.

"It is a magnificent weapon, sir. Rather larger than my own, I admit, but I should be willing to wager on my accuracy at such close quarters."

"What are you doing?" Mr. Moore said nervously as he slowly uncrossed his arms and instinctively leaned back into his corner.

"Why, I should think that would be obvious, my dear," she replied mockingly. "I do so hope that your coachman is careful. Who knows what might happen if a wheel were to hit a hole."

"Put it down," he demanded, trying to sound forceful but failing.

"Whyever would I do that, Mr. Moore?" she asked pertly, an eyebrow raised in surprise. "I am held against my will, so in whose interest would it be for me to lower this weapon? Surely not my own."

"If you would simply submit—"

"Did you really just say that?" Miss Iverson cried angrily. "How dare you? How dare you suggest such a thing! You are insufferable. I can counter that if *you* would simply give up your pretensions, none of this would be happening!"

"Your reputation will be in tatters once the night is through. Why fight the inevitable?" he yelled back at her, fear giving way to stinging anger at her words. He realized now that his aunt had been right about not loading the pistol and fervently wished he had listened. He'd had no intention of using it in any capacity except to frighten his victim, but he had once more underestimated Miss Iverson's self-sustainability. His pride had smarted for days after she had landed her punches at Vauxhall. For how long would he wear the shame of her having the upper hand on him with a gun?

"Thanks to your mask and your hired carriage, I have some hope yet that I will scrape through this night," she said coolly. "And I would remind you that it will cause *you* no small amount of harm to tell anyone what has transpired. Perhaps not as much as it would myself, but enough to see you shunned by much of Society and any female of fortune kept out of your way."

"Would marriage to me really be so distasteful?" he

said peevishly. "When I have loved you for so many years and have waited so long."

"I do not believe you know the meaning of the word 'love,' and in any case I cannot imagine anything more distasteful than marriage to a man who respected me so little that he would abduct me," Miss Iverson said frankly. "I am no simpering miss. Anyone who might claim to know me, indeed love me, would know that. I am firm in my opinions, and my opinion of you is that you care for my dowry and not a jot for me, and I like you just as well."

"I should like to think that affection might grow," he muttered under his breath.

"Rid yourself of the notion. It is a ridiculous one. I know you are not in love with me, Mr. Moore, just as you know I am not—and never will be—in love with you, for I certainly have not offered any encouragement," she declared.

The pistol never wavered for a moment, he realized. In spite of her anger, she did not allow herself to lose focus—and once again Mr. Moore was irritated at her complete lack of femininity. Delicately bred females did not strike gentlemen, they did not ride highly strung blood-horse stallions, and they became hysterical at the sight of pistols. This diminutive dark-haired termagant was making his life unbearable, and he wasn't even married to her yet.

"I will not be forced into marriage with you, Mr. Moore," Miss Iverson said firmly. "Nor with any man who values me and my reputation so little. I believe we are near to Finchley now. You will tell the coachman to set you down on the roadside, and he will convey me home."

"Finchley? How do you—"

"Well, I'm glad to have it so confirmed," she interrupted with a thin laugh. "I had wondered if you might have said the wrong name in order to mislead me, but I see now that I overestimated your abilities."

"I don't underst—"

"Mr. Moore, before we set down my unfortunate maid, you declared that you would not carry her in her hysterical state all the way to Finchley."

His eyes widened for a moment and then immediately narrowed, his jaw stiffened, and his lips pouted like a child about to throw a temper tantrum. It would have amused her if she were not so completely tired of him and the situation in general.

"Pray, do not fall into a fit of hysterics, Mr. Moore. I beg you to remember who holds the gun," she said in an eminently bored voice. "Do as I say and have the driver set you down. You may walk the remaining mile or so to whichever little hole you had planned to drag me to, but I *will* go home."

With an indignant growl and a seething glare, he banged his hand on the door of the coach, and the driver presently halted his horses. She gently reminded him to offer the coachman his instructions before exiting the carriage, which he did by leaning out of the open window and calling up to the man. He continued to scowl at her as he finally opened the door of the coach and disembarked with his hands raised above his head in defeat. The pistol remained trained on him through the window while she called out to the coachman to drive on and quickly, and as the hackney rumbled along the road again at a smarter pace, she smiled with gleeful satisfaction and relief at having trounced her would-be kidnapper not once but twice.

The emotions being experienced by Mr. Moore were not half so invigorating. Stranded in the roadway at least two miles from Finchley, he knew the chances of his being picked up were slim simply because he had deliberately chosen a convoluted route to his destination in an effort to remain unseen on the main carriageways— a circumstance which he now added to the list of stupid ideas that had contributed to this abysmal failure. One foot in front of the other for the next hour, he contemplated how he might dig himself out of the pit he'd been unceremoniously thrown into on his aunt's whim and wondered if by morning all would be at an end.

About twenty minutes later, Miss Iverson stepped halfway out of the hired coach and looked about apprehensively. The dingy lodging house Mr. Moore had directed the carriage driver to go to was well east of the respectable coach houses strung along the main northern highway. With a distrustful gaze she looked up at the coachman, who had remained seated on the box and was looking down at her, awaiting instruction. She had no reason to trust the honesty of the man, but considering all that he'd borne witness to this day, he was clearly able to be bought. With an assertive edge to her voice, she squared her shoulders and stared him down.

"Drive on to one of the posting-houses on the north road, sir," she enunciated clearly. He was about to protest, but when she icily advised that he would be handsomely remunerated for his efforts, he clamped his mouth shut and nodded acquiescence while she climbed back in and slammed the door shut behind her.

As the horses pulled out of the little courtyard at a

sedate walk, Lucilla caught sight of a person at one of the upper windows of the dingy house, but as soon as she looked up at them, the curtain was abruptly drawn shut. She felt a twinge of nerves and worry that she might have been seen. Or worse, recognized. It was too late to remedy the situation, and fretting would not solve anything, so she settled herself back into the coach in anticipation of presently arriving at one of the more reputable inns.

Not five minutes had passed when the coach driver slowed his horses, and Lucilla leaned forward, expecting they had reached a posting house. She had guessed correctly—the unmistakable sound of cobblestones rumbled under the coach, and the usual resonances of a lively posting house stable came to her ears. Grooms were calling out; horses were snorting and shuffling, coach wheels clattering loudly on the pavement. As she looked out over the environs, her gaze landed on a pair of handsome gray horses pulling a phaeton with blue wheels.

"Matthew," she screeched.

Hardly waiting for the hackney to come to a complete halt, she flung open the door and leapt out, running toward the two men who stood animatedly conversing with an ostler. At the sound of her cry, Smithers turned and immediately grasped his companion's arm to draw his attention, and Lucilla found herself face to face not with her cousin, but her brother.

"Edward?" Lucilla said in a faltering voice as she slowed and covered her face with her hands in shock.

"Cilla," he cried in amazement, rushing toward her and catching her up in his arms and holding her tightly while the merrily grinning Smithers sent the curious ostler about his business.

"Where is Matthew?" Lucilla asked confusedly.

"A fine way to greet your brother, I must say!" Edward laughed as he let her go, but as he stepped back he looked her over with sudden concern. "Are you unharmed? Where is that devil, Moore?"

"I expect he is still walking," she replied nonchalantly.

"Walking? Walking where?" he asked suspiciously and then angrily continued, "Don't try to conceal him from me, Cilla. I will find the rake, so help me, God! He will not live the night."

"Oh, do just take me home, please, Ned," Lucilla sighed mournfully. "I don't want to see his stupid face again in my life, much less any time in the immediate future. I have given him a scare well enough, and you may chase the wastrel down another day."

"What d' y' mean y' give him a scare, Miss Cilla?" Smithers asked, his brows raised and his hands on his hips.

With a wry smile, she drew the silver pistol from her pelisse and was pleased to see both men start with surprise.

"How did you come to have a pistol? Have you made a habit of walking armed whilst in the park?" her brother said, wide-eyed, as he took the weapon from her hand and studied it.

"Of course not." She laughed. "Moore had it, thinking to frighten me with it. I contrived to take it from him and had the coach driver abandon him a few miles before we arrived in the village."

"Always bin a knowin' one." Smithers grinned.

"Very clever, very quick."

"Yes," Edward said slowly, eyeing his sister carefully. He weighed up whether it would be prudent to take action against the fiend while he was in the immediate vicinity. It would go very much against the grain to let him go without a confrontation. It rankled already that he had not been allowed to execute a rescue himself. But he could not be unhappy with the result that his sister stood before him, not a hair out of place, and her abductor unsuccessful in his ultimate goal.

After a moment, he begrudgingly decided to cut his losses. Retribution would have to wait—perhaps Lord Iverson would want his share of the pound of flesh to be taken from the creature at fault. For now, it would do to have Lucilla home.

"Well, that is a relief, I must say." She sighed. "Please give the coachman a coin for his trouble, Ned. It would not do to have him mention the events of this evening, yes?"

Her brother grumbled an incoherent and obviously querulous reply, but grumpily handed his coin purse to Smithers with an instruction to pay off the hackney driver. The groom bounded off to complete his task while Edward herded his sister into the posting house in search of a sandwich.

They were back on the road to London within the hour, Lucilla having insisted that her horses be tended to before they returned home. With a blanket drawn about her shoulders, she sat with her hand linked through her brother's arm and her head resting on his shoulder contentedly on the eight-mile journey back home to Grosvenor Street.

At Iverson House, the company had assembled in

the drawing room after dinner. Matthew had been invited to dine with the Russells but found himself too distracted and so sent a note around to his betrothed, excusing himself. So baffled was Miss Russell by the vague and short note that she took a quick early meal before hurrying around to Grosvenor Street.

When she arrived at the house, Miss Russell was horrified to learn the reason for Matthew's confusing letter. Once the tale of the afternoon's events had been recounted to her, she too was able to accurately speculate the identity of the kidnapper, which considerably surprised Matthew.

"Really, my dear, she has always seemed very ill at ease in his company. And he has always been so very overly familiar with her, in spite of receiving absolutely no encouragement," Caroline said frankly. "And I suspect he is not a very patient or personable man underneath that polished exterior. It does not surprise me in the least that he would scheme to do such a thing."

"I know she has never liked the fellow, and I certainly have no great taking for him," Matthew acknowledged. "He'll be sorry when Ned catches him."

She raised an eyebrow at him. The pair sat together at Lucilla's pianoforte, Miss Russell playing an idle tune as they talked. The tension and worry that filled the room influenced her rather more than she realized, for she had to stop herself from playing a melancholy refrain. She glanced around the room at the various occupants and wondered what they were each thinking at the moment.

Lady Iverson was sitting by the Duke of Saliston, who appeared to be putting in a valiant effort to raise the distraught mother's spirits. Lord Iverson stood beside the fire, one hand resting on the mantelshelf, the other holding a glass of port while he stared gloomily into the flames. By now, Matthew was absentmindedly stroking the keys of the fine mahogany Broadwood grand pianoforte.

Lord Hartwell sat alone near the window, staring out into the gathering darkness and speaking to no one. His face was by turns anxious, hopeful, fearful. The sound of clattering hooves had long since been blocked out by the rest of the party, who had at first run to the window at the slightest sound. Only Lord Hartwell now kept up the vigil with determined silence and dignity.

And it was he who observed the grays approaching, and the flash of blue as the wheels of the phaeton turned. They had not reached the house, let alone come to a halt, before he had stood and rushed from the room without a word. His sudden dash drew the gaze of all in the room, but as a certain level of apathy had been reached, no one was prompted to move except Miss Russell. She stood abruptly and watched the young earl hurry from the drawing room with curiosity and hope.

Oliver noticed no one as he flung down the hall and tore the front door open. He trotted down the steps just as the phaeton drew to a halt, and Miss Iverson, feeling the carriage swaying as the horses stopped anxiously, suddenly awoke and lifted her head from her brother's shoulder, blinking as she looked around her and found Lord Hartwell gazing up at her earnestly.

"Olly," she said with a sleepy smile.

"Cilla," he replied hoarsely, reaching up to take her proffered hand.

As she descended the steps, she found herself jerked rather roughly into his arms. This lover-like behavior at first elicited a soft laugh from her, but as she put her arms around his neck, she instead dissolved into tears.

Chapter 28

Still somewhat resentful and prickly after being convinced to allow Mr. Moore an escape, a scandalized Edward Iverson observed the manner of his sister's greeting with a tall, fair young gentleman with widened eyes and a sharp cry of reproof. Smithers put a steadying hand on the young master and shook his head, but it was not quite enough to calm him.

Thankfully, further outburst was prevented by the arrival of Matthew and Miss Russell, and the transfer of Lucilla into the arms of another female, even an unfamiliar person, was decidedly less threatening in Edward's eyes than the stranger she had first embraced so intimately. As soon as she was assured her friend had come to no harm, Miss Russell wasted no time in dragging her into the house to her concerned parents.

Left on the pavement alone, the three young men stared at one another. Edward stared at Oliver, and Oliver stared back at him, while Matthew stood warily looking between them, and it was he who broke the silence as Smithers slowly turned the phaeton in the street and drove the tired grays back to the mews.

"Ned," Matthew said gently. "Ned, this is Lord Hartwell."

"I am pleased to finally make your acquaintance, Mr. Iverson," Oliver said politely, offering a short bow. Edward still wore a suspicious glare, but he nodded and muttered what might pass for a polite response. Sensing his cousin was not entirely accepting of Oliver, Matthew tried one more time to break the ice.

"Uncle Jasper has this evening given Lord Hartwell leave to pay his addresses to Lucilla, Ned," Matthew said informatively, clapping his hand on Oliver's shoulder in a show of friendly comradery. "I came in just as it had all been decided, so Lucilla doesn't know yet. We'll have to remedy that, shan't we, Olly?"

"You're going to marry my sister?" Edward said slowly, his eyes boring into Oliver like a drilling tool. Oliver found himself wincing until the other man suddenly softened and continued, "Lord, good luck to you."

The three young men laughed between themselves, Oliver a little less so than the two almost-brothers, but the tension had evaporated, and he found himself rather giddy with relief at having overcome the hurdle of acceptance from the rather mythical figure that had been the missing Edward Iverson.

Unfortunately, the awkwardness was not over for Edward himself. As the men adjourned to the drawing room, the joyful reunion between the daughter of the house and her distraught parents had begun to calm, and attention was now abundantly available to be devoted to Edward's sudden and fortuitous return. His stepmother burst into tears of joy and relief, and after a tense silence, Lord Iverson wrapped his son in an uncharacteristic bear hug that almost squeezed the breath from his lungs.

Murray brought in two trays with a light meal for each of the inadvertent travelers and the tea tray for the rest of the evening party. Almost as soon as Murray had withdrawn, a soft patting at the door was heard, and

Smithers entered quietly with his hands behind his back and asked for Miss Iverson, who rose immediately and went to the door. The groom whispered to his young mistress and handed her something wrapped in a thick cloth, which she gingerly took from him. He left the room with a punctilious nod and a smile. Lucilla turned hesitantly and found that every occupant of the room was staring at her curiously.

"Heavens, am I so interesting?" She laughed.

"I'm afraid you will be very interesting for quite a while, dear," said her mother in melancholic reply.

"Lord, I hope not. I've no wish at all to be notorious," Lucilla replied. With a flouncing step she marched toward Saliston where he sat in an armchair and held out the wrapped object to him like an offering. "I believe this is yours, sir?"

The Duke of Saliston frowned curiously and slowly took the unknown item from her hands, unsure of what he would find. When he had unwrapped it, he started suddenly and looked up at her in surprise to exclaim, "Where did you get this, Miss Iverson?"

She smiled at him demurely and answered, "It was in Charlie Moore's possession. I had occasion to take it from him, and it enabled me to free myself, so for that, I am grateful. But I thought it would be prudent to return it to its rightful owner."

"Do you mean to say that this man is in some way connected to your abduction, Lucilla?" Edward had stood abruptly, his face red and his expression lividly suspicious. The stabbing glare he received from his sister caused him to flinch back slightly, but he largely stood his ground, though somewhat more precariously than he had at first.

"Of course not, you loon. I suggest no such thing," his sister retorted irritably. "There is a perfectly reasonable explanation, if you would but sit down and let me tell it."

His mother patted his hand reassuringly, and somewhat mollified, Edward sat, still watching the duke guardedly.

"What is it?" Lord Iverson asked, stepping forward and peering at the half-folded cloth. The duke held it out to him, and the silver pistol was revealed to the room, drawing a gasp from both Lady Iverson and Miss Russell, with both of them recoiling instinctively.

"I think perhaps you should start from the beginning, Miss Iverson," the duke said calmly. "I should dearly like to know how you came to have this, as I feel certain that my own is safely locked in its case at my home."

"I feel certain it is too, Duke, which is why I am sure you had nothing to do with Mr. Moore having this in his possession," Lucilla replied.

She then recounted the events that had occurred after Alice had been abandoned near Albany, right up to how she had come to find Edward at Finchley. The company sat mostly silent apart from the occasional gasp from Lady Iverson or a question from Matthew or Caroline. Saliston waited patiently for Lucilla to voice her suspicions regarding the pistol and as she did, he found himself watching Oliver's face instead of hers. The young man betrayed not so much as a flicker of emotion, staring steely eyed at the pistol and then up at his cousin, before looking back at Lucilla, who was watching him with sadness in her eyes.

"I want to believe that Mr. Moore stole the pistol

from your mother, Lord Hartwell," she said gently. "Indeed, if you say it must be so, I am only too happy to be told it."

"I'm afraid I cannot confirm it," he answered with a grim shake of his head. "Unfortunately, my instincts tell me she is quite likely the reason for the entire escapade to begin with. Having failed once to take you, I do not think my cousin would have tried a second time without encouragement or support from someone else. He has always been close to my mother, and it certainly would sit with what I know of her to be so ruthless."

"He has done this before?" Edward cried angrily.

"Sit down and calm yourself, brother," Lucilla replied irritably, glaring at him before glancing concernedly at her mother who was staring at her in utter horror. "Please, Mama, do not be alarmed. I was not harmed and no one knows of it, excepting myself and Lord Hartwell."

"How does Lord Hartwell come to know of it?" Lord Iverson asked sternly.

"It was the evening of the masquerade at Vauxhall. Between us, Caro and I and Miss Craven hatched a plan to wear matching tokens. Somehow, it seems, Mr. Moore was in possession of one of them," she explained haltingly. "I was trying to escape him when Lord Hartwell happened upon us, and Mr. Moore fled. I did not recognize him at the time, but today he admitted it."

"I won't ask why you came to be alone with a masked stranger," Lord Iverson said with determined calm. "I will not ask how you came to free yourself, either. I will simply say that I am glad you have found yourself safe a second time, but I very much hope that there will not be cause for a third serving of such luck."

"Yes, Papa," Lucilla whispered, eyes demurely downcast.

"I think it is time we took our leave, Lord Iverson," Saliston said as he rose from his seat. "I am relieved Miss Iverson is unharmed after the events of this day. Regarding the pistol, it has been a source of great sadness to me that I have been unable to reclaim it before, and I must always regret the circumstances of its return. But I am grateful to you, Miss Iverson, for having it safely home and that it was of use to you in facilitating your own safe return."

Oliver had stood and was hovering behind his cousin as Saliston bid her goodbye and took his leave of the rest of the party. Lucilla turned to Oliver, and he took the hand she offered to him, placing a fleeting kiss on her fingers and gazing at her rather sadly before he spoke and asked if she would allow him to visit her the following morning.

"I expect I shall lie in tomorrow morning, but I will endeavor to be downstairs and presentable before you call," she said with an encouraging smile and a sigh. "It will be much like last time, I imagine. Wondering whether the news of my disgrace has reached the ears of the *ton*."

"Do not let it trouble you, please," Oliver said earnestly. "We are, all of us, glad that you are returned safely. The rest does not matter."

The party broke up, with the duke and Lord Hartwell taking their leave and Miss Russell invited to remain the night. Edward returned with Matthew to his set at Albany, having left all of his belongings there upon his arrival earlier in the afternoon. Iverson House was soon quite quiet after a bustling and stress-laden evening.

Rather earlier in that same evening, in a scrubby posting house off the beaten track in Finchley, Miss Wallace sat in a dirty room, peering out of the window. It had been some time since the nondescript carriage had drawn up before quickly driving away, but she was certain it was Lucilla she had seen leaning out of the vehicle. She hoped she had gotten away from the window before she had been seen, for nothing would have embarrassed her more than being spotted patronizing such a shockingly low establishment. It did not immediately dawn on her to wonder why Miss Iverson had been in an unmarked carriage in the late afternoon, apparently unchaperoned and so far from London, but when she did come to think of it, it struck her as very curious.

Miss Wallace herself had arrived earlier in the afternoon in the company of her mother after they had been bluntly refused admittance at her Uncle Cooke's door. Having been notified of the passing of old Cooke Senior, Lady Wallace had immediately fled her disheveled lodgings on the outskirts of Mayfair. She hastened to the estate her father and brother had purchased north of the city several years earlier, only to find that her brother had no welcome for her. Mother and daughter had been obliged to obtain a room at the nearest dingy inn for the night, with Lady Wallace intending to make another attempt to prevail upon her brother the following day.

Miss Wallace had cried desperately at the news of her grandfather's passing. Indeed, if anyone had borne witness to her tears, they would have concluded that she had been uncommonly fond of her very common grandparent, but in truth, she wept for herself, for she knew she had run out of time and that her horrid, jealous, and spiteful Uncle Cooke would never again come to her aid.

The fact of the matter was that "horrid" Uncle Cooke had had quite enough of being treated with disdain and rudeness by his ungrateful sister, who owed her education and financial security to his mercantile genius. The engaging child of her youth had long since given way to the uptight, haughty, and vain creature that insisted on being addressed as Lady Wallace instead of Sister. Had she made a friend of her brother rather than treating him like an unworthy connection, her reception at his door might have been different.

So Lady Wallace wept, also for selfish reasons. She berated her daughter heartlessly for her failure to secure a match with a wealthy gentleman that would have made it unnecessary for her mother to beg and scrape at the feet of her wealthy brother. She was now bent over the small writing desk and engaged in the task of penning a letter in the hope of softening his heart before her next attempt to approach him. The two women were making an excellent effort at ignoring one another after a hearty row on the subject, and it was during one of these quiet moments that Miss Wallace, staring out into the courtyard, watched a cloaked figure approach the house on foot. As the person came closer, he pulled back his hood, and she recognized the face of Mr. Moore.

"I think I should like to take dinner in the downstairs parlor, Mama," Miss Wallace said pertly as she stood up from the window seat.

"Do what you will. I will not join you," her mother replied, waving a hand at her daughter irritably and not even glancing up from her place at the writing desk as

Miss Wallace left the room with her flouncing step.

She pranced down the narrow dusty staircase, stopping for a moment at a glass where she examined her appearance and tucked a stray curl away before continuing down the hall toward the only parlor the dingy house boasted. She rang the bell to call for the housekeeper, and presently she was attended to by the fat, rough landlord, who grumbled a query on her call and grunted acknowledgment of her request for a dinner tray.

"Was that a knock at the door I heard before?" Miss Wallace asked before the landlord left the parlor, and with another grunt he confirmed the guest they had been waiting for had finally arrived, only two hours later than expected. She glared at the landlord's back with irritation as he stomped out of the room and mulled over how best to put herself in Mr. Moore's way.

She was not alone with her thoughts for long. Only a few moments after the fat innkeeper had left the parlor, Mr. Charles Moore entered it. He seemed to her to be in an ireful mood, for he wore a scowl, and he audibly snarled at the sight of another person in the parlor, but it took only a moment for him to recognize her, and his expression softened slightly.

"Miss Wallace?"

"Oh, Mr. Moore," she exclaimed delightedly, feigning surprise at seeing him. "How ever do you come to be here? And how very fortuitous it is to see one's friends."

"I…I…" he stuttered, blinking quickly and trying to find the right words.

"We are on our way to my grandfather's house for his funeral, I'm afraid," she continued in as mournful a tone as she could muster. She twisted and knotted the handkerchief in her hand, putting on a sad face and sniffling miserably for effect. She had no idea that her act was unnecessary—her words had been quite enough to pique his interest.

"I am so very sorry to hear that, Miss Wallace," he said in a soothing voice as he approached her.

"Oh, thank you."

"I find myself in a rather sad state myself this evening."

"I am sorry to know it," she replied, dabbing her handkerchief at the corner of her bone-dry eye. "Do, please, sit with me. Would it help to unburden yourself?"

Mr. Moore watched her curiously as he took the seat nearest to her chair and wondered what story he would be best to tell in order to garner sympathy. It was so perfect that he had found her, so unbelievably fortunate. It was so important now that he said exactly the right thing.

"I am afraid I have been on a romantic journey this evening, Miss Wallace. A romantic journey that has ended very sadly for me," he declared in a melancholy tone.

"Oh, poor dear. Now you simply must tell me," she cried, reaching out and grasping his hand in hers, inching closer to him from her seat.

Encouraged, he covered her hand with his own and sighed, mostly at his own luck, before he continued.

"Well, I am ashamed to say that I allowed myself to be convinced to act in a manner that is not entirely becoming in a gentleman," he said, sighing again.

"I'm sure that cannot be so."

"I'm afraid it is," he continued, mournfully covering

his eyes with one hand. "You see, this afternoon I set out to elope with Miss Iverson, but at the very last, she could not go through with it and has abandoned me."

Miss Wallace gasped. It was not at all what she had expected to hear, and to say she was shocked would have been to understate her feelings entirely. But it took only a moment for her to realize that if she were very careful and very clever, she might be able to make the most of the young gentleman's obvious disappointment. Clearly, it behooved her to console him in his loss, and condemning Miss Iverson in just the right way might at this moment convince him that she, Miss Wallace, was in every way superior and preferable.

So she did exactly that. With carefully chosen words, she pointed out Miss Iverson's poor form in agreeing to elope, only to jilt him not an hour after their flight. She watched his expression as he allowed himself to be swayed into the belief that he had been ill-used and he deserved so much better than what he had suffered that night. He nodded in grateful agreeance when she proudly declared that she would never have treated him so horribly if *she* had been the one to fly away with him. All the while, Mr. Moore congratulated himself on his luck. It seemed his fortunes had at last turned, and the merchant heiress was now so easily falling into his hands.

Not two hours later, they had reached an agreement to continue Mr. Moore's planned journey to Scotland with the intention to marry one another upon their arrival. They would leave Finchley as soon as Lady Wallace had departed to meet again with her brother, and they would be out of reach by the time she returned or sent to fetch her daughter.

Miss Wallace was sure that once her mother understood the urgency of the situation, she would approve of her daughter's plan, but she still had no intention of confiding in her—Moore found her exceedingly conforming on that score.

When the two young persons retired to their respective chambers that night, they were both delighted with the fruits of their scheming, and entirely unaware that they were completely and utterly deceived by one another.

Chapter 29

Lady Wallace had managed to persuade the innkeeper to drive her to her brother's house in his gig behind a slovenly pony, with the promise of monetary reward at the conclusion of the task, but it unfortunately meant she would be required to begin her journey at a ridiculously early hour of the morning. After breakfast with her mother in the cramped dining room at half seven, Miss Wallace promised faithfully to remain in their bedchamber until her return or the arrival of Uncle Cooke's carriage to retrieve her.

"Everything, our entire future security, rests on this," Lady Wallace muttered fiercely. "I will do whatever I must, though it grieves me greatly. I cannot express how very disappointed I am that you have wasted the Season. Spending so much effort on a young man who clearly had eyes for no one but Lucilla Iverson, you might have at least *tried* to put yourself forward with one or two others. It matters little how rich he is if he is only interested in one woman and you are not her."

"Yes, Mama," Miss Wallace replied demurely, bowing her head and looking away. It hurt her to be spoken to so meanly, but it was hardly anything she had not heard with growing frequently in recent weeks.

For a moment, she thought to match her mother's hostility with the news that she had contracted a match with the very man her mother was speaking of, no less.

But she knew that however pleased her mother might be with the end result, she would not approve of an elopement if she knew of it beforehand. After all, there would be no opportunity for negotiating settlements, no certainty of an agreement once the knot was tied. But Miss Wallace doubted there would be an advantage to his knowing she was penniless herself, and so haste was preferable if not necessary. In this the young couple would have found themselves in complete agreement, had they discussed the subject. Haste was also desirable to Mr. Moore, as the discussion of settlements with her father would necessarily have uncovered his own pecuniary shortfall.

So, as soon as the innkeeper's hairy pony and gig disappeared from view, Miss Wallace raced back up to her bedchamber and hurriedly packed her belongings into her portmanteau, tied on her bonnet, and went back downstairs to meet with her betrothed, at which time it was barely past seven in the morning. He had taken pains earlier in the morning to avoid being seen by her mother by walking round to a nearby public house for his meal, and there he procured a carriage to take them on their journey.

Thankfully he'd lost nothing the previous day, for he'd had the foresight to have his belongings sent to the inn prior to his abduction of Miss Iverson, and he felt fortune was finally smiling on him when his prospective mother-in-law took herself off and his bride excitedly boarded the carriage beside him. It would be several hours at least before Miss Wallace was missed, whether it would be by the return of her mother or the arrival of her uncle's carriage, and in either case they would be well on their way and quite out of reach of possible pursuers.

At the last, unable to leave without explanation, Miss Wallace had penned a letter to her parent and left it conspicuously on her bed. It read:

Dearest Mama,

Please do not be alarmed when you find that I am gone, for I am very well and happy. I am certain that once you have given thought to my letter you will see I had no choice but to take my chance when it presented, and that you will be very happy with the result. You see, it seems Mr. Charles Moore has become resigned to the dissolution of his relationship with that rotten flirt Lucy Iverson. You will be excessively shocked, dear Mama, to know the ridiculously named 'Iverson Jewel' has so far lost her sense of propriety as to actually have eloped with a man! And at the last moment, poor Mr. Moore has found himself jilted, for the horrid girl would not, in the end, keep her word, which comes as no surprise to me, of course.

I find myself the fortunate recipient of his transferred affections, and I am now resolved to marry him immediately. We are bound for Scotland, and I beg you not to follow us, nor send Papa! You will see that this is the best possible solution, for I will return Mrs. Moore, and my husband will inherit a comely estate in Lancashire. It is exactly what you would wish—indeed, what you have wished. I will make you very proud, Mama, at the last.

Your loving daughter,

Tabitha

Lady Wallace, returning from her errand unsuccessful after a row with her brother had lasted several hours, was in no mood for a shock. She had been only irritated to find the bedchamber empty, but upon reading the letter she went off into a dead swoon, and the sound of her dramatic collapse roused the apathetic innkeeper and his wife from downstairs. When they managed to revive her, she wailed hysterically and would not be calmed. The application of a cold bucket of water sufficiently settled the situation, and the landlords, quite tired of their pompous and obviously unhinged guest, requested she settle her bill and take herself off the premises as soon as possible. Thankfully for them, she did just that.

While Mr. Moore had been engaging a coach and ordering his breakfast, he had also busily written an informative note to his aunt, Lady Hartwell, to advise her of the change in his plans and to warn her that Miss Iverson had slipped her leash. He put the note into the hand of a rider bound for London, with a coin and strict instruction to make haste to carry it to Hartwell House in Wimpole Street, where he was sure of further reward for its delivery. By the time the letter was received by Lady Hartwell, her nephew was blissfully lumbering along the road north, and much too far away to hear her shriek of anger and frustration. This unseemly outburst was not solely due to the failure of her plan to rid herself of the threat of her son's marriage, but was linked to several other problems that had now arisen.

Discreet inquiries on her part had uncovered the unpleasant news that Lady and Miss Wallace were not only the pretentious offshoots of a vulgar Cit, but they hadn't even the benefit of financial gain into the bargain and were entirely penniless. Coupled with the untimely arrival at her door of a heavyset debt collector, Lady Hartwell found herself in a singularly bad mood.

The staff in general had become accustomed to receiving such persons, and their orders were always to inform them Lady Hartwell was from home. This morning, a footman informed the collector that his mistress was not in and he would be better to call again another day if the matter was urgent, and so he had inadvertently purchased the lady a reprieve.

Lady Hartwell put a new plan into action. She crushed her nephew's letter between her palms and threw it angrily onto her desk, then jerked the bellpull to summon her butler. When Gibbin arrived, she told him that she was being called out of town on an urgent matter.

"Have my maid arrange my cases immediately, and I want a post chaise at the door within an hour," she instructed him sharply.

"Not the family coach, my lady?" Gibbin enquired curiously, a frown creasing his forehead.

"Is that what I asked for?" she snapped. "No, now move along. Oh, and Gibbin. Have the jewel cases packed with my travel case. I shall want them with me."

"The jewel cases, ma'am? But they have already been taken around to Lord Hartwell at Berkeley Square," the aged butler replied after a slight pause.

"What did you say?" Lady Hartwell turned. Her expression was livid and her entire body rigid with anger.

"The jewel cases were taken around to the duke's residence early this morning, ma'am," Gibbin repeated cautiously. "His lordship sent a note around this morning and requested them. Seeing as he is the young master, we followed his order, ma'am."

"I am mistress here, Gibbin," she screeched furiously. "How dare you take such action without my consent, when I expressly forbade it only yesterday."

The butler stepped backward meekly and muttered what she supposed to be an apology before fleeing the drawing room. With a deliberate step he marched toward the servants' quarters and roused Lady Hartwell's maid into action before sending a footman out to hire a post chaise. Then he softly knocked on the housekeeper's parlor door and waited to be acknowledged.

When he entered the neat little room, he found Mrs. Gibbin arranging the Hartwell family jewelry collection within about a dozen or so velvet-lined boxes of various sizes and shapes. She looked at her husband nervously, and he told her what had happened. With an impatient wave of her hand she went back to checking over the items on the list in her hand and confirmed that everything was in order.

"It is all here, thank the Lord," Mrs. Gibbin breathed a sigh as she checked the final article on her list, a fine silver bejeweled ring. "Will you wait until the woman has gone, then, Norman? It will look less suspicious if you wait, I think."

"Yes, I agree, my dear," the butler nodded. "Now, just make sure that everything is put into that great case there, and I'll have Paul bring the gig around when the woman has gone."

"How lucky that she's taking herself off. Was it the note that arrived? Did you sneak a look at it?"

"It was sealed, I'm afraid, but I cannot imagine it would be for another reason. It is odd she has asked for a hired carriage, though. I wonder what she means by it?" Gibbin speculated.

"Well, it is positively providential, in any case," his wife declared. "And now, after years of putting up with the wench, we'll be free to please ourselves."

"Quite right, my dear."

Within the hour, the staff assembled in the hall to receive parting instructions from their mistress, but Lady Hartwell walked determinedly past them all and out the door, followed closely by her maid. She spoke only to Gibbin, to advise she would send a note when she knew the date of her return, then mounted her hired chaise with the maid and told the driver to move on, leaving the younger staff members thoroughly confused.

The clock had not quite achieved half ten when the post chaise drew away from Hartwell House, and at around the same time, Miss Iverson trotted down the stairs toward the breakfast parlor with Chico at her heels. She found her father seated at the head of the table, studying the *Commercial Journal*. He looked up and greeted her merrily as she arranged a small plate for herself and sat to pour herself a cup of tea.

"Did you sleep well, my dear?"

"Yes, thank you, Papa," she said with a smile. After a moment of silence, she continued, "Dear Papa, I should apologize for not telling you what happened at Vauxhall. It was ill done of me."

"Do not trouble yourself, Cilla. In the end, there appears to have been no harm come from it, and I trust that in a day or two we shall see much the same of this latest kerfuffle," Lord Iverson said airily, going back to his newspaper. His demeanor was so unruffled that his daughter gazed at him curiously for a moment, and she wondered what could possibly make him so carefree in the wake of the previous evening, but as he was consumed by his reading, she decided not to press him. She was about to pick up her own newspaper when the viscount let out a startled exclamation.

"Heavens, what is it, Papa?"

"A notice has caught my attention. Did you check in on your mother before you came down?"

"Yes, she said she would be down in a moment. But what is it, Papa?" Lucilla asked again, mildly concerned.

Her father seemed about to reply when his wife entered the breakfast parlor and drew his attention away. "My dear, have you heard from your friend Lady Wallace of late?"

"I had a note from her yesterday morning. She said she was not well and would not join me for tea this afternoon," Lady Iverson answered lightly.

"What *is* it, Papa?"

"Her father is Cooke, is he not? The merchant-man?" his lordship enquired.

"Yes, that is right, darling."

"Well, I thought so. Seems he's croaked."

"Jasper," Lady Iverson exclaimed in shock.

"He'd been ill, hadn't he? Think I heard her say that," her husband continued, oblivious to her reproachful stare. "Wonder what she and that hoity-toity daughter of hers will do now that the tap's off? Wallace hasn't had sixpence to scratch with for years."

"Jasper, please do not speak so. Oh, poor Lady Wallace," sighed the viscountess mournfully. "I shall write to her immediately. Though I do not at all understand why she did not say so in her note yesterday, for I'm sure I should have understood."

"Do not trouble yourself, Mama," Lucilla said gently. "I am sure Lady Wallace meant no ill in not confiding in you."

At that moment, Murray appeared in the doorway and informed the family that Lord Hartwell had arrived and was requesting an audience with Miss Iverson. Lucilla put down her teacup and stood, but hovered behind her chair uncertainly, watching her mother intently, but Lady Iverson made no movement.

"Mama, are you coming?"

"Whatever for, dearest? He has not asked to see me, surely," her ladyship replied, continuing to scoop jam onto the scone on her plate and ignoring her daughter's wide-eyed stare of surprise.

"Do not keep the young man waiting, Cilla," her father said casually, flicking a page of his newspaper.

Amazed at the apathy she was witnessing in her parents, Lucilla walked from the room slack-jawed and nodded absently as she followed a smiling Murray, who advised her his lordship was waiting in the drawing room. The butler opened the door for her and was about to withdraw when she instructed him to leave the door open and to bring a pot of tea back.

"Good morning, Lord Hartwell. You are very punctual," she greeted him with a sunny smile as he bowed over her hand and responded in kind. "I'm afraid my mother has only just come downstairs and was not inclined to leave her breakfast. Though she usually takes a tray in her room, so I suppose it is not the only odd thing to happen this morning. Please, do sit down. Murray will bring a tea tray presently, if you should care for it?"

"No, I thank you," he replied, watching her face intently as she sat and smoothed her skirts with Chico curling in an unassuming ball beside her feet. He'd never known her to chatter and wondered if she was nervous about being alone with him after the events of the previous day or if it was because she knew what he was about to ask.

She glanced up at him and smiled again. "Are you going to sit?"

"No. Yes. Yes, I will," he stammered and inwardly cursed for allowing himself to become flustered. He sat in the armchair across from her and took a deep breath to steady himself, then looked up to find her watching him with amusement.

Lucilla had finally figured out the reason for her parents' odd behavior in the breakfast room. She wondered if they were now listening from the hall and considered calling out to test her theory, but she decided it was unimportant to verify at the present moment. It suddenly also made sense as to why Lord Hartwell and the duke had been present and privy to the circumstances surrounding her abduction when it seemed that it would have been wiser for her family to have made an excuse to prevent their learning of it. She made a mental note to question Matthew about how Oliver and Saliston had come to know that she'd been kidnapped; he would be the most likely to know.

She sat patiently, her hands clasped neatly in her lap as she watched the young earl with a smile. It would be unladylike to do anything else, and possibly mean and emasculating to apply pressure. So she waited quietly, and after what seemed like an age, he spoke.

"Lucilla, I had intended to wait for the perfect moment to ask you a particular question," he began steadily and deliberately, leaning forward in his seat a little and talking more in the direction of her feet than her face. But it was a promising start, so he continued, "But in light of recent events, I feel that to wait any longer might give rise to gossip. So, although I think you deserve a better setting than your mother's drawing room, it is, unfortunately, the best I can do at short notice."

"Heavens, now you have piqued my interest," she said humorously in an effort to lighten his furrowed brow, but he continued with the same expression.

"Yesterday I spoke with your father, and he very graciously gave me his blessing to address you. I had intended to present you with a gift—I suppose I took my cue from Matthew in that respect. But when he came in and told us that you had been taken..." There was a choked pause as Lord Hartwell recalled the scene. "When he told us that my cousin had taken you, I knew if you were by some miracle returned, I could not wait to select a pretty trinket before asking you to be my wife."

"Lord Hartwell, have you actually just proposed, or am I to wait for it to be phrased as a question?" Lucilla asked, forcing herself to remain straight-faced, but a hint of playfulness managed to peep out, and she had the satisfaction of seeing his face soften and a smile finally appear.

"Lucilla," he said slowly and with a hovering grin, "will you do me the honor of becoming my wife?"

"Lord Hartwell, I am so very glad you have asked, and I should be pleased to accept," Lucilla replied with a provocative smile as she stood and reached out her hands to him, beckoning him forward. He rose and kissed her hands, but she was distracted at that moment by a muffled sound from outside the door that attracted the notice of Chico, who bounded across the room, barking excitedly.

"You can come in now, Papa," she called out, and a moment later both of her parents entered the room and made a show of pretending that they had not, in fact, been eavesdropping.

To Lucilla's surprise, following on her parents' heels were her brother and her cousin.

"Lord, how come you two to be here? Did you sneak in from the back of the house?" she demanded.

"Indeed, we did. Couldn't miss the show," Matthew replied gaily. "Congratulations, old boy. Now it is you who will have the managing of the firebrand."

"Was that a knock at the door?" Edward asked over the excitement.

"Murray will answer it. It is probably Aunt Augusta," Lord Iverson said in reply.

But it was not Lady Edevane who appeared. Instead, it was the Duke of Saliston, and behind him was a little wrinkled man dressed in a servant's garb, but the inhabitants of the room largely took no note of the arrivals except Chico, who whined softly and padded cautiously forward to greet the duke and the stranger.

"George? Gibbin? What do you do here?" Oliver asked confusedly, starting toward his cousin and the old Hartwell family butler.

"I hope we are not intruding, cousin," Saliston said a little stiffly. "I am afraid Gibbin and I arrive unannounced, but we have urgent business, Oliver."

"I am agog with curiosity, George," Lord Hartwell replied, his brows raised and his tone concerned as he glanced from the duke to the old butler.

"Master Oliver—that is, my lord. I bring news," Gibbin said haltingly. "Perhaps it would be best to talk in private?"

"There is no need for that."

Gibbin looked at Saliston and received a nod of

assent.

"Is something amiss?" Lucilla appeared at Oliver's elbow.

"Please accept my congratulations, Miss Iverson," the duke said punctiliously. "We were just hoping for a word with Oliver. But I believe this also concerns you, my dear."

"Indeed? Well, perhaps we ought to sit down," she said brightly.

Introductions were quickly made, and the crowd settled down into a scene rather closely resembling that of the night before, but Lucilla was glad there was no necessity to repeat anything else that had occurred. The duke explained the reason for their unexpected visit.

"Gibbin arrived in Berkeley Square this morning with the items that we requested from your mother yesterday, Oliver," he began. "But he informed me that it was by subversion that he had managed to bring them. Please tell his lordship what happened, Gibbin."

"Yes, your grace," the little old butler said, nodding. "After your visit yesterday, my lord, I asked Lady Hartwell if it would please her to have the articles you requested cleaned before they were delivered to you. But instead of issuing orders to assemble the collection, she informed me there would be no need to do so. It struck an ill note with me, my lord, so I resolved with Mrs. Gibbin to sort through the pieces and ensure that everything was as it ought to be and ready to be sent to you."

"I am most grateful to you, Gibbin," Oliver said graciously. "I am very sorry you were put in such an awkward position. It was not kind of my mother."

"As you say, my lord. But that is not all." Gibbin

swallowed nervously. "This morning, a letter arrived quite early with a rider by express. My lady had been in a precarious humor when she returned from her card party last night, but the letter put her in a proper temper. She called for me to arrange a hired carriage for her and for her maid to pack her possessions, including the jewelry collection that was meant to be sent to you, my lord. I was able to convince her that these had already been delivered to you, which sent her even further into a rage."

"I see."

"After her ladyship left the house, I went into the drawing room and found the note she had received. It was crumpled on the desk, and I thought it might shed light on why Lady Hartwell had been called away so sudden-like."

"I have the letter here, Olly," Saliston interjected, carefully removing a wrinkled paper from his coat and handing it to his young cousin. Oliver took it gingerly and opened it, scanning the page with interest.

The letter said:

Aunt,

As I told you, the girl is untamable. She managed to wrest the pistol from me and I was abandoned on the roadside, but escaped with my life. I cannot but be glad to be rid of the chit.

I have had the good fortune to have stumbled upon Miss W, and I spun a tale that Miss I had jilted me on the road. The girl is so sorry for me that I have found her remarkably willing to continue the journey to Scotland with me in Miss I's stead! I will not argue with destiny, for that can be the only explanation for such luck.

One heiress is as good as another, and this one will

be far easier to keep in check. I know you preferred the other for your own ends, but in the end, you must allow me to be the judge.

I shall return to my father with the chit after the knot is tied and let the gossip die out. Have a care to keep my creditors at bay until I return with the funds to please them. I'll be pleased to assist you in turn.

Wish me well! Your loving nephew,
Charles

Oliver stared at the letter, his face white with fury. In response to the curious looks that were aimed at him, he silently handed the letter to Lord Iverson and apologized for the offense it would no doubt cause him.

"I can only say that I am deeply and grossly ashamed to learn the depth of my mother's involvement in this sorry episode, Lord Iverson," he said sadly when his prospective father-in-law had finished reading the letter.

"You are not to be held accountable for your mother's actions, dear boy."

"Does he mean Miss Wallace?" Lady Iverson asked in a shocked voice as she speedily glanced through the letter. "Oh, heavens, her poor mother will die of shame. And on the heels of her grandfather's passing, too."

"He says here 'one heiress is as good as another'— does he think Tabitha is an heiress?" Lucilla said wonderingly.

"Certainly sounds like it," Matthew said. Having flicked the letter from his aunt's hand, he was now looking through it himself, with Edward leaning over his shoulder.

"Seems the devil is getting his desserts in the end, being married to that jade," Edward remarked smugly.

"Better him than me."

"Last I heard, Sir John was one foot out of debtors' prison," Lord Iverson said tersely.

"Oh, never say so," his wife exclaimed in horror.

"I'm afraid so, my dear, and if it is true that old man Cooke is dead, well, there will be no more money from that quarter. You said yourself that Lady Wallace is always at odds with that nabob brother of hers," the viscount said knowingly. "If she were half as clever as she fancies herself, she would have mended that bridge before the old man turned up his toes."

"Do you mean to tell me that it's likely Tabitha is penniless?" Lucilla asked, to which her father nodded. "And Mr. Moore thinks she is precisely the opposite. Oh, it would be excessively amusing if it were not all so ridiculously absurd."

"It is indeed absurd," Saliston remarked. "But I confess I cannot pity him. Nor any female so stupid as to fall *willingly* into his hands."

"Should we not send someone after them?" Lady Iverson said tremulously, looking at her husband.

"We will tell her mother what we know, but I will not be responsible for the girl, Anne," Lord Iverson said firmly. "It would be very difficult to explain our knowledge of the subject without revealing how we came to know of it, and I will not have Lucilla tarnished to save that little minx."

Lady Iverson had to agree with his reasoning, but it seemed harsh to abandon hope of saving Tabitha from herself. "Perhaps she will come to her senses and return home herself."

"Then the less anyone says about it, the better for her it will be."

Gibbin cleared his throat and the room quieted abruptly.

"I'm afraid there is more to be divulged, my lord," he said softly to his master, prompting Lord Hartwell to sigh loudly.

"Yes, Gibbin?"

"My lord, when Mrs. Gibbin and I were about the task of sorting through the various pieces of jewelry, we noticed several of them were rather lighter than they had any business being."

"It seems your mother has been replacing some of the stones, Olly," Saliston summarized, rubbing his brows in frustration, his arms crossed.

"I believe so, yes," the old butler agreed sadly.

"It certainly explains how she's kept up appearances. And all of the debts we uncovered," the duke continued dryly.

"Yes, I suppose it does," Oliver muttered disgustedly. "I am sorry, Cilla. I had hoped to make a gift of one of them to you, but in light of what Gibbin has discovered, I think we ought first to have everything examined."

"It is not for you to be sorry, my dear. You bear no fault, and I need no gift," Miss Iverson said gently, taking his hand. "I am very sorry this has happened to you."

"My lord, if I may say so, I did think to bring a small item with me. I had occasion to overhear your interview with your mother yesterday, after all, and I thought this might suit your purpose," Gibbin interjected brightly. He put a hand into his pocket and withdrew a ring which he held out to his young master, suddenly seeming excited. "It belonged to your grandmother."

The silver ring was dull with age, but the large square sapphire still glowed, and it was set off by a rim of small diamonds about its face. And it was heavy. Far too heavy to be paste.

"It was a gift from your grandfather upon your father's birth. I feel certain it will pass examination. Lady Hartwell did not like the style, and so it has sat in Mrs. Gibbin's lockbox since Lord Hartwell's passing," the old butler explained, a sentimental smile on his face. "Mrs. Gibbin was your father's nurse, my lord. She was very fond of him, always said so."

"Thank you, Gibbin, you are a treasure," Oliver said kindly as he turned the ring over in his hand and examined its dull glitter. "What do you think of it, Cilla? Do you like it?"

"Like it?" she asked, looking closely at it as he moved it into a ray of light from the window. "How could I not? It is splendid."

Lord Hartwell took her hand and slid the ring onto her finger, a contented smile on his face as she examined it on her hand with delight. Then all of the peace of the moment was ended, for a loud voice suddenly sounded from the doorway, and all of the occupants in the room, who had been watching the young couple with varying degrees of pleasure and satisfaction, were startled by the entrance of Lady Edevane and a loud ruckus raised by the offended Chico.

"Well. I hear there is good news to be had here somewhere, is that right? Well, Lord Hartwell, brought you up to the mark at last, did we? Lord, that is a fine sparkler on your finger, my dear. Careful not to blind me now. Anne, we must go round to the silk warehouses immediately. Edward, move out of my chair, there's a good lad. Where have you been, by the way? Never mind, I'm sure I'll hear all about it another day. Your mama and I must discuss wedding matters. When that is done, we'll have to fix something up for you, too."

Epilogue

Two weeks following that bizarre Friday afternoon, the Iverson family celebrated the union of Mr. Matthew to Miss Caroline Russell. Just one week later, they again gathered to rejoice in the marriage of the Honorable Miss Iverson to Oliver Fairley, the Earl of Hartwell. Excitement and interest were high, and as both events were hosted from the family's London house, many notable members of the ton were present.

The general feeling was initially one of astonishment that the Duke of Saliston should have let such a prize slip through his fingers, but as his young cousin was so personable and well-liked, it was widely accepted and considered to be an exceptional match. Indeed, the two young people were so very obviously happy, and the joining of two pretty faces and fortunes could never be anything but a raging success—except in the eyes of those who could be quickly relegated to the ranks of the bitter and jealous. Unfortunately for the newly wed Mr. and Mrs. Moore, these were the categories into which they would soon be sorted by the majority of their acquaintance.

Immediately upon recovering her wits, Lady Wallace had sent notice for the announcement of her daughter's intended marriage to the *Gazette* in the hope that this might stay the tongues of the gossips and avert possible damage to their joined reputation. After all, the extent of her own knowledge allowed her to believe that her daughter was about to be joined in matrimony to a young man of property and breeding. She might have privately wished for a title to be attached to the union, but it was consolation enough that her fortunes and her daughter's would no longer rest on the mercy of her wretched brother. Lady Wallace resolved to travel instantly to her daughter's new home in Lancashire with the intention of being there to greet her upon her return from Scotland with her new husband.

Upon arrival at the Moore family estate, Lady Wallace was shocked to find it was somewhat closer in size to a gentleman's hunting box than an affluent country home. Morecombe boasted room enough to house no more than fifteen guests at an absolute stretch and was in a state of considerable disrepair. The garden that surrounded the home was a tangle of disordered shrubbery and unclipped lawns, the drive was overgrown with weeds, and the general aspect cried poverty. It was as unlike the grand and stately Gracewood as it was possible for a house to be.

To make matters worse, the elder Mr. Moore had none of his son's charm and made no effort to hide his distaste for Lady Wallace. Before she descended upon his house, he had received word that his son was to marry the daughter of a vulgar upstart, and he was thoroughly disgusted by the idea. When the lady herself arrived at his door, his anger had somewhat lost its edge, for he had learned the extent of the wealth that hovered within reach, though he maintained a level of hostility he intended to ensure Lady Wallace would not become too comfortable with their new familial relationship.

By the time the self-congratulatory young couple

finally presented themselves at Morecombe, all the *ton* knew of the marriage, and no small amount of gossip had begun to make the rounds, largely owing to Lady Wallace and her daughter being widely regarded as rather unpleasant ladies. The family summarily decided to weather the storm of public disapproval from the wilds of Lancashire and prayed their notoriety would die swiftly so that a grand return to London might be made in the new year.

Alas, it was not to be, for the tetchy, troublesome creditors had been fobbed off quite enough and so began to make noise. It was not long before their grumblings reached Lancashire, with the result being an earth-shattering eruption after which the parents-in-law would never again utter a civil word to or about one another, and the irrevocably joined young people were brought to the startling realization they had each made a colossal mistake.

Soon after the news broke within the family, it also began to circulate through London that the charming Charles Moore was, in fact, a penniless gamester, while the new Mrs. Moore was, in fact, not an heiress but an impoverished fortune hunter. This accompanied many a recollection of poor behavior from both parties, with Miss Tabitha Wallace being remembered as a flirtatious and pert little minx and her new husband as a profligate card sharp linked to the ruin of several promising young men of birth and fortune. It soon became widely acquiesced that two such disagreeable young people had come by their just desserts in taking the miscalculated step of eloping to Gretna Green together.

The elder Mr. Moore would be heard on many an occasion mourning the loss of the match of his dreams while loudly comparing his sanctimonious, sharp-faced daughter-in-law to "the pretty Iverson chit" with such regularity that Tabitha Moore's already sour temper worsened and an unpleasant scowl became a permanent fixture upon her face. The younger Mr. Moore would eventually stoop to the level of pleading and begging at the feet of his mother-in-law's brother, and Mr. Cooke ultimately agreed to pay off the ingratiating and encroaching young man's immediate commitments with a warning to never again apply to him for assistance. Lady Wallace eventually retreated to her husband's house to lead a life of quiet contemplation and made no effort to rejoin Society.

And Mrs. Tabitha Moore was transformed from a moderately irritating creature into a vastly irritating one. The only joy in her life came from uttering sniping barbs at her husband until he eventually learned to avoid her company altogether, which, luckily for him, became significantly easier after the arrival of their only daughter. In the months following her marriage, Mrs. Moore sent several fawning letters to the young Countess of Hartwell. Eventually, she received one in reply, which had the effect of immediately halting all efforts to assume a relationship. So humiliated was she by the contents of the letter that she burned it immediately and never told another soul of its existence.

It was not a particularly long letter, and though it was politely worded, it fanned the glowing embers of Tabitha's discontent and shame, and ensured the words would remain in her memory long after the physical letter was gone. It read:

Mrs. Moore,

How delightful that sounds! Though I must admit I

do not regret that it is not myself to whom the name is now assigned, I hope it satisfies you. Indeed, I am sure it suits you far better than it should have suited me.

Alas, I am forbidden to write to you again but this once, for my own dear husband feels so dreadfully hurt by the actions of your husband, his cousin. To discover that Charles was in league with the Dowager Lady Hartwell to rob my dear husband of his fortune was a bitter pill to swallow, and his actions against my person? It is too much, and Hartwell will not have anything more to do with him. I confess it is not a difficult condition for me to accept, for your husband's behavior is certainly unforgivable, and so we must part.

I must beg you now not to write me again, but please believe that I wish you all the happiness that you surely deserve in this world.

Sincerely yours,
The Countess of Hartwell

A word about the author...

Victoria Clarke is a historical romance writer and author of this novel. A competitive horsewoman and equine insurance specialist, Victoria has spent the majority of her years reading novels of all styles from young adult to historical, science fiction to fantasy. Her favorite genre is Regency romance, particularly the works of Georgette Heyer and Jane Austen, and her debut novel is inspired by the novels of these two great authors.

Visit her at:

victoriaclarkeauthor.com

www.ingramcontent.com/pod-product-compliance
Lightning Source LLC
Chambersburg PA
CBHW072306020726
47501CB00002B/414